# KENYA

# KENYA

A NOVEL

John Halkin

BEAUFORT BOOKS
*Publishers*
New York

Library of Congress Cataloging-in-Publication Data

Halkin, John.
Kenya.

1. Kenya—History—1885-1963—Fiction. I. Title
PR6058.A4445K4    1986    823'.914    85-26743
ISBN 0-8253-0349-4

Published in the United States by
Beaufort Books Publishers, New York.

Printed in the U.S.A.    First American Edition, 1986

10  9  8  7  6  5  4  3  2  1

Published in the United States by
Beaufort Books Publishers, New York.

# A NOTE ON SOURCES

The characters in this story are all fictional and are not based on any actual person, alive or dead. But the railway was built, settlers settled, Africans found their territory invaded, their way of life changed. For details of these events the author has relied on numerous conversations with Africans, Indians and Europeans in present-day Kenya, as well as wide reading of personal memoirs, biographies and histories too numerous to list. Of these, M. F. Hill's *Permanent Way* (East African Lit Bureau, 1977), the official history of the railway, should be specially mentioned. For details of Gikuyu life in earlier days, the author is particularly indebted to Jomo Kenyatta's *Facing Mount Kenya: Tribal Life of the Kikuyu* (Secker & Warburg, 1969), Godfrey Muriuki's *History of the Kikuyu* (Nairobi, 1974), and L. S. B. Leakey's monumental *Southern Kikuyu before 1903* (Academic Press, 1977 & 1978) among other sources.

# SPELLING

For the purposes of this book the spelling *Gikuyu* has been adopted (following Jomo Kenyatta) rather than *Kikuyu*, although both forms are in use. Similarly, the author has used *Maasai* rather than Masai.

First came the traders, explorers and missionaries making their way around the African coast, probing inland along the rivers and caravan routes, some seeking the source of the Nile, some seeking fortunes in ivory . . . Then came the flag, the rivalries, the European hunger for expansion, until in 1884–5 a conference in Berlin – to which no Africans were invited – divided the dark continent into 'spheres of influence'. One of the new, straight lines appearing on maps of the east coast of Africa demarcated British East (now Kenya) from German East (now Tanzania) and on each side of this line the race began to build a railway westwards into the very heart of the continent, to Lake Victoria, in an attempt to achieve a controlling influence in Uganda, astride the upper reaches of the Nile . . .

# Book One

Young Scottish engineer, sent to Kenya
to build a railroad, during the latter
part of the nineteenth century, must
contend with hostile natives, fights
among the workers, and a collegue with
whom he is forced to share his wife's
affections.

John Philip Andrewes glanced anxiously at his young
wife's drawn, white face and felt relieved to see her relax
into a smile as their ship, the SS *Arabella*, cautiously eased
her way through the narrow channel leading into Mombasa
harbour. Above, the solid walls of the old Portuguese fort
were sharply outlined against the clear blue sky, guarding
the approach. Ahead, the channel widened into a lagoon
busy with Arab *dhows* whose single, broad sails rippled
gently in the warm breeze. The scene must have remained
unchanged for centuries, he thought. Only the slow throb
of the SS *Arabella*'s engine and the pungent smell of coal
smoke from her funnels served as reminders that Queen
Victoria was on the throne and the year was 1896.

'It's beautiful!' Hester cried excitedly as the town came
into view with its white, flat-roofed houses nestling among
tall palms and luscious mango-trees. 'John, look at those
hills – so green! Oh, I never imagined anything like it!'
She clutched his arm and snuggled up to him. 'And your
son will be born here! I'm thankful for that. It's been my
constant nightmare I'd have our first baby in the middle
of a storm on board this ship.'

'We shoulda listened to your father an' let ye stay in
Liverpool.'

'That's nonsense, John, and you know it!' Her dark eyes
flashed with indignation. 'What d'you think I'd be doing,
left behind? I'm no sit-at-home wife – where my man goes,
I go too!'

But she did not look well and that was the truth. Her
face had a sickly pallor, emphasized by her rich brown
hair, and she was so swollen, Andrewes feared the baby
might arrive at any moment. Almost a year they had been
married and he had not yet lost that odd sense of disbelief
whenever he thought about it. When they had first met

she had been just twenty, daughter of a Baptist minister – a gaunt man with brooding eyes and an Old Testament look – and she had never spent so much as a single night away from home, though her work among the Liverpool poor, helping her sister and aunt, had given her more experience of life than many an older woman. He had been attracted immediately – that determined chin, her cheerful common sense . . . She was full of laughter. Full, too, of romantic ideas about the East which he had indulged more than willingly. Her interest had flattered him.

'Will ye no' come back to India wi' me?' he had asked one day by way of a proposal.

And she had accepted, though her father had been none too pleased.

It was natural enough, though, for a parent – a widower at that – to be worried. Andrewes was eleven years her senior and only a few months back from India, where he had worked on the Railway. He was a giant of a man, well over six feet tall, brawny, and spoke with a down-to-earth, almost brusque Scottish accent; by her side he felt clumsy, awkward . . . But Hester had been more than a match for her father, authoritative though he was in the pulpit. She had brushed aside his objections and within a few weeks they were married.

But when it came to returning to India there were snags. His old job had been filled and there were no other vacancies, not right away. Except . . . how would he feel about East Africa? They were desperate for engineers for the proposed Uganda Railway and with his record . . .

He'd have to go alone, of course. The railway was to be constructed across wild country – unmapped, most of it – with every imaginable danger. A challenge, though, for the right man. They aimed to start on the coast at Mombasa and strike over six hundred miles inland, into the very heart of Africa, to establish a vital lifeline for the new British Protectorate of Uganda.

'As for taking your wife – my dear fellow, it's out of the question. It's no-man's-land out there!'

'Do they think I'll melt or what?' Hester had scoffed

when he told her. 'While you've been down in London I've been hunting through the old missionary magazines we keep in the loft. Florence Baker went with *her* husband to the source of the Nile – that's Uganda, isn't it? – so I'm going with mine. You get back to London and tell them you'll not take the job unless I travel with you. You'll need to be firm, John.'

So he had been firm and, after a long argument, the gentlemen of the Foreign Office had reluctantly agreed, though only on condition that Andrews paid for his wife's passage himself.

Just about everything had gone wrong on the voyage out, which had taken eight weeks longer than expected. In the Bay of Biscay they had run into one of the worst storms in living memory; giant waves had washed over the little cargo steamer, tossing it about mercilessly, while they had stayed below beneath the battened-down hatches and prayed to God that He might spare their lives. Later, off the coast of Portugal, the engine had started to give trouble and for the best part of a day they had drifted helplessly. At last they had managed to get up enough steam to limp into harbour where they spent three weeks waiting for replacement parts from London.

Then twice in the Mediterranean sudden gales had blown up, each lasting several hours, and in the Suez Canal they had been plagued by a sandstorm. Sand everywhere. In their clothes, their shoes, their ears, their hair, their bedding . . . Even in the food they ate. They had reached the Red Sea before the wind dropped sufficiently for it to be worthwhile shaking everything out and sweeping up. More than once Hester had declared that she had no intention of allowing *her* son to be born on board ship, not after all that.

'Even if I have to hold him in by force,' she had added, daring him to laugh. Her face had been flushed and obstinate, her eyes alert for the slightest twitch of his lips.

Now, as the throb of the engine stopped and the SS *Arabella* rode gently on the smooth water of Mombasa harbour, she smiled at him.

'We've arrived,' she said softly.

A word of command, and the anchor rattled out. Immediately a multitude of small boats and canoes surrounded them, their occupants vociferously competing for attention. Andrewes picked one out at random. A ladder was thrown over the side for him to clamber down to it.

'I'll never be able to get down that,' Hester objected. 'Not the way I am.'

'Never you mind, Mrs Andrewes!' the burly first mate reassured her. He had plenty of children of his own, as he never tired of boasting; ay, an' gran'children too. 'We're fixin' somethin' up for you special. Be ready by the time your man's back. You're in good hands on this ship, you know that.'

'I'll go first to the Railway Office to enquire what arrangements they've made.' Andrewes swung his leg briskly over the rail. 'I'll no' delay. Perhaps ye could tell our son to wait another couple o' hours. If he can!'

The laugh in her eyes did not quite hide her uneasiness as she held on to the rail. 'Don't be too long,' she whispered. 'Nor too fussy, either. Just find a place quickly, so long as it's on land.'

Once down the ladder and in the boat he looked up to see her still gripping the rail. Suddenly he felt a stab of uncertainty. Of fear, even. What if she started her labour while he was still away? With no doctor on board . . . no other woman . . . If it went wrong he might never see her alive again.

She was waving to him and he waved back.

'Hurry!' he snapped at the boatman.

The man merely grinned, gap-toothed, in reply and pulled gently on his stern oar as if he had all eternity at his disposal.

The intense sun burned into his skin and the dazzling sea hurt his eyes, making it difficult for him to keep Hester in sight as she stood there on deck, still watching. *Lord God, may no harm come to her!*

For a second the boatman rested on his oar and began explaining something to him, pointing towards the town.

'Will ye no' hurry!' he urged irritably.

That triggered off a fresh stream of words, though nothing he could understand. Before leaving London he had invested in a copy of Steere's *Handbook of the Swahili Language* to study during those long days at sea, but he had not settled to it. He had never been a man for reading.

In spite of his anxiety he was eager to see Mombasa at close quarters. On board they had talked about it often enough, he and Hester, and questioned the first mate, who had been there several times before. They had built up a picture of a charming Arab-style town spiced with the inevitable mixture of races and cultures typical of ports serving the Indian Ocean. Since biblical times ships had used its natural harbour. Vasco da Gama had investigated Mombasa island, hugging the African coast before setting out on the perilous crossing to India, and he had narrowly missed death when his locally-recruited pilot plotted to wreck his ship on the reefs. Over the centuries, control of Mombasa had changed hands several times; now it was part of the newly-established British East African Protectorate. The island itself, together with a ten-mile coastal strip, still legally belonged to the Sultan of Zanzibar, to whom an annual rent was paid. In acknowledgement of his rightful ownership, the British authorities planted no flagstaff in Mombasa soil and the Union Jack was flown only from the tops of buildings.

The boat scraped the bottom of the landing steps. Throwing the man some money, Andrewes jumped ashore and looked around for someone to direct him.

But there was no one about. The town seemed to be quietly slumbering. Attractive enough, though. Tall white houses with dark, carved doorways; windows shuttered against the fierce sunlight; graceful wooden verandas around the upper storeys . . . And, incongruously, down the centre of each cramped street ran railway lines – a narrow gauge, no more than two feet – partly overgrown with grass and weeds.

Yet not everyone could be asleep, he thought as he stared about him. The heat was oppressive. Sweat trickled

15

down his neck, soaking into his shirt collar. His light jacket felt as restrictive as a warm winter overcoat.

It was dreamlike – the brilliant light, the closed buildings . . .

Suddenly the dream was shattered by the clamour of triumphant shouting accompanied by wild drumming. Around the corner came a procession of about fifty men – mostly tall, strong Africans but with a scattering of turbaned Indians among them – dressed in a riotous variety of clothes, dancing, chanting, excitedly showing off the great elephant tusks they were carrying; each must have weighed a hundredweight at least, and there were nigh on forty of them. The leader, striding along purposefully, was a squat, red-faced European in tattered clothes, the bottoms of his trousers bound up in frayed puttees, worn-out boots, a rifle slung on his shoulder and a stained sun helmet. He did not even deign to glance in Andrewes' direction.

But at least his arrival woke the town up. People thronged out of the houses on every side to see what was happening. Every race on earth was represented – Africans, Arabs, Greeks, Indians, even a couple of other Europeans. Tall and muscular; short and wiry; fat, thin, healthy, sickly; men, women, children, bairns on the arm, bairns at the breast . . .

'A fortune there, I reckon, the price o' ivory bein' what it is,' said a soft Irish voice at Andrewes' shoulder. 'Sure it'll have cost him a pretty penny, a caravan o' fifty men at least . . . maybe a couple o' dozen more when he set out . . . they don't all come back alive . . . But I'm told he's been away fourteen months or thereabouts, as far as Lake Rudolph. Ay, it's a handsome profit he'll be making.'

'An' slaughtered many a fine beast,' Andrewes commented.

'Nature's riches, provided for the use o' mankind,' the Irishman replied mildly. 'Sure, an' didn't the Almighty make that clear to Adam an' Eve in the Garden of Eden?' He stuck out his hand. 'The name's Ed Muldoon. I'm thinkin' you're fresh ashore from that steamer out there in the harbour?'

'I'm glad to meet ye, Mr Muldoon. I'm John Philip Andrewes.'

Ed Muldoon's grip matched Andrewes' own. His fingers were rough and gnarled, as though accustomed to heavy work from an early age, and he wore a shabby, white suit which sat uneasily on his broad shoulders. His small, dark eyes shifted constantly as they talked.

'I've a wife on board anxious to get ashore as soon as there's accommodation ready for her,' Andrewes said, distrusting the man instinctively. 'So if ye'll—'

'Missionaries?' Ed Muldoon interrupted. 'Protestant missionaries? Holy Mother o' God, they're arrivin' in this part o' the dark continent like flies around a honey pot! Sure, an' good luck, I say! I'm Church o' Rome myself when I can spare the time to be anythin' at all. But here's hopin', John Philip Andrewes, when you make your way to the bara – which is what we call the interior, around this latitude – you'll both live long enough to make your first convert.'

'What makes ye say we're missionaries?'

'Who else but a missionary wi' the love o' God in his heart would be daft enough to bring a wife to Africa? Don't be misled by Mombasa now, John Philip Andrewes. What you see here is the last outpost o' civilization as we know it. One foot outside this town an' if you're not stung to death by insects, cut down by disease, eaten by lions or Lord knows what other wild animal, sure it'll only be to die wi' a spear in your side from one o' the heathen brethren you aim to lead into the ways o' the Almighty.'

Andrewes laughed.

'It's no yarn I'm spinnin',' said Muldoon darkly. He belched and the whisky was strong on his breath.

'Ye've a great way o' makin' a man feel his journey's been worthwhile, but I'm no missionary, Mr Muldoon, an' I'd be obliged if ye could direct me to the Railway Office. The sooner I can check what arrangements they've made, the better.'

Muldoon's delighted smile revealed the stains on his teeth. 'It's on the railway y'are then? An engineer, maybe? Put your hand there, Mr Andrewes – my mistake, I'm sure!' He seized Andrewes' hand again and shook it heartily. 'Now you'll find the Railway Office on the far side o' the island at Kilindini, some three miles from here.'

'We need a place urgently to—,' Andrewes began.

'Sure, there's plenty o' room to pitch your tent. You were not expectin' anythin' grander, were you?'

'An' it's three miles, ye say?'

'Take you no more'n twenty minutes on a ghari.' He pointed. 'A trolley like the one you see there. They run on these rails, an' with a couple o' stout Swahilis to push 'em, you'll be at the Railway Office in no time at all. Jesus Christ, man, it's no hardship, not compared with what's in front o' you.'

'My wife's in no fit condition,' Andrewes answered shortly, reluctant to say more. He glanced back across the harbour to where the steamer was anchored, remembering her last words as he had climbed over the side. *Just find somewhere quickly.*

The rowdy procession, still shouting excitedly, had come to a stop outside a building he took to be the custom house. As each man deposited his load of ivory, the red-faced hunter handed him some money for the night, explaining in a parade ground voice that they would all receive their full pay after the sale the following morning. He paused after each phrase for his words to be repeated in Swahili.

Muldoon was looking impatient. 'What ails her? If she's sick she'd best remain on board ship.'

'That's just what she refuses to do. An' she's no' sick, Mr Muldoon, but expectin' our first bairn any minute now, too far gone to be transported three miles across any island. So if ye canna help me, I'd be obliged if ye'd step aside an' allow me to find someone else who can.'

'Sure, an' isn't it help I'm offerin'? What you need's a room to rent, an' who better to find one for you?' He turned to call out something in rapid Swahili to a group of men lounging beneath the shade of a tree; one stood up and replied – a brief exchange – then ambled away. 'Run, you bastard!' Muldoon bawled after him. 'Kimbia! Upesi!'

'The best we can get, mind!' Andrewes told him sharply. 'I'll no' be havin' my wife givin' birth in some harbour brothel.'

'I'm doin' my best for you, Mr Andrewes.' Muldoon scowled, making no attempt to hide his annoyance. 'In the meantime, while I'm seekin' out a palace good enough for the young prince to enter this vale o' tears, I suggest you start fetchin' her off that steamer.'

'Ay. Ay, ye're right.'

'Correct me if I'm wrong, but your father was a lord, I'd guess. Or a Member o' Parliament, which is worse.'

'He was a railway engineer, same as meself. An' I owe ye an apology, Mr Muldoon. I'd no wish to appear ungrateful.'

'No offence taken, Mr Andrewes.' He grinned suddenly. 'Sure, an' welcome to Africa!'

# TWO

Kamau had overheard part of the conversation. A fine-featured man dressed in a clean white *kanzu*, he had been lounging in the shade against the custom house wall when the SS *Arabella* nosed her way into harbour, the dark smoke from her funnels blackening the sky. Every day saw the arrival of some new ship bringing yet more strangers from across the sea, just as his father Ngengi had foretold. Indians, most of them; but they came at the behest of the white men

The sight of Andrewes coming ashore stirred a memory in Kamau's mind of someone his father had often described – a man taller than most, strongly-built, with short hair the colour of sand growing down both cheeks. His pale eyes, too, gave the impression of taking everything in while hardly moving. This could not be the same man of course, for he had died long ago; 'Master of the Meat' they had called him – Bwana Nyama – because of the care he took when carving up the carcases of animals he had hunted.

But the newcomer was sufficiently like him to arouse Kamau's interest; he had edged nearer to find out more about him. Was he perhaps of the same family as Bwana Nyama? Kamau thought back over his father's stories but could remember no mention of the white man having brothers or relations of any kind. Except Ngengi himself.

As a boy, Kamau had never tired of listening to Ngengi's tales. He had been born a Gikuyu and grown up with no thought other than to spend his life with his own people, as was the custom. Then one day an Arab trading caravan arrived at his village, demanding food and water. After they had eaten they also explained how they needed more porters to help carry the many fine tusks of ivory down to the great sea. Two young men had volunteered immediately but the others held back, fearing they might never see their homes again.

The Arabs leading the caravan had been gentle-seeming men with delicate, pale skins. They wore strange garments down to their feet and lengths of cloth wound about their heads, quite unlike anything the villagers had ever seen before. In their hands they carried long ornate sticks which they used for hunting; when they saw wildebeeste or zebra, they would raise the sticks and cause them to bark like thunder. The animals would fall down dead at the sound.

Old Ngengi had always laughed when he reached this point in the story. Invariably he held his own gun in his hand and stroked the barrel, remembering.

No one in the village did any work the day the caravan left. There was so much to talk over. It had been as though a plague of locusts had descended upon them, one man said. Everyone agreed, but at the same time they were thankful it had not been worse. The next harvest would replace the food which had been eaten, while the volunteers had been two of the more troublesome young men. Few would regret their going.

It was not until the first streaks of dawn broke across the sky the following day that they realized something was wrong. The signs were hard to explain. An unaccustomed quietness. Vultures alighting on the rooftops, folding their wings with an elegant patience. A slight rustle in the grass.

The men were already reaching for their spears when the first shots rang out. Two of them fell dead.

The slaughter was remorseless. One by one the warriors were picked off by musket fire until finally the village itself was rushed by the attackers, who set the houses alight and cut down all who resisted – men, women and children alike. Then they divided the survivors into two groups. On one side they gathered the old, the sick, the wounded and the very young. And killed them.

A hush always fell on his audience when Ngengi recounted the details, as though anxious that they should never be forgotten. Babies were held up by their feet and their skulls smashed against a tree. Their mothers, screaming and kicking, were knocked to the ground to be disembowelled on the spot. Any wounded were despatched with jabbing spear thrusts to the heart while the aged had their throats cut. Two of the most venerable men of the village were cheerfully beheaded by a grinning rhinoceros of a man, one of the caravan's *askaris*.

Ngengi, still only a boy, had been in the second group. Terrified, he had watched the annihilation of his whole world. Never before had he experienced such agonizing bewilderment and anger, such deep pain and frustrated fury, such great emptiness of soul. With him in the group were the remaining able-bodied villagers, those who were still alive, including any children old enough to work. Their captors roped them together, kicking and beating them into submission, and then forced them to pick up the ivory tusks and other loads. The Arab traders in charge looked on, unconcerned, issuing an order from time to time but allowing their armed Swahili *askaris* to take care of the details.

For many days the prisoners were made to walk in single file through forests and grasslands, with their masters constantly bullying them on. Of Ngengi's family, only Nyakweya – his father's younger wife – was still alive. He occasionally caught glimpses of her in the line somewhere ahead of him. His mother, heavy with yet another child, had been butchered before his eyes together with his two sisters and his baby brother. His father had been one of the first to die in defence of the village.

On the fourth day Nyakweya stumbled and dropped the tusk she was carrying. The rhinoceros-man strode up and began to hit her savagely about the head; then he picked up the tusk and thrust it at her again. She staggered under its weight and gradually sank to her knees, too exhausted to go on any farther. Impatiently, the rhinoceros-man reached for his knife, cut her free from the ropes, and stabbed her to death.

Some voices were raised shrilly in protest but they soon fell silent when he turned towards them threateningly. As for Ngengi himself, he had been too numb to react at all.

That night, exhausted as he was, he could not sleep; in his mind he was reliving the horrors of the past few days over and over again. Then, moving restlessly on the hard ground, he felt something sharp and uncomfortable digging into his back – a rock, firmly embedded in the turf. Only slowly did he realize he might use it to free himself – yet to what end? How long could he survive in this distant country by himself before either a wild animal or starvation killed him?

But after a time he began to rub one of the ropes against the rock, working cautiously in order not to wake the others. Eventually it frayed and the strands parted. He was free from the prisoner in front of him but still tied to the man behind, and this second rope proved much more troublesome. It was almost dawn before he succeeded in breaking through it.

For a few moments he lay quietly, listening to the disturbed sleep of the others, some muttering, some sobbing . . . From his captors came only the sound of snores competing with the night shrillness of the insects. Moving very slowly and carefully, he began to creep away.

'You – stop!'

He did not wait to see who had spotted him. Staggering to his feet he ran as best he could between the trees. In full daylight he would never have got away, but the sun still hovered on the horizon and the shadows were deep. On he went, using whatever cover he could find until the trees thinned out and ahead of him lay an endless expanse of waving grassland, pink-tinged by the sun's first rays.

At first he thought it was hopeless. He was trapped. Then, unexpectedly, an impala stood up in the midst of all that grass with only its head and part of its neck visible, and he realized it was an ideal place to hide. He slipped in amongst the grass, wriggling forward on his belly like a snake until he was far away from the trees, and there he lay totally concealed.

How long he stayed there he never knew. At first he had heard his pursuers calling to each other, but their voices became more and more distant, eventually stopping altogether. Then he slept. A real sleep this time: the sleep of a free man. Once or twice he awoke and wondered what he should do next; perhaps the traders were still lurking there, waiting for him to emerge. The second time he risked raising his head, only to see a lion, its forepaws up on some rocks, keenly surveying the scene. Fortunately he was downwind of it and he ducked back into cover.

The next time he awoke it was to find himself staring at a dirty pair of leather boots, the first he had ever seen, though he was to get to know these boots intimately during the coming years. The white man wearing them seemed as big as an elephant and twice as frightening in his thick smelly clothes and sun hat. But he treated the boy kindly, ordering his people to give him some food and make sure he was looked after.

This was Bwana Nyama, they told him importantly as they threw him some meat. They grinned when they saw how hungrily he tore at it with his teeth.

Nevertheless, Ngengi had felt he had no reason to trust the white hunter and his worst fears were confirmed when – later the same day – they came across the Arab traders setting up camp. Bwana Nyama greeted them like old friends and hardly even glanced at the miserable villagers sitting exhausted on the ground, still strung together. Some, in fact, had by then been secured in pairs by means of wooden yokes across their necks.

Then the traders' voices became hard and persistent as they pointed to him. It was clear they were demanding him back and the white man was refusing. Some of his party began fingering their guns uneasily, though they were outnumbered more than three to one by the Arabs' party. At last the tension eased, quite unexpectedly. Some glinting metal pieces changed hands and Ngengi understood that the white man had bought him.

Telling about it all years later, Ngengi always had his audience rolling about with laughter at his imitation of the way Bwana Nyama spoke and strutted about. Kamau remembered every nuance of the mimicry, every gesture –

24

and when Andrewes had stepped ashore in Mombasa it might have been the same man, returned from the dead.

Ngengi had stayed many years with Bwana Nyama, cleaning those same leather boots, washing his clothes, preparing his food, accompanying him on countless hunting safaris, learning to shoot straight, twice saving his life, nursing him when sick, and in the end travelling with him to India where he died. In his will they found the words: *To my friend Ngengi I bequeath his liberty.*

On his return, Ngengi had lived first in Zanzibar where he had been much in demand among white travellers as *askari* and headman. Sometimes he was with them on safari for two years or more, yet in spite of these long absences he managed to acquire several wives, many children, and a great reputation for story-telling.

Later, he had moved to Mombasa where he collected four more wives, the youngest being a lovely Maasai girl who, like himself, had been captured by traders and sold into slavery. This was Kamau's mother and she was his favourite. By that time Ngengi's hair was grey but he devoted his old age to teaching Kamau everything he knew.

'Look out for the white man,' he would often say – Kamau thought of his words whenever he sat watching the steamers creeping into Mombasa harbour – 'for they are like the first scattered raindrops at the beginning of a storm. Now one . . . now two . . . now three . . . until the day comes when they flood the entire land and take it from us. And that will be the day of the long rains.'

Over on the ship something was happening. Kamau strained his eyes to see what it was. The boatmen in the harbour were resting on their oars, watching; men crowded along the rails of the Arab *dhows*.

A cargo tray was being slowly raised from the deck. It bore a white woman seated on a chair, her long skirts flapping in the light breeze. With one hand she held her sun helmet in place; with the other she clutched a furled umbrella.

25

'Steady as she goes!' came a man's voice across the water. 'Right – now over the side with 'er, but slowly! Slow, now! Slowly does it!'

The derrick edged around until the tray was clear of the deck. Kamau moved away from the custom house for a better view and recognized Andrewes standing up in the small boat beneath the tray, reaching out to steady it as it came down.

One of the other men on the harbour wall, a Swahili, called out some mocking remark, he couldn't hear what. His friends laughed.

Every week brought fresh evidence, Kamau thought. *The day of the long rains.* And now they had their women with them. Clearing his throat, he spat into the water and turned away.

# THREE

Swaying at the end of the derrick, Hester now felt grateful that she was sitting down, although at first she had tried to persuade them she could just as easily remain standing, holding on to the ropes. The mate had refused to listen.

'It'd be an irresponsible act, ma'am, an' one I'd want no part of.' He had explained how they planned to fix a comfortable chair to the cargo tray, screwing it down firmly like a throne on a dais. 'Then we'll strap you round the waist wi' a leather belt to make sure you don't slip off, like, an' you'll leave this ship as safe as steppin' out o' your own carriage back in Liverpool.'

'But I've never had a carriage of my own!' she had laughed.

'Ay, but you will one day, I've no doubt.'

The cargo tray was moving again. She caught her breath, desperately trying to convince herself there could be no danger of it tipping her into the sea. Had any woman ever arrived in Africa in such a manner before, off-loaded like so much freight?

Looking down, she could see her husband standing precariously in the small boat, waiting to steady the tray as it came within reach. Her stomach shifted uneasily and, with the taste of fear in her mouth, she tightened her grip on the curved handle of her umbrella. Its sharp point dug into the soft wood of the tray, helping to give her some slight sense of security. Oh, if only she had not refused to climb down that ladder!

Those first pains had come and gone, a false alarm, and she regretted now having troubled anyone. Not that she had told them, though it had been clear enough from their faces that they guessed.

'Now, lass, this is the tricky bit,' John was coaxing her

as the tray slowed in its descent to stop level with the gunwale. 'Jus' stay still till I have ye steady.'

He caught hold of the rope secured to one corner of the tray, indicating that the boatman should grab the other. The sun was hot on her face; her new pith helmet felt heavy and cumbersome. No shade anywhere, and the water's glare hurt her eyes. As for the tiny boat, it swam unevenly up and down, up and down . . .

'Are ye ready, my love?' he was saying. 'Undo the strap now an' stand up. Ye've only to take one step forward, then down into the boat. I can hold ye.'

Her head was aching; in spite of the heat the perspiration felt cold on her body. John's eyes were searching her face, worried. She took a deep breath, determined not to be defeated.

'Are ye all right? Because if ye're no'—'

'What a way to travel!' she tried to joke. 'Her Majesty – Queen Hester!'

Undoing the belt at her waist she stood for a second and then stepped down into the boat, with John grasping her wrist to steady her. Her head was high, her back straight, and she was conscious that the great bulge of her pregnancy preceded her regally.

The boat rocked and curtsied beneath her feet as it took her weight; then a quick surge of chatter arose from all the other small craft around, together with a cheer from the crew of the steamer, who were watching from the deck above.

'Let's go now!' John told the boatman, pointing to the quayside. 'An' this time put some muscle in it, will ye?'

Hester smiled at him, not wishing to speak. With an effort she managed to wave to the crew. Then she closed her eyes and prayed they would reach land before she fainted. John was explaining something and she tried to listen, but his voice was so far away . . . so far . . . Where the pains had attacked earlier she again felt twinges of discomfort as though . . . No! It was real pain again. *Real.*

She gasped, vaguely aware of John leaning towards her, anxiously asking if she . . . But she could not answer, whatever it was. Again it twisted inside her, that excruciating pain; it was all she could do not to cry out.

Why . . . why was she here in this eggshell of a boat under the tropical sun instead of in a cool, shady bedroom with clean white sheets and filmy lace curtains to diffuse the light? Another spasm shot through her and she clung to the sides, allowing the umbrella to fall to her feet. If only she could summon up some legendary genie to transport her in the twinkling of an eye to . . . oh, anywhere rather than that boat, even back to the poky little room in Liverpool she had shared with her sister.

'Come on, lass. Let's see if we can manage the steps.' He spoke gently, placing his hand under her arm to help her stand up. The boat was scraping lightly against the stone of the quayside. 'I'd carry ye, if I thought it'd do any good, but ye might be better off on your own two feet. Slowly now, we've plenty o' time.'

The pain throbbed through her once more. 'I don't think we have,' she murmured.

'What's that, lass?'

Clutching his arm, she managed to get on to the landing steps. Perspiration was pouring off her, yet at the same time she was shivering uncontrollably. Hesitantly she began to climb, pausing on each step to gather fresh strength, determined to reach the top.

'Three more now. Jus' three more, my love.'

But she stopped – with a swift intake of breath as the pain explored her again; not a pointed stab this time, but long and drawn out, moving through her. She must have moaned because John's voice suddenly sharpened with worry. He grasped her arm more tightly.

How she managed those last three steps she would never know, but vaguely she realized people were crowding around her, chattering excitedly in a strange language, and that someone was plucking at her sleeve to lead her towards the shade of a nearby tree. They helped her sit down on a packing case as yet another pain cut into her; this time she kept it to herself, gritting her teeth and pressing her lips tight together. One young African woman spoke to her, wiped some of the sweat from her neck and forehead. Her black, oval face revealed that she knew only too well what the white *memsabu* was going through. Hester looked at her warm, sympathetic eyes and a bond of trust immediately formed between the two women.

'An' haven't I searched the whole town o' Mombasa an' not a room to be found anywhere?'

An Irishman, she thought amazed. He was talking to John and protesting vigorously. Then he turned on his heel and came over to her.

'Sure, that's the way, Cabby!' he gave his approval to the young African woman. 'Look after her as best you can!' He raised his sun helmet with an exaggerated gesture. 'Muldoon's the name, ma'am. Ed Muldoon, at your service. As I've jus' been explainin' to your husband, there's not a palace to be rented anywhere on the island, but sure Cabby'll take care o' you.'

'Nyokabi,' the young woman corrected him.

'That's right – Cabby. You'll soon get the hang o' these savage names, though for the most part the poor creatures'll answer to whatever you care to call 'em.'

'Mr Muldoon is offerin' his own quarters,' John informed her apologetically. 'It's more'n a mile away on the far side o' town, but we dinna seem to have much choice.'

'It's very kind of him,' Hester answered weakly.

'Rough an' ready, ma'am. Bachelor quarters. But I'll clear my people out an' tidy it all up a bit for you. An' I've taken the liberty of sendin' for Mrs MacPherson, the missionary's wife, though they say she's away on the mainland, so it could take a while before she gets back.'

'Yes . . .' Hester tried to disguise the agony of the next pains, which were slicing into her like a knife. 'Thank you . . .' Oh, if only she could lie down, if only all those people would go away . . .

John took hold of her hand, his voice filled with concern. 'I'm sorry, lass, it's no' exactly what we planned for our first bairn an' I'm no' too certain how it'll go wi' only meself to help ye, but—'

30

'Cabby will help me,' she said emphatically, surprised he should think anything else. 'Can't you see she wants to?'

'Muldoon's orders. She's his kept woman.'

'Aren't I yours?' she retorted.

'Ye're my wife, an' there's all the difference i' the world. Besides, my love, I doubt if she knows anything about medical care.'

'Nor did Eve in the Bible when she had her first. John, women have been having babies since the world began.'

'Ay, well let's pray this Mrs MacPherson arrives in time.' He sounded unconvinced and helpless. 'Now if we can get ye across to this ghari . . .'

She took a breath. 'Yes.'

Leaning heavily on his arm, she walked unsteadily towards the *ghari* which, as far as she could see, was a simple railway trolley bearing two benches placed back-to-back with a canopy above them to provide some shade. Once there, John lifted her aboard as though she were no weight at all. She sunk on to the bench feeling dizzy, ready to faint at any second. John sat beside her, with Ed Muldoon behind. Two muscular Africans began to push the *ghari* along the rails.

'They've been ordered to go slowly an' try not to jolt us,' Muldoon explained, 'but only the Almighty knows how much they understand. At times it's beyond me.'

'What about Cabby?'

That last pain was slighter, almost bearable, so perhaps it had been another false start. Or . . . '*Ooo-ah!*' she groaned involuntarily as the next flashed through her like forked lightning. No false alarm, that one.

'Cabby can run alongside o' us,' Muldoon was telling her cheerfully. 'A fine pair o' legs, has Cabby. Best on the coast!'

'For God's sake let's move!' she heard John snapping as she slumped against him.

'Mother o' God, an' isn't that what we're doing?'

The *ghari* was rumbling along the track, picking up speed and swaying crazily. Hester held John's jacket lapel

31

crumpled in her clenched fist, digging her fingernails into it with each new spasm. Her face and neck were soaking wet. Then came the sound of more voices – men shouting, and John replying in a language she had never heard him speak before. The *ghari* was stopping. Hands lifted her down, but she was so faint from the heat and intense pain, she was hardly conscious of what was happening.

'This gentleman is a merchant from India.' John's voice sounded as though he were in some deep cave a thousand miles away; his arm held her up as he half-carried her towards the shade. 'He's heard about our problem an' he's kindly offerin' us a room.'

India – that was the magic name, she thought as she floated away. And John had enchanted her with it. Temples and holy men . . . the smell of spices . . . rich colours under a brilliant sun . . . She had listened, spell-bound, as the fog descended over the Mersey to hide the dark buildings of Liverpool in a blanket of choking greyness. The pictures he painted had made her long for the sun, that tropical sun he described so vividly, and she had spoken to her father on the subject, how she might become a missionary and . . . Oh, not with any burning desire to convert the heathen – though that was a duty the Good Lord had laid upon all Christians – but because she yearned for that warmth she had not yet experienced, those exotic colours, the mystery, the variety . . .

'Pray about it,' her father had advised drily, seeing into her soul only too clearly. 'If it is truly the will of God, He will let you know. Unambiguously.'

Then John, a few days later, had said, 'Marry me?' Quite simply, with no romantic gestures or ceremony. Just those two words – *Marry me?* And she had known there could only be one answer.

'John?'

'Ye'll be better off here, my love.' He wiped her face gently with a cloth dampened in a bowl of cool water. 'An' once Mrs MacPherson arrives, everything'll be fine.'

'Where's Cabby?' She could not understand why she was not on the *ghari* any longer but lying on a bed, an iron bed with creaking springs and great brass knobs. 'Is Cabby here?'

'She's outside.'

'I want Cabby here,' she insisted sharply.

Then she heard herself screaming as the pain clawed into her. '*Oh no, no!*' And again . . . and again . . .

The sight of Hester suffering there on the bed, tended by Cabby and two other African women from the Indian merchant's household, made Andrewes feel completely useless. He tried to help, fetching a towel, holding the bowl of water, but he knew he was only in the way. Yet he was reluctant to leave before the missionary's wife got there. She at least, he thought gloomily, would understand the need for hygiene. Every so often the three women glanced in his direction, outraged that he was still lingering in the bedroom, until at length Cabby ordered him out with a stream of incomprehensible Swahili. No mistaking her meaning. This was women's business and men were not welcome.

Downstairs in the lower room he found the Indian merchant waiting for him. He was a well-fleshed man with soft, light-brown features; earlier, he had introduced himself as 'One Roshan, from Bombay,' but Andrewes had hardly taken it in.

'I am trusting everything is to your satisfaction, Sahib?' he enquired, but not obsequiously. 'Set your mind at rest, Sahib. My women are having much experience in the delivery of children.'

*She might die.* The thought went round and round in his mind; he could not rid himself of it. *She might die.* He nodded at Roshan and went outside, restlessly, where he found Muldoon still waiting about, sitting in the shade.

'They take their time about it, these womenfolk.' Muldoon eyed him curiously. 'A man now – he'd be wantin' to get it over an' done with as quick as he could. Not women, though.'

Andrewes did not bother to answer.

'I heard you speakin' the Hindoo lingo jus' now, Mr

33

Andrewes,' the man persisted. 'Out there long, were you? Born in those parts, perhaps?'

Another *ghari* could be heard approaching, its metal wheels rasping against the rails. Andrewes roused himself.

'Will that be Mrs MacPherson now?' She was not to be expected before dusk, Muldoon had told him, but he could well have been misinformed. 'I must admit, Mr Muldoon, I'll feel much happier once she's here.'

But when the *ghari*, powered by two strapping Swahilis, came into sight around the corner he saw that its passenger was a tall, thin Englishman clad in a light-coloured suit and sun helmet, his legs crossed, and one arm draped negligently over the back of the bench.

'Mother o' God, if it isn't William Carpenter in person!' Muldoon made no attempt to hide his dislike. 'He'll be wantin' to know why you neglected to report to the Railway Office directly you landed.'

The *ghari* slowed down to a stop. As Carpenter descended from it, Andrewes heard a cry from inside, followed by the raised voices of the African women. He wanted to hurry in, but Carpenter blocked the way.

'Afternoon, Muldoon . . . Roshan . . . And you must be Andrewes, I presume? We expected you six weeks ago.' He sported a pale blond moustache, as carefully tended as a weeping willow in a landscaped garden. 'But now you've deigned to arrive it would've been a matter of courtesy to call at the Railway Office before organizing quarters.'

Andrewes stiffened. 'May I ask whom I've the pleasure of addressin'?'

'Carpenter,' the man barked. 'William Carpenter, Comptroller of Construction, Uganda Railway.'

'Ay, then ye're jus' the man I want to meet,' Andrewes said. 'I imagine the Railway Office must've made some arrangements for our accommodation?'

Though the Englishman was a slender six feet tall, Andrewes had the advantage of him by three inches and from the look on his face he was obviously uneasy about it. He flushed.

'You're under a misapprehension, Mr Andrewes. No

34

arrangements have been made for accommodation, as you'll not be staying in Mombasa. Your work will be at railhead, living under canvas.'

'Ye've no' heard then that Mrs Andrewes is in labour? Had our steamer no' been delayed, we'd have arrived on the coast in good time to find something suitable. As things are, we'd have been lost wi'out Mr Roshan's aid.' He returned Carpenter's glare unmoved. 'An' Mr Muldoon's.'

'I fail to understand how the Foreign Office could agree to your bringing your wife with you.'

'Ye dinna ken my wife,' Andrewes said briefly.

More cries from inside the house, and those women's voices again. Excited? Afraid?

'I don't doubt you're a first class engineer,' Carpenter went on wryly. 'The reports from India indicate that much. But East Africa's different, as you'll soon discover. You speak Hindustani?'

With the question his tone sharpened and for the first time Andrewes realized the man was deeply worried about something.

'Ay, well enough.'

'Good, I'd hoped you might.' He spoke briskly, as if trying to hide his fears. 'Now the situation is this. We had a message from railhead this morning reporting trouble among the Indian coolies. Our engineer-in-charge, Jackson, had been attacked and injured. It seemed also that his assistant, Murray, was in a bad way. They requested medical help and we sent the M.O., Dr Carson, up the line together with a couple of armed *askaris*, but on arrival he reported back by telegraph that the coolies were completely out of hand. In a state of mutiny, in fact. He must have been in the middle of that message when the line went dead.'

'Oh, they'd cut it,' Muldoon observed sagely. 'First thing they'd do.'

Carpenter ignored the interruption. 'Nothing else we can do today, it'll be dark shortly, but you're to set out at first light, Andrewes, and see what's going on. Sorry to push you into this so soon, but there's no other Hindustanispeaker available for the moment, and I can't afford any hold-up in the work.'

'Ay, but my wife?'

'An' am I not here to make sure no harm comes to her?' Muldoon offered eagerly, his dark eyes flickering from one face to the other. 'As for the young prince, when His Highness sees fit to be born, I'll—'

He broke off and his face lit up as the baby's first cries were heard.

Andrewes pushed past him and strode into the house, up the narrow stairs, bursting into the bedroom. 'Hester, are ye—?' Then he breathed with relief as he saw her.

She was half-sitting, half-lying in the bed, her drawn face looking ghostly against the tumbling long brown hair which spread profusely over her pillow. But her eyes were bright with happiness as she looked first at him and then down at the wrinkled, reddish, wee bairn that Nyokabi was placing in her arms.

'John – come and meet your baby,' she said simply. 'She's a girl!'

# FOUR

Andrewes passed most of that night anxiously watching over Hester as she slept and praying that the problems at the railhead camp might sort themselves out, that he would not have to leave her to fend for herself and the bairn. They had pulled out a drawer from the chest-of-drawers and made a wee bed in it to serve as a cradle. In his eyes the bairn seemed incredibly small, by far the smallest he had ever seen, and so fragile – though Hester merely smiled at him fondly when he voiced his doubts and said all new-born babies were that tiny. Maybe she was right.

Yet she had been so swollen while she was expecting, it was hard to believe such a wee bundle o' nothing had been the cause of it. *His* daughter. The life he'd set in motion. Yet already a real person, as much a person now as she would be when she'd grown up and was turning the heads of all the men in sight.

Even men such as Muldoon. For a moment his mind clouded. In so many ways a son would have been easier. He crossed to the open window and stared out into the darkness, enjoying the mellow freshness of the light breeze from the Indian Ocean, knowing in his heart that a railhead camp was no place for a daughter to grow up.

The first glimmers of light were edging into the dark sky when an Indian *jemadar* arrived to conduct him to the Railway Office on the far side of the island. By the time they got there the sun had already edged its way above the horizon and splashes of pale orange skimmed over the waves.

Carpenter was in the telegraph office, rattling at the key impatiently. He turned as Andrewes entered.

'Line's still dead I'm afraid, so there's no alternative – you'll have to go up there, though I admit I don't feel happy about it.' He stared at Andrewes doubtfully. 'Not because you've chosen this moment to start a family, don't think that! But you are new to Africa, you need time to settle in and get your bearings, find out what's what . . . Well, it can't be helped. At least you're accustomed to dealing with native labour, after India.'

Andrewes followed him out of the office towards the siding where the brand-new F-Class locomotive was already getting up steam. Construction work on the railway, he explained, was already behind schedule; to date only twenty miles of track had been laid and a full-scale mutiny among the Indian coolies had to be avoided at all costs. When the project had started earlier that year, Carpenter said, it had been impossible to foresee the difficulties. All supplies had to be brought in by sea. Mombasa harbour was unsuitable, but there was a natural, deep-water creek at Kilindini where steamers could anchor, though their cargoes were carried ashore by lighter. One of the first tasks was to build a jetty to allow ships to unload alongside. Everything had to be imported, even the timbers needed for the long wooden viaduct which temporarily carried the track from Mombasa island to the mainland.

Carpenter paused, pointing across to it proudly 'We've placed orders for an iron bridge, you understand, but we're rather pleased with our timber causeway. Over half a mile long and 1,700 feet high, the only one of its kind in Africa. Know how long it took us to put it up, once all the bits and pieces were here? Ninety-two days! They say you're a good engineer, Mr Andrewes – well, let's see if you can beat that for a record!'

And this was the first stride, he went on, along a road which eventually – if it all worked out – would end some 600 miles inland on the shores of Lake Victoria. 'It's a revolution. To go there now you'd have to recruit a caravan of porters and askaris, you'd have a four month trek on foot over rough country, in danger of being attacked on the way . . . But, believe me, the railway will change all that.'

'Ay,' Andrewes grunted, hardly listening to the man. 'But right now it'd be more to the point if ye could tell me what to expect at railhead. Ye had no hint this was likely to happen?'

'None. Oh, we'd a few minor problems, but nothing serious . . . I'm sending you, Mr Andrewes, because you've the right background and you speak the language. I don't want to turn out the army, that could be the worst move, but I can spare you four sepoys. They're just two weeks off the boat from Bombay, so don't expect a lot. Oh, and there's this chappie . . .'

A group of Africans stood at the side of the track and one stepped forward to address Carpenter in quick, musical Swahili. His skin seemed a shade darker than most – a young man, perhaps in his late twenties, with alert eyes and a finely-shaped face. Even in his loose white *kanzu* he looked muscular and athletic, while on his shoulder he carried a single-shot Snider slung from a strap of animal hide.

'For some reason he insists on being taken on as your askari,' Carpenter was saying lightly, with a dismissive laugh. 'I told him it'd be your decision, on your pay-roll, but it's not a bad idea in the circumstances. Someone to watch your back, at any rate. We do know him, by the way. He's been on three or four safaris, including survey parties. Reliable, as they go. Handles a gun better than most.'

'For a trial period, maybe,' Andrewes agreed. Something in the man's appearance pleased him. His eyes were intelligent, and there was nothing sullen about his expression.

'Ten rupees a month will do for a start.' Carpenter translated it into halting Swahili and a slight argument developed; but then the man gave in. 'That's settled, though you may have to pay more later if you decide to keep him. His name's Kamau.'

'Kamau?' Andrewes nodded, then turned towards the Indian engine driver to greet him in Hindustani. The single inspection coach which – with the locomotive –

made up the entire train was familiar Indian rolling stock and he commented on it to the driver, bringing a smile to his face. Kamau could ride on the ledge between the rear buffers, he decided; the four sepoys could travel inside with him. 'Right, we'll be on our way.'

As he unslung his new Winchester repeating rifle he became aware that Carpenter was eyeing it with some interest.

'One thing you should remember about Africa, Mr Andrewes,' he said by way of farewell. 'Personality wins here. Guns may get you out of a jam, but when the chips are down personality wins every time.'

Watching him from the inspection coach, Andrewes could not help feeling Carpenter looked absurdly out of place in his immaculate white suit and smart pith helmet. Around him stood stacks of railway equipment and old crates. For a moment he hesitated, raising his hand as if to give a military salute; then he changed his mind and doffed the pith helmet instead, civilian fashion. Correctly.

The little train seemed to quiver apprehensively as it eased its way across the timber viaduct but once on the mainland it plucked up courage and moved steadily along the newly-laid track which, after a mile or two, began to climb into the hills, passing plantations of coconut palms and mangoes set against a backdrop of thick forest. As the line curved he caught tantalizing glimpses of Mombasa town. Somewhere among those rooftops . . .

Hester had slept only fitfully that night and he'd felt grateful Cabby was there, though as for the bairn, she'd not have been lustier if she had been born in Balmoral Castle with all the royal doctors in attendance.

'We should call her Cabby, don't you think, John?' Hester had suggested, almost in a whisper, her face still pale and strained. 'Or Nyo—'

'Nyokabi!' With a flash of white teeth the girl had acknowledged Hester's attempt to pronounce her name. 'Nyokabi!'

He prayed to God he would find them both still alive and well on his return, whenever that might be.

For several minutes the town remained visible. The sparkling Indian Ocean beyond merged into the blue sky, dissolving the horizon. Then the line suddenly twisted into a forest whose thick trees and high, spreading ferns blocked the view. Reluctantly, Andrewes turned his attention to the four sepoys in the carriage with him, clutching their rifles nervously between their knees.

'Have any o' ye been up to railhead before?' he asked in Hindustani, thinking they might be able to tell him something of the layout of the camps.

None had.

'This is no mutiny, Sahib,' one volunteered – a thin, wiry man with sad eyes and red-stained teeth. His name was Patel, he said, and already he regretted having left Bombay for this uncomfortable adventure. 'Our people say the railway camp has been attacked by savages.'

'What savages?'

'Black men from the forest. These are terrible people, I have heard. Their women are impure, unbelievers in any faith, who do not cover themselves but wear only ornaments of brass and iron. And the men shave their heads to present a most frightening appearance in an exceedingly ugly fashion. They shoot poisoned arrows – one scratch will kill. They say even an elephant may be destroyed by one such arrow, so potent are they.'

Patel was looking at him slily and Andrewes suspected he might merely be trying to test out the new Sahib's courage. 'Ye canna tell me ye witnessed this wi' your own eyes,' he commented.

'I hope never to witness such a thing, Sahib,' replied Patel gravely, shifting his grip on his rifle. 'We can shoot them down before they come too close.'

'Ye'll no' fire till I gi' the order!' Andrewes snapped, looking at each one in turn. 'D'ye understand?'

One stray shot, he thought, could bring all hell down on his head.

For the next twenty minutes or so no word was spoken. The four sepoys occasionally glanced at each other and shifted about on the hard seats, but they remained silent.

41

Andrewes stared out grimly at the variegated landscape. The forest gave way patchily to stretches of low shrubs spotted with yellow and purple flowers. The heat was stifling and the movement of the train created hardly any breeze at all.

Then a change in the rhythm of the wheels clacking over the rails alerted them to the fact that they were slowing down. Patel leaned out of one of the windows, his rifle ready. Andrewes checked the other side. Nothing to be seen. As the train came quietly to a halt he jumped down to investigate.

'Sahib – one mile still to go, Sahib!' the engine driver reported, keeping his voice low. 'Perhaps not so much. It is possible now for you to continue on foot from this present place.'

'That's what ye advise, is it?'

'The noise from the train will be warning them you are coming, Sahib, so it is best you approach on foot with caution.'

As the driver was speaking, Andrews noticed that his new African *askari* had unobtrusively taken up a position a yard or two behind him. *Someone to watch your back,* Carpenter had said. A deep silence lay on the countryside around; the only human sounds came from the low voices of the sepoys.

A slight hiss of steam from the engine. In the distance, a bird call, taken up yet again from even farther off. Among the foliage a vague rustle . . . the light humming and scraping of a myriad insects . . .

Andrewes remembered uneasily some of the tales he had heard about African hunters who could stalk their prey so discreetly that not a twig broke underfoot, not a movement was heard . . . The driver was right, of course. The sound of the approaching train would give any trouble-makers ample warning.

'When we arrive at railhead,' he said, 'is there one place which is visible from the whole camp, where everyone can see us?'

The driver looked at him doubtfully. 'Near the water tower, Sahib, the ground is continuing to rise.'

'Then that's where we stop, understand?'

'But Sahib—'

'When it first comes into sight, sound the whistle – one good long blast. I want everyone to see us. Then, as we get closer, a second blast on the whistle. And a third when we stop.'

'Sahib, they will kill you. I am knowing them very well.' He shook his head, uncomprehending. 'For myself, they will understand I am obeying your orders and they will be sparing me. But, Sahib, you are having a wife and a new-born baby . . .'

'Ye heard my instructions,' Andrewes told him.

'Then it is not in my hands.' The driver hoisted himself on to the engine again and muttered something to the fireman who was stoking up with more logs.

As the train jerked forward once more Andrewes tried to work out the details of his plan, which so far was little more than a hunch. According to Carpenter, almost a thousand Indian coolies were employed at the railhead at that time; their main encampment was on one side of the line, opposite the water tower, although there was a secondary, smaller camp a little distance away on the other side. One thing was clear – there was nothing to be gained by arriving on foot. A single British engineer with four Indian sepoys and an African *askari* would immediately be swamped by a mob of that size. His only chance lay in boldness.

Over the last quarter of a mile the ground levelled out and the train began to gather speed for a while; then, unexpectedly, the driver sounded the whistle – a long, shrill blast. On the left of the track Andrewes caught a glimpse of a wooden stockade surrounding a small camp; no sign of coolies.

A second blast on the whistle. Almost immediately the brakes were applied and the flanged metal wheels skidded, screeching, over the rails.

43

The train stopped – a third blast, short and peremptory; then a loud hiss of escaping steam.

Following his instructions, the sepoys immediately jumped out and took up their positions, two on each side of the track with their backs to the train. Andrewes straightened his jacket, put on his sun helmet, and stepped out on to the little platform at the end of the coach.

A crowd of several hundred men had gathered, with more still arriving. Some sat or squatted in the shade; others stood in small groups, watching to see what was going to happen. Taking his time, Andrewes climbed down from the coach, went a few paces towards them, and then stopped, keeping to the high ground. The crowd shifted a little, spreading, and he was glad that Kamau had joined him a step or two behind. He waited, warily, for the coolies to make the next move.

About two dozen men separated themselves from the rest and came purposefully up the slope towards him. They were armed with heavy sticks, though at least two had rifles. Andrewes stood firm, holding his own gun loosely in one hand as though unaware of any threat; if he betrayed the least sign of his nervousness they would wash over him like a tidal wave. The tactic worked and they straggled to a halt about three yards away.

'Is today a holiday?' he called out to them in Hindustani, making no attempt to hide his displeasure. 'Why is no one working? Where is Jackson Sahib? And Doctor Sahib?'

'Alas, Jackson Sahib is not well at all,' one man replied, also in Hindustani but imitating the white man's accent. Clearly this was the acknowledged wag of the group – a lean, bare-headed young man dressed in a faded, striped *dhoti* which was ragged at the edges. 'He was struck down yesterday by Allah the Merciful and even now Doctor Sahib is at his tent.'

A few of the others laughed, but most stared at Andrewes and his sepoys with undisguised contempt. One among them appeared to be their leader. Taller than the rest, he sported a tightly-knotted turban and a fringe of dark beard.

44

On his shoulder he carried a sledgehammer, as though on his way to work.

'Jackson Sahib needs no visitors,' he said, blocking the way. Grinning, he looked Andrewes up and down while the others fell back, leaving the ground clear for him. 'So you can be returning to Mombasa.'

Andrewes ignored him, addressing himself to the crowd at large. 'My name is Andrewes,' he announced. 'I have come here from India jus' as ye have. Perhaps some o' ye knew me there?'

His gaze took in each group in turn but there was no response. The sun was high, glaring hotly into his eyes; the coolies had fallen silent. One false move, he knew, and he'd be dead. That crowd would close in around him, beat him into the ground . . . His rifle would be useless against them. With cold deliberation he handed the Winchester to Kamau and, unarmed, took a pace towards the ringleader, who was now holding the sledgehammer with both hands, ready to use it.

'Take me to Jackson Sahib.'

The Indian stared at him insolently.

'Well? I havena got all day.'

The man's eyes dropped and he blew his nose, pressing one nostril with a forefinger and emitting a stream of white mucus from the other; it hit the soil close to Andrewes' boots. With a face-saving leer he then shifted aside to allow the new Sahib to pass.

From among the crowd came a low murmur of disappointment. Some began to drift away. Hiding his relief, Andrewes considered retrieving the Winchester, then decided against; the gesture had paid off so far, and provided his *askari* stayed close at hand . . . Yet what if the coolies had threatened him directly? How much loyalty could he expect for ten rupees a month?

The wag in the striped *dhoti* scurried towards him. 'Sahib, I shall accompany you to the tent of Jackson Sahib in person. My name is Abdul Hakim and I deeply respect the manner in which you faced Ratnam, a very dangerous man. And you had no weapon, which is most wonderful.'

Andrewes was well acquainted with his kind. Not an ounce of courage anywhere in his make-up, though in its place a deep-rooted instinct for survival which probably served him better than any act of bravery.

'Very well, Abdul Hakim,' he decided, his eyes searching among the others and picking out the two with rifles. 'And these two men can come along with us.'

'Yes, Sahib.'

'Let 'em walk ahead.'

The sullen knots of coolies allowed him to pass unmolested. Several seemed awed at his height and hastily moved out of the way.

'It was indeed a most unfortunate accident which befell Jackson Sahib,' Abdul Hakim explained in flowery Hindustani, half-running alongside him and gesticulating as he talked. 'Of course we were all exceedingly full of pity, though I must apologize that some hot-heads in our midst took advantage of the situation to stir up much trouble.'

'Who cut the telegraph wires?'

'Oh no, Sahib!' Abdul Hakim did his best to sound shocked; obviously the rebels had chosen their spokesman well. 'This cutting was the work of people from the village – very bad people, Sahib, you would not believe! They are cause of many problems.'

'Such as?'

'Those stories I could not repeat, Sahib.'

Jackson's tent stood with three others in a clearing some distance from the main encampment, totally unprotected by any stockade or fortification. To one side, a thick grove of trees offered ample cover to any would-be attacker – though Abdul Hakim said there was a Christian mission village and plantation beyond it; while on the other side, and clearly the reason why the site had been chosen, was an uneven outcrop of rock sprouting rough grass and ferns, with a miniature waterfall tumbling down through its crevices into a transparent pool below. It was an idyllic setting, yet foolhardy.

As they approached, a stout, balding man emerged from the main tent, his glasses glinting in the hot sunlight. His plump face lit up and he hurried forward to grasp Andrewes' hand.

'Ah, you must be the relief expedition! Very glad to see you. Very glad.' His voice was rounded and plummy, his handshake vigorous. 'You're quicker than I imagined, but none too soon, I can assure you of that. No, none too soon. Nasty business, this. Very nasty. I'm Carson, by the way. Dr Carson. My two patients are in the tent.'

'Badly hurt?'

'You might say that.' He gazed at Kamau, Abdul Hakim and the two others with the rifles. 'How many men did you bring with you? More than these four, surely? Though I think I've seen this man before.'

Abdul Hakim grinned at him.

'I'm a railway engineer, no' a soldier,' Andrewes informed him briefly. 'Andrewes. John Philip Andrewes.'

Dr Carson regarded him doubtfully and his well-trimmed moustache seemed to droop at the sides in disappointment. 'You're still welcome, of course. Very welcome. But what we need right now is a detachment of troops with a maxim gun. A whiff of grapeshot, as the great Emperor Bonaparte once put it. Only way to control a mob.'

'Ay, but dead men canna work.' Andrewes eyed Dr Carson distastefully. 'An' I think as a medical man your interest lies surely in savin' life rather than destroyin' it.'

'Not been long in Africa, have you?' said Dr Carson pointedly. 'But come an' see my two patients. No doubt they'll be able to put you right.'

Turning to the two men with the rifles, Andrewes instructed them to stand guard outside the tent, but they were not to shoot; if anyone came near, let Abdul Hakim fetch him. They both nodded vigorously, yet were obviously not at ease handling the guns. Probably stolen, Andrewes thought; though it was still too soon to start asking questions. The situation could easily blow up in his face even now.

'Ready?' Dr Carson demanded with heavy sarcasm.

'Ay.'

Inside the tent he found the two patients lying on camp beds set a couple of feet apart. Between them was a low table with bottles and medical implements; the whole tent stank like a field hospital.

'What d'you think, Jackson – we've a visitor from the outside world! Meet John Philip Andrewes, another railway engineer freshly arrived in the dark continent. He's come to raise the siege an' restore order. Unarmed, you'll observe.'

'Must be an idiot.' Jackson's head was swathed in sweat-soaked bandages and his arm was in a sling; he propped himself up on his good elbow and examined Andrewes disdainfully. 'Who the hell sent you up here – Carpenter? The best he could do?'

'Jackson had a lump o' rock thrown at him,' Dr Carson commented, displaying little sympathy. 'Caught him on the left temple. Next thing he knew they were rioting, knocking him about, trampling over him. The right arm's broken . . . bruises over much of the body . . . I telegraphed Mombasa for help an' what do they send? *You!*'

'What started the trouble?' asked Andrewes.

'Going to put it right, are you?' Jackson jeered, wincing as he shifted about on the camp bed. 'By yourself? Jesus Christ give me patience. Listen – get on the wrong side o' that lot an' they'll stick a knife between your ribs before you notice it.'

The man on the second camp bed groaned. He was lying on his back, his face bloodless, his eyes open but seeing nothing; dark spittle dribbled from the corners of his mouth.

'That's our surveyor, Murray,' the doctor said calmly. 'That's how I found him when I got here yesterday. Why I wasn't sent for earlier I can't understand.'

'What have ye diagnosed?'

'Africa, that's what I've diagnosed. That's what we're all suffering from – bloody Africa. But don't get me wrong. If I can get him down to Mombasa he might live. I've seen worse.'

Jackson interrupted him violently. 'Murray's dying,

anyone can tell that. It's a missionary he needs now, not a doctor. Or maybe Andrewes knows the funeral service?'

'Ay, well the first thing is to get the men back to work,' Andrewes replied briefly. Pushing past Dr Carson he left the tent without waiting to listen to Jackson's jibes.

Outside, the warm air seemed fresh and clean after that stench of sickness. The little waterfall churned and gurgled, its spray breaking the light into rainbow patches. Through the branches a slight breeze was whispering. He could still hear Jackson and Carson arguing and was glad to be away from it.

The moment he emerged Kamau stepped forward and stood close to him. He held the Winchester in his hands; his own Snider was slung from his shoulder. Abdul Hakim and the two men with the stolen rifles had been joined by several more Indians, some frowning sulkily but others looking merely curious about what the new Sahib was going to do next.

'If the men have any grievances, now is the time to talk everythin' over!' he announced in Hindustani, choosing his words carefully. 'I have only jus' arrived here, so I need help from all o' ye to understand the problems. An' we can make a start now. Abdul Hakim, will ye tell all the jemadars I am here by the waterfall an' ready to listen to them.'

Abdul Hakim bustled forward eagerly, his waggish face one bright smile; two of the *jemadars* were already there among the onlookers, he said, but he would send messengers for the others.

'Call me when they are ready.'

He turned to Kamau. With a gun in his hands he would have felt more secure, but he had no wish to give the impression he was threatening them. In any case, he knew the feeling was deceptive. At the most he might manage one shot before they killed him. It was a tight-rope he was walking. His decisions had to be right the first time; there would be no second chance.

'What-ever-ye-do,' he said to Kamau slowly in English, praying to God the man would understand him and

49

regretting the time he had frittered away on board ship when he should have been studying Swahili, 'dinna-fire-a-shot. If-trouble, warn-me. But-no-shoot – savey?'

Kamau smiled and said something in Swahili; then he paused, as if waiting for a reply.

'I—' Andrewes started, but then he gave up. 'Och, jus' dinna shoot anyone, d'ye understand? Nay, I dinna suppose ye do.'

He lifted the flap and went into the tent again. Jackson and Dr Carson looked at him cynically.

'You've decided you're safer in here with us, I imagine,' Dr Carson remarked sarcastically. 'You're quick on the uptake, Andrewes, I'll say that for you. Unlike our masters in Mombasa. When did you land?'

'Yesterday.' It seemed a week already, with all that had happened.

'Twenty-four hours, is that right? Makes you an old Africa hand by now, what d'you say, Jackson?'

With his one good hand Jackson retrieved a glass from among the medicine bottles and poured himself a whisky. 'Be bloody lucky if he lives till tomorrow. Christ, you wouldn't think they've a maxim gun in Fort Jesus. It's soldiers we need up here, not a—'

He stopped in mid-sentence and drained his glass.

'You speak their tongue, it seems,' Dr Carson commented. 'Heard you at it out there. That's something, I suppose.'

'I was ten years in India,' said Andrewes. 'Long enough to know ye wouldna get this sort o' trouble if ye handled the men the right way.' He tried to sound more confident than he felt.

Jackson's expression hardened. Keeping his eyes on Andrewes, he poured more whisky. On the other bed, Murray was groaning again.

'Not my department,' Dr Carson was saying. 'Jackson's the engineer-in-charge.'

'I begin to understand why they rioted. D'ye have rifles?'

'We did, till the coolies stole 'em. Though we've still got the shotguns.'

50

'Loaded?'

'Naturally.'

'Ay well, if ye wish to stay alive there'll be no shootin' – d'ye hear me? Ye'll gain nothin' by starting a massacre.'

Jackson intervened. 'You weren't listening, Andrewes. I'm the engineer-in-charge here, an' that means I give the orders.'

'Ay, ye've made that plain enough.' Andrewes turned and left the tent without giving him a chance to reply.

At the waterfall roughly a hundred men had gathered. He climbed the rocks to a point where everyone could see him and waited for silence, at the same time searching the crowd for any sign of Ratnam with his sledgehammer. But he was not among them and Andrewes sensed with some relief that the general mood was more curiosity than anger. They would notice he was still unarmed, though Kamau had also positioned himself on the rocks a couple of yards away, where he stood partly hidden by the giant ferns.

Speaking in Hindustani, Andrewes began to explain that he wanted to hear about their grievances from their own mouths. He was new to Africa, he said, and still had much to learn about the country, but he had worked for many years in India and was pleased to find himself again among people he knew and respected. When the railway had been built many of them would return home with the money they had earned. But some would wish to settle in this new land. Their right to do so was clearly stated in the contract, and for them the railway would be a vital link with the coast.

'Now we have this problem which is troublin' us,' he continued. He was holding their attention, he felt, which was half the battle. 'As I explained, I want to hear from ye how it came about, an' what wrongs need to be put right. But no work has been done today, an' the sun is already high. No work means no money. Now I ask your advice an' your help. Let us talk again when the sun is settin', this evenin' – but in the meantime, late as it is, let the men get back to work now an' they'll be paid for a full day.'

It was a gamble. Had the crowd been hostile it would

never have worked. As it was, two or three of the *jemadars* voiced objections but the others overruled them. It was almost as if a great sigh of relief was sweeping through the camp as each one called his gang together and organized the return to work. Andrewes remained on the rock for some time watching the bustle of activity. He was under no illusions about his victory. That evening he would have to face them again; the arguments could be long and bitter.

No, it was a skirmish he had won, not the whole campaign. And now he would have to inform Mombasa. Would Carpenter pass the news on to Hester, he wondered – or would he leave her to worry in ignorance? Luckily Roshan could be trusted, he was convinced of that. The Roshan family had been trading on this coast for three generations at least, he had been told, and were highly respected.

'They are lifting the rails, Sahib!' Abdul Hakim told him excitedly as they heard the men's voices chanting a work song in the distance. 'They know they are meeting you again this evening you will not be disappointing them.'

'I only hope ye're right!' Andrewes said in English as he jumped down from the rock.

He retrieved his Winchester from Kamau and slung it on his shoulder. Its weight was reassuring; unlike some, he had never been a lover of guns, but nor did he despise them. Pausing briefly at the tent, he glanced inside to explain the situation and that a train would be organized to get them back to Mombasa. Jackson started some blustering reply but Andrewes dropped the flap again impatiently. Ordering Abdul Hakim and the men with the stolen rifles to lead the way, he went back to the train.

The four sepoys were lounging in the shade, yawning and talking. As they saw Andrewes approaching they scrambled to their feet. Patel snapped out a command to bring them to attention.

'Nothing to report, Sahib!' He grinned with a wide flash of stained teeth. 'No trouble here. Do we return to Mombasa?'

'We stay.' Andrewes turned to the men with the stolen

guns. 'Ay, now these rifles – ye've looked after 'em well. I'm pleased. But ye'll no' be wishin' to lose a day's pay, so if ye'll place the guns by the train ye can get back to work.'

The men were too surprised to resist. He had given no order, spoken no word of reproach, nor asked how they had acquired the guns in the first place. One stepped back as if to protest but Kamau was behind him; the four sepoys spread out, ready. They had no choice but to lay the guns down as instructed and then back away, relieved they had got off so lightly.

Once they had gone, Andrewes ordered Abdul Hakim to take him to the traffic manager's hut where the telegraph equipment had been temporarily installed. He found papers torn up and strewn across the floor, pages ripped from the logbook and furniture overturned, but miraculously the telegraph itself was undamaged. Even the wire was intact inside the hut, although outside it had been pulled loose from the terminals.

'Abdul Hakim, d'ye know how to repair the line?'

'No, Sahib.'

'Then pick up that coil o' wire an' I'll teach ye.'

Half-an-hour later Andrewes had made contact with Mombasa. He reported that he was investigating the cause of the disturbance but in the meantime work had been resumed. More details to follow. His message was acknowledged and he was about to get up from the table when Mombasa began a lengthy reply, mostly routine instructions, but ending: YOU WILL WISH TO KNOW THAT YOUR WIFE AND DAUGHTER ARE BOTH DOING WELL AND SEND THEIR WARMEST REGARDS STOP CONGRATULATIONS STOP I AWAIT YOUR FULL REPORT CARPENTER ENDS.

Straightening up, Andrewes became conscious that Kamau had been watching him closely, his quick eyes following every move. 'Ay, maybe ye think this is white man's magic,' he said, though realizing his words would not be understood. 'If so, ye'd be wrong. What ye see is science an' engineerin' which is available to anyone takin' the trouble to reach out for it.'

53

Kamau's fingers touched the morse key, then he looked up at Andrewes and made some answer in Swahili.

'Ay, no doubt ye're right, whatever it was ye said!' Andrewes remarked drily.

The two men laughed, as if satisfied they had made a kind of contact in spite of the language problem, and then Andrewes went out of the hut to give his orders to Patel. He had a nagging feeling that fresh trouble was just below the surface and the sepoys would need to mount a permanent guard over the telegraph. As for the men in the tent, his mind was already made up. Dr Carson could take Murray down to Mombasa that same day if he wished, but Andrewes was prepared to hold on to Jackson even against his will until he could let Carpenter have his own full report. Let Jackson get there first, he thought, and he might just as well pack up to catch the next boat out.

Left alone in the hut, Kamau read the message which Andrewes had painstakingly written out as each morse letter came through on the telegraph. Some of the words were unfamiliar but he understood the gist of it well enough. Ngengi had taught him English through the many stories he told about Bwana Nyama whose words he had frequently quoted in the way he had originally spoken them. And reading, too – tracing the letters in the dust with the end of a stick. But at the same time he had uttered a warning.

'You need cunning if you work for the white man,' he had said. 'Bwana Nyama was different, and I learned these things from him, but with the others it is wise to keep them secret. When you work for them or travel with them on safari, remember this. The clever man observes everything, but reveals nothing.'

54

# FIVE

Murray died the same day and they buried him in a grove of trees beyond the waterfall. Dr Carson read the service from a tattered Book of Common Prayer which he produced from the depths of his medical bag, while Andrewes, Jackson and two Muslim gravediggers formed the meagre congregation. His was the third Christian grave in that little clearing; the other two were marked by simple wooden crosses against which the termites were already beginning to establish new colonies.

'Thank Christ that's finished!' Jackson declared roughly as the short ceremony ended and the two Indians started to shovel the reddish soil back into the grave. 'I need a drink!'

He limped off towards the tent.

Andrews watched him go without comment. The sun was already dipping below the horizon, tingeing the pale sky with smears of crimson. That meant his daughter was now a full day old, he thought. Well, they were better off in Mombasa for the time being. They should stay down there some months at least.

A slight breeze had sprung up, a welcome relief from the heat, carrying with it the pungent smells of the hundreds of cooking fires, familiar smells of hot spices which brought back memories of his years in India. When the small chorus of cicadas started up he might have been back there. Only the sight of Kamau standing a few yards away, as watchful as ever, reminded him that this was Africa. Yet he wondered why the man never relaxed. Did he too suspect more trouble?

Then, from somewhere hidden deep in the forest came the sound of drumming, a low steady pulse with quicker, higher-pitched rhythms woven intricately around it. They had said there was a mission village in that direction;

but when Andrewes had suggested asking the missionary to conduct the funeral service Jackson had snorted scornfully.

'Not a real bloody missionary,' he had said. 'A Bombay African. Makes me spew to see 'em dressed up in our sort of clothes.'

'Mainly a settlement for freed slaves, that village,' Dr Carson had explained, displaying a shade less hostility since the coolies had returned to work. 'No way they can get home, of course, even if they can remember where they came from. Now we're meddling in their lives again, building a railway. Ask me, we're ruining Africa. Ruining the place.'

Andrewes had not argued, having other things on his mind, but it would take more than Carson to shake his faith in railways. They brought change where change was needed – witness the achievements in Britain. Or India. Anywhere in the world. He often thought of his own father, who had worked with Brunel in his heyday. On a Sunday evening before the coal fire, after he had closed his Bible or one of those books on political economy he used to read, he would explain to his sons how the steam engine was undermining the old relationship between master and man. It would topple the inherited, unjust social order and replace it with something better.

'Before the invention o' the steam engine,' he would say once he got into his stride, 'the life o' man was nasty, brutish an' short. Ay, an' superstitious into the bargain. Now wi' railways an' factories we may still be a long way off paradise, d'ye ken – but, laddie, at leas' we now hae a sportin' chance!'

Andrews glanced at Dr Carson who was still gazing pensively at the newly-filled grave. 'Ye've no idea what Murray died of?'

'No.' A moment's pause. 'An' if I could give it a name, that'd be no help. We know too little, Andrewes. For the past seven years or more I've been watching men die on this coast. I've sailed it between here an' the Cape three times as ship's doctor. Then I was in Zanzibar, Mombasa . . . an' right into the interior with Lugard, as far as Uganda. I'm still trying to get my book together on that trip. An' now this crazy business – building a railway, I ask you! For what purpose? It's lunatic. They can't even use local labour but have to import these coolies from India. You like India, I suppose? Well, I like Africa – the way it was.'

'Thought ye hated it.'

'That too.' He changed the subject abruptly. 'Think you'll be able to settle this trouble?'

'Maybe.'

Together they walked back through the trees towards the waterfall where Andrewes perched on a rock and explained how he had been trying to sift truth from falsehood in the stories the *jemadars* had told him.

'Between you an' me,' Dr Carson said, filling his pipe from a battered tobacco tin, 'Jackson got on the wrong side o' these coolies the first day he came up here to railhead. He'd been used to dealing with Irish navvies. When he's got to put down fighting between Hindus an' Muslims he's lost.'

'Trouble involvin' the village, from all they say.'

The drumming still throbbed on the air; maybe it held a meaning, but there was no one who could tell him.

'They're mostly freed slaves in that village, as I was explaining. That's been British policy over the past few years, to free the slaves – give 'em a scrap o' paper to prove it's all legal, then turn 'em loose. Leave 'em to scratch what sort o' living they can from the soil. Or starve. It's not unknown for some freed slaves to sell their papers to the highest bidder an' then go back to their previous owners – Indian merchants, Zanzibaris, Arab traders . . . At least that way they could be sure of a meal every day. So who can blame 'em?'

But with the building of the railway suddenly bringing hordes of coolies into the neighbourhood, Dr Carson continued, the villages around now had a market for the food they grew. And for other services. The local women were enticed to the camp and inevitably there were quarrels. Jackson had intervened, heavy-handedly.

'He forbade the women to set foot in the camp again an' fined the troublemakers a day's pay. Really laid down the law. Which led to this mess. Can't ignore it either, now it's happened.' He sucked on his pipe, emitting clouds of thick smoke. 'According to Jackson, the fellow you want to watch out for is a brute of a man with muscles like a prize fighter. Often carries a sledgehammer round with him . . . You know, you should take up a pipe while you're out here, Andrewes. Keeps the insects off.'

Andrewes' tent was nearer the main camp than the others; the site was suggested by Abdul Hakim after long discussion with two of the *jemadars*, and that in itself was some indication that they were beginning to accept him. Abdul Hakim also recruited a personal servant, an older man called Ali who, he said, was an excellent cook. 'Of either Indian or British food, whichever you are requiring, Sahib.' He was extremely thin, with hardly any teeth; his eyes had a dreamy look as though he spent most of his time smoking *bhang*, and yet Abdul Hakim had been right about his cooking.

After he had eaten, Andrewes sat outside his tent in the cool of the evening. There was a steady murmur of men's voices from the camp, punctuated by an occasional loud laugh or the sudden flaring of what sounded like a quarrel, though it died down again immediately. Soon he expected the *jemadars* would arrive; not all of them, for he had heard they were electing spokesmen, yet they would have to find some face-saving formula.

With the sound of the voices, the cicadas, the smell of the spices, he again had this strange feeling that he was back in India, that he had only to reach out and Gita would be there, still alive. Her gentle features were hidden only by the darkness; at any moment he expected to see the laugh in her eyes, or her slim arm rising to adjust the *sari* over her shoulder. It had seemed then that their life together must go on for ever and ever; but now here he was in

58

East Africa less than two years later, with an English wife and a new-born child not twenty miles away down in Mombasa. A wife he loved, as he'd loved Gita.

One day, he knew, he would have to tell Hester about it all. She had a right to know, after all.

But not yet.

The *jemadars* arrived quietly and stood in the semi-darkness just outside the circle of light cast by the safari lamp, waiting for him to invite them to approach. He welcomed them and, after a long exchange of polite words, asked them to explain what had caused the trouble. One had obviously been appointed to do most of the talking, although the others joined in to enlarge on a point or to express their indignation. As he had expected, the discussion took many hours and it was not until they all felt everything had been said that a conclusion could be reached. He pointed out that some give-and-take was necessary, and this they accepted. After a quick consultation among themselves they solemnly undertook to make sure there would be no more trouble with the villagers; they would punish any offenders themselves. For his part Andrewes agreed to forget the fine of one day's pay which Jackson had imposed. It was as good a settlement as anyone could expect, he felt. Get them back to work, Carpenter had said; which is what he had done, with no loss of face on either side.

But as they left, one *jemadar* lingered behind to explain privately how there was much bad feeling among the men; in his opinion it would be a miracle if they accepted the agreement. He knew for certain some hot-heads were planning more disruption. 'But I can always be telling you what they say, Sahib.'

Andrewes looked at him cynically; he'd come across this type often enough before. 'If they're the men who attacked Jackson Sahib, ye've a duty to point 'em out to me now.'

'Sahib, with so much confusion, who could be certain of the identities of such men?'

'I'll find 'em out sooner or later,' Andrewes was amused

in spite of himself, but he tried not to let the *jemadar* spot it. 'Ye can tell 'em I said so.'

By the next morning there was no evidence at railhead that any disturbance had ever taken place. Work was proceeding normally on each of the main sites. True, the men glanced around as he stood watching them, but there was nothing hostile or secretive in their expressions. He stayed for some time, observing the gang spacing out the sleepers, and waited until the next lot had brought up the rails, dropping them into place, to be followed by the men carrying the fishplates, keys, nuts and bolts to secure them. Nothing to grumble at there.

After a while he went to the traffic manager's hut to send off his report to Mombasa. As he tapped it out letter by letter he noticed that Kamau was taking it all in. Would there be enough words in Swahili, he wondered, to explain the principles on which the telegraph was based? Perhaps not.

Carpenter's reply started with the news that Mrs MacPherson, the missionary's wife, was looking after Hester and Gaby. The name 'Gaby' surprised him; a misspelling of Cabby, perhaps? She had said something about calling the bairn Cabby, though he would have preferred Hester Mary.

As the telegraph chattered on, he jotted down the full message. He was to despatch the train back to Mombasa ... TO FETCH YOUR ASSISTANT TIM WILTON NEWLY ARRIVED FROM ZANZIBAR ... and Dr Carson was to advise whether Jackson's injuries might not be better treated on the coast.

From outside came a sudden noise. Kamau swung around to position himself silently near the door. But it was Abdul Hakim who came in.

Kamau's nervous, Andrewes thought. Perhaps rightly so. He remembered the *jemadar's* warning.

The engine driver had already been getting up a good head of steam and was anxious to go. Andrewes added a few more sentences to the handwritten report he was

60

preparing for Carpenter and gave it to Patel with instructions that he was to hand it to the Comptroller in person and no one else. With it was a list of stores which Patel should bring with him on the return journey, and a note for Hester.

Once the train had left, Andrewes ordered Kamau and Abdul Hakim to go with him to inspect the ground where track would have to be laid during the coming weeks. Part of the route led through a narrow gorge where gangs of coolies were already busy levelling the boulder-strewn earth and chipping away at the cliff sides. Beyond the gorge they came to several deep potholes in the rock, each about two feet in diameter with perfectly rounded rims like basins. Here they stopped and gazed at the breathtaking view of a vast, flat, dry plain covered in part with dense low scrub but broken here and there by bleak stretches of brown grass and exposed red soil. A few stunted trees stood, isolated, against the horizon.

'Nyika,' said Kamau.

'Taru Desert,' Abdul Hakim confirmed cheerfully with a sweep of his arm. 'Bad country. Many travellers die of thirst.'

Yes, water would be the main problem, Andrewes realized. An advance party had already cut a wide swathe through the scrub, like a red razor slash, ready for the track-layers; but after three or four miles they had stopped. It was not going to be easy.

Abdul Hakim was touching his arm. 'Meat!' he whispered excitedly, pointing.

On the very edge of the wilderness was a big flat-topped acacia casting a wide circle of shade; beneath it was a small gazelle, grazing, every movement precise and delicate. Andrewes watched for a few seconds, fascinated by it; then, conscious of what was expected of him, he reluctantly unslung his rifle. But the sound of the lever as he rammed a cartridge into the breech was sharp against the desert air, echoing off the rocks, and the little gazelle suddenly sprang off gracefully to rejoin the rest of the herd well out of range.

61

Kamau's face was immobile, betraying nothing; Abdul Hakim was openly disappointed. Andrewes realized he had made a mistake. He'd been content to let the gazelle live, but that was not how they saw it. Reputations were easily won or lost in a railhead camp and his was now open to question.

At that moment a large bird came swooping across the sky in front of them. Andrewes held it in his sights, following the line of flight, and squeezed the trigger. The bird plummeted to the ground a couple of hundred yards away and with an excited whoop Abdul Hakim scrambled down over the rocks to retrieve it. When he returned he held it out at arm's length, its wings spread but lifeless, its neck no more than a raw stump. The bullet had taken the head off, leaving the plump flesh unspoiled.

'Give it to Ali,' Andrewes instructed, cutting across Abdul Hakim's chatter. It had been a freak shot, he knew, but news of it would spread through the camp in no time, which could do him no harm. 'It'll do for my supper.'

Kamau remained impassive. Ay, like a dour Scot, Andrewes thought; unreasonably, it irritated him.

He turned on his heel and went back towards the gorge. This long, straight gap in the rocky hill-top was Nature's free gift to the railway; a man-made cutting would have involved many months of hard toil. But it was only just about wide enough for a train to pass through and Jackson had rightly set the men to drilling and chipping away at the high cliff walls to remove all protruberances, smoothing them down to provide maximum width.

He stopped to examine one apparently finished section but his thoughts were elsewhere. This job was going to be a challenge, he could feel it stirring in his blood already, that old fever; yet how, he wondered, was he going to break the news to Hester that she and the bairn would have to stay in Mombasa without him for a while? Maybe a year, even.

Then, out of the corner of his eye, he noticed something swinging towards him. Instinctively he stepped back to avoid it, but only just in time. The sledgehammer missed

62

his leg by less than half an inch as it smashed into the rock, throwing up a shower of chips and dust. If he had been a fraction of a second slower moving out of the way, he would be lying on the ground with a shattered leg.

'Sahib should be more careful!' Ratnam was staring at him insolently and rubbing the fringe of his beard with the back of his hand. 'There was almost being an accident. Andrewes Sahib is surely not wishing to join Jackson Sahib in his tent.'

It was a direct challenge, and he could not have chosen a worse place. They were standing about half-way through the gorge, which was several hundred yards long. On either side the coolies had stopped work to look on, expectantly. It was plain from their faces that they would not hesitate to kill him, and there was nothing to stop them arranging a fall of rocks to make the death look accidental. Yet he could not refuse the challenge, that was out of the question.

'Ay, I reckoned ye were responsible,' Andrewes said, sizing him up and not liking what he saw. 'I'll be sendin' ye to Mombasa for trial.'

Ratnam shook his head, grinning. 'Why are you afraid, Sahib? Do you think I will hurt you?'

Andrewes ignored the taunt. 'Jemadar!' he called out. 'I am takin' this man with me.'

From a safe distance the *jemadar* shouted back, 'I saw nothing, Sahib! Nothing at all!' He turned as if to hurry off but the other coolies prevented him from leaving.

'Now you begin to understand, Sahib.' Ratnam cleared his throat and spat. 'No one will help you.'

Andrewes calmly slipped his Winchester from his shoulder though he knew it was only a gesture. Ratnam was already holding the sledgehammer up ready to use it; his biceps bulged and an almost holy smile crossed his face. If he even attempted to get a cartridge into the breech the gun would be knocked out of his hand and his knuckles shattered beyond mending. There was no room to step back either; behind him was the solid rock face.

Still smiling, Ratnam was raising the sledgehammer

63

even farther, aiming it directly at Andrewes' head, when a shot rang out from the top of the cliff opposite. The bullet splintered the haft close to Ratnam's fingers and, stupified, he dropped it.

Andrewes allowed himself a split second to glance up and see Kamau outlined against the skyline, already reloading.

But Ratnam had recovered and was coming back at him, his eyes dark with hatred. Andrewes abandoned the Winchester and landed a hard punch across his jaw. It would have felled any ordinary man, but Ratnam merely grunted, hesitated briefly, and then charged at him like an enraged elephant. Andrewes dodged his first blow, but took the second on his shoulder. Its force jarred through him.

But the memory of that sledgehammer drove him on and he hit out again . . . his left . . . his right . . . his right again . . . every blow smashing into the thug's face. He was quicker on his feet too, dodging about to avoid that massive fist. Ratnam stood no chance against that avalanche of punches; eventually, after one caught him unintentionally on the throat, he staggered back against the cliff, crumpled, and fell.

He lay motionless for no longer than two or three seconds before attempting to get to his feet again, unsteadily. Andrewes watched him cagily; pains shot through his chest as he gasped in the warm dusty air.

'Sahib, it is not wise to be letting him stand up!' a voice called out urgently behind him. 'Please not to let him get up, Sahib!'

Andrewes ignored the advice and waited until his opponent was properly on his feet before going in to finish him off. Ratnam's next move caught him completely off guard. Holding his two fists together. he swung them with all his force against the side of Andrewes' head and might well have cracked open his skull against the cliff, spattering his brains across the gorge, had he not ducked in time. As it was, those powerful knuckles grazed his temple with the impact of a passing bullet. He reeled back dizzily.

But Ratnam had placed his whole weight behind that blow and now his right fist rammed against the rock. Andrewes heard him cry out in pain; as his eyes cleared, he saw the hand was bleeding profusely.

The two men faced each other. The crowd of coolies watching fell silent.

'Be sensible, man!' Andrewes told him. His head throbbed wildly and his shoulder was aching. 'Let me go get Doctor Sahib to look at that hand before we send ye down to Mom—'

With a deep grunt of rage, Ratnam lashed out with his left hand, his fingers apart and aimed straight at Andrewes' eyes. But by now he was too unsteady. Andrewes' left caught him just below the ribs; his right followed immediately with a steam-hammer blow to the jaw. Ratnam twisted helplessly and the back of his head banged against the rock as he went down. This time he was out cold.

'Sahib! Sahib! Are you needing help, Sahib?' Abdul Hakim shouted angrily as he hurried towards him. 'I have only just heard, Sahib! Oh, this is most unfortunate. Are you unhurt?'

'Abdul Hakim, now ye're here, ye can do something for me.' His head swam as he stooped to retrieve his sun helmet and the Winchester. 'Go to the traffic manager's hut. I need two sepoys here immediately. One must stay wi' the telegraph, an' two come here – d'ye understand?'

Abdul Hakim's lips spread into a wide grin. 'Oh most definitely, Sahib, most definitely! I am running!' With that, he ambled off, choosing his route carefully through the loose rocks scattered over the gorge bed. 'This Sahib, he is shooting a bird out of the sky with his rifle, then he is felling a rhinoceros with his fist!'

High on the cliff-top Kamau stood motionless, his single-shot Snider rifle still held ready for the slightest hint of trouble. Handles a gun better than most, Carpenter had said of him. Had he really known how good a shot the man was, Andrewes wondered. And where had he learned?

By the time Abdul Hakim returned with the two sepoys Ratnam was already regaining consciousness. He winced

65

and spat as they pulled his arms behind his back, hand-cuffed him, then hauled him to his feet.

'Ye'll be sent under guard to stand trial in Mombasa,' Andrewes informed him briefly. 'If ye wish, Doctor Sahib may take a look at your hand before ye go.'

Ratnam stared back, refusing to answer; he was clearly in pain.

Andrewes ordered the *jemadar* to get the rest of the men back to work, then marched his prisoner off towards railhead. A whooping whistle in the distance announced the approach of the train back from Mombasa; the sooner he could send Ratnam on his way, the better. The sun was already high in the sky and the sweat was uncomfortable on his grimy skin. Given any choice he would go directly to the waterfall to plunge in and wash himself clean, but there were other things to do first.

'Andrewes, what the hell've you been up to?' came Jackson's voice as he neared the water tower. 'Been falling off a cliff?' Then he noticed Ratnam. 'Ay, that's the brute – you've nobbled him! Good work, Andrewes! Now wait till I get him down to Mombasa; it'll be fifty lashes at least if I have anything to do with it. I'll teach him to attack a white man! He'll rue the day he was born.'

'Where's Carson?' Andrewes demanded brusequely, interrupting his tirade. 'I'd like him to take a look at his injured hand.'

'Given my way, I'd have those hands amputated for daring to raise 'em against his betters,' said Jackson.

'Ye're no' to lay a finger on the prisoner, d'ye hear?' Andrewes roared at him, his patience snapping. 'He's to have a fair trial an' ye can have your say then. But I'll break ye in half if I hear ye've indulged in any private act o' vengeance before the prisoner's handed over to the proper authorities.'

Jackson's face flushed a deep red beneath his bandages. 'Any time you like, Andrewes. If that's the way you want it.'

With one more blast on the whistle the train arrived and cut the confrontation short. Its wheels screamed over the rails as the driver applied the brakes. The moment it stopped, a lank athletic young man jumped down from the passenger coach with his solar topee still in his hand. He had a shock of blond hair and pale blue eyes contrasting strangely with his deep sun-tan; his white suit looked clean and new, as if he were expecting a cricket match rather than a railhead camp. Once he had adjusted his helmet and straightened his jacket, he strode across towards Andrewes, holding out his hand.

'I'm Tim Wilton,' he introduced himself, smiling disarmingly. 'They said in Mombasa you might be expecting me. I'm to be your assistant, Mr Andrewes. Heard about you in India, don't you know? I'm honoured.'

Andrewes grasped his hand; he had a firm enough grip, for all his airs. 'A bit o' help'll no' come amiss. Glad ye're here.'

Wilton's eye fell on Ratnam, in handcuffs and still bleeding. 'Trouble?'

'A wee spot o' bother,' Andrewes admitted, instinctively liking the newcomer. 'I reckon things'll sort themselves out once we've moved railhead on a few miles.'

He stood naked under the waterfall, allowing the stinging water to wash over him. His shoulder ached where Ratnam had hit him and a blue-black-yellow bruise was gradually spreading over the skin. Kamau sat on the rocks nearby.

'I have ye to thank for my life!' Andrewes called out cheerfully as he came out of the water refreshed and began to dress. 'If ye hadna been on that cliff-top keepin' watch . . . Ay, ye dinna ken what I mean, but – what do they say in Swahili?' He had made a point of asking Dr Carson. 'Ay, that's it – asante! Asante, Kamau!'

Kamau came up to him and contemplated the bruise. Then he said something abruptly in Swahili, turned, and went off among the trees, leaving Andrewes wondering if he had offended him in some way. It was an hour later before he returned bearing a handful of leaves, fungi and bark which he proceeded to crush into a pot and cook slowly over a fire. When it was ready he indicated with gestures that Andrewes was to remove his jacket and shirt.

'Ye dinna mean no harm, I take it,' Andrewes said, complying reluctantly.

'Dawa,' Kamau told him, applying the hot mess to the bruised skin.

'Ye're burnin' the hide off me!' the Scot protested vehemently. But he let him continue.

# SIX

Gaby . . .?

Hester woke up with a start and propped herself up on her elbow to look anxiously at the makeshift cradle, a roughly-made drawer placed on top of a chest at the side of her bed. But her baby daughter was still asleep, her little eyes tight shut, the flesh around them wrinkling, her cheeks delicately rosy and slightly puffed out. Gaby, short for Gabriella – it was a good name, Hester thought as she gazed at her, and the nearest she could get to 'Cabby' without being completely barbarous.

Four days old already, four that evening . . .

She lay back against the pillows, wondering if she had strength enough to get to the Railway Office by herself. Yet she was determined to do it, determined to speak to Carpenter.

It was unbearably stuffy in that room at the Indian merchant's house, in spite of the open windows looking out across the lagoon; the air was as motionless as in a dream. Tiny beads of perspiration covered her skin, attracting a mosquito – maybe that was what had disturbed her, its high-pitched whine in her ear; she slapped at it as it explored her neck, squashing its elegant body, smearing blood over her fingers, her *own* blood on which it had gorged itself. Too late, though. It left a reddening, itchy spot behind.

To her mind, mosquitoes *were* elegant. She had tried to explain it to Muldoon when he had visited her that morning, true to some promise he'd made to John. He had merely laughed roughly and said they were a bloody nuisance. It made her uncomfortable the way he haunted her bedroom, always with the feeble excuse that he had something interesting to tell her – that the railhead mutiny was over, that John would soon be returning to Mombasa to find somewhere more permanent for her to live while he was away working on the railway . . . And he would eye her low-cut nightdress, saying not to mind him if it was time to feed the baby but to carry on, he'd no objection.

'Perhaps not, but I have!' she had retorted, exasperated.

But each time he had been reluctant to leave until Nyokabi had chased him out of the room; then she heard the two of them whispering and giggling outside the door, and she felt she wanted to march out there to send them packing. Back home in Liverpool she had seen plenty like him swaggering along the dingy streets or lurching into public houses, drinking the money they should rightfully have given to their wives. She had known how to deal with them, too. Their wives had turned to her for help, young as she was. Everyone there had recognized her as the minister's daughter and she had been able to walk safely through even the roughest quarters.

It had fascinated John, she remembered. He had never tired of hearing her talk about it and questioned her endlessly about the people she visited, his eyes exploring her face as though he could hardly believe some of the things she told him. And she had often answered impatiently, not wanting to waste their precious time together on such commonplaces when he might be telling her more about India and the other lands he'd seen. From her earliest days she had loved tales of travel in exotic places; she had devoured accounts by missionaries and explorers; even kept a print of David Livingstone over her bed, and had it with her now in her luggage.

'You're sure it's not just his traveller's yarns you've fallen for?' her father had demanded drily when she announced she wanted to marry John.

She had been furious – *of course* she was sure! Her father must have been blind not to read it in her face.

Oh yes, she was so sure. She had never before known anything like that mysterious excitement she had felt when they were first introduced, that strange sense of recognition . . . And John had experienced it too, she had seen it in his eyes as he held her hand in his.

During those first weeks they had talked for long hours as if no one else in the world mattered and her sister Mary had busied herself with her sewing at the other side of the room, pretending not to notice when their hands touched. When she was younger she had always hated the thought of marriage, repelled by the idea of tying herself for life to one person whose every little gesture would become so familiar and predictable, it would drive her mad. But John was different. She felt she could never get to know him completely, he was too complex a person. Those unexpected areas of reserve . . . those moments when an intense sadness seemed to lurk behind his smile . . . Perhaps that was why she loved him so much. He was older, certainly, more experienced in life, strong, someone who could really care for her; yet at the same time he was often so unexpectedly vulnerable – a man she could respect, yet also a man who needed her.

When he had eventually asked her to marry him – yes, that had been one of his more awkward moments. He had been so brusque, she almost burst out laughing, but she had controlled the laugh just in time, said simply, 'Yes' – matching his tone almost – and he had looked so happy . . .

She lay back on the pillow as she allowed her thoughts to wander. Through the open window the sky was so blue, it was almost unbelievable. She had not yet set foot outside that room but she could sense already that she was going to love Mombasa with its clamour of voices in their lilting foreign tongue, the aromatic smells as the meals were being cooked, the call from the mosque, even the welcoming, enveloping warmth. But she meant to enjoy it *with* John and not be left down here while he sweated it out in some rough construction camp. He would want the best for her, she knew that, but she was determined to stay with him whatever the discomforts.

She raised herself on her arm again to look at Gaby. 'We're not going to let him run away on his own, are we?' she confided as those big baby eyes opened wide – lovely brown eyes which reminded Hester of her mother. 'If your

Papa wants to go off building railways he'll have to take us along too.'

Gaby gave a massive, toothless yawn, then began to whimper. Hester swung her legs out of bed, picked her up, and opened her nightdress for the feed. The baby's lips had just closed contentedly around her swollen pink nipple when Mrs MacPherson, the missionary's wife came in. She stayed so long that Hester could not get to the Railway Office that day.

The following morning, even though she still felt very weak, Hester dressed carefully and went out, leaving Gaby in Nyokabi's care. The air in the narrow street was baking hot; her high-necked blouse and long white linen skirt seemed unduly restricting after four days of wearing only a loose nightdress. Her pith helmet, too, was uncomfortably heavy on her head, though she knew well enough the dangers of direct exposure to the tropical sun. Mr Roshan, the Indian merchant, hurried out after her, concerned; when he heard where she wanted to go, he sent out a servant to find a trolley and a couple of stout Swahilis to push it. Then he held out a hand to help her up on to its bench seat. She was glad to sit down again beneath the shade of its canopy and welcomed the rush of air against her face as they set off.

She found the Railway Office to be a low building with wide verandas but with a corrugated iron roof which made it unbearably hot. Carpenter was in his shirt sleeves working at his desk when she entered unannounced. He seemed flustered to see her and immediately put on his jacket before leading her out to a cool veranda facing the wide creek. Some distance off-shore a smoky freighter was dropping anchor.

'I can offer you some fresh lime juice which is very passable, ma'am,' Carpenter suggested when she had settled into one of the canvas chairs. She sensed a hint of disapproval in his manner, as though he felt her very presence might disrupt the vital work of constructing the railway.

Yet, as they drank the lime juice and she explained how she wished to join her husband at the railhead camp, he raised no real objection.

'You'll find no home comforts, ma'am,' he warned her mildly. 'A simple, rough life. But that's your decision and your husband's. Tho' I imagine you must have thought over what you were in for before you came out here. I'll fetch you some paper and you can draft out a message which we'll telegraph to him.'

As she wrote it out he began, awkwardly, to tell her something about his own wife who had stayed behind in England. She lived in a grey stone house in the Cotswolds, he said, and hunted. Hester made no comment; it was a life she found impossible to visualize, although she had once seen paintings of fox hunting scenes at the Walker Art Gallery in Liverpool and had found them distasteful.

Carpenter glanced at the message when she handed it to him and said he would send her the reply as soon as it came through. It was time for her to leave, he was implying, and let the men get on with men's work. She stood up graciously and allowed him to lead her to where the trolley was waiting. As far as she could see very little work *was* going on at that moment; a few wagons stood idly on the shining rails, partly loaded; a couple of Indian coolies squatted, talking energetically, beneath a rough thatched shelter covering some boxes of stores; nothing else.

Back at Roshan's house Hester began getting her things together in order to pack ready for the journey. After a few minutes Mrs MacPherson looked in; she was strongly against Hester taking her new-born baby up to railhead – 'Poor wee mite!' – and started going over all her arguments yet again.

Hester refused to listen. 'I'd like Nyokabi to come with me,' she said, setting her chin in determination.

'That girl!'

'She's been very kind, and if she's willing to go on looking after Gaby . . .'

Mrs MacPherson made no attempt to hide how deeply

shocked she was at the suggestion. She was an angular woman, about thirty, with a sharp, tense face; her every movement betrayed her disapproval. 'Perhaps you don't realize, my dear, that the girl is a . . . Well, she's not all she might be.'

Ed Muldoon heard the remark as he came through the door with the air of a man who knew how to make himself at home. Oh, she'd be glad to get away from him, Hester thought as he stood, wide-legged, snorting at the missionary's wife.

'Not all she might be, is it? Mrs MacPherson, I mean no disrespect, but I'm thinkin' Cabby's a lot more'n you'll ever be.'

A violent red flush spread over her face and neck. 'Mr Muldoon, I'll thank you not to be personal.'

'No offence meant I'm sure, Mrs MacPherson.' He grinned at her discomfort. 'An' Mrs Andrewes, sure if it's my Cabby you're wantin' to steal away from me, who am I to deny you? Though, if you mus' know, she's light-fingered. A darlin' girl but light-fingered an' you might have to be takin' the whip to her.'

'I'm certain she's stolen nothing of mine!' Hester answered him warmly. 'Will you ask her if she'll come?'

A quick exchange in Swahili followed, then he shook his head, delighted. 'She says no. It'd break the dear girl's heart to be leavin' me, an' that's the truth o' the matter.'

Mrs MacPherson intervened. 'The truth is,' she said tartly, 'the girl would like to be with you, Mrs Andrewes, but she refuses to leave Mombasa. Her very words, and if you ask me, you'd be sensible to follow her example.'

'I've made up my mind,' Hester told her obstinately. 'So there's no point in arguing, is there?'

'I brought you the reply from your husband,' Muldoon announced suddenly, producing a crumpled piece of paper from his pocket. 'Carpenter asked me to bring it as I was passin', like, but with all this goin' on I'd almost forgot. You'll be unpackin' again when you see what he says.'

'You've read it?' All her anger blazed up at him.

'Sure, wasn't I there when it came through on the railway telegraph?'

What made it worse was that John's reply was not the joyous welcome she had hoped for, but a cool message in staccato telegraphese stating that several coolies had gone down with malaria, two dead, and begging her to remain in Mombasa for the time being as conditions in the camp were not suitable. SEA AIR HEALTHIER FOR BOTH OF YOU LOVE JOHN. She read the words twice before impulsively sitting down at the table and scribbling a hasty answer at the foot of the paper. WE SHALL BOTH ARRIVE ON FIRST SUPPLY TRAIN TOMORROW MORNING – LOVE HESTER. She tore off this part of the paper, folded it and handed it to Muldoon.

'Mr Muldoon, will you be so kind as to return to the Railway Office and have them telegraph this today.' She added, 'You may of course read it yourself if you wish. I shall not object.'

'You'll not be forgettin' every favour has its price, I hope?' he said impudently, winking. 'But sure for a lovely lady like yourself wouldn't I go to the end o' the world an' back?'

Once he had gone, Mrs MacPherson started to finger through Hester's clothes, rejecting some as being unsuitable for the *bara*, as she called the country beyond the coastal strip, and setting to one side those of which she approved. She had obviously abandoned all attempts to persuade Hester to stay.

'You'll have to watch the baby's little folds of flesh under the chin, under the arms, places like that, for signs of rash. That'll be prickly heat. In that case, wash with a very mild solution of permanganate, and make sure you dry her properly. Use talcum if you have any. Oh, and by the way, that heavy sun helmet you've been wearing, we find they're not very becoming, my dear, so we usually wear a felt hat, a double terai, and I'm sure you'd be a lot more comfortable in one of these . . .'

Very early the next morning, while the sun was still

throwing its elongated dawn shadows across the street, the trolley was already outside Roshan's house. Roshan himself stood contentedly near the door as Muldoon helped Hester climb up with the baby on her arm. She arranged herself carefully on the wooden bench and shook away his hand. Much to her distaste he travelled with her as far as the Railway Office; whichever way she turned her head she was unable to escape his foul breath. She bent over Gaby, her face shaded by the new double terai she was wearing – it was held in place over her high hair-do by a light scarf tied in a flowing bow beneath her chin – and she could have sworn the baby smiled at her.

Luckily Muldoon was unable to accompany her to railhead – 'Though I hope you'll not be thinkin' me negligent in my duty,' he actually apologized – as he had to supervise the unloading of the freighter which now lay at anchor just off-shore. It was his job, it seemed, to organize the transport of stores and materials – 'So we'll have the pleasure o' meetin' often enough.' He set up a great clamour making sure that all Hester's luggage was on board, save the two boxes she was leaving in Mombasa, while she stood expressing her thanks to the cool, elegantly-polite Carpenter.

At last there she was, sitting comfortably in her compartment as the little train rode gently over the wooden viaduct, and relieved to be away from both of them. She would miss Cabby, and Mrs MacPherson had been nice enough in her straight-laced way – well-meaning at any rate, fussing over the fact that it was only six days, less than that, since the baby was born, and far too early for her to be getting up – but it felt so good to be on the move once more, knowing she would soon be seeing John again. Would he be angry, she wondered, that she'd taken matters into her own hands in spite of his message? She had never seen him angry, not yet. How much she still had to learn about him!

# SEVEN

But John was not angry in the least. As the train slowed
down she could see him standing at the side of the track
together with a small group of Indian coolies, and he
swung himself up into the compartment even before it
stopped. A moment's anxious glance at her face, and at
the baby, and he gave a broad smile.

'She's a bonnie wee lass!'

'John – your forehead! What have they done to you?'

She caught her breath as she saw the long, discoloured
bruise, all black and purple and yellow, starting above one
eye and spreading down his temple towards the cheek bone.

'Nay, that's all over an' done with!' He tried to laugh it
off but as he helped her gather her things together she
noticed how his knuckles were swollen too, and the skin
broken. Yet he refused to talk about it. 'I'm more than
glad to see ye, my love,' he said gently, 'though I canna
say ye're wise to come here wi' the bairn.'

'But here I am!' she declared stubbornly.

'Aye, an' I'm no' sorry, though ye'll find things a wee
bit rough an' ready, d'ye ken.'

He almost lifted her down from the train and she became
aware for the first time of what he meant. The station
consisted of nothing more than a patch of cleared ground,
a couple of wooden huts and a metal water tower to serve
the locomotives. Beyond it, stretching over the hillside like
a vast rubbish dump, and smelling like one too, was the
'camp'. In the intense heat it seemed to blur into a haze,
and she felt her legs weakening.

But John's arm was already around her and he lifted her,
still holding the baby, into a sort of hammock carried by two
of the coolies. She was conscious of them grinning as they
took her weight, but she was too exhausted to mind.

In this litter she and Gaby were borne through the camp

while John walked alongside explaining how most of the men were still at work; she would see how overcrowded it became when they all returned. It was a nightmare experience. Bundles of personal belongings, cooking utensils, boxes and bags lay scattered about among the makeshift shacks in which they somehow managed to live. Over everything hung a vile stench which seemed made up of human sweat, decaying food, excreta, stale cooking spices and the Lord alone knew what else.

As for the flies – she was forced to cover Gaby's little face to keep them off, they were so persistent.

Then – much to her relief – they began to climb farther up the hillside until they were well clear of the camp itself and at length reached a glade on the very edge of the forest. The coolies stopped and lowered the litter gently to the ground. John helped her stand up.

'Best I can offer ye, I fear,' he apologised uncertainly. 'An' this is only for a week or two. Who knows what the next place'll be like.'

Hester steadied herself on his arm as she gazed around. 'But, John, it's beautiful!' she protested, trying to hide her doubts. 'And you can hardly smell that horrid camp at all up here.'

Without that camp, she thought, it would have been an idyllic spot. The high trees were whispering promises of coolness and shade, while to one side was a great tumbling cluster of massive boulders between which a waterfall dropped down into a tiny pool, sending out constantly widening ripples which lapped against the stones. In the centre of the glade stood a tent with a table and camp chairs set out in front of it; behind, four or five Africans were busy constructing a high, curving screen of interwoven twigs and leaves held together between upright staves.

'That wall'll offer ye some privacy,' John was saying, 'though there'll be others comin' to fetch water from time to time. Ye understand this is a workin' camp, my love, an'—'

'This is much better than I expected, John,' she lied to reassure him; though the truth was, she'd been so intent on rejoining him, she hadn't given it all that much thought.

Perhaps he had been right after all and she should have stayed in Mombasa.

He summoned one of the Africans across, a handsome-looking man dressed in a long white robe who – to her surprise – stooped to pick up a rifle before approaching. 'This is Kamau,' he told her. 'Kamau is in our employ, d'ye ken, no' the railway's. It'll be his job to see ye an' the bairn come to no harm.'

'How d'you do, Kamau?' But should she shake hands with him, she wondered.

The African looked at her gravely. She hesitantly held out her hand and he touched it briefly and spoke what sounded like words of welcome, though she did not understand them. Then he returned to supervising the work on the screen, leaving her with the absurd sensation that she had just been presented to *him*, rather than the other way round.

The coolies carrying the luggage arrived and, while John was busy telling them where to put everything, she sank into one of the canvas chairs. Gaby was still dozing on her arm in spite of all that was going on – yet had she been right to come? She had longed to be with John again – and the moment she'd seen that bruise on his face she had been in no doubt about it at all – but what about Gaby? That camp with its disgusting smells, and those fat, overfed flies – it must be a hotbed of every imaginable disease. She gazed down on the healthy, pink, baby complexion, that skin which was so smooth and soft, and suddenly in her mind's eye saw it covered with sores. She shuddered deeply.

'My love!' John was standing by her, alarmed. 'D'ye no' feel well?'

'I'm . . . all right . . .' Then she added, 'It's very hot, that's all.'

'Ali has made some tea,' he said kindly. 'Ali cooks for us. One thing I *can* promise ye, he's a first-rate cook.'

She made an effort and smiled, feeling oddly light-headed.

Ali, with the tray in his frail hands, responded with a friendly grin which revealed his toothless gums, stained an unnatural red. And there was something unusual about his eyes, she felt, as he bent down for a second to look at the baby, as though he could see into her very soul. It was an unnerving experience. He set out the mugs on the camp table, his movements very slow and deliberate; he was mere skin and bone, with seemingly no flesh on him anywhere.

'The tea will do ye good,' John said, handing it to her. 'An' then mebbe ye should lie down awhile.'

'After I've fed Gaby . . .'

'Ay . . .' He eased open the lid of the tin and spooned out some sugar. 'Hester, my love . . . I have to tell ye the next place may no' be as suitable as this one an' . . . Ay, well what I wish to say is . . .'

'No,' she interrupted firmly. 'No, John, I'm staying with you.'

'Ay, but if ye should change your mind at any time, d'ye ken, perhaps on account o' the wee bairn . . . ye've only to give the word.'

The expression in his eyes betrayed how worried he must be feeling. Impulsively she reached forward and took his hand, turning it over to kiss the bruises and cuts on the knuckles. 'I canna leave ye alone five minutes wi'out ye get yesel' into a brawl!' She teased him affectionately, imitating his accent.

'Ay, lass!' he laughed contentedly, for the first time relaxing a little. 'It's good to see ye. But ye will rest awhile afterwards, won't ye – d'ye promise?'

As it turned out, Hester stayed in bed for the next two days, eating practically nothing and getting up only to feed Gaby. One of the Indian coolies had made a little cot out of fragments of a discarded packing case and a strip of old canvas; Hester placed it at the side of her camp bed where she had only to turn her head to see into it. Gaby was as good as gold, sleeping most of the time, and hardly ever crying, even when she was awake.

During that time everything seemed vague and unreal, particularly in the evening when she lay under her mosquito net listening to the murmur of voices from the crowded camp rising and falling like the surging of waves, sometimes with African drumming coming insistently from the forest as a counterpoint, pulsing through her blood. In the daytime, John was away working on a new section of track which, he tried to explain, stretched for several miles into the Taru Desert; but as she had so far seen nothing faintly resembling desert, and as the trees were heavy with leaves and the waterfall gurgled ceaselessly, she found it impossible to visualize what he meant.

Every couple of hours Ali came to the tent entrance to enquire if she needed anything. His total knowledge of English consisted of the two words *please* and *water*, so her attempts to communicate with him were not too successful.

Her only other visitor was a tubby, bald man who introduced himself as Dr Carson, the camp's medical officer; he brought an aura of stale pipe smoke into the tent. But he tickled Gaby – who was far too young to respond to that kind of approach – and pronounced her healthy; then he produced a stethoscope and proceeded to examine Hester herself. When he had finished he told her she was a fool for getting up so soon after having the baby, and an even bigger fool for having quit Mombasa for this God-forsaken hole, but there was nothing wrong with her, she'd been damned lucky, that's all, and she should take things easy till her strength came back.

'An' make sure that Indian bearer o' yours boils the water,' he added in his gruff, matter-of-fact manner – and she liked him for it. 'Never let a drop pass your lips which hasn't been boiled first.'

He turned to go; then paused, raising the flap of the tent.

'Glad to have you on station, ma'am, all the same. An' I wish you good morning.'

After the second day Hester began to feel well enough again to get up and take charge of things. With Ali's leisurely help she cleaned out the tent, then opened one of her boxes for fresh linen and some more suitable crockery than John had been using. Then she went to inspect the area at the back where Ali did his cooking; he listened patiently as this new *memsahib* instructed him to wash the pots and dishes more thoroughly and grinned at her

81

uncomprehendingly, leaving her with the feeling that he had won that round. But it was a start, she thought.

And if she used one of her boxes in the tent as a dressing table, perhaps with a little cloth over it and the mirror and maybe that framed photograph of her father . . . It would make it seem more homely, even though they would only be staying there for a week or two.

However, when it came to the point they did not move on as quickly as John had forecast. They had hit a snag, he said; work had not progressed as quickly as he'd hoped and . . . well, no point in bothering her with the details but . . . She could see he was reluctant to discuss his problems with her, and the realization came as a shock; it was not what she had expected. They had been so close so far, sharing everything; yet now it was a question of his work he said they were his worries, not hers. She felt hurt.

She tried to show an intelligent interest, even tried insisting, until one day he took her to a place where they could look out across this Taru Desert he'd talked so much about. They left Gaby in Ali's care for a couple of hours – the old man was father and grandfather many times over, John explained, and it was true he seemed alert to her every need – and walked along the track until they came to a deep, narrow gorge where they began to climb up a winding path to a narrow, rocky plateau. She gasped aloud at the unexpected sight of that flat, red plain stretching for miles and miles until it lost itself in a dusty haze where the horizon should have been.

'Lack o' water's the main difficulty,' John grunted. He passed her his field glasses and pointed down to the dead straight railway line which seemed to cut the plain in half, the metal rails a scintillating silver in the hard sunlight – like the Archangel Gabriel's sword, she thought, remembering those Sunday School lessons she had taught back home.

'D'ye see that wee train down there?' John went on. 'That's the water train, d'ye ken. Most o' the coolies are still transported out before sunrise each mornin', but they canna work too long wi' no water to drink, an' it's brought up twice a day in tankers from a river thirty miles back.'

82

'What about our waterfall?' The moment the words had passed her lips she realized what his answer must be. It was their only source of pure water, and the level of the pool was already lower than it had been; every evening a steady stream of coolies came to fill their *debes* and cooking pots.

'It's dryin' up, have ye no' noticed?' he replied shortly. 'Accordin' to the local villagers we'll be lucky if it lasts through to the next rains. Have ye no' spotted how the grass is turnin' brown in patches?'

'What shall we do then?'

'Och, we'll be movin' on i' the next few days.'

Yet another week passed before the move finally took place – the first of many, as Hester later realized. The coolies went ahead. Early one morning she heard them leaving the camp as usual to work at railhead, but only half the gangs returned; the following day more left, until only a small contingent of about 300 men remained behind. The evenings seemed inexpressibly quiet as the great stillness of Africa swallowed up any tiny little sound which dared to disturb it.

Her own journey came the next day. Ali, helped by a young coolie who had introduced himself as Abdul Hakim, organized the transfer of her luggage and tent to the waiting train, where it was loaded into a wagon already filled with various railway supplies. For her comfort, John had ordered the inspection coach to be added to the train; Hester paused to fold her parasol and hand it to Abdul Hakim before hitching up her long skirt and clambering aboard with Gaby on her arm.

At times on its way across that dry, barren landscape the train must have reached a full twenty miles an hour. A steady, baking hot breeze blew through the coach. She tried closing all the shutters to keep it out, but it soon became unbearably stuffy and she had to open one or two again. What worried her most was how to protect Gaby from the terrible, coarse dust which got everywhere; soon the baby clothes were red with it; it was almost impossible to keep it away from her little face.

Looking out, she suddenly began to understand why

John had seemed so tense during the past weeks. It must have been like the torments of hell working in that desert day after day.

Long stretches were covered with a thick tangle of stunted, skeletal thorn trees, bare of leaves and even of bark. The first gangs must have hacked their way through these pale nightmare forests inch by inch to clear the route for the railway. Then came miles of flat, desolate, empty land where the only shade was provided by the occasional, isolated acacia, while all around the exposed red earth lay open to the sun. But why, she mused, hadn't he told her more about it? Why had he kept this side of it to himself? As if he wanted to shield her from the worst side of his work – was that it?

When the train eventually arrived he was waiting there beside the track, just as on that first day. As she appeared on the little platform at the end of the coach he burst out laughing.

'Ye're a fine sight, d'ye ken that?' Still amused, he helped her down. 'So ye've been baptized by the desert now? An' wee Gaby too? That's a sign ye really belong to the railway.'

She glanced down and saw that her fresh blouse was now a patchy brick red, and she shuddered to think what her face and hair looked like. 'I hope there's enough water to clean up properly!' she retorted tartly, but her eyes sought his tenderly as she spoke and her own laughter suddenly bubbled out of her. 'Oh, John, do I really look as bad as that!'

'Ay, but dinna fash yesel', my love – we've all the water we need an' more.' He took the baby from her arm while she opened her parasol to shade her face from the sun. 'Now come an' see your new wee home an' tell me how ye like it!'

The main camp site was near the bank of the Voi river and it looked very different from the one they had left. It was still an untidy sprawl but many of the shacks and tents were grouped together like little villages; several were surrounded by high thorn fences – *bomas*, John called them – and others were under construction.

'Water!' Hester exclaimed as they approached the river, and her spirits soared as she saw it. Occasionally on that morning's journey through the desert they had crossed what appeared to be eroded river beds which had dried up long ago, and she had begun to fear she would never see flowing water again. Now here was a vast expanse of it – muddy and unattractive in places, but enough for everyone. As she watched, a log on the mud flat bestirred itself and, with an idle swish of its tail, slithered into the current. 'It wasn't . . . John, *was* it?'

'Ay, ye'll have to watch out for crocodiles,' he said drily. 'Now, we've a step or two to go before we get to the spot I reckoned best for us.'

About a quarter of a mile farther upstream, well clear of the main coolie camp, they came to a thick *boma* of strongly interwoven thorn branches. Inside the high fence was a roughly-made hut with a thatched roof.

'It's no' exactly Buckingham Palace,' he began to apologize, 'but we'll be livin' here only two or three months at the most, d'ye ken . . .'

'John – it's our first home!' she cried, delighted. It looked so picturesque with its thatch extending raggedly over the uneven timber walls. 'Not counting the tent, of course.'

'Ay, we canna count the tent. Though to my way o' thinkin' if we were to put the tent up alongside the hut – just there – we'd then have two rooms, d'ye no agree?'

'Then it *will* be Buckingham Palace!' she declared, aware yet again of those puzzling signs of doubt in his eyes, as though he felt he was letting her down in some way. She kissed him, running her fingers over his cheek. 'John, I *am* happy with . . . all this . . . truly I am.' And she added, laughing again, 'Though it's a bit like Robinson Crusoe, isn't it? What do you think, Gaby?'

Gaby stared back at her gravely with those big, wide-awake eyes of hers and playfully bubbled out the spittle from between her little rosy lips.

It took no time at all for Ali and Abdul Hakim to set up Gaby's cot and the two camp beds in the cool, windowless hut, while Kamau, in a fresh white *kanzu* – how he'd

85

already found time to change after the journey Hester had no idea – and with his rifle slung as always from his shoulder, stood outside watching them without lifting a finger to help. But Hester's thoughts were elsewhere, still worrying about John. Perhaps now they were so much closer to the work sites she could go and watch, see some of construction problems for herself, *prove* she was interested . . . Perhaps that would help.

She went the next day. After feeding Gaby and putting her down to sleep, leaving Ali in charge of her, she summoned Kamau and explained in halting Swahili – learned from John's book – that he was to accompany her to the railway. The sun was fierce, but she did not relax her pace until they had reached the line and followed it to a point where a wide swathe had been cut through thick scrub and high grass. Here the line stopped and a gang of coolies was working on the next section, laying out a straggling row of new sleepers one next to the other like dominoes. Several of the men glanced at her curiously, passing remarks among themselves and laughing. In their eyes she must have seemed terribly out of place with her parasol, her double terai, her white blouse and pale grey skirt, yet she felt anything but elegant in that heat. The perspiration ran down her skin in little rivulets; her waistband was soaked through. What torture it must be, she thought, doing hard physical work on top of it all.

She watched the little engine shunting a long low wagon over the finished stretch of line, with men running alongside shouting instructions to the driver. It edged its way along until, after one great, urgent shout, it stopped with its wheels just inches from the end. A fresh gang clambered aboard, their bared brown bodies gleaming, and began to ease down one of the new rails it was carrying, co-ordinating their movements with a rhythmic chant as they played it out foot by foot. It must have been some thirty feet long, she estimated, and burning hot in that sunshine, to judge from their care in taking hold of it. Some tried to protect themselves with rags, others had no more than their bare hands, yet they had to manhandle that rail off the wagon, bearing its full weight as they positioned it along the sleepers.

Then they turned to the second rail, working quickly, noisily, urged on by shouts from a turbanned *jemadar* standing well away to one side. But as the last few feet cleared the end of the wagon they were unable to hold it; a couple of the men called out a quick warning, but too late. The man behind them stumbled and fell, with the rail landing heavily across his ankle.

He screamed in agony.

For a second no one else seemed to move; then, as others in the gang went to help him, Hester saw a young Englishman running up, appearing from somewhere beyond the train. Nervously, feeling she ought to be doing something, she watched him elbowing the coolies aside. He bawled out some impatient orders in Hindustani; most of the men sheepishly moved back from the rail while he – with four or five of those who were nearest – lifted it away from the injured man.

'Let me through! No, don't touch him, not till we've had a look at his leg!' Impulsively, Hester pushed her way through the little crowd of coolies and went down on her knees to examine the wound. The bone was badly fractured, with the torn edge protruding through the skin. 'We need a stretcher.'

The Englishman nodded and snapped out some more orders which she did not understand, though they certainly had an effect. Some of the coolies hurried off, to return almost immediately carrying a crate-lid; a few bent nails still stuck out dangerously around its edges. But it would do well enough.

'Gently with him!' she warned.

She held the broken leg carefully with both hands as the other coolies raised him on to this improvized stretcher. Again he screamed at the pain, and she tried to calm him down, talking soothingly for a moment or two before allowing them to take him away to the hospital tent.

'He'll be in good hands now,' the young Englishman told her reassuringly. 'Nasty accident, but we're very grateful for your help. My name's Wilton, by the way. You must be Mrs Andrewes.'

'Yes.' Should she go after them, she wondered, just to make certain?

'We haven't met because I've been out here with the advance party during the past few weeks. Mr Andrewes may have told you.'

'Yes . . .' What unusually pale blue eyes he had, she thought inconsequentially. Yes, she would go, she made up her mind. 'Excuse me, Mr Wilton, but I think I'll . . .'

'Of course, Mrs Andrewes, and thank you once again, ma'am.' He raised his sun helmet, standing aside to allow her to pass.

Calling Kamau to follow her, she hurried after the men with the stretcher. She had blood on her hands and skirt, but that could not be helped. The expression on that poor man's face haunted her. So vulnerable . . . so frightened . . . There might well be no more she could do, perhaps Dr Carson would send her packing; yet on the other hand, she thought, merely being there might be of some use. She couldn't just do nothing.

That night, lying sleepless in her thatched hut, Hester found herself thinking once more of those pale blue eyes – almost unnaturally pale against his bronze skin. He was quite unlike any other man she had met on the railway. Jackson, now back from sick leave in Mombasa, seemed coarse and uncouth; Muldoon . . . in some indefinable way she feared Muldoon and could not explain to herself why. If anything happened to John, any accident, and she had to rely on Muldoon . . . But it didn't bear thinking about.

And at least Mr Wilton might be someone she could talk with, she decided as she turned over to try and get some sleep. Yes, he was quite different from the others.

# EIGHT

The railway was inexorably pushed on, mile after mile through desert, forest and grassland. Word had come from London that nothing could be allowed to delay it. If they met any obstacle which could not be overcome immediately, they should lay a temporary track around it, leaving the more permanent work to be completed later. It was inefficient and expensive, as Andrewes knew only too well, but the politicians had their reasons. He could guess well enough what they were too, though no one would bother to consult a mere engineer on the matter. However much the fine gentlemen in London might talk about trade, the real purpose of the railway was to carry troops rapidly and securely into the heart of Africa, to Uganda and the Nile.

Day after day the work went on and the coolie force grew until – some twelve months after Andrewes had first stepped ashore in East Africa – it numbered more than six thousand men employed on the line to build earthworks, level the ground, cut through the rock and lay the tracks. Ratnam, of course, had gone, shipped back to India to serve a sentence of several years' hard labour, and there was no more talk of mutiny. Luckily, Tim Wilton had turned out to be a very competent assistant whose easy, relaxed manner made him very popular with the men.

The main problem had been supplies. Not everything could yet be carried up from the coast by rail as they were still short of locomotives; a long engineering strike in Britain had held up delivery of more F-Class engines, while the secondhand N-Class they had been obliged to import from India had needed extensive repairs. As for the gangs working on sites ahead of railhead, the Office had envisaged the use of pack animals to transport their food, water and materials, and Ed Muldoon – whose department

89

it was – had purchased hundreds of camels, donkeys and oxen. But within a few weeks most of them had died.

Yet as Andrewes rode over each completed section of line in the inspection coach, or aboard one of the trolleys, he experienced a strong sense of contentment. In fact, the bigger the obstacles, the greater his satisfaction at having overcome them.

Kamau, too, he suspected, shared these feelings in his own unspoken way. He remembered that time, months earlier, when the track had at last reached the Voi river and they had stood together on the hillside looking back at the gleaming rails. 'Ay, the *nyika*, as ye call it, will no' be too much of a problem for travellers now,' he'd said aloud.

And Kamau had glanced at him with quick intelligent eyes, seeming to agree, almost as if he understood English. Impossible, of course, though the thought had crossed Andrewes' mind several times.

Yet on the other hand Hester seemed to take it all for granted, this engineering miracle. At one time she had gone almost daily to watch the work in progress and he had tried to explain some of the technical questions involved; but those conversations invariably ended unsatisfactorily, with her declaring her wide-eyed faith in his ability to find the right solution to whatever problem was troubling him at the time – a faith which was not necessarily justified, he thought ruefully.

Sometimes he watched her as she fed Gaby and wondered what was really going on in her mind. Some regret, maybe? Back in Liverpool he had often described the sort of bungalow she might expect if they went to India – on a cool hillside perhaps, with a spacious garden for the children . . . He had desperately wanted it for her. Instead, all he'd been able to offer her was a thatched hut and a tent in one railhead camp after another; camps which were notorious for their fights and drunkenness, and for the lechery which made prostitutes of African village girls. Even of boys.

Hester never complained. The flies, the dust, the often stale water, the thirst, the constant danger of disease, dysentery, ulcers, ticks which clung to the skin to suck blood, jiggers which burrowed under the toenails – to his amazement she took them all in her stride. He would not have been surprised if she had decided to pack up and catch the next boat home; instead, she started helping Dr Carson in the hospital tent. The patients were usually Indian coolies, and they trusted her though she spoke not a word of their language; she had a gift, Dr Carson said, for calming them down after the shock of an accident. But then she developed a fever and was advised not to breast-feed until her temperature had gone down again as there was some chance she might have been infected by one of the patients. At that, Andrewes had put his foot down and insisted Gaby must come first. Reluctantly Hester agreed that the risks were too great, and gave up the work.

As for Gaby herself, they were lucky she had suffered from nothing more than prickly heat and some short-lived but dramatic bouts of fever. She was a great favourite with Ali, who watched over her as though she were his own grandchild; even Kamau, normally distant and grave – though he'd a wife and child of his own in Mombasa – had sometimes been seen coaxing a smile out of her.

They had now moved on as far as Tsavo river, where work on the diversion of the line down the hillside to the temporary wooden bridge – still under construction – was proving particularly difficult, so when the signal came through that the first hundred miles of track as far as Voi were to be officially opened for paying passengers Andrewes welcomed the chance of taking a few days off to see them arrive. Hester and Gaby – now fourteen months old and never still for a second – travelled with him.

The newly-completed Voi station – with platforms and waiting rooms, everything as it should be – was specially decorated for the occasion with flags and bunting. An Indian station master had been installed and he waited now – as pleased as punch in his spotless uniform – for the first scheduled train to arrive.

'It'll be somethin' for Gaby to remember when she's grown up!' Andrewes commented seriously, looking at his watch. He would never admit it to anyone, but he always felt a touch of pride at moments like this. 'D'ye see, Gaby, that's the direction the train'll come from . . .' He pointed. 'Ye'll be able to tell your grandchildren all about this day, the launchin' o' the Uganda railway!'

Hester laughed, her eyes darting over his face as if she longed to tease him but felt she had better not. Not just then. 'You expect too much, John! She's only a baby still!'

He held Gaby on his arm to make sure she could see everything. She gurgled with pleasure as she heard the chugging of the engine approaching. Not even the triumphant shrillness of the whistle shocked her as the train slowed down, clanking to a stop; she merely opened her eyes a little wider and chuckled as the steam hissed through the valve.

'Ay, ye're a railway engineer's daughter, no doubt about it!' he told her complacently. 'Like all the Andrewes ye've steam in your blood. Though as a lassie it's no' a line o' work they'll encourage ye to take up – more's the pity if ye're capable.'

Her tiny fists lashed out affectionately in the direction of his face, forcing him to jerk his head away, laughing.

'Now you know what she thinks of your nonsense!' said Hester, taking her from him. 'A railway engineer indeed! When this job's finished we're off to India where she'll marry a handsome, and *very* rich, young man who never gets his hands dirty.'

In spite of all the flags, the cheers and general excitement only two paying passengers had travelled on this first train and they had chosen to ride at least part of the way on the cow catcher in front of the engine, to which a wooden seat had been secured. It gave them the best possible view of any game they might pass and they had made good use of it too, for the first of their belongings to be unloaded was an ostrich they had shot.

Both men were covered in thick red dust. One – probably in his mid-twenties, Andrewes estimated – was clean-shaven, with mouse-coloured hair and a weather-bronzed, open-air face; his older companion was short, lean, with several days' growth of dark beard, and obviously in a foul mood. He jumped down from the train and began trying to enlist the help of three or four Africans standing nearby who merely stared at him blankly.

'Our first customers . . .' Andrewes felt disappointed. No bands, no speeches. They should have had a band at least. And Carpenter should have travelled up with them.

As it was, the only representative of the Mombasa Office was Ed Muldoon. He strode across to greet them, gripping Andrewes' hand firmly.

'King John! – an' here was I expectin' you'd be miles away at railhead! An' the lovely Mrs Andrewes – you're keepin' well, I hope? There's mail for you bein' unloaded at this very minute. Letters an' newspapers both, plenty o' readin' matter.' He held on to her hand a little too long and Andrewes noticed how she pulled it away from him. 'An' how's my fairy princess?'

Gaby regarded him with big dark eyes but no glimmer of a smile. He grinned at her with a display of nicotine-stained teeth.

'Ye've had company, I see?' Andrewes nodded in the direction of the two men. He let the nickname 'King John' pass without comment.

'Master Carpenter was so delighted, he sat down there an' then to get off a report to London, an' me standin' waitin' wi' papers for him to sign. Mother o' God, he understands nothin'.'

'Who are they?'

'The young'un's name is Hans de Jong, he says, an' they're plannin' on farmin' out here in the wilderness – would you credit that now?' Muldoon was scornful. 'They hold a title deed to the land if you please, signed by the Commissioner – who never in his life set eyes on it – sayin' it's all theirs for the next twenty-one years, renewable!'

'Ye sound like ye disapprove?'

'An' do I not?' Indignation flashed in his small dark eyes. 'Did not the English come to Ireland wi' a scrap o' paper in one hand an' a gun in the other? An' wasn't my own family starvin' to death in the Great Famine while

English landlords grew fat sellin' good Irish food in Liverpool an' Manchester an' the like?'

'Ay, but this is Africa, no' Ireland, d'ye ken.'

'An' aren't the English the English wherever they go? Did anyone think to ask permission o' the natives o' these parts?'

'The allocation o' land's controlled by law, as well ye know.' The man was getting under his skin. 'The Regulations—'

'Sure I saw the Regulations – printed in London, aren't they always?' Then, with a quick laugh, he broke off the argument and turned to Hester. 'Mrs Andrewes, I'm sorry. You're lookin' a picture today, you an' the pretty princess! Anythin' you ever need from Mombasa, you've only to let me know an' you'll have it within a week. For a beautiful lady like yourself there's nothin' I'd not be doin'.'

Hester's smile at the blarney seemed almost absent-minded. 'D'you think those men really have a chance of farming here?'

'Sure they're convinced they can, but aren't they both from the Cape, as they never tire o' tellin' the whole world an' don't they know all there is to know an' a lot more besides?' He cleared his throat as though about to spit contemptuously but thought better of it. 'I beg your pardon, Mrs Andrewes, but I'll be sheddin' no tears if they fall flat on their faces . . . *Hey!*'

He broke off abruptly and, yelling a stream of abusive Swahili, ran towards the rear of the train where a freight wagon was being unloaded. Andrewes – half-amused, half-annoyed, at his nonsense – could not at first see what was wrong, but then he noticed how the coolies were fooling around, carelessly slinging the boxes from one man to the next before dumping them untidily on to the platform.

'If that's blastin' gear they're unloadin' . . .!' he exclaimed, worried.

Then he relaxed as Muldoon reached them and brought the sky-larking to a stop. His blistering comments on their behaviour could be heard by everyone on the situation.

'Kamau came up on the train,' Hester was trying to say.

'Ay, I was expectin' him.' He was still watching the cool-

94

ies, now at work again under Muldoon's supervision; not that he distrusted the Irishman, as a transport manager he had his good points so long as he stayed off the whisky . . . But the off-loading now appeared to be going ahead in an orderly fashion and he turned back apologetically to Hester. 'I'm sorry, my love – ye were sayin' about Kamau?'

'John!' she reproached him.

It was only then he realized his *askari* was not alone but had brought his wife and child back from Mombasa with him. Although he was dressed coastal style in his usual long white *kanzu*, his wife – obviously from the interior – wore a loose cloth secured over one shoulder, with numerous bangles on her arms and row upon row of necklaces about her neck. The lobes of her ears were pierced and held round, wooden plugs.

'Njeri,' Kamau introduced her, his face as grave and expressionless as always. It was impossible ever to see into his thoughts.

Njeri's eyes flickered up to meet Andrewes' for a second in a cool appraisal which left him feeling none too sure he was passing the test. Then she dropped them again modestly, with an almost secret smile on her lips.

'Ay, ye're welcome, Njeri,' he said awkwardly.

Hester said something in Swahili – her command of the language astounded him, she'd picked it up so quickly – and pointed to the two children, who were standing gazing at each other, fascinated.

Kamau's son was perhaps a year or two older than Gaby and he had inherited his father's seriousness. He remained quite motionless, his big black eyes fixed on her face as she tried to say something in her usual baby talk. Taking hold of his hand, she attempted to coax him to go with her towards the dead ostrich which lay a few yards away along the platform. But he still gazed at her until suddenly – she was unsteady on her feet – she tottered and then flopped down on her bottom.

Njeri smiled, a big flash of her white teeth, swooping her son up into her arms, telling him something in her own rapid language – not Swahili, Andrewes could hear that much –

and nodding towards Gaby as she talked. Then, glancing at Andrewes, she held the boy up for him to see better.

'Ngengi,' she told him. Another wide flash of white teeth, her eyes lively. 'Gaby – Ngengi!'

They had taken to each other immediately, those two children, Hester thought as she sat in the train the following morning keeping an eye on Gaby, who was climbing on the seat. The little boy would be someone for her to play with back at the railhead camp; no harm in that while they were still little.

The train moved slowly through the flat open country, scorched, thirsty, longing for rain, with only the odd isolated acacia showing up unexpectedly green against the dry grass. A little distance away the vultures were circling; a kill, probably. The seats in this coach ran lengthwise down both sides, unlike those at home, and as usual they had it to themselves – a little family apartment with a W.C. and small kitchen next to it. John sat opposite her, deep in official papers, always working. 'King John', as Muldoon called him mockingly, though it never seemed to bother him. Perhaps he even secretly enjoyed the title.

But Muldoon disturbed her. The previous night – sleeping again in the *boma* in which they had lived all those months ago – she had lain awake for long hours thinking about it. Whenever they met he greeted her with some flattery or other; he would keep hold of her hand just those few seconds too long, yet not enough for it to be obvious to anyone else, and when he withdrew, it was lingeringly, his rough fingers gliding over hers.

She was uncertain how to deal with it, that was the trouble. A direct approach she would have turned down flat, but this was so . . . so insinuating . . .

John was watching her over his papers; she smiled at him, confused, almost – illogically – fearing he could read her mind.

'My love, ye were miles away,' he said gently, a hint of a laugh in his voice. 'An' I wonder where – Liverpool?'

She shook her head. 'Muldoon,' she admitted, curious

to know how he would react; they had never openly spoken of him before. With a smile she bent over Gaby who had fallen asleep on the seat.

'He's a mite too fond o' the bottle if ye ask me. But if ye're contemplatin' that offer o' his to bring ye somethin' special from Mombasa—'

'Not that.' What should she tell him? Anything at all? 'It's what he was saying about land,' she plunged on, withdrawing from the brink.

'My love, this is a new America!' John seemed amused. 'Ye should read the reports o' those who've been ahead wi' the survey parties – thousands upon thousands o' empty acres, they say.'

'Empty?'

A hundred yards or so from the side of the track stood three Africans armed with bows, naked but for the cloth about their loins. Each man carried a short sword at his waist; coils of wire looped around their arms and legs glinted in the sun. Hester waved to them but they ignored her. They looked so dignified, she thought.

'I'd imagine those arrows are poisoned,' John commented, watching them keenly. 'They're from villages up in those hills yonder. Ye canna honestly say they own this land we're travellin' over, no' the way we use the word *own*.'

'Perhaps they're convinced they do.'

'Ay, but they canna halt the course o' history, that's for sure. Did I ne'er tell ye about my ol' grannie in Scotland? Och, she'd her stories o' how English lords dispossessed the crofters, my family among 'em, an' I'm no' sayin' she was wrong. But wi' out that I might still've been plantin' barley, tendin' sheep an' the like instead o' buildin' railways – an' then I ne'er woulda met ye at all!'

Hester refused to laugh. 'I've heard my father preach that all land belongs to God, meaning it's blasphemy for any one person to claim ownership.'

'Ay – a dreamer, your father. Though I've the greatest respect for him, d'ye ken.' He turned back to his papers.

John was much too matter-of-fact, she decided, dissatisfied, staring moodily at the herd of zebra which cantered

97

alongside the train for several yards. Beyond them were half-a-dozen giraffes, sharp against the skyline as they fed from the upper branches of the acacias. Surely he too must sometimes feel they were intruders, coming here with their railway, scarring the land. In her heart she knew it was magic, this country, even when the sun was at its highest, killing the shadows.

In her early letters to her father she had tried to express something of this feeling, to share her experience with him. She had described one evening near Voi when she and John had looked out across the forest of pale, dwarfed thorn trees and how they had become part of a fantastic, mysterious world as the moonlight had eerily brought them to life. But when his reply arrived weeks later it contained warnings against the spiritual dangers of isolation, and he urged her not to neglect her Bible.

Yet John had shared that experience, and been moved by it, without ever speaking of it. Her hand had reached out for his and he had held it gently. Knowing.

At railhead Andrewes found everything in confusion. The coolies surrounded the train, clamouring to tell him something even before it had stopped. 'A great calamity, Sahib! We shall all be eaten in our beds!' 'Oh, may Allah protect us, Sahib!' 'We are being punished for coming here with the railway, Sahib! To this place where we do not belong!' Then Tim Wilton approached, pushing his way through the crowd of men as Andrewes sprang down from the step.

'Mr Andrewes, thank God you've come back!' he exclaimed, concern showing in his pale blue eyes. His face looked drawn and white as though he had not slept all night. 'Perhaps your presence will reassure the men, because I'm damned if I can.'

'If ye could tell me what's been goin' on, Mr Wilton?' Andrewes spoke brusquely and bawled at the men to stand back.

'We've a lion on the prowl. A man-eater. Two men dead – we found their remains next morning. One severely injured. Dr Carson doesn't think he can save him.'

98

'When did it happen?'

Tim Wilton explained how two nights earlier a lion had broken into one of the coolie huts, seized a man by the leg and tugged him out through the flimsy leaf walls. His screams had alerted his companions in the hut but they had been unable to save him. Several gangs had then been taken away from work on the track and set to thickening the protective thorn *boma* around each group of huts, but the man-eater had returned again the following night to claim another victim.

'I followed the trail as soon as it was light and found the body. Not a pretty sight. No trace of the lion, though. The whole camp's in a panic. They're refusing to work.'

Hester came out on to the little platform outside their coach. As Andrewes took Gaby from her he had a sudden vision of them being dragged off helplessly from their tent. Only a couple of months earlier he had heard of a survey engineer, a man called O'Hara, being attacked while asleep, and his wife had spent the rest of the night cowering with fright, unable to save him, unable either to shut out the terrible sounds of the lion gnawing at her husband's body.

Tim Wilton hurried forward to help Hester descend the steps. She jumped down, touching his arm lightly as she landed.

'Thank you, Mr Wilton!' she said, accepting his polite gesture but demonstrating her independence at the same time. 'You must've had an awful couple of days.'

'We've doubled the thickness of your thorn *boma* and strengthened it with railway sleepers. I only hope it's enough.'

'I think I'll be spending the night sitting up with a shotgun,' she replied, shuddering. She held out her arms for Gaby and hugged her close. 'Of all the ways to go I think that's the worst.'

'Kamau can stay wi' ye in the *boma*,' Andrewes decided.

'And you, John?'

'Mr Wilton an' I had best stay up an' wait for the beast, I reckon. D'ye no' agree, Mr Wilton?'

# NINE

The first task was to unload the fresh stores and medical supplies brought up on the train. Andrewes spotted three of the *jemadars* nearby and summoned them across. The victims had not been men from their gangs, they said, but everyone had heard the screams. The whole camp was on edge and work on their section of the track had stopped. Then Abdul Hakim hurried up, adjusting his usual striped *dhoti* and proclaiming that this was a very bad situation, very bad, but now Andrewes Sahib had returned something would be done about it.

'Ay, we must take precautions,' Andrewes agreed after listening patiently for some minutes, 'so I'll leave ye to see to the unloadin' while I go with Wilton Sahib to check the *bomas.*'

The *jemadars* regarded him doubtfully for a moment, but then they bustled away, shouting to their men that there was work to be done, so look sharp about it.

'We'll need to bag that lion, Mr Wilton, if we're to avoid trouble.' He did not feel at all confident about it; with several thousand men in the camp, it was a lion's larder. 'Let's start with the *boma* attacked last night.'

'You have the edge on all of us, speaking Hindustani like that,' Tim Wilton commented as they made their way through the sprawling camp. 'I could follow the gist, but I'll never achieve your fluency, more's the pity.'

'I was there ten years. An' at times with hardly any call to speak English.' But had Wilson heard rumours in India, he wondered; sooner or later the gossip would catch up on him.

He had still told Hester nothing about Gita. Some nights he woke up and found himself reaching out for her, vividly convinced she lay next to him, only to touch Hester's voluminous nightdress. Often he had persuaded himself he must find a suitable moment the next day to confess that he had lived for years with an Indian woman, discreetly, as man and wife – closer than that, even – and that her death was the reason why he had thrown up his job and returned to England. But when the next day came he always backed away from it, reluctant to cause Hester any unhappiness.

Tim Wilton cut across his thoughts as they reached the thorn fence. 'You can see where the lion pulled him through.'

Andrewes examined the sides of the gap, the thorns discoloured with blood, some even with shreds of flesh on them. 'They've no' repaired it either.'

'They'll not be sleeping here again – would you?'

'Maybe they're right.'

He inspected the thatched hut inside the *boma*, then returned to the gap. If the lion came back that night . . .

Nearby was a thick baobab tree, its massive trunk two or three yards in diameter; the juncture where it divided into several large branches formed a natural platform, big enough for two or three men. He scanned it carefully, remembering another baobab nearer the coast which had turned out to be infested with wild bees.

Tim Wilton was becoming restless. 'You're not proposing to spent the night up there?'

'Unless ye've a better suggestion. It's my guess the lion will be back to the same spot hoping for another victim.'

'Not with no one sleeping there. You'd need bait to coax him to come close enough.'

'Are ye volunteerin', Mr Wilton?'

Tim Wilton gave him a big, disarming grin. 'Division of labour, don't you know? I'll take the tree.'

'Thought ye might.'

Andrewes surveyed the *boma* again, making certain that gap was the only weak point. Summoning a gang of coolies, he ordered them to strengthen several of the thinner patches and sent one man off to requisition a live goat. It must have smelled danger even outside the *boma*, for it dug in its heels and refused to go any farther. Three men were needed to drag it inside, protesting loudly, and secure it to the stake which had been firmly fixed into the ground. Inspecting it, Andrewes' foot brushed against an empty kerosene *debe* lying with the other rubbish behind a hut.

'Will ye arrange for this tin to be cut into wee pieces,' he requested, 'which ye can then string together to hang up in the gap? D'ye ken what I'm after? Like Christmas decorations – something that'll clatter when the lion goes through?'

'You mean *if*,' Tim Wilton said.

Andrewes spent the next hours walking about the camp trying to reassure the men, checking the security of their *bomas* and advising them to keep their fires going all night. No time to get over to the second camp which was a couple of miles away on the far bank of the river, but the smoke smudges against the pale sky were more numerous than usual. Tonight, he thought grimly, it could well be their turn. None of his business, though: Jackson was in charge over there, with Jimmy Hathaway, the telegraphy wizard, for company.

The sun was already low in the sky before Andrewes got back to his own *boma* – 'Buckingham Palace' Hester still called it wherever they went; the name had caught her fancy. Before sitting down to eat he inspected every inch of the high, thick fence, probing it with his rifle to make quite sure. It seemed strong enough.

'If I'm right, ye've nothin' to fear,' he said after explaining his plan briefly. 'But, Hester love, I dinna want ye takin' any chances. Make sure the fire's kept high. Kamau will stay wi' ye, an' his family should sleep here. An' I've been thinkin' about Gaby . . .'

He took another mouthful of the stew Ali had cooked and chewed on it stolidly. He had little appetite and the meat was tough.

'It's you I'm worried about,' Hester said.

'I'm goin' to make a wee hammock for Gaby so she'll be out o' reach o' the lion, or anythin' else.'

'She'll fall out, John!' she protested.

'No' if we tie her in.' He took her hand. 'For her own safety, lass. If ye'd seen the injured man ye'd know that—'

'I have seen him,' she stated calmly. 'I helped Dr Carson change the dressings. John . . . I . . .'

His face betrayed his sudden anger.

'I can't just stand aside and do nothing,' she defended herself. 'Dr Carson has enough on his hands.'

'Ye'd agreed that'd all finished.'

'I gave in to you. You insisted.'

'He said himself it wasna wise wi' a bairn to look after . . .'

'That was weeks ago!' Her temper flared but she controlled it immediately. 'John, two of the Indian medical orderlies are down with malaria. It was the least I could do.'

She was right, he knew; ay, but wrong too. There was Gaby.

'There are no infectious cases at the moment,' she said, reading his thoughts. 'Only the men hurt in that accident last week, and I'm hardly likely to catch a broken leg, am I?'

He dodged the argument; it wasn't the right time. 'Ye must do as ye think fit, my love. I'll no' dictate to ye.'

Hester laughed. 'What else d'you do all day long – *King John*?' Teasing, she assumed a grave face and imitated his voice. '*Ay, that's what we'll do, lass, so see ye get on wi' it!*'

He caught her by the shoulders, swung her around and kissed her, much to Ali's disgust. This was not the behaviour expected of a Sahib in public. 'Finished?' he asked, indicating the dishes.

'Ay, ye can take 'em. But bring me that old kit-bag from the tent first. I'll use it for the hammock.'

Ali brought it. Andrewes slit it open down one side; then, with the point of his knife, he made a series of small holes for the ropes, which Hester helped him to thread through. They slung the improvised hammock from the roof posts inside the thatched hut and Andrewes lifted Gaby gently into it. She was fast asleep and did not wake up save for muttering a few incoherent protests as he fastened the flaps around her.

'There – she'll no' fall out o' that, an' she's well out o' reach,' he said contentedly when he had finished. 'Though she may find it a bit warm an' show signs o' prickly heat in the morning. Now, ye've got the shotgun, my love, an' . . .'

Hester was still gazing at Gaby, snug in her little ham-

103

mock. 'John, I've waited for the right moment to tell you.' She spoke softly, not raising her eyes. 'We're expecting another.'

Andrewes experienced a sudden flood of mixed emotions – pleasure – excitement . . . Yes, and fear. 'My love, why did ye no' say it earlier?'

'I wanted to see Dr Carson first. That's why I went to the hospital tent.'

'A wee brother for Gaby . . . She'd like that.' Yet his mind was filled with doubts. Another bairn while they were still living in these camps? And all the dangers for Hester . . . 'My love, we'll need to take extra care, d'ye ken?'

'Both of us,' she reminded him gently. 'So don't put yourself into unnecessary danger tonight – please, dearest? Aren't you happy about it?'

'Ay, lass, of course I'm happy, but if only things were different.' He began to check the shotgun. 'Now, it's loaded an'—'

'John – look!'

To the west the sun was touching the flat tops of the acacias, a great scarlet disc colouring the whole sky, but Hester was pointing south. There, hanging miraculously in mid-air above a layer of cloud, was the dome of Kilimanjaro, a dazzling white slightly tinged with pink. It was an awe-inspiring sight and caught Andrewes completely unawares. He stared at it spell-bound, the gun still in his hands.

'Home of the gods,' Hester murmured to herself, but then she was always quoting one poet or other. 'So easy to believe.'

'Ay,' Andrewes added drily, 'an' to think Queen Victoria went an' made a present o' that to the Kaiser. That's somethin' she'd no' have done if she'd ever seen it wi' her own eyes. Mebbe Muldoon is no' so wrong after all.'

Hester smiled, linking her arm through his. 'It's a good omen for the baby, seeking Kilimanjaro,' she told him firmly as the sun dropped slowly behind the horizon and the vision faded.

He gave her the gun.

'Ye've fired a few shots already, so remember what I taught ye – take aim calmly, no hurryin', an' only squeeze the trigger when ye've the beast firmly in your sights. An' trust Kamau – he's a first-class shot – but ye've two barrels an' he's only got one. Remember he needs to reload each time. But it's all a question o' keepin' your head.'

'And of you keeping yours, John,' she said, but he hardly listened.

The lion was out there somewhere, that was certain, lurking just beyond the bounds of the camp. Waiting for the darkness which was now on them. And there was not all that much he could do to stop it.

Kamau squatted in the shadows away from the firelight, close to the sealed entrance to the *boma*, his rifle between his knees. Beyond the fire sat Memsabu Andrewes with the shotgun, her eyes dreamy as she stared into the flames. Why white people had to stand everything on its head he would never know. They understood so much about mastering the world around them yet they never paused to hear what the earth was telling them. Now they had to insult him by leaving him here among the womenfolk.

Were they perhaps punishing him, he wondered, for bringing Njeri and the *toto* to live at the railhead camp? But she had nagged him unceasingly about the heat of Mombasa, the discomforts of living there now he was away from her for so long, how she yearned for the morning mists on the ridges, the cold bite in the air and the unhurried music of Gikuyu voices around her. And so he had agreed to bring her, knowing that within a season or two the railway would arrive at the very border of Gikuyu country.

And then?

The prophecy warned the Gikuyu to do nothing, the railway could not be defeated; but old men, distrusting change, would recall past battles; hot blood coursed through the veins of young warriors . . .

Kamau remembered how reluctant they had been to accept him on the ridge where he had first met Njeri. He had travelled through the country twice accompanying white men on their hunting safaris, camped on scrubland nearby, spoken to them in the Gikuyu tongue – arousing their suspicions – and at last met one elder who recalled hearing of his father from someone he knew on another ridge a long distance away. Only then had they really decided to make him welcome; they had offered him food from the same calabash and made him drunk on honey beer.

On his second visit he had noticed a young woman looking at him as he came from the stream, though as their eyes met she tossed her head and turned away. She had a strong face, full of character; her name was Njeri, a friend explained, and she was still unmarried. Having turned down two suitors, he had added jokingly, no other man had risked asking her, fearing her sharp tongue.

Kamau had thought no more about it until one night she came to the hut where he was sleeping and lay down beside him. He took her, discovering that she was still a virgin. Then, as they talked together throughout the night, keeping their voices low, he began to understand what she had done. It was called *kuheera*, he remembered from what Ngengi had told him years earlier. A woman finding herself unmarried, unwanted, might visit a married man in his hut and offer herself; if he had sex with her, it was understood that he would take steps to make her one of his wives. Although Kamau was not married at that time, she had used this custom because he was a stranger who would not be staying on the ridge for long.

The discussions with her family about the correct procedure went on for many days. The normal enquiries about his own background and suitability had to be waived; eventually, after consultations with the best-known medicine man in the district, the marriage had been agreed. Kamau had used up practically his entire stock of trade goods – bangles, coloured beads, knives, even a couple of blankets – in bartering for the thirty sheep which he paid over as security for the success of the marriage; then he had returned to the coast taking his new bride with him, happy in her company, enjoying her sarcastic comments about the white hunters, but also feeling he had at last established a genuine bond with his own people.

In time, she gave birth to their first son and they named him Ngengi after Kamau's father, in accordance with Gikuyu custom. Now he was three years old by the white man's reckoning.

The medicine man had foretold sons, he remembered as he gazed across the fire at Memsabu Andrewes who was almost asleep, sitting there on her canvas chair with the shotgun across her lap. Behind her, he could just see the outline of the rough lean-to shelter where Njeri and Ngengi were to spend the night. Left here with the women . . .

Kamau stood up and threw more wood on the fire; it crackled fiercely, throwing out a shower of sparks. Had the insult been intended? Or had Andrewes, with a white man's blindness, not even realized what he was doing?

Hester stirred and opened her eyes as she heard the fresh logs sizzling and snapping when the flames licked them. Perhaps she should go to bed, she thought, leaving Kamau on guard as John had intended. Yet she would not be able to sleep for thinking of him sitting up there in the baobab tree, waiting for the lion to walk into their trap. Which she did not believe it would.

The fire shifted, throwing off intense heat which forced her to move her chair farther back; the smoke brought tears to her eyes.

What if they heard the lion but could not see it? And what if they decided to come down from the tree to investigate and . . . The memory sprang back into her mind of that poor coolie in the hospital tent, his flesh exposed and raw, and Dr Carson muttering to himself what a miracle it was gangrene had not yet set in, amazing how the man was still alive, still 'clinging to life' as he had put it, might even last through till morning . . .

The thought of John lying there . . . or Tim Wilton . . . either of them . . . She shuddered.

Then: *Mr* Wilton, she corrected herself silently. Though

with that frank, easy friendliness it was much easier to think of him as Tim. Gaby had taken to him right away. He was younger than John of course, perhaps no more than a couple of years older than herself. John had more – well, her father had called it *gravitas* – and he lived for the railway too, whereas Mr Wilton took it all more lightly. That first time they had seen Kilimanjaro some weeks earlier . . . She had been reading in her Palgrave's Golden Treasury, one of the few books she had with her, and still held it in her hand. He had noticed it.

'You like poetry?' he had asked, surprised. Looking up towards the mountain, he had started to recite:

> The splendour falls on castle walls
> And snowy summits old in story:
> The long light shakes across the lakes,
> And the wild cataract leaps in glory . . .

'Tennyson,' he had explained, breaking off quickly. 'Not completely right, I'm afraid.'

She thought about it drowsily as the fire moved again and the fiercely burning logs seemed to abandon all resistance. He had promised to lend her the book. She must remind him.

A shot, then two more in rapid succession.

She was on her feet immediately, gripping the gun. Kamau, by the entrance to the *boma*, held out a hand warning her to remain still. The thorn fence was some fifteen feet high and nothing could be seen over the top of it, only the dark sky which was suddenly filled with birds screeching their protests. From the coolies' quarters came a murmur of men's voices.

'Oh, if only we knew what was happening!' she exclaimed, feeling it was not right for her to be cooped up there in the *boma* while John was outside in danger.

But the voices died down after about five minutes or so. The birds returned to their slumber among the treetops, and the camp became quiet again.

So they didn't kill it after all, she thought, sinking into her canvas camp chair again. Kamau was watching her, unblinking. 'Lion not dead,' she commented in poor Swahili.

But he said nothing.

Not far from the great baobab tree, Jevangee lay uneasily awake in the roughly-constructed hut of leaves and thatch which he shared with eight other workers in his gang, most of them from the same neighbourhood back home in India. One was snoring, an endless row of hefty, disturbed snorts – like an animal, Jevangee thought – but he suspected the rest were still awake. They must have heard the sahibs' guns.

Hunting the lion, the *jedmadar* had explained importantly. Just as, in India, sahibs went after the tigers which harrassed the villagers.

As a child, he had often witnessed the start of a hunt with the white sahibs resplendent in spotless solar topees and riding breeches. One man in the village had described how these sahibs needed fresh clothing for each different time of day, each different job, and a bath whenever they changed. No one knew why. But Jevangee had marvelled most at the beautifully-groomed horses, each one led by its own *syce*, its jingling harness sparkling in the sunlight. Then the host of gun-bearers and other attendants – how could anyone possess enough money to pay so many?

His own father's poor patch of land could hardly support their family of six brothers and four sisters. At times he would pick up a handful of soil and watch it crumble into dust to be blown away by the wind. He should work for the white sahib, the family decided. With his fine looks and lithe body he should do well in a sahib's household. As the youngest brother it was his duty, they said.

No household wanted him, though, so he stayed in the village and worked the land as best he could. After two more bad harvests, with his father in debt to the money-lenders, there was no alternative. The Uganda Railway project was recruiting labour and Jevangee had to go.

Here he was, he thought, a stranger in a hostile land. He stared up into the darkness and tried not to listen to that loud, uneven snoring which sent shivers down his spine. Here, even the sun shone differently. The moon and the stars looked down at him as though wondering what he was doing so far away from home. Yet – he could almost hear his father's voice – by the time the railway was completed he might have sent home sufficient rupees to pay off the debt *and* buy better land.

When he arrived back in India, what a rejoicing there would be, what a—

He smelled the lion before he heard it, a hot stale smell as it pushed through the flimsy leaf walls of the hut. Wet drops of its saliva dribbled on to his face, a paw rested heavily on his chest. His nerves alive with shock, not daring to breathe, not daring to move, he prayed it would step right over him, take one of the others, not him, oh please not . . .

But that wild shriek was *his* voice, that warm slobbering mouth was closing around *his* shoulder, those hard teeth were burning into *his* flesh, gripping him savagely, crunching into the bones – *his* bones. Dimly he was aware of panic in the hut, the other men yelling for help, but *he* was the victim, thrashing about to save himself, uselessly, his head swimming, confused, in agony.

He was being dragged out through the wall. He could feel the stakes which formed the framework of the hut shredding his skin off him as he was relentlessly pulled through. Oh, that pain was unbelievable . . . and his shoulder, too – a throbbing, vicious, open rawness. He could do nothing to fight it, not against that brute strength. Helplessly his mouth tried to form the words of prayers he had been taught, his mind seemed for brief moments to leave his body, looking down on it as it was tugged across the rough ground, as though no longer his.

Someone was trying to free him, lashing out at the lion with a pick handle. The beast dropped him, standing over him, snarling . . .

'Must get away . . . get away . . .' He tried to concentrate his mind. Crawl. Roll over . . . if only he could . . .

Then he was free! Miraculously the lion had gone,

though he could hear a squeal of terror somewhere, and he knew he had to run to safety, anywhere away from that place. That temple in the centre of his village, that's where he would be safe once he could get to it. If he could only stand, push himself up on to his knees even . . .

But the lion was over him again. He heard himself screaming in uncontrollable agony as its teeth clamped sharply into his thigh. The pain shot through his body in spasms, again and again, until his yelling declined to a pathetic whimpering, a longing to die . . . oh, quickly – *please!*

Now he was being drawn through the fence. Thorns tore into him like red-hot needles probing his flesh, and his skull cracked . . . cracked . . . cracked . . . as it was jolted over tree roots and rocks. Oh, why was he still conscious? *Why?* Not even the prayers helped him any longer; the words would not come.

In the tall, tangled grass the movement stopped. The lion was licking . . . sucking . . . at the bites where its teeth had dug deepest. Then it bit again; he felt his flesh being ripped from him. Pain signals reached his brain, he knew it hurt . . . somewhere . . . as those strong incisors savaged his belly: but it was all far away by now. He had reached the village temple. He could see its familiar walls, the carvings around the door, and he slipped gratefully into unconsciousness knowing he was home at last.

Andrewes had heard the screams but it was not until the following morning that he came across Jevangee's gruesome remains beneath a tree about half a mile from the camp. He steeled himself as they reassembled all that was left of the poor man for burial. The eyes stared out from the smashed skull, accusingly; shreds of raw meat clung to the exposed rib-cage; the pelvis lay a yard or two away from the rest of the body, with one leg still tenuously attached to it by stringy sinews. The other was missing.

He felt sick, convinced the whole business was his fault. The lion had returned to the deserted *boma* just as they had hoped, brushing against the scraps of tin hanging in the gap; the moment they heard the clatter he and Tim Wilton had opened fire simultaneously from the tree. But somehow the lion had escaped. They had waited, uncertain whether to risk coming down. The camp became quiet again – except for the goat which kept up a steady, irritating bleat – until the screams and yells from Jevangee's hut some twenty minutes later. They hurried across, but too late.

Much too late, he thought bitterly as the *askaris* gathered the last fragments, wrapping them in some old sacking. If that had been Hester? The lion might just as easily have found a weak spot in the Buckingham Palace *boma* and . . .

He turned to find Tim Wilton had retreated a few paces to vomit near a thorn bush. A few threads from the dead man's clothes were hanging from the long, needle-like thorns and moving gently in the slight breeze.

'When ye're ready, Mr Wilton!' he snapped, angrily.

'I beg your pardon.' Tim Wilton hurried back, wiping his mouth and glancing down at his clothes to make sure he had not soiled them. 'Two nights without sleep – and then *that*.' He nodded towards the sack.

'We'll take Kamau an' a couple o' others to see how far we can track the beast.' He spoke brusquely, hiding his feelings.

He issued orders to the Indian coolies to transport Jevangee's remains back to the camp for formal identification. Dr Carson would need to write a report on the death for the Railway Office in Mombasa and the man's few belongings, anything of value, would be despatched to his family in India, together with his teeth. Ay, that anonymous coolie will be mourned wi' more ceremony, Andrewes thought, than any o' us, no doubt o' that.

'Which way d'ye reckon it went, Kamau?' He repeated the question in pidgin Swahili. 'Simba wapi?'

Silently Kamau pointed towards the thickest clump of thorn trees. Tiny speckles of blood – was it blood? – marked out a path through the undergrowth.

Andrewes led, with Kamau close behind; Tim Wilton with his Indian gun-bearer Sharma brought up the rear.

After a few yards it was no longer possible to walk upright and they were forced on to their hands and knees to avoid the low thorn branches. He cursed under his breath as he tried to free himself from the thorns entangled in his clothing, holding him back. For some reason neither Kamau nor Sharma had the same difficulty. Perhaps they were more adept at pressing themselves close to the ground as they wormed their way forward.

Eventually the trees thinned out. Much to his relief Andrewes was able to stand again. Patches of bare rock protruded through the hard soil over which a scattering of animal droppings baked in the heat. Through the trees ahead the water of the Tsavo sparkled in the morning sunlight.

'Same pattern as last time!' Tim Wilton exclaimed, frustrated. 'We track him so far, then lose him. It's my bet he hangs out along the river bank somewhere.'

In the distance they could hear the men from the other camp back at work, their hammers chipping at the rock walls of a cutting through which the railway was to pass when the permanent bridge was built. 'Out! Out! Everyone out!' came Jackson's voice faintly on the breeze. 'At the double if you don't want your balls blown off!' Then a few short moments of silence followed by a muffled explosion. Farther upriver birds flew into the air, squawking and circling.

They took the other direction along the bank towards the point where the river curved and twisted between massive clusters of giant boulders, some smooth, some half-overgrown with thick vegetation. As they got closer, Andrewes caught a glimpse of white on the lower rocks. It could well be clothing, he thought. Or on the other hand . . .

He signed to the others to spread out and be on the alert. Kamau indicated that he could try to get nearer to it. Knowing how silently he moved, Andrewes waved back in agreement. A turbulent breeze blew over the rocks towards them; it would be impossible for any animal concealed there to scent their presence. But as Kamau approached, the lizards sunning themselves on the boulders suddenly scurried away and the birds seemed to fall silent.

He reached the white patch. Andrewes held his rifle ready. Tim Wilton, tense, was a few yards to his left, with Sharma just beyond him. Now was the moment.

Kamau went on, passing the whiteness, then suddenly stopped and gestured urgently for them to join him. They crept forward cautiously while Kamau dropped out of sight behind a boulder. That white patch was clothing after all, Andrewes noted grimly. A man's clothes, scattered about untidily. Another victim – but this time the lion would not get away with it.

As they came up to where Kamau lay concealed they dropped down and eased themselves forward on their stomachs to see what awaited them beyond the rocks which fell away sharply down to the river bank. There, amongst the leaves of a sturdy tree, was the pale full moon of someone's backside.

They stared at it in disbelief, then collapsed into loud laughter. Whoever it was, at least he was still alive.

'King John, is that you, you bastard?' came the flat Manchester tones from the tree. 'Can't tha do something to help instead o' laughing like a daft bugger? It's no bloody joke – get that animal away from me.'

Snuffing harmlessly among the roots was an ugly-looking warthog with a tufted tail and curved tusks.

'I can't get down,' the plaintive voice said.

That only started them laughing again. Jimmy Hathaway had a reputation for being so scared of animals, even a pet gazelle would send him dashing for cover. No one had ever seen him with a gun either; he probably didn't own one. Small, wiry, with a worried, ferret-like face, he relied on his quick wit to get him out of awkward situations; that, and the fact that he was a telegraphy genius who had only to twist two bits of wire together to get a message along them, made him one of the most popular men on the railway.

'What are ye doin' there wi' no clothes on?' Andrewes

demanded with a wink at the others, making no move to dispose of the warthog. 'Ye're no' decent, man! D'ye ken?'

'I was about to take a bath in river.' Jimmy had still not shifted; as he spoke, only his naked bottom was visible. 'What else could I do but climb up to get out of its way? Be reasonable, King John. Please . . .'

'I hope ye're tellin' me the truth.' He kept his voice grave. 'Ye're no' pullin' our legs, Jimmy? There's somethin' about that expression ye're wearin' on your face . . . What d'ye think, Mr Wilton?'

'Oh, absolutely!' Tim Wilton spluttered, unable to control himself.

'It *is* your face I'm addressin'?' Andrewes enquired. 'Wi' that lopsided grin?'

'King John, I'm covered wi' scratches an' I've got insects all over me, sucking my blood . . . oh, please, King John . . .'

'Try jumping down on the warthog's back, Jimmy! I'll lay you five to one you can't ride him back to the camp.' Tim Wilton exploded into laughter again. 'You – you – you might even win, you've the build of a jockey, don't you know!'

'Tha's not funny!' He was beginning to lose his temper.

Andrewes raised the Winchester and put a bullet through the warthog's head. They could use the meat anyway, he reflected. What with the trip to Voi, and now being taken up with the man-eater, the needs of the larder had been neglected.

Jimmy climbed painfully down the tree, shivering as he looked at the dead animal. 'See them tusks?' he demanded, hurt. 'Vicious, they are. A foot long if they're an inch. He could've ripped insides out o' me wi' them tusks.'

'I think this one's a lady,' Andrewes commented. He pulled the carcase over.

'Then that explains a lot,' said Jimmy darkly. 'It explains one helluva lot.'

# TEN

Either the maneater had the luck of the Devil or it was too sly for them, that much was obvious. Every attempt to trap it during the next few weeks ended in failure. Andrewes stayed up several nights running on watch, either perched in a tree or – once – concealed in a brake van, but all to no avail. Night after night it raided a different part of the camp, keeping well clear of his hiding place; night after night the screams of the next unfortunate victim told him that he had failed yet again. Tim Wilton suggested leaving meat for the beast beyond the camp perimeter. The two of them went out and shot countless zebra, wildebeeste, giraffe, anything in sight and left it lying in a wide circle where the lion could find it. But no, one skinny living coolie was more to its taste than any amount of well-fleshed, dead game. Only the hyenas and marabou storks benefitted from that slaughter.

To make matters worse, Jackson came storming over to taunt him about his 'bloody feeble efforts'. It was only with difficulty Andrewes managed to control his temper; if Hester and Gaby hadn't been living at the camp he would have worked out all his anger and frustration on the man, beaten him to a pulp . . . As it was, he merely said Jackson should go ahead and track the lion down himself if that was what he wanted.

But Jackson had no better luck than anyone else. He organized a three day hunt from which he returned with enough to keep both camps in meat for a month – but no lion. And the coolies showed no surprise. According to them it was no natural beast, this lion, but some African god bent on exacting vengeance on them for bringing the railway to his country.

Even Hester commented on it.

She had been helping at the hospital tent again – 'Only

while the orderlies are off sick,' she had excused herself, aware of his disapproval – where Dr Carson had been amputating toes. 'Three more men this morning, one toe each. Dr Carson has explained to them over and over again how jiggers get under their toenails to lay their eggs, and that's the cause of the inflamation, and they should wear shoes . . . But they never listen. They think it's some African curse on them they can do nothing about – like the lion.'

Andrewes took her hand in his, stroking it as he talked. 'My love, ye dinna think ye might stay clear o' the tent now ye're expectin' again?'

But she was stubborn, refusing even to talk it over. 'If there was any real danger, Dr Carson would be the first to say.'

He gave up, not wishing to quarrel, knowing that once her mind was set, nothing would change it.

That was a night the lion chose not to appear. In fact, its visits gradually became fewer until at one point a full seven nights had passed with no sign of it. The atmosphere in the camp brightened, though he sensed how the fear remained as an undercurrent, however normal things seemed.

Work on diverting the track down a gentler gradient to meet the temporary bridge was going well. Another couple of months and he would be ready to move on, leaving the specialist engineer – not yet arrived from India – to take charge of constructing the more permanent girder bridge across the Tsavo. Some advance work had already been done along the route the line was to take, but it was high time Andrewes had a look for himself.

'If ye've no objection, lass,' he apologized to Hester. He felt uneasy about leaving her and the bairn alone while there was still some chance the lion might return. 'It might be six or seven days I'll be away. It seems there's a chance o' recruitin' extra labour among the Wakamba – so I'm told, at any rate, an' . . .'

'Oh, John, of course you must go – it's your job!' She seemed astonished that he should even hesitate. 'I have my shotgun. And it's no timid English rose you married! If that's what you wanted you shouldn't have come to Liverpool for a bride!'

'I shall need Kamau wi' me to help make contact wi' the Wakamba . . .' He regarded her uncertainly. 'Though I've instructed one o' the sepoys – Patel – to sleep at the *boma*.'

She was almost laughing at him, her eyes sparkling yet, at the same time, gentle. 'Oh, John, I do love you – but it's going to be all right, really it is. I could ask Mr Wilton to keep an eye on things. Or Dr Carson – though he really has enough to do.'

'Ay . . . But I'll be away no longer than I can help, ye can count on that.'

He took only a small party with him – fifteen men in all counting *askaris* and porters. Instinctively he had felt Kamau should act as headman and guide. The choice was a good one. He obviously knew the country well, finding his way without difficulty through the long grass and entangled bushes. His manner was different too; his seriousness dropped away and he became almost eager and open.

Ay, ye're in your element on safari, I can see that, Andrewes thought approvingly, and he could understand why. In spite of long hot hours on foot, walking in single file along narrow paths no more than a couple of feet wide, he could already feel something of this great continent's power to draw men to it. Away from railhead and the Indian coolies, he was at last face-to-face with Africa as it really was.

He let Kamau decide where they should camp for the night. The men were immediately set to gathering a good supply of wood; once the fires were alight, they started work cutting down several strong thorn trees for the *boma*. The whole area was teeming with wild life and they had already spotted one lion among the long grass, though it had slunk away, ignoring them. Andrewes took three *askaris* with him to hunt for meat and brought down an eland. The moment it fell the *askaris* rushed forward to cut its throat, Muslim fashion, to drain out the blood before it died, or their religion would not have allowed them to touch the flesh. Then they carried it back to the camp where the *boma* was almost finished.

As they sat around the fire that evening eating the roasted eland, tearing at the meat with their teeth and grinning contentedly at each other, Andrewes realized that the tensions of the past weeks had at last begun to slip away from him. Of course Hester would be all right, there were plenty of people around to look after her, and she really was improving with that gun. He thought back to when he had first met her in Liverpool. After Gita's death – leaving him desolate, terribly alone, hating his own existence – he had gone through a black period when he had drunk himself into a stupor every night just to blot it all out. He had deliberately picked fights to wallow in the punishment, and finally abandoned his job to work his passage back to Britain as a stoker on board a tramp steamer – though there'd been enough money in his account for a first class ticket on one of the new luxury ships if he'd felt so inclined. But at that time he had been unable to face all the silly chatter and frippery; he'd preferred to shovel coal. A good job too. Coming through the Red Sea and the Suez canal in that stoker's hell-hole he had sweated the drink out of his system and started the climb back to life. By the time they docked in London he was in control again – as scarred, in his soul, as any pugilist, but definitely in control. In Liverpool, staying with his cousin, he'd even been able to talk about India again. And he'd met Hester . . . Her eyes dancing, the laugh in her voice, that strong chin . . . ay, an' at the same time so full o' commonsense. He'd witnessed once how she dealt with two down-and-outs who had come begging – her evident sympathy for them as she saw through the yarns they were spinning – perhaps that had been the day he began to realize . . . to visualize – they might make a match for each other, he and Hester.

*Ay, that was it!*

He accepted another eland chop from Kamau and sat

there with it still hot between his fingers as he stared into the flames of the roaring fire remembering that smoky coal fire in her father's drawing room where they had talked those long hours. But he had not wanted this for her, not the way it was at the camp. A house at least – that's what she needed. Four solid walls.

And Gita would have understood, he thought, as an Indian, better than most.

By midday the following day they had reached a river which, Kamau indicated, would be the best location for their next camp. Andrewes agreed. Using the survey party's maps, they were keeping to the proposed route for the railway and he had it in mind to check some of their readings.

But as they were setting up the tents he noticed movements in the long grass and was reaching for the Winchester when Kamau stopped him. An African came out of the grass silently, then another, and a third, until they were surrounded by them – the men quite naked and armed with bows, the women wearing small pubic aprons, with bangles on their arms and legs. Their faces seemed handsome at first, but when they spoke Andrewes saw how their front teeth were filed to sharp points with wide gaps in between, giving them a very threatening appearance.

'Wakamba,' Kamau said.

As they came closer, the railway *askaris* and porters called out that they wished to barter for beans and *posho* meal, but the Wakamba ignored them and they fell silent again.

Remaining a few yards off, the Wakamba grouped together as if defensively. A moment's uncertain pause, then one of their number – an older warrior bearing an air of great authority – stepped forward to face Kamau. To everyone's astonishment they greeted each other as long lost brothers; the air rang with their words, their questions and answers, their laughter, their exclamations of genuine delight at meeting again. Then another man, even older, his face heavy with wrinkles, started to sing. The women joined in, chanting the chorus.

Andrewes waited, intrigued, to see what would happen next. His whole party of *askaris* and porters suddenly relaxed, laughing and congratulating each other as they witnessed how warmly the Wakamba were welcoming Kamau. Discreetly, they laid their weapons aside.

Kamau led the other warrior across to introduce him to Andrewes. 'Mbiti,' he said, adding in Swahili that they were all to be the Wakamba's guests.

For Andrewes, accustomed to taking charge of things, the next two days were bewildering. He was shown every consideration, but without doubt here Kamau was 'king' – or treated as such. It puzzled him. Over the months he had gradually come to understand that unlike the other *askaris*, mostly Swahilis, Kamau was a Gikuyu and the son of a man brought down to the coast as a slave by Arab traders. How much more was there to know? And how much more was there to this mysterious country, glibly named British East?

Here he was experiencing a new world. Thoughts of the railway – subduing everything in its path, pushing on with its clanking engines, its rushing steam – all dissipated. Mbiti took him to the village whose round, grass huts snuggled into the landscape. The women were already at work on a great feast of welcome, while the men came to share their calabashes of home-brewed beer with him explaining everything at length, telling him of Kamau's great achievements – whatever they might be, for he did not understand a word of it.

Once darkness fell and they had eaten their fill the praise songs began again, the *lili, lili, lili* of the women's joyous chorus, the dancing, and the men – firelight gleaming red on their glistening black skins – pressed more and more drink on him until slowly it took control. He slumbered, and they guided him away, stumbling, to a place where he could sleep.

At the first hint of dawn he awoke to find the grass walls and roof around him alive with busy insects. Yet they belonged there; they were not intruders – and nor, he now felt, was he. As a boy he had slept a few nights once in a crofter's cottage which, it had seemed, grew out of the land itself . . . ay, that was it.

They came to take him hunting, their way, tracking a wildebeeste silently on foot – with himself lumbering clumsily behind – until Mbiti loosed an arrow which caused it to stand shivering for a brief moment, then drop down paralysed, and die. Poison on the arrow-head, of course; they were known for their poison. But they clamoured for him too to demonstrate his own skills. He chose his target with care – a group of Grant's gazelle – and brought down two with quick shots from his Winchester, flicking the lever rapidly.

And back at the village that evening – more feasting, drinking, talking around the crackling fire. Two of the men challenged each other in rapid cross-talk; one dropped out and another joined in; then a third . . . And the bursts of admiration, the applause for the winner: a riddle competition, Kamau explained as another calabash of drink was handed around.

Early the following morning they left again for Tsavo, well supplied with food for the journey, still feeling dazed and warmed by their welcome. For the first couple of hours Mbiti and some of the other Wakamba walked with them to see them well on their way; then the final farewells and they were left to trek on their own again. The march seemed longer than before, the ground harder, the scrub thicker, but at last – later than estimated – they arrived back at the *boma* they had built four days earlier.

But they had achieved their objective, Andrewes thought, contented, before he slept. Mbiti had promised to recruit all the labour needed for the railway; no shortage of volunteers once Kamau had talked to them. Without Kamau – ay, well that was a mystery. He had often noticed, wherever they were, how Kamau would slip away to make contact with local African villagers – those up in the Taita Hills, the mission people near the first railhead camp . . . Many he may have met before during his safari days. But the Wakamba? He had questioned the other *askaris* and pieced together a story, as far as he understood it at all, that Mbiti's village had been at war with a Maasai group, something to do with stealing cattle, and Kamau had helped to end the fighting, acted as a go-between. Now he was Mbiti's blood brother. But maybe that wasna the case at all, maybe he had it all wrong; it was no' too easy, followin' that rapid Swahili – even assumin' the *askaris* were sure o' their facts, which he doubted. Perhaps he'd never know any more than that.

As their caravan neared the camp he spotted Hester coming to meet him, looking so fresh and happy, it did his heart good to see her. She brought Gaby with her too and he thanked God nothing had happened to them while he had been away. The nagging fear that something might go wrong had never left him.

'No, of course not!' she insisted, mocking him, in answer to his very first question. 'The lion would never call while the master's away – didn't you know that?' Her eyes caressed his face and she tucked her arm through his as they walked. 'But there is news – *real* news! We're to have the Indian army here, coming up from Mombasa by rail.'

'When do we expect 'em?' He had heard rumours the first contingent might be on its way.

'Later today – so you'd better have a wash and get into clean clothes. You look like the reddleman again!'

'Ay, this dust . . . It's short notice.'

'The telegraph line was out of order again. A couple of hundred yards of wire was stolen between here and Voi, and Mr Hathaway only managed to replace it this morning. This was the first signal to come through.'

'Ay . . . but we canna blame 'em stealin' it. Och, if ye'd only been wi' me this time, Hester love. But what wi' Gaby an' ye expectin' again . . .

'Oh?' she teased, flirting with him. 'Mr Wilton's been very attentive. Lent me his Tennyson again. Should I read you some?'

'I couldna promise to stay awake, lass.' He slipped his

arm affectionately about her shoulders. 'It's good to see ye again. Why did the army have to choose today to come here?'

The whole camp gathered at railhead to await the arrival of the train that afternoon – Tim Wilton in a newly-pressed white suit, Jackson bullying the coolies to stand well back from the track, Jimmy Hathaway bustling into the telegraph hut every couple of minutes . . . Gaby held out her arms to be lifted up to her father's shoulders the moment the whistle was heard, but little Ngengi – Kamau's *toto* – pressed closer to his parents, shy of the commotion.

The train pulled in, belching out smoke and wood ash. Immediately the cleared ground at the track-side was crowded with Indian soldiers, straightening their uniforms, putting on little pillbox hats and retrieving rifles as the *halvidars* shouted their orders, strutting up and down making sure every man was on his toes. The platoons were fell in and brought to attention, though not smartly enough for the *halvidar-major*, who yelled at them to watch their spacing, the straightness of the line, the angle of their caps . . . Shoulder – *arms!* Order . . . *arms!* A hundred rifle butts hit the ground as one. Would they still keep that up after their two months' march to Uganda, Andrewes mused. It was an open secret they were bound for Uganda where the British-led Sudanese troops had mutinied, murdering three of their officers. That sort of news travelled fast in Africa.

The British officers in charge of this expeditionary force swaggered down from their coaches at a more leisurely pace, stared arrogantly at the railway coolies, then turned their backs to give orders for the unloading of their personal baggage. At first it seemed they were deliberately ignoring the engineers who had gathered to greet them. Andrewes waited, the cold anger gnawing at him.

But it was Hester who gave voice to his feelings. 'Think they're the lords of creation, don't they? Look at the blond one with the Dundreary whiskers – straight out of Punch! I'd like to see him down a few streets I know in Liverpool.'

'My love, he'll hear ye!' Andrewes warned, amused that

124

her reaction was the same as his. Spit and polish, shining boots, regulation puttees – he'd seen it all so often in India.

A fresh round of yelling from the *halvidars* and a smart bringing-together of heels announced that the force was ready for the officers' instructions. Subalterns joined their platoons. The little blond major stood stiffly before them, speaking in a barely audible voice, then marched towards Andrewes, saluted and introduced himself.

'Major Arbuthnot, Uganda Relief Force. You're Mr Andrewes, I take it? And this is Mrs Andrewes? Your servant, ma'am.' He touched her hand, performing a little half-bow over it. 'We'll need to camp here for a couple of days while the train returns to Mombasa for the rest of our force, together with our supplies.'

'Then ye'd best pitch your tents on the far side o' the river where the ground's cleared for the new station,' Andrewes advised coolly. Ed Muldoon had arrived with them, he noted, and was now supervising the disembarkation of the horses down a sloping board set against the door of the freight wagon in which they had travelled. 'Ye'd best tell your men to build a good strong fence. We've a rogue lion i' the neighbourhood which has—'

'A lion, by Jove!' The major's face lit up. 'So there's good sport hereabouts? We must see if we can't flush him out for you while we're here, what?'

'Ay, we'd be grateful,' Andrewes replied drily. He introduced the others. 'Mr Jackson . . . Dr Carson . . . an' Mr Hathaway, who keeps us i' touch wi' the outside world . . . an' Mr Wilton, my assistant . . . Mr Wilton will show ye the site I suggested for your camp.'

Major Arbuthnot stiffened. 'That's a decision I'll make for myself if you don't mind, what?'

'Andrewes can never leave off interferin' in other folk's business,' Jackson sneered. He still held a grudge from their first meeting and made no bones about it. 'Glad to see you here, Major. It's time someone put King John in his place, an' you're just the man.'

The major stared him up and down without speaking – Jackson was twice his size and looked as though he had survived many a rough-house – but then addressed himself to Andrewes. 'King John they call you? King of the Uganda Railway, what?'

Andrewes ignored the question. 'When ye've settled in, perhaps ye'd care to dine wi' us tonight? I shot a fine eland earlier today, so there's plenty. Ye're all heartily invited, all the officers.'

'A pleasure – King John! A royal command, what?'

The presence of the army had a disturbing effect on the railhead camp from the start. They pitched their tents on the site of the new station as Andrewes had suggested – the major barked a few words of approval later in the evening – but social contact with the coolies was officially discouraged. Only the Indian traders serving camps up and down the line were allowed to visit the sepoys. But the bugle calls, the yells of command, and the sight of the Union Jack fluttering at the top of a temporary flagpost made it impossible to ignore them. Soon a rumour flew about among the coolies that the Railway Office was about to reduce their wages and the army had been called in to ensure there was no trouble. Another explanation was that they planned to bring all East Africa under British rule, placing it under the jurisdiction of the Viceroy of India: were they not already paid in rupees, subject to Indian law, and was there not enough land here for any Indian who dared cross the ocean to take it?

Abdul Hakim conveyed both these stories to Andrewes with considerable enjoyment, and in ornate Hindustani. His tone of voice was shocked yet diplomatic; his dark eyes looked mischievous.

'What else has Jackson Sahib been saying?' Andrewes had to scotch the rumours right away before there was trouble.

'He said—' Abdul Hakim stopped short, realizing he had betrayed himself. 'Sahib!' he exclaimed reproachfully.

'Ay, I guessed as much. But ye can tell your friends they'll know the truth when they see the army march off in two day's time.' Was the man deliberately trying to stir something up?

He brooded over it that evening while he sat in the *boma* with his guests. Across the fire he could see Jackson biting with relish into his eland steak, then wiping the back of his hand across his thick lips and pugilist's nose. He was entertaining the officers with vivid accounts of the man-eater, making out Tim Wilton and Andrewes himself to be incompetent clowns who should never be allowed to handle a gun, though he built up his own exploits well enough. But Andrewes refused to rise to the bait.

'Only one way to deal wi' trouble in Africa – anywhere in the Empire, come to that – the maxim gun! That's my belief.' Jackson buried his face in the steak again; then, chewing, 'Shoot 'em down, Slaughter the buggers till they crawl on their knees an' beg you to stop. It's good to see you gentlemen here. Now we'll have some order.'

'Mother o' God, he means like Cromwell in Ireland!' Muldoon joined in with a sideways grin at Hester who sat quietly near the door of the hut, listening out for Gaby.

'I say nothing against the Irish. I know how to deal with the Irish. Irish navvies. Any Irish.'

'Sure you do!' Muldoon taunted him, his speech slurred. 'An' one fine day this Irishman here'll be dealin' with you.'

'Drunk or sober?'

'You sayin' I'm drunk?'

'You sayin' you're not?'

'Sure, an' haven't I put better men than you under the ground?' Muldoon boasted, relaxed. 'There's not a port anywhere in the world where they don't know me, from New York to New South Wales an' back. When the right time comes, Jackson – an' I choose the time, remember that, the time *an'* the place – you can have the choice o' weapons. Knives, rhino whips, bottles, bare fists, you name it.'

'But not now,' Hester intervened firmly.

'What's wrong wi' now?' Jackson blustered, getting to his feet. 'Why not now?'

'In the presence of a lady?' Muldoon mocked him lazily. 'Fightin', when we should be drinkin' her health? Sit down, man, an' let's drink to Mrs Andrewes an' King John who've come all this way to Africa to found their own dynasty, long may it last!'

'I'll drink to that, what?' The little major stood up with the light of the flames dancing over him. 'A first class meal you provided, ma'am. Charming hostess. Excellent hospitality. Let's all raise our glasses!'

The guests drank solemnly, casting grotesque shadows against the thorn fence behind them. A sliver of moon had appeared among the few stars but it gave very little light. The night insects shrilled, almost drowning the voices from the camp.

'As for killing natives, I've thought this over many a time,' Major Arbuthnot announced as he resumed his seat. 'As I see it, our British Empire is based on the principle of self-interest. Must be, wouldn't work else. We show the natives they've everything to gain if they co-operate, and everything to lose if they don't, what? That means short, sharp disciplinary action when they rebel, but know when to hold your hand. Make them understand it's in their own interest, that's the secret. Greatest thing in the world, the British Empire. Africa, India, West Indies, Canada, Australia, Singapore, Hong Kong – sun never sets on it! At its heart – Great Britain herself! Workshop of the world, leader in industry, inventions, science, government . . . Mother of Parliaments. Democracy. And our beloved Queen, God bless her, what?'

His words were greeted by a terrified scream coming from only a few yards away, just outside the *boma*. For seconds everyone was shocked into silence; then, as the scream was repeated, Andrewes grabbed his rifle.

'He's back!' he snapped at the major bitterly. 'Left us alone for more'n a fortnight, an' now he's back. Let's get after him.'

Weeks later, Hester remembered that evening as she sat day-dreaming over Mr Wilton's Tennyson, unable to concentrate. Even with the help of the army they had not been able to destroy the lion. They had found the track, a trail of blood and torn clothing, then lost it again among the thorn trees. One of the *jemardars* this time, a man John liked and respected; the next morning his body had been discovered disembowelled, chewed up, drained of its blood.

It had a charmed life, that lion. The officers had swept the country hunting for it. Their total bag, sickeningly displayed on the river bank – consisted of five zebra, five giraffes, one rhinoceros, three eland, seven Grant's gazelles, a Kirk's dik-dik, two duikers, ten buffaloes, a white-bearded gnu, and three warthogs, two of them little more than piglets with stripes down their backs. Hester had noted it all down at the time, distressed at the slaughter. The sepoys had been kept busy without rest transporting it all, cutting it up . . .

No lion, of course.

Then the army had left. The bugles had sounded reveille an hour earlier than on the previous days. Commands bawled out briskly. Drums tapping out the pace of the march. Major Arbuthnot had thanked them stiffly, stroking his blond sidewhiskers with a forefinger to hide his embarrassment at having to go through these formalities. Then he had wheeled his horse about and ridden off.

She had tried one afternoon to describe it in a letter to her father, the smart uniforms, the major's clipped speech, the pompous way he strutted about, the bugles and drills, how the visit had brought a touch of Empire into their lives, all the details – except Jackson's quarrel, of course, that would never have done.

But what did he do with her letters, she wondered. While she still lived at home the church would sometimes hold a special day of prayer for missionaries in Africa. Their letters would be read aloud from the pulpit – were hers? Or did he keep them to himself, ashamed perhaps of what he called her romanticism? Uneasy at her sense of humour, which did not match his?

Not that she told him everything in those letters, not by any means. She had tried to describe how the railway line grew steadily westwards like a long iron tentacle – he had written back to question the word tentacle, saying he was sure she had not quite meant it that way – but she said very little about the realities of the railhead camp, the constant fights among the coolies, and African girls they brought in as prostitutes, the young boys she glimpsed . . . Nor about the smoking of *bhang* which made them blissfully unaware of anything going on around them; nor the drinking of home-made toddy which made them aggressive, ready to pick a quarrel with anyone, and might one day turn them blind. She could imagine his reaction! The suggestion that God might be calling her to set up a mission among these men – *if only you could hear Him* – mixed with reproaches that this was clearly no place to bring up her daughter.

He would be right about that, of course. She closed the Tennyson and stared at the thorn fence, thinking it over. Gaby was with Njeri, who was washing clothes down by the river somewhere, and Ngengi was with them. He was completely in love with Gaby, never took his eyes off her, and he was a sturdy little boy too, getting on for four years old now. The atmosphere of that camp could not be good for him either. The leers of some of the men brutalized by long absence from their own families . . .

'Mrs Andrewes . . .'

She looked up sharply, annoyed.

'Mrs Andrewes, I'm sorry to be disturbin' you in your thoughts o' home, like . . . It *was* Liverpool you were daydreamin' about? I guessed as much – a darlin' city!'

Ed Muldoon's white suit gave the appearance of having been freshly laundered, though frayed at the cuffs; a flowery handkerchief protruded from the breast pocket and he wore a stiff butterfly collar with a spotted necktie. He had obviously gone to great lengths to smarten himself up and she wondered why; it was not an improvement.

'I thought you were in Mombasa,' she said.

'Mombasa one day, here the next . . .' He had been drinking, it was in his voice, and he smiled at her, overeager to please. 'Moving food supplies up an' down the line. Six thousand men take a lot o' feeding.'

'I suppose so.' She remembered now having heard the whistle when the train arrived a couple of hours earlier.

He stood there awkwardly, obviously not knowing what to say next; in his hand he clutched a small leather bag like a doctor's and the sight of it vividly brought back those terrible first days at Roshan's house, his persistent visiting, eyeing her nightdress. The Mombasa doctor too, bustling in on the third day with his apologies for having been away on safari, had astonished her by pausing in his examination to gaze on her full breasts, ripe with milk, exclaiming, 'Magnificent! Truly magnificent!' Several seconds had passed before he remembered the stethoscope in his hands. Oh, she hated this place and all it did to people! *Hated it.*

'You must excuse me, Mr Muldoon, I've one or two things to do,' she went on hurriedly. 'John will be back soon, should I tell him you'd like a word?'

'King John? Oh, he'll have his hands full till sundown from what I hear. He's a mile away on the other side o' the river where they're having trouble wi' one o' the traction engines. They say it's overturned, but he's the man to sort it out, you can be sure o' that.' He stopped, then blinked at her, an odd look on his face, part hang-dog, part expectant. 'I . . . It's you I came to see, to apologize, Mrs Andrewes, for our behaviour that night, Jackson an' me. Sure it was unforgivable.'

She laughed, feeling suddenly relieved. If that was all . . . 'I'd forgotten it already,' she exclaimed, meaning to be gracious. But from the quick change in his expression she realized she had made a mistake.

'I noticed the way you looked at me across the firelight – oh, you were beautiful, Hester! Really beautiful!' He came closer; the whisky was heavy on his breath. 'An' about Jackson, we shared an understanding, you an' me, that night?'

'Mr Muldoon, I think you'd better go.'

'Oh, there's no one around to see us, an' look, I've brought you something from Mombasa like I said I would.' He fumbled with the catch of the leather bag. 'Couldn't go down to Mombasa without thinking o' you, could I now?'

He wrenched the bag open and covered the little camp table with tins of butter, tea, coffee, sugar, condensed milk, until finally he came to a flat package in brown paper which he began to unwrap. It was a white silk blouse with delicate pearl buttons and fine lace on the front and cuffs.

'Specially for you, Hester darlin' – so tell me you like it!'

She was so shocked, she could not think what to say. Was he trying to . . . to *buy* her? No . . . no . . . it couldn't be that . . . She was confused . . . all these months, and he had still not realized how much she disliked him. She flushed hot with shame.

'You must have taken leave of your senses!' She started thrusting the tins of food back into the leather bag. 'I don't want them, I don't want anything from you, and certainly not that blouse.'

'An' didn't I order it specially for you, though it took some weeks in coming? Perhaps I . . . I . . .' He faltered, but then the whisky must have given him courage. 'I'm a fool waitin' till now to tell you, but there it is. I love you, Hester. I love you.'

There was only one way to regain control of the situation, she decided. She stepped back from him and spoke firmly. 'Mr Muldoon, you know you've been drinking, and you also know I could never accept any presents from you, even though they are kindly meant.'

'An' what's wrong wi' the blouse? Didn't I pay a fortune for it?' His face became purple with anger.

'I can't take it.' Then, foolishly, she added, 'I'm sorry.'

'Hester . . . you an' me . . . Holy Mary, you'll not be denyin' that between you an' me . . . Ever since Mombasa when we used to sit talking while you were feeding your lovely new baby . . .'

'We never did!' Her temper flared. 'Now take your blouse and go! Go on!'

'Oh – Lady Muck!' His small dark eyes taunted her, daring her to try and stop him. 'I've met plenty in Liverpool like you, Hester darlin'! No need to come the high an' mighty wi' me, 'cos I can read what's in your face, in spite o' your fine words. You're pantin' for it!'

He seized her shoulder in an iron grip and tried to kiss her on the lips.

'No . . . no . . .' She twisted her head this way, that way, struggling to avoid his mouth, despising her own weakness. 'Oh, please . . .'

'Yes . . . yes . . .!' he mocked her, grinning. 'You've had this coming a long time now. But then it's what you wanted, isn't it? It's what you like, a touch o' the rough! King John's too gentle!'

'No . . .' It was useless; he held her so firmly she could do nothing. 'If I scream for help you know what that'll mean, don't you? So be sensible – let me go now, and I promise you I'll say nothing.' Another mistake.

'An' who'd take your word anyhow?' He belched his whisky into her face; his eyes gleamed with excitement. 'But, sure, this is what you've always dreamed of, an' I was the idiot not seeing it – the way you looked at me across that fire . . . Wake up in the night all hot an' bothered, darlin'?' He released one shoulder and began to explore her breasts.

She could not believe it was happening to her. Struggling for breath, she screamed out her terror. 'Oh, help me, somebody! Help!'

His hard, massive hand slapped her across the face. 'Try that again an' I'll break your neck, d'you hear?'

She staggered back, tasting the blood in her mouth. His eyes were pitiless. Saliva dripped from his open lips as he threw his sun helmet on the ground and stripped off his jacket . . . that spotless jacket . . . Nervously she watched every move, trying to edge away towards the entrance on the far side of the *boma*.

'Now what d'you say we do this daycent like, inside the tent wi' the flaps down? A cosy little love nest, eh?'

She dodged away from him, for a brief moment convinced she could escape, but he grabbed her easily, ripping the top of her dress.

'Come on now, be a good girl . . . into the tent . . .' His voice was deceptively gentle; he held her firmly, bruising her arms. 'Or is it a lick o' the kiboko you're beggin' for? A nice little lick o' the whip jus' to get the blood excited? Oh me darlin' Hester, I bet King John doesn't know what

133

you're really like, all hot an' ready for what I've got for you!'

He was enjoying himself! The bastard was enjoying himself! Furiously she hit at him with her small fists, which had no more effect against his strength than a flea bite against an elephant. Taking the remains of her bodice in his paw, he peeled it off, leaving her naked to the waist. A smile of fierce pleasure broke across his face at the sight of her breasts.

Something snapped inside her head. Screaming did no good, but all the gutter language she had ever heard in the back streets of Liverpool came to her lips in one long stream of abuse as she fought him. But it only encouraged him. He was delighted.

'I knew there was passion in you, me darlin', buried deep down, jus' longing for someone like me to come an' release it . . .' He was pushing her towards the entrance to the tent. 'Now we'll jus' get rid o' this Lancashire cotton . . .'

She was like a doll in his hands, he could pick her up, put her down, her muscles useless against his. Desperately she tried to force herself to think. She had to do *something* . . . a gun . . . a knife . . . anything . . .

Then, backing away, she tripped over one of the guy ropes and fell heavily. He dropped down on top of her with his full weight, knocking the breath out of her, still tugging at her skirt till it was above her knees, groping between her legs, his fingernails tearing into the one remaining layer of cloth. She screamed again. Again and again – not knowing how else to help herself, his whisky fumes choking her.

His fingers were on her – *in* her . . . *oh God, NO!*

Oh, why didn't he leave her alone? If only she had a knife she could . . . But she only had to yield, let him do it, and her nightmare would be over. The thought shocked through her; she grasped at it, rejected it, but then what else could she do? She closed her eyes, unable to hold back the tears.

He must have sensed her resistance had gone because

he suddenly shifted, fumbling at his trousers. *Oh, John . . . Gaby . . .* But his move knocked her hand against a tent peg, loose in the ground. Her fingers closed around it. She watched him, waiting for the right moment. *Mustn't let him do it,* her mind insisted with feverish clarity, her determination restored. *Mustn't let him get inside me, whatever else —* He turned and, grabbing the chance, she lashed out at his genitals with the peg, using all the strength she could summon up.

But his hand came down, seized her wrist, twisting it; she gasped at the pain. Cried out. The peg dropped down somewhere. It was useless. Muldoon lowered himself over her, grunting, his eyes bulging as he groped again with his coarse hand to—

She saw the movement flash past her eyes as the rifle butt hit him hard between the shoulders. He shuddered, twitched, and rolled away. Unbelieving, she stared up to see Kamau standing there, holding the gun ready to hit him again.

Hester crawled into the tent on her hands and knees, clutching at the few remaining rags of cloth. They hardly covered her. Pains shot through her whole body as her stomach heaved and she vomited on to the ground; she sobbed bitterly with shame and humiliation, not thinking at first what the pains might mean. Not caring, even — wasn't she hurting all over, and most of all inside herself? But that wetness on her legs, that was blood — *her* blood. And . . . She had lost the baby.

Outside, Muldoon was bawling angrily at Kamau who stood in front of the tent, his rifle still threatening.

*Shoot him,* she prayed. *Oh God, please, let Kamau shoot him. Dead.*

# ELEVEN

The news that Ed Muldoon had ordered a detachment of railway sepoys to seize Kamau and handcuff him to a tree to be whipped spread through the camp like a lightning flash. A small crowd of coolies immediately gathered to observe the punishment, chattering to each other excitedly. None of them took much notice of the naked black infant who crawled between their legs to get to the front; they did not know he was Kamau's child.

The African had attacked a white man – unprovoked, some said – a crime no native could be allowed to get away with. He was lucky to escape with a beating, they told each other. Ed Muldoon was generally liked in spite of his roughness and heavy drinking; they gasped when he stripped off his shirt and they saw the ugly blue-black bruise between his shoulder blades. Whatever the circumstances – and no one knew them for certain – there was no doubt Kamau was guilty.

Ngengi looked on fearfully as the white man picked up his long whip of hippopotamus hide, flicking his wrist to make it snake out and *Crack!* in the air. The crowd held its breath.

'Now, you heathen bastard, you're about to learn a lesson you'll never forget, not as long as you live.' Muldoon's face was scarlet with rage. His dark eyes swept dangerously across the crowd, resting for a moment on Ngengi; then he drank deeply from a bottle and tossed it away empty. 'This is goin' to be the thrashin' o' your life.'

Scared, Ngengi bit his lip. His father stood embracing the tree, his arms about the trunk, his wrists manacled together; his face was calm, almost disdainful, as though taking no interest in the proceedings. He winced as the first lash of the whip cut into his back, but only momentarily, recovering himself immediately. At the second and third lashes he did not so much as flicker an eyelid.

The weals began to seep blood. Muldoon paused when he saw it, grinning, and wiped his forehead with the back of his hand before raising the whip again. The crowd watched, silently.

With difficulty, Ngengi held back his tears as the long rawhide whip rippled out for the fourth time and the tip caught the side of his father's throat, leaving a line of blood as Muldoon withdrew it with a sharp, vicious tug.

'Holy Mother o' God!' he exclaimed, his eyes gleaming with excitement. 'One more o' those, an' you'll be dead before I've had time to teach you that lesson.'

He cracked the whip once, twice, and Ngengi felt so sure that this time the white man intended something even more terrible, he could stand it no longer. With a high-pitched cry of despair he launched himself at Muldoon, beating away at him with his tiny fists, throwing him off his stroke. The whip whistled harmlessly through the air.

'Another o' the brood, is it? Push off before I smash your skull.'

Ngengi felt his shoulder wrenched as Muldoon shoved him roughly aside but he was not going to give up so easily. He threw his arms around the man's leg, clinging to it and biting through the thick cloth.

'Christ, you vicious little bugger!' Muldoon swore. 'Will you leave me be?'

His ears sang as Muldoon slapped him hard about the head, sending him sprawling on the ground where he lay bemused, frustrated, sobbing his heart out with shame. Another whiplash. Through his tears he saw more weals across his father's back, bleeding profusely.

But the whipping stopped; the crowd stirred with an outburst of voices like a gusty wind which then died down to a whisper. 'King John,' somebody said.

Andrewes had been working a couple of miles away on the far side of the river when the message reached him that Hester was in trouble. The young Indian coolie sent to fetch him could not say exactly what was wrong, only that he should return to the camp immediately. Every imaginable fear raced through his mind. The lion, perhaps? Or she had fallen ill with – what? Malaria? Blackwater fever? Plague, even? 'Plucky little woman, your wife,' the little blond major had said; it had been plain from his tone he was reproaching Andrewes for bringing her here at all. Didn't they all?

When he reached the *boma* he found her in bed, and Dr Carson in attendance. Her face was covered with scratches and bruises, her eyes red from crying. He dropped to his knees beside the camp bed. 'My love, did ye fall, was that it?'

'Now try not to excite her,' Dr Carson began, but she interrupted him.

'I've lost our baby, John.' Her speech was slow, as though in a dream. 'I'm sorry.'

He tried to comfort her, awkwardly, not really understanding. 'But these things happen, my love. It's no' your fault. Now we must make sure ye get well an'—'

Dr Carson took his arm and guided him out of the tent, warning him with a look not to say any more. Once outside, he explained he had given her laudanum to calm her down. 'It's shock, mainly. Physically I think she'll get over it.' He stopped, as if unwilling to go on. 'Nobody told you?'

'Told me what, man? How did she get that bruise on her face?' Fears and half-formed questions raced through his mind as Dr Carson hesitated. 'Jesus Christ, was she in an accident or what?'

'Muldoon assaulted her.'

As Dr Carson gave him the details – the little he knew – Andrewes' anger hardened within him, ice-cold. He pushed Carson aside and strode towards the clearing from which he could hear the sound of the whiplash punctuated by Muldoon's slurred voice. He found Kamau handcuffed to a tree with Muldoon standing behind him, letting his long whip dance over the ground, then making it suddenly shoot out, like a venomous snake, to draw blood.

Thoroughly enjoying himself, too. The crowd of coolies gasped with each blow, but the handful of Africans looked on sullenly, silently, while Kamau's small son, Ngengi, lay crying on the ground nearby.

Andrewes took it all in with one glance.

'Muldoon!' His voice was whip-crack hard. 'I'm told ye attacked my wife?'

Muldoon turned and an odd, twisted expression crossed his face, half fear, half mockery. 'Sure, an' if she isn't the most darlin' creature in all Africa! Hester an' me, we've long had eyes for one another, surely you knew that now?'

The whip curled out and wrapped itself viciously around Andrewes' shoulders, cutting through his shirt, razor-sharp, but he caught hold of it. It sliced into his palm as he tugged it away. He hammered his right fist into that mean, grinning face. Muldoon staggered back, then recovered and charged towards him. Andrewes' next punch caught him hard on the temple, stopping him in his tracks, dazed. But Andrewes was out to punish. He pounded the man mercilessly until at last he fell headlong to the ground.

Not even that was enough to break Andrewes' fury. Harshly, he ordered the sepoys to release Kamau and pass him the handcuffs.

'Yes, Sahib! Yes, Sahib!' They obeyed hastily, subdued by what they had just witnessed.

Breathing heavily, Muldoon managed to get to his feet but Andrewes immediately grabbed him by the neck, slammed him hard against the tree and handcuffed him to it. His head drooped against the bark, his eyes closed, all resistance gone.

No one moved to hand Andrewes the whip, but nor did anyone try to stop him. He and Muldoon might have been there alone, settling this thing between them. Each lash left its weal across Muldoon's back; with each lash his bitterness increased – bitterness with himself for exposing Hester to this danger, bitterness that he had not been there to protect her.

He could have killed Muldoon – *lash* – with his bare hands – *lash* – but that would have been too quick – *lash*

– too easy – let him stay alive and – *lash* – take what was coming to him – *lash* – let him suffer the pain – *lash* – the humiliation – learn what it was like to be degraded – *lash* – let him . . .

'That's sufficient now, King John.' Dr Carson held out his hand for the whip. 'Go to your wife. She needs you.'

Andrewes stared at him, hardly aware of what he was saying, the anger and bewilderment still seething unappeased within him; but he let him take the whip and went back to the *boma*. The coolies cleared out of his way, saying nothing.

He found Hester in a heavy, drugged sleep brought about by the laudanum. Taking Gaby on his lap, he sat watching over her, brooding. The bruises on her face were darkening and her features looked drawn, exhausted – hardly recognizable, in fact. And he was to blame, he was convinced; he should never have brought her here in the first place. Not into this wilderness.

'Och, lass,' he whispered. 'I'll make it right by ye, if it kills me. I'll get ye a kingdom, I promise ye that. A real kingdom.'

'Mama?' Gaby was struggling to get down. 'Mama sleep?'

'Ay,' he said shortly, holding her still. 'Let Mama sleep.'

Kamau decided to leave that same night. It would not be an easy journey, he knew. His back was badly lacerated and ached fiercely; every move was an effort as the pains shot through him. Njeri had cried out in shock and disbelief when she saw the wounds. She begged him to stay at the camp at least until they had started to heal a little, but that was impossible. Kamau knew in his heart that by morning they must no longer be there.

He dressed in Gikuyu fashion, abandoning his long white *kanzu* which he allowed Njeri to tear up to make bundles for their few belongings, together with food for the journey. But he checked his rifle carefully, that single-shot Snider which had once been his father's. Andrewes had come to him in the evening, proposing to buy him a new

Martini-Henry as compensation for what had happened. Kamau had merely listened without reacting. The Martini-Henry was also a single-shot gun, he noted, and he toyed with the idea of stealing into the *boma* after dark to take the Winchester. But that would only bring them after him.

'We go,' he said quietly.

It was pitch dark, but his instinct led him by the right paths through the trees, skirting the camp. They crossed the river by means of the temporary bridge and had already left railhead well behind them before the moon appeared, shining weakly. They walked in silence with Kamau in front, his rifle half-cocked in case of trouble, then little Ngengi carrying one of the bundles, and Njeri bringing up the rear. By travelling only at night, and taking cover in the daytime, Kamau reckoned they had a good chance of reaching his friends among the Wakamba unharmed. It would be a slow journey, fraught with danger from hunting parties and wild animals alike. Yet he had no choice.

Andrewes was at Hester's side the moment she woke up in the morning, but he was shocked and hurt by the way she regarded him – that cool, appraising look, neither wanting him nor rejecting him, as though he didn't exist for her any longer. All she could bring herself to say was, 'Hello, John.' Tired, uninterested . . . Then she fell silent, brooding. Trying to hide his anxiety, he went to fetch Gaby; much to his relief she smiled and held out her arms for the bairn, who snuggled up to her.

'I'll send Dr Carson to ye,' he decided, stooping awkwardly in the tent.

'Why? I'm not ill.' She avoided his eyes, and whispered something to Gaby. 'We'll be up and dressed the second you're out of here.'

'Dwesst,' Gaby confirmed.

Andrewes went out, feeling bewildered and uncertain of himself. She was sick, his mind reasoned; it was going to take her time to get over it. Yet once a woman had made the decision to shut a man out, there was not much he could do.

He fetched the Winchester, took a pocketful of cartridges and went in search of Dr Carson, finding him on his way to the hospital tent.

'You're lucky Muldoon's still alive,' Carson greeted him. 'As it is, we're sending him to Mombasa this morning, so if you want to lay charges, now's the time.'

'That'll be Mrs Andrewes' decision.'

'How is she?'

'Ay, well, she's . . .' Andrewes hesitated. 'She's no' hersel'.'

'What would you expect?' the doctor asked drily. 'But I'll go an' have a word with her. You know, I suppose, your *askari*'s gone?'

'Ay.' He'd not been surprised, either; he'd suspected as much the previous evening when he'd enquired after him.

'You'll not see him again. The first sign of trouble, they always disappear, these askaris. They melt into the veldt.' The phrase seemed to please him. 'That's about it, they melt into the veldt.'

'I'd hoped this one might be different.'

'They're none of 'em different, take my word. Now I'll just look in on Mrs Andrewes, though I'm afraid time's the only cure. Not all that much a doctor can do.'

'Ay, well, whate'er ye can . . .'

He hesitated, thinking he should go with the doctor, but then he decided against it. Best leave her be awhile. She'd let him know if she wanted him. If – the idea nagged at him, torturing him – she could ever face a man again.

But he was in no mood for work either. He brushed aside Tim Wilton's concerned enquiries – the lad seemed genuinely upset, too – and asked him to take over for the day. He needed to be alone, away from those curious, sidelong glances from the coolies, away from everybody . . .

He headed out along the river bank towards that spot among the rocks where they had once come across Jimmy Hathaway marooned up a tree: an odd wee man, Jimmy, who woke up every day thanking the Almighty for bringing him to Africa, well out of the reach of his wife back in Manchester. From all he said – and at times he had them rocking with laughter at his tales, unbelievable, mostly – she was a large, well-fleshed woman and twice his size. How they came to marry he had never explained, though he had fathered four children on her. 'Ee, I said to meself, that's more'n enough for any man, so I signed on for Uganda Railway. Nowt else I could do. Only way to stop 'er breeding.' It became a catchword throughout the camp: *Only way to stop 'er breeding!*

The lizards scrambled to safety as Andrewes climbed over the boulders, choosing a place to sit where he could look at the river. Thin clouds covered the sky that morning, but enough sunlight was filtering through to warm the stone. According to Kamau the rains were overdue; crops were parched and there was a danger of famine. They lived from one harvest to the next, these people, keeping nothing in store; if one harvest failed . . .

No need for Kamau to run off like that though, Andrewes brooded. Hurt pride, no doubt. He had lost face.

'Ay, mebbe Carson's right an' he'll no' come back at all,' he muttered aloud. It was a lonely spot; no one could overhear him. 'Treated him as a friend, no' as a servant – but ye live an' learn. I should hae killed Muldoon – ay, an' that's what's botherin' Hester too, though she'd ne'er admit it. Against her Christian upbringin', but deep down she wants him dead. An' I let him live.'

Then a suspicion thrust itself painfully into his mind – had Muldoon attacked Gita, would he no' be lyin' dead by now? He rejected the thought. It was impossible. Were his feelin's for Hester no' jus' as strong? Had he no' once dreamed o' Gita still alive, an' them all livin' together, the three o' them?

He came down from the rocks, still arguing with himself. Suddenly – it was no more than an instinct – he knew he was in danger. He swung around, simultaneously cocking the Winchester with a quick pull on the lever.

The lion stood high on the rocks he had just left. Fortunately the wind was in his direction or it would have scented him and been on his back before he had realized it was happening. It crouched as if to spring; he fired, immediately pumping in another round. It recoiled, snarling, and then launched itself at him.

Andrewes jumped aside, stumbling into the shallows, and shooting again, desperately. It roared its agony as the shot went home; then it backed away, manoeuvring, crouching, its determined eyes fixed on him. His fingers felt for the lever again but there was not enough time. The lion sprang at him, he could smell its breath, almost see down its throat as he brought the gun around and slammed the butt between its eyes. Blood and saliva from its open mouth spurted over him, but the blow forced it to retreat again.

The break lasted no more than a second, but that was long enough to get the next round into the breech and fire. The bullet went through the eye and the lion dropped dead on the spot. Examining the carcase later he found his first round buried in its shoulder; the second had shattered its upper jaw, practically severing the tongue.

The firing attracted Tim Wilton, Jackson and others who came running to find out what was going on. When they saw the dead lion they were loud in their congratulations; even Jackson managed a compliment, seizing his hand, and a couple of coolies were organized to secure the paws to a long pole and carry the trophy back to the camp. Andrewes followed them, dazed. The coolies everywhere stopped work to sing his praises, dancing around with delight.

Hester, hearing the commotion, came out of the tent as they brought him back to the *boma*. His clothes were spattered with the lion's blood, his sleeve was soaked in it. She ran to him, pale, almost hysterical. 'Oh, John, what's happened? Oh, John, my love . . . your arm . . .'

He put his arms around her, both arms, trying to calm her down, repeating that he was unhurt, he'd been lucky, while Tim Wilton spluttered out excitedly, 'He's killed the lion! Your husband's killed the lion!' Then, suddenly comprehending, he herded the others discreetly out of the *boma*, leaving Andrewes alone with his wife.

144

Her voice trembled, uncertain of herself. 'You'd better get out of those things then.'

When he stripped off his jacket and shirt she noticed the cut from the whip across his shoulders and touched it gently with her finger-tips. But she asked no questions about it. Perhaps someone had told her – Dr Carson?

All this time Gaby looked on, wide-eyed, wonderingly, but with not a tear, not at all upset by all the excitement. Andrewes picked her up, and hugged Hester with his free arm. 'Everything's all right, isn't it, Gaby?' he smiled, trying to convince himself that it had to be, otherwise there was no future for any of them.

Gaby gurgled. Hester rested her face against his shoulder for a moment, then took her from him. 'Come on, darling, let Papa get washed. He's filthy.'

But it was not until Gaby was asleep that night that she felt able to talk to him, and then only haltingly. 'I don't want to . . . to say anything about it . . . not to anybody . . . but you've a right to know.'

'Only if ye're ready, my love.' He did not want to hear it, he felt, not the details; yet he had to know.

'You've a right,' she repeated firmly, looking away from him. 'He . . . Came here to . . . to woo me, I suppose. Brought me presents. A silk blouse. What he imagined, I don't know . . . He was drunker than usual, and all dressed up, and . . . When I refused he tried to rape me. That's all.'

'Ay, an' he knocked ye about!' The bruises on her swollen face bore witness to it. He clenched his fists, knowing he had not finished with Muldoon, not by a long chalk. 'I was asked if ye want to lay charges.'

'No.'

'Why no', for God's sake?' His voice rose sharply, but he controlled himself again. It did no good to shout, not after what she had been through.

'Oh, John, d'you really want me to stand up in a courtroom and go through it all again – blow by blow? While the men sit there gloating?'

'Nay, my love. Nay, but—'

She sat closer to him and took his hand. 'John . . . I . . . I mean . . . he didn't succeed, you know. He didn't . . . you know what I'm trying to say . . .'

Andrewes held her close, his feelings in confusion. 'Lass, d'ye think I'd love ye any the less? D'ye really think that? 'Cos if ye do, ye're wrong.'

She was crying. Her shoulders shook as though she would never stop. 'John . . .' she said at last. 'Oh John . . . I'm not wrong . . .'

# Book Two

# ONE

After that nightmare experience Hester knew that something very deep inside her had changed. During the following months she turned it over in her mind time and time again. Up till that day, it now seemed to her, she had been terribly innocent, vulnerable without knowing it, never for one moment imagining anything could possibly harm her. All that was now shattered. She felt older. Cynical.

She often felt afraid, too. She had only to catch a certain expression on a man's face, or hear that note in his voice, in a turn of phrase, and the fear would shiver through her once more. Her helplessness as she struggled with Muldoon, the insanity in his eyes – it all came back to her, however much she tried to suppress it.

John had despatched the sepoy Patel to Mombasa with a note for Mr Roshan, the Indian merchant, to find a gun for her – something small. She protested half-heartedly that it was not necessary, but he insisted; when Patel returned with a single-shot derringer pistol so tiny, she could conceal it in a handkerchief, she accepted it without any further argument. Not that she had the slightest intention of shooting anyone, whatever the circumstances, but the mere knowledge it was there was reassuring.

He took her out along the river to practise firing it well away from the camp, using what he called 'Jimmy Hathaway's tree' as a target. After three or four shots her fingers ached with holding it. 'A lady's life preserver,' John called it, because of the mother-of-pearl handle.

'A lady of the town, you mean!' she retorted. It was small enough to be tucked into a garter. 'I hope I never have to use it.'

'Ye'll no' be havin' any more trouble from Muldoon at any rate. Accordin' to Patel he's quit British East altogether. It seems when the Mombasa doctor called to examine him, Muldoon kicked him out o' his quarters, got himself dressed, an' was last seen boardin' a German steamer bound for Dar es Salaam, draggin' that African girl Cabby wi' him. It's my guess we'll no' be runnin' into him again.'

But John did not understand – how could he? – and there was no way she could explain. It was more than Muldoon; it was any man. They all had that madness in them, that brutal violence. Even John himself – though he'd be the first to deny it.

He worried about her, she could see that. Even brought forward the date of their next move, saying a change of scene would help her forget; and it was true she was relieved to escape at last from the monotony of those grey thorn trees and the weary whining of the wind among their branches. The new camp site was so different. From her tent she could look out across wide plains covered with high grass rippling like water in the breeze. Though there was little enough actual water. The river bed was dried up and cracked; once again the tankers had to be brought into use.

Yet there must be waterholes somewhere, she thought; those plains teemed with wild life, too numerous to count. She pointed them all out to Gaby, teaching her how to identify each kind – gazelle, impala, eland, zebra, giraffe, wildebeeste, and others whose names she had not yet learned herself. At times she felt there was something healing in just watching them; they made human problems seem that much less significant.

Or the problems of railway humans, at least.

One day the camp was invaded by more Africans than she had ever seen gathered together before – handsome Wakamba men armed with poison-tipped arrows. John welcomed them as old friends – with relief she realized they must be the new labour force he was expecting – and she heard him attempting to ask for news about Kamau, though they either knew nothing of were pretending not to understand. Then Gaby toddled boldly up to them, fascinated; but one man smiled at her, revealing his devilish, filed teeth, and she began to yell with fright. Yet once John had set them to work clearing the ground for the new stretch of track she saw very little of them, and a couple of weeks later many had gone.

'An experiment, lass, that's all – using African labour,' he explained as they sat talking it over, looking up at the star-rich sky and listening to the cry of the hyenas from across the plains. 'Thought I'd give it a try, but they're no' too keen.'

Even when they were alone he kept the conversation on neutral topics, she thought resentfully – as though afraid she might break down if he relaxed with her. He had become reluctant to touch her; for weeks he had given her no more than a chaste goodnight kiss and then gone to his own camp bed on the other side of the tent. Did she disgust him now Muldoon's hands had been on her, she wondered, hurt; or was he trying to be kind . . . over-cautious . . .?

That same night, as he bent over to kiss her as usual, she put her arms around his neck and held on to him just long enough to . . . well, to let him know . . . Yet without making it seemed like a brazen invitation – which it was, of course.

He drew back, apologizing awkwardly. 'I dinna wish to force mysel' on ye, lass, if ye're no' ready . . . d'ye ken . . .'

'Oh, John, I love you!' she whispered urgently, her arms tightened around him. Her thoughts were in a turmoil, wanting him . . . and yet scared . . . 'John, can't you understand I need you? To wipe out all that dirt and . . . and . . . to show me you don't despise me for what happened.'

'Nay, Hester love, how can ye say that?'

'But men do despise women who . . . Don't they?'

He kissed her lips gently, holding her to him and stroking her head, comforting her. She felt so secure with him, belonging to him wholly. When he unbuttoned her nightdress and his hand slipped inside, taking her breast, that sensation in her nipple as she responded to his touch was like . . . oh, it was like returning home after a long absence . . . she was almost purring like a contented kitten.

A hungry kitten . . . She was quivering expectantly, longingly, as his fingers searched for her . . . found her . . . her legs parting . . . But in the back of her mind that doubt was still there, that fear she was determined to overcome. *No!* she told herself, almost crying the word aloud. *She was not going to let Muldoon spoil this part of her marriage for the rest of her life.*

But if only they had a wide double bed instead of this narrow camp bed which groaned and protested as he lowered himself over her and it took his weight. The spars dug into her thighs, distracting her. It had never seemed important before, but now she was conscious of it and the fears – the distaste – took over. She fought back, closing her eyes tightly and forcing herself to remember those first nights after their wedding, how lovingly John had taken her, how exciting it had been discovering those new secrets about her own body . . . and John's . . .

Afterwards, as John lay with her satisfied, falling asleep with his head on her shoulder in spite of that cramped, narrow bed, she knew she had won. Not a total victory: the ghost of Muldoon had still been there, taunting her. But next time would be better . . . and the time after that . . .

John's work on the railway had become an obsession with him. He talked of nothing else but problems with rolling stock, calculations about the next section of track, how white ants were eating into the timber sleepers, which now had to be replaced by metal ones. He lived it twenty four hours a day and even mumbled about it in his sleep. Several times she discovered him with Gaby on his knee, trying to explain – with the help of rough drawings – exactly how a steam locomotive worked.

'But she's much too young!' she laughed, protesting.

'Nay, lass, she's gettin' to be a big girl now!' He put an arm affectionately about her waist, holding both her and

Gaby tightly as if afraid he might lose them. 'It's high time I told her these things.'

A couple of weeks later they moved camp again, another thirty miles farther on across the grassy plains. The railway was growing like a long, thin taproot into the very soul of the continent. And as they settled into their tent at the new site she announced that she was pregnant once more, which led to their first quarrel.

It was about her work at the hospital tent – naturally. There was a steady stream of patients, mostly with ulcers, and Dr Carson needed all the help he could get. No one seemed to know what caused these ulcers, but they usually started with a scratch or an insect bite and, if left untreated too long, they ate into the leg until there was no alternative but to amputate. So, sickened by the foul smell, she helped Dr Carson clean away the greyish matter, then bathed the sores in permanganate of potash. Tens, even hundreds, of coolies passed through her hands. It was not pleasant work, as she told John often enough, but not heavy either – and she could not sit around idly when there was so much to do, could she?

'My love, it's your health an' the baby's I'm worried about,' he insisted – but for once that concern in his voice irritated her and she snapped back at him. He replied by *ordering* her not to go the hospital tent. She demanded to know how he was going to stop her. And he went to bed that night sullen and moody, deep in his own thoughts no doubt, while she felt hot, angry, stubborn, and intent on not giving in to him.

Yet the next morning she caught herself actually humming a tune as she bandaged a cut leg – Dr Carson had just put in half-a-dozen stitches – and realized that she was happy about it. She was still annoyed with John, of course, but at least he'd risked a quarrel with her. Since Muldoon, he had treated her as if he was walking on eggs – so carefully! So cautious, as if afraid she would break down at the first cross word. Now, suddenly, he was his old domineering self again, and – however contrary it seemed – she loved him for it.

She lost the baby a fortnight later.

There was no telling why. She'd had a touch of fever, which may have had something to do with it; at least, Dr Carson thought so. But she felt her whole life had emptied out again. Just drained away. Everything looked desolate to her; no hope anywhere.

For three days she stayed inside her tent, not getting up, hardly taking any notice of Gaby even, but letting Ali look after her. What was the point even of living any longer? Nothing seemed worth any effort.

Then, on the fourth day, she dressed and went outside to stare across that wind-swept grass yellowing through lack of rain, with no sign of any break in the white, hot sky. She saw herself dying out there, her bones bleaching under the pitiless sun. A few yards from the camp the vultures were circling – swooping down, then rising again in a ghastly circus with pieces of red, raw meat dangling obscenely from their beaks. She went nearer to investigate. A dead giraffe lay stretched out on the ground as they tore out its guts. The sight nauseated her; everything about life nauseated her – the brutality of it all . . . the futility . . . In her disgust, she took a quick aim at the vultures and discharged both barrels of the shotgun at them.

'Mrs Andrewes, are you all ri—?' Tim Wilton came running up behind her, stopping when he saw the giraffe. 'It's best not to look, don't you know! Should I—?'

He took the shotgun off her and held out his hand for the fresh cartridges to reload it.

'It didn't do much good,' she said. She had brought down three vultures; the rest were already gathering again.

'We all feed off something – some other creature!' he commented lightly. 'Doesn't do to brood over it, though. You'd see it with quite different eyes if you'd grown up on a farm!'

'Did you?'

'As good as. But I missed you, don't you know? I've had a parcel from home – several books that might interest you. One of them is *Jude the Obscure*, have you heard of it? It's caused quite a scandal, they say. Then there's back copies of the *Illustrated London News*. You should see the new fashions – big floppy hats with giant ostrich feathers stuck in them!'

He seemed, almost imperceptibly, to be drawing her away from that scene with the dead giraffe as he chattered on amiably about the latest news from London, the things people were talking about and the fact that Christmas was only two weeks away and what were they going to do about it this year? He was so relaxed, so eager and frank, that she felt the waves of depression slipping away from her and that inner tension easing.

' . . . so I thought we might all have dinner at my tent, if you could spare Ali to cook it for us. My mother sent me a tin of Christmas pudding from Fortnum's, and of course there's . . .'

Her tears came without warning, uncontrollably. 'I'm . . . I'm sorry,' she murmured through her sobs, and she felt all her misery breaking out at last, great heaves as the weeping took over. 'I . . . I feel so . . . so stupid!'

He led her to a rock where she could sit down. 'Just let it all come out . . . take your time, there's no hurry . . . no one can see you here . . .' His voice was so friendly and understanding, she thought, sniffing. Like an older brother.

A fresh paroxysm of tears shook her . . . oh, she blamed Africa for it all . . . she had lost two babies now, and perhaps she might never have another, it would always be like this . . . and Muldoon, yes, she blamed Africa for him too . . . and for that insane force that drove John to work incessantly, taking no rest, forgetting how to relax . . . She loved him so deeply, even the way he was now – and he needed her, she knew that – but at times she yearned for the John she had known back in England, or on the ship, before this job had taken him over so totally.

Tim Wilton stood near her, waiting patiently, seeming hardly embarrassed even but taking it so naturally. He lent her a clean handkerchief – her own was soaked through.

'I'm sorry,' she apologized again, trying to smile. She blew her nose, hard. 'It's so silly, but I think I feel better now.'

The weeks rolled on. Twice the long rains had been expected; twice they failed to arrive. A few isolated showers dampened the ground, but nothing more. Then one day a fresh wind blew up and brought loose grey clouds billowing over the horizon. Within half-an-hour solid sheets of rain battered the dry earth, soaking into the black cotton soil to make it a quagmire of treacherous mud, dripping through the tent canvas, drenching everything. Gaby wanted to stand out in it – a new experience, this stinging hard rain, and so cool! When Hester, sliding about helplessly on the black mud, tried to fetch her in, she too began to enjoy it. She raised her face, closed her eyes, and offered herself to that exuberant flood of rain. It streamed over her, flattening her hair, saturating her clothes, renewing her . . .

But it passed. Already by the following evening the water had drained away; soon the soil was as dry as before, crumbling to dust when she touched it. The only lasting effect was that a mile of newly-laid track had to be taken up again and re-sited.

A few days later the first group of starving Africans arrived to ask for food; a heart-breaking sight they were, too – their bodies little more than loose bags of skin covering emaciated skeletons. There were some three dozen of them, Hester counted, men, women and children. One woman, hardly more than a girl, held up her baby, which was whimpering pathetically, almost wasted away, but it died before Hester could do anything to help.

She summoned Ali to boil a *debe* of water while she checked to see what food could be spared. They had precious little themselves, but she sacrificed her last two tins of condensed milk together with some meal. It made a thin gruel which they ate hungrily, but it was not enough.

Then John returned from supervising work on the track. 'We've got to do something!' she insisted defensively before he could speak. 'John, we can't let them die!'

As they stood there, one little boy vomited the gruel he had just eaten, then shuddered and collapsed. Within seconds he was dead. The others looked on passively, resigned.

'Ye're right, lass,' John said quietly.

He summoned a few coolies to build a rough shelter where the Africans could rest in the shade; at the same time, he sent out Patel and Abdul Hakim to search out what food they could find, though supplies from Mombasa were overdue and there was little enough in the camp.

'No shortage o' meat on the plains, though,' he assured her, fetching his Winchester. 'Though much o' the game is already on the move, searchin' for water.'

He set out with Tim Wilton and within an hour or so Hester heard the sound of the first shots carried faintly over the grassland. Soon the Swahili meat bearers were arriving back carrying a buck and three fine eland.

The next day a second group of starving Wakamba turned up at the camp; a third followed within twenty four hours, begging for help. Hester did her best, working herself so hard, she dropped exhausted each night on to her bed, yet unable to sleep for thinking of those who had died, and others who might not last till morning.

A missionary travelling through – a gaunt man with worried, sunken eyes, who introduced himself as the Reverend Henry Taylor – reported that thousands were dying as a result of the drought. Crops had failed for the second year in succession, sheep and cattle had long ago been slaughtered, and people were reduced to eating roots. The men no longer had enough strength for hunting. He asked John if the railway could get him down to Mombasa to buy food for his mission station and the neighbouring villages; with his thirty porters already worn out after more than a month of travelling on foot, he doubted if they would ever reach the coast otherwise.

John listened grimly to all he had to say, asked a few questions and then set about drafting a long report to the Railway Office in Mombasa. But when the reply came through, Hester saw immediately from his face that something was wrong.

'They dinna believe me, d'ye credit that!' His voice was bitter with contempt. 'That idiot Carpenter thinks I'm exaggeratin'. Ye can read his reply for yesel'.'

157

She took the paper, but its message was so depressing, she could hardly speak. 'SUGGEST YOU OVER-ESTI-MATE NUMBERS AFFECTED BY FAMINE,' she read, dismayed. 'NO FUNDS ALLOCATED FOR ADDI-TIONAL FOOD SUPPLIES NOR OTHER LOCAL CHARITIES. STOP.'

'My love, if ye can manage on your own a wee while, I'm goin' to Mombasa mesel' to sort this out. An' the Reverend Mr Taylor can accompany me. Ye'll get the food ye need, dinna fret yesel'. My wife's doin' good work here, Mr Taylor, an' deserves all the help she can get.'

Hester felt herself flushing with pleasure at his words and some of her tiredness seemed to drop away. She kissed him warmly and then went to check on the broth she had instructed Ali to cook. At least they still had some fresh meat.

But John was away for a week and every day more starving Africans arrived until she no longer knew what to do with them all. Tim Wilton recruited a gang of coolies to build extra shelters where at least they could lie out of the sun; but he was also away for many hours hunting, though what he brought back was scarcely enough. Yet there were good moments too: one little boy – she had no idea how old he was – had been on the point of death when she first saw him, but she had nursed him gently, coaxing him back to life, and was rewarded on the third day when suddenly he smiled at her, his eyes brightening. For a few hours she persuaded herself she had succeeded; then he relapsed, and she went yet again to plead with Dr Carson to use some of his precious stock medicine.

'Mrs Andrewes, what good would it do?' he argued with her, refusing to change his mind. 'It would maybe prolong his life by one more day. Two, at the most. Then, if you or Gaby fell ill, I'd not have enough medicine left to treat you with.'

Depressed, angry, she went back to the shelter where the boy was lying, only to find Tim Wilton with him. He knew how much she cared for this special patient, whose mother had died on the very day they had reached the

158

camp. Together they sat with him, leaving him only when the time came to supervise the issue of gruel to the others, until late that evening he slipped away into death.

They covered the body and left it lying where it was, inside the stockade where it would be safe from the hyenas. It was a clear night, the sky a mass of milky stars, and no moon. They walked silently towards the tents.

When they stopped, Hester's hand rested for a second on his arm as she said simply, 'Thank you for staying with him.' Without thinking, she leaned forward and kissed him on the cheek, just as she had kissed John that time. Her lips brushed the corner of his mouth, and he turned his head to meet her kiss, slipping his arms around her tenderly.

'No, Tim!' she whispered softly, breaking away from him, twisting her mouth away from his. 'No, that isn't what I meant.'

He was immediately apologetic, confused, saying he didn't know what had come over him, until she stopped him with a little laugh, insisting it was her fault, they were both tired, not themselves . . . But it must not happen again; it wasn't right. With a quick sisterly peck, she said goodnight and left him standing there.

She did not feel in the least guilty, she decided as she prepared for bed. If anything, she felt pleased. Contented, even. It was his fault, of course: it was so easy to relax with him, she had hardly known what she was doing. He took life as it came, never worrying too much – unlike John. For John everything was a challenge; perhaps that was what she loved about him most. She found him exciting, stimulating . . . But with Tim Wilton she could stop trying for a few hours, and that was such a relief.

Of course, he would never build an empire, she was sure, and John would. John was very special.

Before turning down the lamp she bent over Gaby who was sleeping soundly, her thumb in her mouth, her cheeks rosy. The thought of that poor little boy came back into her mind; if only she'd been able to keep him alive . . .

And she wondered, as she settled into her camp bed, if the drought would ever end.

Gaby developed a fever the very day John was expected back. He came to the tent looking for her, disappointed not to find both of them at railhead to meet him; when he saw her flushed little face, he squatted down on his heels and took her hand in his, but she hardly smiled. Hester held his arm, glad he was back.

'It's a high temperature, that's all we know,' she told him outside the tent, the worry gnawing at her. 'I asked Dr Carson to look at her, but he said he can't be sure what it is. He tried giving her quinine – a little, not very much – but she couldn't keep it down.'

'I'll have a word wi' him.'

Immediately, that defensive feeling flooded back into her. 'I've not been neglecting her, John, however busy I've been.'

'My love, did I say ye had?'

'It's always possible she may have caught something off those poor people, but I don't really think—'

He interrupted her, taking both her hands in his. 'Hester, d'ye no wish to hear my news? We persuaded Carpenter to send a cable to London, an' they've agreed to finance an extra cargo o' rice from India, wi' probably more to follow. I've brought up two wagon-loads o' *posho* wi' me, so there'll be enough to keep things tickin' over awhile.'

'Oh, John, you're wonderful!' she cried, delighted that at last there would be enough food for them. 'That's going to make all the difference. While you've been in Mombasa, there's not been one day without at least three deaths.'

'Wi' the same symptoms as Gaby?'

'D'you imagine that isn't the first thing I thought of? No, the symptoms weren't the same.' She looked at him anxiously; whatever she said to reassure him – and herself – she knew it was at least possible those starving Wakamba had brought diseases into the camp with them.

'I'll speak to Dr Carson,' he said again, as if that could make any difference; yet, irrationally, she felt it might.

Gaby grew worse and by nightfall she recognized neither of them. Her fever became frighteningly high. On Dr Carson's advice they sponged her down at regular intervals, but it seemed to make little difference. Her temperature had dropped a little by morning, only to rise again a few hours later. Hester sat watching over her, blaming herself for the time she had spent with the Wakamba instead of caring for her own daughter; blaming herself, too, for what had happened with Tim Wilton. Now, if Gaby did not recover, how would she ever live with herself? Was that what God really had in store for her?

John left her alone for a couple of hours while he went to inspect the work on the new track. 'They're managin' fine an' Mr Wilton's keepin' an eye on things,' he said when he got back, keeping his voice low. She could see from his face – so drawn and unusually pale – how worried he must be. 'Now ye've your own folk to tend to.'

'But I can't leave Gaby!'

'Ye'll crack up if ye dinna take a wee break.' His eyes held that familiar concerned look as they examined her face and he spoke so mildly she was moved. 'I'll stay here till ye get done.'

Perhaps he was right, she thought wearily; she had to make sure they were fed properly. If only she knew what was the right thing to do. She got up from the camp chair. 'But I'll not be very long,' she said, going.

It was that night Gaby became delirious, impatiently shaking her head from left to right . . . left to right . . . left to right . . . as though attempting to rid herself of unwelcome dreams, and mumbling long strings of words which made no sense whatsoever. Hester sat next to the bed, frightened, yet feeling there was nothing she could do, decisions were out of her hands – she knew now she was going to lose Gaby as well. And if Gaby was taken, how long would John stay? Ever since Muldoon . . . oh, that was her fault too . . . she should never have encouraged him – yes, without even knowing it she must have encouraged him, just as she'd encouraged Tim Wilton that night . . .

John stood just behind her, his hand resting on her shoulder. 'Why no' lie down awhile, my love? I'll sit up.'

'No.' She put her hand over his, holding on to it.

What was he really thinking, she wondered. She'd never known, he kept so much to himself. Sometimes in those early days she had heard him muttering restlessly as he slept, that Indian language again, and he would reach out for her, stroking her neck, her throat . . .

He took a quick step forward, yet quietly, to look at Gaby. Hester was seized by panic; she felt she were about to choke. Then he relaxed again. 'She's asleep,' he whispered.

'You're certain?'

She fell on to her knees by the side of the bed, listening for Gaby's breath. No, she couldn't hear it . . . and her face was pale too, as if all the blood had drained out of it. She wanted to hug her child to her and wail out her misery, but John was whispering something . . . restraining her . . . Her fingers searched for Gaby's pulse the way Dr Carson had taught her, holding her wrist gently. And . . . she was alive! The pulse was steady, even strong, caressing her finger-tips, and the fever had gone.

'Oh, thank God,' she breathed in genuine prayer. 'Oh, thank you, God!'

John helped her up, enclosing her in his arms, and she pressed against him as the tension inside her gave way, running down like an old spring, and she knew everything was going to be all right again.

# TWO

Once more the camp moved on across those vast, open plains. Now they caught their first occasional glimpse of Maasai herdsmen, lonely figures leaning on their long spears, sharply outlined against the horizon, reminding Andrewes of the Scottish shepherds he had known as a child. Never before had any railway grown so rapidly, he thought with pride, over such wild country. But the going would not always be so easy: somewhere ahead – according to the survey reports – the ground would begin to rise more steeply to a point where it suddenly plunged headlong down into the Rift Valley some 1,500 feet below. A route had been worked out for the railway to follow but it was now time, he decided, to check on some of the problems for himself.

He took Tim Wilton, with him and left Jackson in charge of the work at the railhead. Everything was going with a swing and the man was a good enough engineer to handle any difficulties, whatever his shortcomings when it came to dealing with the coolies. And young Wilton would be good company, he thought. There would be quite a few engineering conundrums to be talked over when they came to the Rift Valley, and Wilton always had interesting ideas to contribute. Hester liked him too, which pleased Andrewes; there was little enough social life for her at the camp.

They set out before dawn with a few porters and *askaris*. It was pleasant enough walking at that time of day; in fact, there was quite a nip in the air. The plains here were 5,000 feet above sea level and there was much talk of encouraging British settlers to farm the area once the railway was fully operational. By the afternoon they were ready to pitch their tents for the night. They took their time over washing and eating, went off to hunt for meat – bringing down a couple of gazelles – and then sat discussing some of the trickier supply problems caused by the war in South Africa against the Boers. Every cubic foot of shipping space was taken up by the military, and there was no telling what the outcome would be. But away from railhead everything seemed less urgent and Andrewes retired early to his camp bed relieved to be free of it all for a week or two.

On their fifth day they found a place for their tents on some slightly higher ground overlooking a papyrus swamp. It would be an ideal spot to build a house, Andrewes mused as they sat eating their meal beneath the umbrella-like shade of a spreading thorn tree. In one direction – far enough away to be free of mosquitoes – was the gleaming water of the swamp itself, broken up by clusters of fan-shaped papyrus; in another, a wide vista of flat plains and distant hills. Nearby was a Maasai *manyatta* whose circular, boundary wall of dried mud and cow-dung was splintered by hundreds of tiny cracks like an old man's face. He had already made friendly contact with the Maasai living there, trading a bag of *posho* meal for fresh milk.

Ay, Hester would love a house here, he thought, an idea taking shape in his mind. He would have brought her with him on this trip, only she was expecting again and Dr Carson had said she had better not exert herself too much, having lost two already. Thank God she was at last over that business with Muldoon; at least her depressions had passed – since Gaby's illness, was it? Or since having to organize relief for the drought victims? Whatever had jerked her out of it, she was practically her old self again. A little brisker, perhaps. And tougher.

She needed a home of her own, that was it. Something more solid than a tent and a grass hut. And this might be the spot to build it.

It had an effect on Tim Wilton too, that location. Maybe it was the lowing of the Maasai cattle that brought it on, or the loud croaking of the swamp frogs as darkness fell – whatever it was, he started reminiscing about his life back in England. The country vicarage where he had grown up, youngest of eight, incurring his father's displeasure by taking up engineering instead of studying Latin to become a schoolmaster; the village church; cricket; the muddy lanes; and his sister who was married to a curate in the next parish . . . Andrewes only half-listened.

'Ye realize, we'll need to do some hard thinkin' when we reach the Rift Valley?' he interrupted at last, growing bored. 'The surveyors have already changed their minds twice about the route. Their latest idea cuts out the steeper gradients an' the need for reversin' stations, but it's goin' to take quite a while to construct. In the meantime, we're bein' pressed to reach Lake Victoria before Parliament goes back on its word an' stops the money. The railway has a lot o' enemies in Westminster.'

'I've been talking too much,' Tim Wilton admitted sheepishly.

'Ay, it's time we both got some sleep.'

Continuing towards the Rift Valley they climbed steadily for the next day or so. Gradually the whole landscape changed to one of rolling hills, one peak after the next – the home of the Gikuyu, his *askaris* told him nervously. He stopped to examine them through his field glasses, wondering if that was where Kamau had taken refuge with his family. There had been no news of him since he left, not so much as a whisper.

Then – without warning, when it seemed they might still have another hour's walk ahead of them – the ground suddenly gave way dramatically in an almost sheer drop. Deep below them was an extensive plain stretching for mile upon mile before losing itself in the dusty heat haze. The Rift Valley.

'Ay,' Andrewes breathed, lost for words. He felt he was standing on a cliff-top and looking out over a vast inland sea. It was going to be a headache carrying the line down those rock-strewn slopes and ledges. He examined the survey map. 'Now it seems they've estimated the line could follow a route over in that direction over there . . . The pity is, if we could only be layin' track along the bed o' the valley while this work's goin' on it wouldna hold us up too

165

much, but we'd ne'er get the material down there. Unless . . .'

The thought seemed to strike Tim Wilton simultaneously. 'A funicular!' he joined in with enthusiasm. 'We could run rails straight down to the bottom, never mind the gradient, and haul the wagons up and down by cable. I've seen something similar in Switzerland. We'd need to build the engine house on top here, wind the cables round a drum and . . .'

'An' the other work proceeds as planned, d'ye mean?'

'That's right – this'd only be temporary, till the main track is laid, don't you know?'

'It might work,' Andrewes agreed cautiously, wanting to give Tim Wilton his head. 'But the wagons'd be carryin' some very heavy equipment. Let's get a few figures down on paper an' see what they tell us. An' we have to reckon the time it'll take to construct.'

'It could save months in the long run!' His face was flushed with excitement. 'D'you think these gradients in the surveyors' report can be trusted?'

'I'd no' wish to stop ye takin' your own readin's.'

He tramped off along the cliff-side, leaving Tim Wilton to get on with it. That suggestion of an engine-house – ay, his own idea had been a steam-powered winch but wi' two sets o' rails laid side by side in order to make use o' the empty wagons comin' up to counter-weight the full ones goin' down. An' the whole thing taken in several stages perhaps . . . Ay, well the calculations'd reveal a few problems, no doubt. Yet the lad was right to look excited: this was the sort o' engineerin' challenge that could make or break a reputation.

Workshops . . .

The wagons would need adapting to carry their loads level while their wheels were at that crazy angle. The ideal location would be near that swamp before the ground started to climb again. Plenty of water there, with room for a wee marshalling yard where they could make up trains, turn engines, everything necessary . . . 'Nairobi,' the *man-*

166

*yatta* Maasai had called it – the 'cold water' – which was as good a name as any for a railway depot.

Hester could have her house by the thorn tree. In his notebook he sketched the approximate route of the railway in relation to the swamp, placing the station, workshops, living quarters . . . Ay, the house would be in a good position, he thought, an' they'd leave the tree standin'.

'Mr Wilton!' Andrewes called across to his assistant, who was busy setting up his theodolite and issuing instructions to the Swahili porters. 'I'm thinkin' if your father could see ye right now he'd mebbe understand ye better – an' offer up a prayer perhaps.'

Tim waved a hand in reply, laughing, but concentrated on his work.

'My father-in-law's in that line o' business himsel'.' Andrewes went on expansively. 'Baptist minister in Liverpool, d'ye ken, wi' a church the size o' some cathedral, preachin' to nigh on a thousand congregation every Sunday evenin'. Ye ne'er see anythin' like that in your village.'

'Mrs Andrewes was telling me!' he called back.

'Ay. Ay, she would.'

He looked again at the rough plan he had drawn in his notebook, adding details here and there. They would need to shift the *manyatta*, which might take a few days' negotiation. No trouble, though. There had been no serious opposition anywhere so far – some minor raids mainly for theft, some complaints about coolies debauching local girls, but nothing more.

But this 'Nairobi' would be no camp, he thought. More like a wee town.

Among the Gikuyu on the ridges the approach of the red strangers had become the subject of endless discussion. Ngengi lay awake at night listening to the men talking about it – though the murmur of their voices, the smoky warmth of the crackling log fire and the knowledge that he was now big enough to sleep here in his father's *thingira* – as the hut was called – rather than with his mother and

167

sister, all helped to give him a cosy, secure feeling that nothing could go wrong any more.

It had not always been that way. At first, the people of the ridge had been very suspicious. They accepted Njeri without question – was she not one of them? – but Kamau they treated as a stranger. Those elders who were members of the *kiama* council met to decide if he could be allowed to stay. No one knew what words were spoken at that meeting – the *kiama*'s doings were secret and not to be spread about in idle chatter, but Ngengi could well imagine what his father had said. Had he not heard his views often before?

'First,' he would say, 'I am Gikuyu. My father was Gikuyu and that counts among our people. Let me remind you how our race began. In the beginning, our father Gikuyu emerged from the great hole in the ground and was led by Ngai up to the very peaks of Kere-Nyaga to show him the wonders of the country which was to be his. And he pointed out a group of fig trees where Gikuyu was to live.

'So Gikuyu came down the mountain and made his way to these fig trees, and there Ngai gave him a wife whose name was Mumbi. They lived happily together. She bore him nine daughters who grew up and became young women, old enough to marry. Gikuyu appealed to Ngai for help in finding husbands for his daughters and Ngai said he should sacrifice a ram beneath one particular tree in the sacred grove, smearing its blood and fat on the bark before burning the flesh. This he did, and, when he had finished, he saw nine handsome young men standing there.

'His daughters were delighted. They declared themselves ready to marry these young men on one condition – that they, the women, should head the household. And so it was, and from them are descended the nine clans of the Gikuyu. For many generations they lived in this way with the women in control until the day came when they began to mistreat their men, inflicting all kinds of injustices upon them, and – as the men were weaker – they were unable to defend themselves. But these injustices were too great to bear, so they met and plotted together so to flatter

168

and woo the women that they all became pregnant at the same time, for this is when women are most vulnerable. The plot succeeded. As a result, men were able to gain the upper hand; since then, men have always been the leaders in Gikuyu.

'As my father is Gikuyu, therefore I am Gikuyu,' he always concluded this part of his discourse. But he went on, 'As all of you know, my mother was a Maasai woman, and thus I have the strength of two great nations. In these days when the red strangers come into our land we need to draw all people together, or we shall be made slaves.'

It must have been arguments such as these which Kamau had used when he appeared before the *kiama*, and he must have spoken well, for they had allowed him to stay as a tenant – he often explained these things to Ngengi, wanting him to understand – on the land of one of the wealthier elders. He was respected, too. Men listened to his stories, talked over his advice . . . Yet Ngengi still had that picture of him in his mind, shackled to a tree to be whipped by that white man at the railway camp, that 'red stranger' as he had learned to call them. Time and time again he woke up in the middle of the night thinking about it, unable to sleep, frustrated with rage and deep shame.

As for that red stranger himself, The-Man-of-Thirst, he had groaned and writhed as King John beat him till he sagged, unconscious, against the tree. But Ngengi took no pleasure in that memory. The man was still alive.

And it was all long, long ago . . .

In the *thingira* the men were discussing the misfortunes suffered by the ridge over many seasons now. Crops had been poor because of uncertain rainfall, though they knew it had been worse in the plains – had not people come to them begging for food, ready to barter their last few possessions in exchange for a morsel to eat? Many farms had been left, too dry for crops to grow, and their families had taken refuge on the ridges or deeper in the forest. Most had already known suffering earlier from the plague of locusts, or from *mutungu* – that terrible disease which could wipe out whole villages. There were still some who caught

169

it and had to be isolated in special huts in the forest, as Ngengi knew only too well; earlier that year his father had visited one such man, hearing he was getting better, to obtain pus from his sores which he had then pressed into Ngengi's leg with the point of a sharp thorn. The evil was weak, having already been defeated by the sick man, he had explained; now it would learn that Ngengi's spirit was also too strong for it and in future he would be safe. But three days later Ngengi had experienced a high fever and felt he was about to join the many who had already died, though he soon recovered.

So many things had gone wrong on the ridge. Muthoga, the oldest among the men and famous in his youth for his prowess against Maasai raiders, summed it all up for them.

'Is it not clear,' he said, looking around their faces, red-tinged by the firelight, 'that our troubles started when the red strangers first appeared in our land? They came in ones or twos to trade, or to hunt for elephant tusks. We did not allow them to enter our forests, but when we heard the sound of their guns we went out to meet them, our women bartered food with them, and so they continued on their journeys. But when they had passed our cattle fell sick and died – yes, and the cattle of the Maasai too, which made them greedy to steal ours. Now the day has come when these red strangers have returned with many more men. They build villages for themselves and their iron snake creeps across the country. Have we ever tried to stop them? No, we have tended to our crops, kept to our forests, looked after our own affairs – but they have brought disease, they have taken away the rain. Among some clans of the Gikuyu the farms are desolate and the people are dying. Truly it is said, snakes grow fat while men sleep.'

'That is so,' confirmed Mukiro, one of the younger men who was not known to be talkative. 'We trusted them, and this is our punishment.'

'We were warned,' came Chege's high-pitched voice out of the darkness. Since he had become an elder he spoke more insistently than ever. 'Remember the prophecy made by Mugo wa Kabiro.'

'Our children are hungry and we have no food to put in their mouths!' Muthoga cried in an attempt to regain their attention. His tetchiness betrayed his dislike of being interrupted. 'As you say, Chege, we did not heed the prophecy made many generations ago. My own father told me of it, and he had it from his father – that strangers would come to our land out of the great water, and they would have light-coloured skins and be dressed like butterflies. They would carry sticks that made fire and bring with them an iron snake which would breathe fire, and when that day came the land would be stricken with famine.'

'The young warriors on all the ridges are becoming restless,' said Mukiro, speaking for the second time. 'They ask why we allow these red strangers to move among us. If the Maasai attack, do we not defend our homes and our cattle? If the Wakamba attack, do we not defend our women? Why, then, should we not destroy this iron snake and kill these red strangers who bring so much affliction?'

For a moment all the men in the *thingira* fell silent, impressed by his words. They knew he did not talk idly, but had authority among the warriors.

'Remember the prophecy warned that we must not act hastily, but wait,' Kamau answered him flatly. 'I have seen this iron snake. I have ridden on its back. And these sticks that make fire – they cannot be fought with spears.'

Ngengi could sense their suspicion – had not Kamau lived with these red strangers, shared their food, perhaps sold himself to them? Of course none of them could know of the rifle he kept buried under the hardened floor of his *thingira*, carefully smeared with fat and wrapped in an antelope skin. But Ngengi knew and he had been sworn to secrecy: because, as his father had said, 'The time is not yet.'

'Is Kamau afraid?' asked Chege.

Patient as always, his father ignored the jibe. 'The red strangers brought a magic over the great water with them, stronger than any we have learned from our forefathers.

But it does not belong to them alone. We can all learn it, though it may take many long years to acquire their skills.'

'If we do that,' Chege objected, 'the purity of the Gikuyu will suffer. Our people will no longer be the same.'

'That is true,' he agreed. 'Was not my own father changed when he became the slave of men armed with sticks that make fire? Later he crossed the great water, perhaps the first of the Gikuyu to do so, and saw many things with his own eyes. He used to say when I was a child that a man should fight only when he knows he can win, or when he has no choice. Does the lion attack the elephant?'

'But we have no other choice!' Muthoga cut in, his querulous voice rising in anger. 'Is it not clear that our people will continue to die until we have expelled the red strangers from the land? We have word that warriors from the ridges beyond the hilltop are preparing to attack, and some have already taken oaths. Are we to join them? Or are we so divided among ourselves because some among us have no stomach for a fight? Let me remind you all – when Ngai took Gikuyu to the peaks of Kere-Nyaga to show him the hills and valleys, the ridges, the streams, did he say, "Hold back, Gikuyu, all this is for the red strangers, so make way for them?" No, Ngai showed Gikuyu the land for himself and his children – for ever.'

No one disagreed, not even Kamau. Ngengi thrilled as he heard the words, vowing he would never forget them – yet why did his father not speak? He knew so much more than the other men: why did he now remain silent?

Far into the night they talked. Ngengi listened drowsily, only half-paying attention as he puzzled over this one question. The answer was clear enough, though he hated admitting it even to himself. Whatever their words, the people of the ridge still refused in their hearts to accept Kamau as one of them.

# THREE

Practically everyone for miles around the new little town of Nairobi must have come in specially to see the races, Hester thought as she waited for Ali to find a suitably shady spot for the canvas chair he was carrying. John was supervising him fussily, but she let him take charge, pleased to have him with her for once.

Several young officers of the King's African Rifles were already there, excitedly talking over the details of the course and setting out markers on the broad, open plain. With them was William Carpenter, Comptroller of the Railway, up from Mombasa. Hester had seen him arrive a few days earlier, so smothered in red dust from the railway journey he looked like one of those terrifying illustrations in the Grimm's Fairy Tales she had read as a child. Hans de Jong was there too, the young Cape Town Dutchman she had first seen at Voi some years ago, and with him a short, thin man with an unpleasant face, his partner, whose name she did not know. And Dr Carson, Jimmy Hathaway, Mr Jackson . . .

'Oh, it's going to be lovely! she cried happily. 'It's like living in a real town for once, though it's a pity Mr Wilton can't be here. Oh, and just look at those two!'

Two young officers had harnessed a couple of unwilling horses to a cart, but they were rearing up in protest and defeating all attempts to bring them under control.

Gaby, just five years old – already! – and with long, auburn hair scattered over her shoulders, danced about trying to attract the attention of her baby brother Michael. For a few brief months she had resented his arrival, perhaps fearing her parents would no longer love her now they had a new baby, then to Hester's relief that mood gave way to a fascination with her new role as elder sister. She had sent off a long letter to Liverpool with a photograph Tim Wilton had taken of her and the two children together, just to show how well they all looked.

*But at least,* her father had written in his last letter, barely disguising his disapproval of her life in Africa, *at least you now have a proper postal address.*

Nairobi – odd how it already felt like home! Her house might be little better than a large shed whose once bright corrugated iron roof had now rusted to a shabby brown, but she had sewn curtains, buying material from Indian traders, added cushions and a bedspread . . . It made a big difference; after dark, in the soft light of the oil lamp, it looked almost cosy. The flies were a nuisance, though – swarms of them got in everywhere and you could scarcely serve a plate of soup without some dropping into it. Then the swamp frogs kept everyone awake at night and, recently, there had been rats. Hardly surprising, though, when rubbish was merely dumped outside the houses for the hyenas to scavenge. Nature's own refuse collectors, someone called them.

But then she had made a garden behind the house, employing a couple of Gikuyus to break the ground and sow seed sent out specially from England. From Carter's, near Reading. After his first meal of her own home-grown potatoes, brussels sprouts and beans, with her own flowers on the table, John had complimented her warmly, 'Ay, lass, we'll make somethin' o' this country yet, see if we dinna!'

Of course he was away much of the time, either at the Rift Valley escarpment – he and Tim Wilton were so proud of that funicular, an awkward-looking device she had thought when she saw it, but she supposed it was necessary for lowering the heavy material down into the valley – or visiting the various construction camps along the line, dashing here and there. At times she had the impression even his dreams were about more viaducts and earthworks. He talked more about a new locomotive out from England than ever about his own son.

But that's the way he was – and, secretly, she had observed him playing with the baby too, a bit awkward and clumsy, making a train out of some small blocks of wood. And she had loved him for it, elephant though he was in many ways.

In truth, Nairobi was little more than a railway depot. The station itself consisted of a wooden platform in front of a warehouse with a rusty roof; a little tower had been built on top of it and equipped with a large clock – and there it was, in the middle of Africa, where zebras, giraffes or even a rhino might wander across the track at any time! Whenever a train arrived the whole population turned out to watch. Swarms of Africans appeared from nowhere, naked but for a few ornaments or strips of animal hide, armed with spears, and gazing impassively at the disembarking passengers streaked with red dust. As for the other buildings – offices, stores, workshops – they stood in straight lines along either side of a wide, deeply-rutted track which some wag had dubbed 'Victoria Road' and, at the far end, was the Indian bazaar quarter: noisy by night, unsavoury by day. Most people were convinced the flies originated in the bazaar, and it was only a few months since Dr Carson and his Indian assistants had managed to stamp out an epidemic of smallpox among the coolies. No wonder the army had moved their camp to a hillside a couple of miles away.

Already quite a crowd had gathered on the plain outside the township where the race meeting was to take place. John selected a shady knoll beneath a spreading acacia where they could watch in comfort with a good view of the winning post. He would not be riding himself, being too heavy to inflict on any horse fast enough to take part. Gaby was becoming impatient.

'If ye canna see too well, I'll lift ye on my shoulders,' he attempted to reassure her. 'The second race is the one to watch out for. Remember that, now!'

'Why not the first? I want to be the first!'

'Gaby!' Hester laughed reproachfully. 'Not everyone can be first.'

'I want to be. I'm always going to be first.' She tossed the auburn hair back from her face. 'And it's my cup!'

'The cup goes to the winner,' John explained for about the fiftieth time, 'but it's in your honour, wee lass. That's why we called it the Gabriella Cup – an' when ye're an old, old lady wi' grey hair an' wrinkles, I prophesy they'll still be ridin' for the Gabriella Cup!'

The laughter bubbled out of her and Hester smiled as she listened to them. He had suggested the Cup as a joke a few days earlier while trying to describe to Gaby what happened at a race meeting, and the following morning he had gone into the bazaar to buy this tawdry brass bowl from Patel's store. Carpenter, on behalf of the race committee, had accepted it enthusiastically.

'My love, look who's arrived!' John exclaimed suddenly.

A man on horseback trotted towards them; Hester shielded her eyes against the sun to see who it was.

'It's Major Arbuthnot – d'ye remember?' John's voice boomed out across the field and several people turned to see who he was talking about. 'Indian Army – the Uganda relief expedition.'

'Now of 3rd battalion, Queen's African Rifles. Got here yesterday.' The little major dismounted, as blond as ever, and red-faced. 'How d'you do, ma'am? Often think back with pleasure to those days in Tsavo and your excellent hospitality, what? A last touch of civilization before our forced march. Heard you bagged that lion, Andrewes. Jolly good show. Though I'm told you'd a deal of trouble later with the man-eaters of Tsavo – held up work on the railway and I don't know what!'

'Ay, luckily we'd moved on by then,' John said, 'an' someone else had to deal wi' them. Are ye racin'?'

'Hope to. What's this Gabriella Cup?'

'Meet Gabriella in person!' John introduced her proudly.

'Well, well . . . not your baby, ma'am? Not the little girl I used to . . . Bless me, you've grown!' The little major struggled valiantly to present himself as a jovial uncle. Gaby regarded him gravely, not uttering a word. 'I'll win your Cup, young lady or die in the attempt, what? Damme if I don't!'

The contestants in the first race were summoned to the

starting line by a young officer blowing a hunting horn. Only five horses were entered and Hester had never seen such a mixed bunch. Not that her father would ever have allowed them to go to the races in Liverpool, but many a fine lady and gentleman rode along Princes Avenue on a Sunday morning – and what fine mounts they had been! As for these – one might have been at home pulling a cart along the Dock Road; another, a roan mare, seemed more interested in cropping the grass than in racing.

'Isn't that Mr Hathaway?' Hester exclaimed in surprise, shading her eyes to see who was on the roan.

John chuckled, greatly amused. 'Ay, an' scared out o' his wits too. He's the right height an' weight for a jockey but they'd a de'il of a time persuadin' him.'

The young officer with the horn had some difficulty getting the riders to line up properly, but at last he was satisfied. He drew his revolver and fired into the air.

Major Arbuthnot was first away, riding in fine style; the others followed close behind – Hans de Jong, then Carpenter, immaculate in the saddle as his horse kept its place with an easy canter, then an officer whose name Hester did not know, and finally Jimmy Hathaway, crouched over the roan's neck and giving the impression he was hanging on for dear life. Indeed, he may have been: his roan had been startled by the gun, reared up on its hind legs, and dashed after the others in obvious panic.

As the horses came around the order of the field changed. Major Arbuthnot fought hard to keep the lead but Hans de Jong was slowly overtaking him. Carpenter was in trouble as his mount was clearly refusing to gallop. It cantered elegantly around the course in last place. But the real eye-opener was Jimmy Hathaway, now third behind Hans de Jong, but still gaining.

At first the spectators had looked on with only mild interest, but now they were caught up in a fever of excitement, shouting and waving their arms, urging the horses on. On the far side of the field Hester spotted Abdul Hakim collecting last minute bets from the Indian watchers. Her own heart was in her mouth too as Jimmy

177

Hathaway on the roan came into the lead, with Hans de Jong only a half a neck behind him. She stood up, her fist clenched and pressed into her mouth; on her arm Michael was whimpering, but she took no notice.

He made it!

Jimmy Hathaway passed the winning post just ahead of Hans de Jong; Major Arbuthnot came third, though some way back. William Carpenter, Comptroller of the Railway, was last past the post, still cantering, with not a hair out of place.

'Oh, John, aren't you sorry you were not riding?' Hester gasped with relief as she sat down. 'I am! Oh, if only I could ride this afternoon!'

'Nay, lass,' he shook his head. 'It's men who ride races, no' womenfolk.'

'Papa, why?' asked Gaby.

'Too risky, wee lass. If somethin' went wrong . . .'

'Isn't it risky for men too?'

'Ay, but women take enough risks goin' about their natural business wi'out facin' more. Now let's go an' offer our congratulations to Mr Hathaway.'

They found Jimmy Hathaway transformed by his success and now determined to ride in the next race as well – the Gabriella Cup. But Carpenter, having persuaded him to take part in the first place, was insisting that the roan mare was too old to run twice.

'You've upheld the honour of the Railway, Mr Hathaway,' he explained briskly. 'That was all I asked, and we're grateful to you. Andrewes here is too heavy, but you've a jockey's build. We couldn't leave it all to the military. Never hear the last.'

Jimmy Hathaway was scarcely listening. 'Ee, but I didn't know what grand fun it'd be! When horse really got movin' an' started passin' others like that, I thought to meself – ee, this is the life, I thought.'

'Congratulations, Mr Hathaway,' said Hester warmly. 'If I ever take up gambling, I'll put my money on you.'

'You had nothing on the race, Mrs Andrewes?' Carpenter enquired politely.

178

'No.' Suddenly she felt cold, as she always did whenever he addressed her; beneath those easy good manners there was – nothing. 'No, I . . . don't.'

John came to her aid. 'My wife's family didna back horses.'

'Oh?' Again that withdrawal, that distance.

'Then what did they back?' Jackson had joined them while they were talking and overheard the last few words; he laughed roughly. 'What did they back, eh?'

Before anyone could reply, the horn sounded again to call the contestants for the next race.

'Here we go, that's me!' Jackson announced, boasting. 'The Gabriella Cup! If I win it, young Gaby, I'll expect a big kiss! You'll not be tellin' me, Andrewes, your wife's family don't go in for kisses?'

'I'll see ye in hell first,' John replied darkly.

Carpenter went back to the acacia with them, saying he was dropping out of this race. The shadow had moved with the sun and John shifted the chair for Hester; she sank into it gratefully. That encounter with Jackson had brought back the whole Muldoon thing again. She had told John she was over it, didn't think of it any longer, but that was not true. She still carried the derringer in her purse, loaded.

'I'm told you've developed a fine garden, Mrs Andrewes,' Carpenter was saying.

'Yes.' She forced herself to pay attention, but did not look at him; instead, she held the baby on her knees, jigging him up and down till he smiled toothlessly at her. 'You see, Gaby – he likes that!'

'He's my brother,' Gaby told Carpenter importantly. 'His name's Michael.'

'A fine little fellow.' Carpenter sounded almost irritated at the change of subject. 'Ever thought of a farm, Mrs Andrewes? The country's crying out for settlers of the right sort. No shortage of labour either, not with the hut tax. These Africans will need to work for cash if they're to pay it.'

'Why should they pay it?'

179

'The cost of the administration . . .' he began.

'*Our* administration. In their eyes we don't belong here.'

'It's one rupee a year for each hut – hardly a fortune.'

'Would you pay it?' she demanded hotly. 'In their place?'

John seemed amused, guessing that she was deliberately needling Carpenter: the Southerner, as she referred to him scathingly. He represented everything she – with her Welsh family and Liverpool nonconformist background – despised most.

'D'ye see, they're linin' up, Gaby!' he pointed out, lifting her to his shoulder. 'Eight horses this time. For the Gabriella Cup!'

'I don't want Mr Jackson to win,' she said firmly.

'I'm sure he won't,' Hester reassured her. If that man so much as laid a finger on her . . . She hated those small, mean eyes and disjointed nose, no doubt broken in some bar-room brawl.

'Damned decent of you presenting this Cup,' Carpenter was telling John. He had no way with children at all, she thought. 'Gives chaps something to compete for. Maybe we should put all this on a formal basis next time. Start a racing club. Members, subscriptions, that sort of thing.'

The young officer had drawn his revolver again, aiming it at the sky. One horse pranced forward and had to be coaxed back by its rider. Jimmy Hathaway's roan mare was tearing at another mouthful of the rough grass. Jackson was on a bay which stood quietly with the others, neither giving trouble nor showing any interest in the proceedings.

Then the revolver was fired. They were off!

Six of the horses made a businesslike start, urged on by their riders, with Hans de Jong in the lead, but once again Jimmy's mare reared up at the sound of the shot, thoroughly frightened, almost unseating him, before galloping off in pursuit. Jackson's bay remained stolidly rooted to the spot until he managed to whip some life into it.

'He'll do that poor beast an injury, beatin' it like that,'

John frowned. 'If a horse doesna wish to race, all the beatin' in the world will no' change its mind.'

'He should be disqualified!' Hester declared; then she added sweetly, 'Don't you agree, Mr Carpenter?'

'He's almost caught up though,' Carpenter pointed out. 'Hathaway's only just ahead.'

It was true. Jackson's bay was showing an unexpected turn of speed. It overtook Jimmy Hathaway, and then the two riders ahead of him. He was still whipping it furiously, determined to bully his way into the lead. Major Arbuthnot yelled something across at him as they drew parallel, Hester could not hear what.

As the horses passed the acacia where they were watching, Hans de Jong still held the first place, with Jackson immediately behind him. Major Arbuthnot had fallen back to fourth and Jimmy Hathaway was one of the last. He was standing in the stirrups, bending low over the mare's back, his face determined, his lips moving urgently.

'Hathaway! Ye're doin' fine!' John called out encouragingly. He turned to Carpenter. 'Ye're right, that mare's dead tired. He'll ne'er make it.'

But those last horses, once bunched up together, now began to spread out. Jimmy Hathaway saw an opening and took it. Without using his stock at all – he seemed to be murmuring words of magic into the mare's ear – he moved up to sixth place . . . fifth . . . fourth . . .

Jackson, becoming aware of the threat, belaboured his bay again with renewed vigour. At the same time Hans de Jong's mount was obviously tiring and could no longer hold the pace he had been setting.

Hester was dismayed. 'Oh no! Oh, please God . . .!'

The outcome of the race now looked terrifyingly clear. Jackson was in the lead, with Hans de Jong still holding on to second place and Jimmy Hathaway coming third. Then the bay appeared to stumble. A gasp went up from the onlookers as Jackson flew over its head and landed on the turf, narrowly missing the hooves of the other horses. Riderless, his bay galloped after them.

Once again the final moments were to be fought out

between Jimmy Hathaway and Hans de Jong. But one of the young officers was gaining ground too, a man with a sharp, angular face and humourless eyes – Hester had often seen him around in Nairobi though she didn't know his name. Again Jimmy Hathaway whispered into the roan mare's ear, but in vain. The young officer drew ahead, way out in front now, with – yes, it was Major Arbuthnot! – coming up behind him. For a few yards they were neck and neck. Then Major Arbuthnot was . . . was he? Yes, it was Major Arbuthnot, by a nose!

Above the cheers the organizing officer announced, 'The Gabriella Cup has been won by Major Arbuthnot on Hercules!'

The little blond major emerged from the confusion of horses and riders to trot towards the knoll where Gaby stood solemnly holding the Indian bowl in her hands.

'Say congratulations,' Hester reminded her. Over towards the winning post she could see Jackson limping across the grass towards his bay which had followed the race faithfully, coming in last, and she thanked God he had not won. Beyond him in the distance, hardly more than a cloud of dust, someone else was approaching on horseback – a latecomer for the races? Or . . .? Why did she suddenly feel uneasy?

'Con . . . ga . . . lations!' Gaby was saying in a loud clear voice as she offered him the bowl. 'I'm glad you won. You're my favourite.'

The major drew himself up to his full height, saluting formally. 'Thank you, Miss Andrewes.' He smiled almost slily at Hester. 'A fine daughter, Mrs Andrewes. Wouldn't mind betting she'll break a few hearts when she's bigger, what?' He groomed his Dundreary whiskers with a forefinger.

Across the field Jackson was struggling between two officers trying to restrain him from beating his horse. They wrenched the stock out of his hand.

'Fellow's a maniac!' the major commented. 'Drew blood, what? A long open wound. Hardly believe my eyes when I saw it. No way to treat a horse.'

The latecomer galloped across the grass towards the little knot of officers, reining in his horse as he reached them. There was a quick exchange of words, too far off for Hester to hear, then they pointed in her direction. Immediately, the rider turned his horse's head and came over.

'Captain Burns!' the major exclaimed. 'Well, he's missed two, but maybe he's entered for the hurdles!'

Hester laughed politely, relaxing. She knew Captain Burns slightly. His small talk consisted of listing the numerous animals he had slaughtered, with a detailed account of which gun or ammunition he had used. His lean, hard face was furrowed with deep-set lines, giving it the appearance of having been put together in sections, an impression reinforced by the fact that his protruding chin was not positioned centrally to the rest of the design but slightly to the left.

He jumped down from his horse, saluted, and took Major Arbuthnot aside for a private word. Then he had not come for the races after all, she thought. The major summoned Carpenter and John to join them; for a few minutes they were in deep conversation, then she heard John's voice raised.

'I'll no' stay behind! The man's my assistant. Ye dinna think I can bide here an' do nothin'!'

If there was one thing Hester hated, it was men with grave faces talking over some crisis and assuming women were unable to contribute. She called Ali over to take care of Gaby, then went across to force them to take notice of her. They fell silent.

'Will nobody tell me what's going on?'

No one answered.

'John?'

'Ay, ye've a right to know, lass . . .' he began.

Major Arbuthnot stopped him. 'Mrs Andrewes, it might perhaps be best if you—'

'Major, it'll be the talk o' Nairobi within half-an-hour. Ye canna keep secrets in Africa.'

'I wished only to spare the lady.'

'Ay, but the lady in question is my wife,' John reminded

him pointedly. 'My love, Tim Wilton an' his party were ambushed a couple o' days ago by Gikuyu – the news has just come in by runner. When the runner left he was still alive, but wounded. He lost at least ten men killed, an' some mutilated.'

Her shock at the news held her paralysed. Tim . . . She wanted to ask where he was, how badly hurt, she wanted to go to him . . . 'Has no one . . .?' Her voice was hardly more than a whisper. 'Has no one gone to help him?'

'Seems he's holed up still waitin' to be relieved – if he isna dead already.'

'It's an army matter, ma'am,' Major Arbuthnot intervened briskly. 'I'll be leading the force myself. In the meanwhile, I'd be grateful if you'd explain to your husband that his duty lies here in Nairobi. At your side, ma'am.'

'I sent young Wilton out there, an' I'll bring him back!' John exploded angrily before she could reply. 'I'll no' be interferin' wi' the military side o' things, but I've a duty to look after my own people. I'm comin' along wi' ye, major. An' Mr Carpenter, I'd be grateful if ye'd announce the postponement o' the remainin' races till further notice.'

'Mrs Andrewes . . .' the major pleaded.

'But of course he must go!' she exploded at him, hardly able to restrain herself. She felt so helpless, standing there with the baby in her arms, so tied down, frustrated she could not go with them when Tim was in trouble. 'John,' she pleaded, 'you will make sure he's all right, won't you? And be careful, dearest. I want you both here alive.'

# FOUR

Maybe he should have known better than to send young Wilton out with only a dozen *askaris* and a handful of porters, Andrewes brooded moodily as he marched with the relief force, but the railway was desperately short of timber for the wood-burning locomotives and Wilton had an eye for that sort of thing.

The column consisted of some fifty African riflemen armed with single-shot Martini-Henry .450 rifles, porters, and a Maasai levy of just over a hundred spearmen. Major Arbuthnot was in command. With him were Captain Burns, Lt Smythe – a cheerful youngster who had competed for the Gabriella Cup and come in sixth – and Dr Hume, the dour medical officer from Glasgow. Progress was slow and Andrewes did not hide his impatience when Arbuthnot called a halt.

'The men need a rest and so do you, King John,' he insisted sharply. 'They'll march all the better for it, and fight better too.'

By dawn they were ready to move again. Fearing an ambush on the narrow forest paths, Major Arbuthnot divided his force into smaller units of about twenty spearmen and eight riflemen each, ordering them to follow separate routes through the trees.

But however silently they walked, Andrewes knew it needed only the slightest of rustles or the crack of a twig to betray their presence to any enemy with sharp ears. The low, overhanging branches forced him to stoop awkwardly as he moved forward, and he swore under his breath as one swung back at him, scraping his face. Somewhere in the tree-tops a bird kept up its persistent, mocking call. Then it stopped: an uneasy quiet.

A high-pitched, agonized shriek broke the silence. It shocked through the forest again and again, twisting in his

185

guts until it slowly subsided into a series of equally terrifying, squealing sobs.

He pushed on past Major Arbuthnot, following the sound, and discovered one of the Swahili riflemen trapped in a deep, narrow pit in the centre of the path, impaled on the sharpened, bamboo stakes with which it was spiked. Its opening must have been concealed under a cover of twigs and leaves which gave way the moment he trod of them. His screeching cries were hideous to hear.

'Ye'll need to get him out, man, an' soon!' Andrewes snapped, his nerves raw.

One wrong step now, he knew, and half their force would desert them. He beckoned the two tallest Maasai spearmen to help him grasp the victim beneath the arms to ease him out of the pit; but his shrieks stabbed into his brain like sharp knives and the two Maasai looked at him uneasily, as if they also would prefer to end the poor fellow's suffering on the spot with a quick spear thrust.

But they lifted him out and laid him on the ground, his squat muscular figure a mass of lacerations. Dr Hume had hurried up to join them; he shook his head reproachfully when he saw the wounds. There was bleeding from the testicles, the rectum, the lower abdomen, the navel, his side beneath the rib-cage, and half a dozen other places.

'D'ye think I can work miracles?' Dr Hume puffed out his sunken cheeks, dark with stubble, then expelled the air slowly from his pursed lips – a grotesque habit Andrewes found irritating. 'Internal bleeding, too. Only the Almighty knows what organs are damaged.'

'Thank God he's stopped screaming, what?' The major was pale under his sunburn.

But as he spoke, the man let out one long shrill cry, drew in a deep, shuddering breath, and then went limp.

'He's dead.' Dr Hume stood up and brushed the dust from his knees. 'Next time you find someone in one o' these pits – an' they're vicious, I've ne'er seen anythin' so vicious – cut his throat, will ye? It'd be kinder.'

Already the black ants were exploring the blood patches and beginning to encroach on the body itself.

'An' look at them buggers!' the doctor exclaimed, disgusted.

The major turned away. 'Right, you men!' he called out in a clear, steady voice. 'Keep a sharp look-out, there may be more traps like that one. And watch for any movement among the trees. We're going on.'

The body was left lying by the edge of the pit as a warning to those who came after them, and the ants took possession of it. Sickened, Andrewes turned away.

As they pushed forward the sun filtered down through the trees, throwing weird patterns of light and shade. The air was stifling; insects swarmed in dancing clouds, getting into the eyes, the nostrils, the ears . . . Rustles deep in the forest whispered the presence of other people though they saw no one, only the occasional pit-trap which the men in front, probing the ground ahead with long sticks cut from the bushes, managed to uncover before anyone fell in.

The blond major was becoming edgy. 'I could swear they're watching us,' he confided in Andrewes at one point. 'Feel it in my bones, what? Somewhere among the trees, if only we could spot them. But then they know this country like the back of their hands, while we have to trust a guide who may have no better idea than I do.'

A sudden squawking some distance away seemed to confirm his fears. A bird disturbed by – what?

Andrewes ducked again to avoid a branch and thought he saw something. A man's face? An animal? Or were the 'eyes' merely the effect of sunlight on the leaves? He peered through the thick undergrowth; whatever it was, it had gone.

Then, ahead, another pit-trap claimed a victim. A scream of terror. Moaning. Wailing out a string of incomprehensible words which gave way to sudden ear-piercing yells as the sharp bamboos penetrated. The forest filled with the screaming echoes.

Hurrying forward, he was just in time to see the tall Maasai standing on the edge of the pit trying to help the man suddenly pitch over, dead with an arrow between his shoulders. Andrewes stopped, feeling the menace all around him.

'Down!' the major barked. 'Everyone down!'

He dropped to the ground just in time – the arrow meant for him quivered in the tree trunk where he had been standing – but in the same instant he spotted a movement and fired blindly at it. He pumped round after round into the forest as the fear gripped him. If only he could see what he was fighting against . . . The others were shooting too, but the enemy remained invisible and the shower of arrows stopped abruptly.

While the major checked the casualties Andrewes went cautiously among the trees, uncertain whether the attackers had withdrawn or were merely lying low. Then he came across three bodies – Gikuyus. One must have been killed by his first shot: he lay arched over a low bush, his mouth and unseeing eyes wide open, and a deep red wound in his throat. Andrewes left him where he was and returned to tell the major what he had found.

'Three dead – that's some consolation, what? I'm afraid we lost two riflemen and three Maasai, not counting the man in the pit. Hume here says they're using poisoned arrows.'

'Ay, fresh poison too, judging by the speedy reaction,' Dr Hume agreed. 'When it gets into the blood the victim's paralysed an' dies o' suffocation. But what I canna understand is this hit-an'-run attack. No' like 'em. No' normally.'

'It makes some sense, though,' Andrewes commented. 'They'd no' stand a chance in pitched battle against guns.'

'Not on their side, are you what?' the major demanded irritably. 'Because it sounds as though you are.'

'A student o' military tactics, major.' Andrewes spoke lightly, looking down on his pale blond head. 'An' the sooner we're out o' these trees, the happier I'll feel.'

'I'd just remind you, *King John*,' Arbuthnot stressed the words sarcastically, 'that you're here on sufferance. You've no military experience to contribute, to my knowledge, what?' He stared up at Andrewes, his face reddening, and then gave the order to move on.

The path seemed to be leading them through the thickest part of the forest. Andrewes was beginning to wonder if their guide really knew where he was heading when – after about another half-hour – the trees began to thin out and they eventually reached more open country where the ground rose and fell steeply in a series of bumpy hills. There, already in position on the nearest slopes, was Lt Smythe's party. Over towards the south, also just emerging from the forest, was the unit commanded by Captain Burns.

Lt Smythe saluted smartly as Major Arbuthnot approached. He had a relaxed, cool way about him which was immediately likeable. Nothing pompous. None of the parade ground manners which so many officers displayed – though, as he had explained to Andrewes in camp the previous evening, he had been through Sandhurst and served three years on the North-West Frontier before transferring at his own request to the King's African Rifles.

'There's a fortified camp on the far side, Sir, visible from the top here,' he was explaining. 'I spotted some movement inside, but no one has ventured out yet. I've posted a couple of men to keep an eye on it.'

'We'll take a look, what?' The major turned to Andrewes. 'You too, if you can keep your head down.'

They climbed up to the summit, dropping down flat for the last few feet in order not to be seen against the skyline. The *boma* was on raised ground on the other side of the valley, not too far from where the forest began again. The major examined it carefully, then handed his field glasses to Andrewes.

'Couple of tents inside,' he said.

'Ay, that'll be Wilton, right enough.' He was about to hand the glasses back when something about the ground outside the *boma* attracted his attention. 'On the left there. Graves?'

The major took the glasses. 'Could be. Time for a display of strength, what?'

The main force had now assembled on the hillside out of sight of the valley. The major ordered Captain Burns to station a dozen of the best riflemen on the high ground to watch out for Gikuyu while the remainder, in two parties, were to make their way to the gentler slopes at either side of the hill. Once they were in position, he gave the signal for them to march down into the valley, converging on the *boma*.

'Pity we've no bagpipes to scare the shit out of 'em, what?' He strutted along importantly, keeping pace with Andrewes' easy strides. 'D'you play the pipes?'

'I'd an uncle who did,' Andrewes admitted, 'though he was ne'er too popular wi' the rest o' the family.'

But even without bagpipes it was an impressive sight. In the lead were the riflemen, mostly Swahilis, in their pill-box hats and dark jumpers. Behind them came the Maasai warriors, about fifty in each column, with shining spears and long hide shields, their hair greased and twisted into pigtails, and short goat-skin togas draped over one shoulder. The porters brought up the rear with their headloads.

Half-way across the valley the major called a brief halt. He stood with Andrewes in front of his army, drew his revolver and fired three shots in the air. Immediately, two railway *askaris* appeared at the entrance to the *boma*, waving their rifles in greeting. Others joined them, chattering excitedly as they saw the columns.

'Well, King John, your subjects have recognized you,' the major commented drily. 'No doubt about our welcome, what? *Forward – march!*'

Outside the *boma* Andrewes noted the newly-dug graves and prayed that one was not Tim Wilton's. He waited while the major issued his orders. Then Dr Hume came up and the three of them went in together, apprehensive of what they might find.

Tim Wilton – still alive, thank God – lay on a camp bed in the first tent, his face hot and flushed, a cut down his right cheek, his pale blue eyes bloodshot; his right leg was crudely bandaged with two spear shafts serving as splints, held in place by strips of torn linen. His hands and fore-arms were also bandaged, although somehow he was managing to grip his rifle which he pointed directly at Andrewes as he entered.

'Ye've no need o' that now, Mr Wilton!' Andrewes remarked cheerfully to disguise how relieved he felt. 'I heard in Nairobi ye were on the point o' dyin'! I'm grateful ye awaited our arrival.'

'King John – am I glad to see you!' His voice sounded very unsteady. 'And it's . . .'

'Major Arbuthnot. Delighted we got here in time. We met in Tsavo, you remember? Some years ago? And this is Dr Hume, whose orders are to bring you back to health with the least inconvenience to everyone concerned. A first-rate medico, whatever they say.'

Tim Wilton went on, troubled, 'There's precious little ammunition left, and they keep coming back and back . . . One more . . . attack . . . we'll not be able to hold out any longer . . .'

'We can handle them, what?' the major assured him.

'But with so few rounds left . . .' He was exhausted.

'Ye've a high fever, lad,' Andrewes observed gently, 'but ye can take it easy now. The army's here, an' we'll have ye back in Nairobi as soon as Dr Hume says ye can travel. Gaby's waitin' to see ye, an' ye know how impatient she can get.'

'If ye gentlemen'd kindly leave us,' Dr Hume intervened testily, 'it's time I examined my patient.'

'My report, must make my report,' Tim Wilton gabbled, holding on to Andrewes' wrist, his eyes unnaturally intense.

Andrewes glanced at Dr Hume, who nodded his consent. The account was confused, repetitive, the outpourings of a sick man, but gradually it emerged that the first attack had come at dawn one morning, quite unexpected, as there had been no previous contact with any Africans in the district, which they had assumed to be uninhabited. It had been a terrifying sight as some fifty men had advanced out of the forest, yelling and springing in the air. Several porters had gone down under the hail of poisoned arrows; then the Gikuyus had rushed the survivors with spears and short swords. The fight was desperate. Most of his men were armed only with bush knives. The railway *askaris* had rifles, but they were so vastly outnumbered they were in danger of being overrun at any moment. Tim Wilton had kept firing until he ran out of ammunition, when they closed in and cut him down. After it was all over, Sharma, his gun-bearer, reported that four Indian coolies had been killed and disembowelled, together with five Swahili porters and one *askari*. Ten Gikuyus lay dead.

'Since then the men have kept to the *boma*, except to fetch water,' he ended, beaten. 'We sent a runner, he volunteered, we didn't expect him to get through, and they've been back to attack and again . . . and again . . . and if—'

'Mr Wilton, your runner did get to Nairobi, else we'd not be here, what?' The major's manner was practical, almost bracing. 'Now we'd best leave you to Dr Hume. He'll see you right.' And, outside the tent, he added quietly to Andrewes, 'Ask me, he's bloody lucky to be alive. No smell of gangrene, though. That's something.'

He marched off briskly to make sure his orders were being carried out, leaving Andrewes to check on the rest of the railway party.

They all had injuries to show. The gun-bearer, Sharma, had escaped with a disfiguring cut across the temple; others had wounds on their arms or legs, and one of the burliest of the porters, a squat, thickset Swahili with a scowling face, had lost several fingers, though the stumps appeared to be healing well. He had 'a healing touch', Sharma explained, and had treated several of the men, including Tim Wilton.

Then they showed him the remaining stores, grinning proudly as he counted the ammunition – no more left than six rounds per man – and saw that the food supply was practically exhausted. But they were laughing happily, congratulating each other; they had expected to die that day but knew now they were safe – could they not hear the wee major outside the *boma*, briskly shouting his orders? Ay, thought Andrewes, maybe. Maybe.

Dr Hume emerged from the tent. 'His leg's in a right mess. I may have to amputate but I'm hoping not to.' He glanced around the other men. 'I'd best be takin' a look at these, too. King John – bloody stupid nickname, I dinna ken how ye pu' up wi' it – your friend's as strong as an ox an' it's my guess he'll live. Only a guess, mind.'

'An' his hands?'

'Ay, they'll do. Wounds seem clean enough, an' once we get rid o' the muck he's pu' on them . . . Looks like bark from a tree mixed up wi' mushrooms or somethin' – some kind o' fungus.' Honest Scottish disgust showed on his face. 'Says he go' it from one o' the porters.'

'This man?' Andrewes summoned the burly porter across for Dr Hume to examine the stumps which had once been fingers. 'Healin' nicely, d'ye see? An' Tim Wilton too – no gangrene . . .'

He questioned the man in Swahili.

'What's he say?' Dr Hume demanded irritably.

'Learned it from his father in Zanzibar. Seems he was a slave owned by an Arab healer o' some sort. Ay, they dinna teach ye that i' the Edinburgh School o' Medicine, though I reckon my grannie mighta seen sense in it.' Andrewes recognized the anger in Dr Hume's eyes, so he added a sweetener. 'We face the same problems, you an' I, Dr Hume. Ye're a medical man, I'm an engineer, yet we're both o' us surrounded wi' superstitions an' habits o' mind that go back centuries.'

Outside the *boma* the men had already started clearing the land for the construction of a new thorn fence to embrace the entire hillock, big enough for them all to camp inside. Andrewes watched them for a while. They worked rapidly, spurred on by the major's repeated reminders that their own safety depended on it being finished by nightfall. He knew what he was doing all right, Andrewes noted approvingly – making good use of the natural contours of the ground, ensuring a clear field of fire in all directions.

As an extra precaution he was planning a network of barbed trip wires outside the fence. Necessary, too.

The surrounding hills were ideal terrain for the enemy. Although some were fairly bare, others were covered with low scrub thick enough to conceal any number of men; to one side, dense forest came within three hundred yards of the *boma*. It must have been these trees which first attracted Tim Wilton to the site. Andrewes was no expert on timber, but they looked ideal for railway use. It was a good spot too in other ways, with a stream nearby and plenty of open land in the valley. First-rate farming country. And to the east the valley widened, offering a panoramic view of rolling countryside reaching to a distant horizon of chubby white clouds.

Andrewes was about to return to Tim Wilton's tent when he glimpsed a movement among the trees – a shadowy form, nothing more.

'Major!' he called, keeping his voice down and flicking the lever of his Winchester to force a cartridge up the spout.

Major Arbuthnot was at his side in an instant, his revolver in his hand. Around him, a chorus of clicks announced that the riflemen were also alert to the danger. Then came a low moaning sound, as of someone in agony.

The men glanced at each other uneasily. Again the sound was heard, but this time it grew to become a loud protesting bellow. Andrewes suddenly realized what it was. Laughing, he relaxed, but most of the men remained on their guard until the cattle began emerging from among the trees.

They came out into the open in a seemingly endless procession, some stopping to graze, only to be butted on by more moving up behind them. To one side, an untidy straggle of goats also arrived from the forest, bleating their objections as one of Captain Burns' men urged them on with a long, slim stick.

'Back to work!' the major roared, his face reddening at the outburst of laughter and chatter from the men. 'Get those men back to work!'

Lt Smythe took up the order and repeated it, making sure it was obeyed.

In the meantime, Captain Burns had arrived from the forest, a twisted smile of triumph on his lined face. 'Came across 'em in a glade not half-an-hour from here,' he reported to the major with a quick nod in Andrewes' direction. 'Obviously hidden there to be out of danger, with four men an' some boys to look after 'em. Taken completely by surprise of course – though they put up quite a fight, I will say that for 'em. We killed three o' the men an' a couple o' lads – pity, that. The rest ran off when they realized they'd no chance. No casualties on our side.'

'Huh,' the major grunted, pleased.

'Brave, though, 'pon my word!' Captain Burns went on. 'Damned if I'd fancy hand-to-hand, not armed as they were, against trained riflemen an' a levy of Maasai *morani*.'

'I reckon,' Andrewes thought aloud, gazing at the cattle. 'we can expect an attack either tonight or early tomorrow. Ye've a grand haul there, an' they'll be comin' to get 'em back.'

'King John's right,' the major agreed, 'so our first task is to get them out of sight. We'll coral the lot inside Wilton's *boma* – less a few we'll slaughter now to feed the men.'

The sun was touching the tops of the trees by the time the new fortification was finished: a squashed egg-shape of thorns following the natural lines of the hillside, completely enclosing Tim Wilton's original, small *boma*. The only entrance faced away from the forest; once the Maasai had driven the cattle inside, the major ordered a tangle of barbed wire to be placed in front of it. Guards were posted to take the first watch while the rest of the men had their meal.

Andrewes went into Tim Wilton's tent, now moved to a fresh position, and found him asleep, feverishly pouring out a stream of anxious talk, mostly impossible to understand. If he died . . . well, Andrewes liked him well enough himself, everyone did, but how could he break the news to

Hester who regarded him – ay, almost like a brother. It would not be easy.

But then would any of them get back alive, he wondered moodily. Who could tell how many were massing in the forest? Leaving the tent, he went to exchange a word or two with the men on watch. It was only a matter of time, he felt. Ay, only a matter of time.

An hour later the moon came up, flooding its pale light over the cleared ground. One man claimed to have observed a couple of rhinos ambling towards the stream, though no-one else had seen them. But, in contrast, the shadows of the scrubland seemed even deeper, and that was where the enemy would assemble. It was impossible to hear anything, either, over the row set up by the cattle in the small *boma*.

Lt Smythe joined him. 'Checking the guards?'

'Ay.'

'Just listen to those cows!' There was an eager laugh in the young man's voice; Andrewes realized he was enjoying the situation, probably looking forward to some action.

'I've no' seen the major a while.'

'Oh, he's eating – a roast steak the size of your hat!' He lowered his voice. 'For a small man he has a giant of an appetite, don't you think? I say, it was your daughter who presented the Cup, wasn't it?'

'Ay – Gaby.'

'Thought so.'

The guard next to them suddenly choked, his breath rasping in his throat as he tried to speak; he staggered and fell, an arrow through his neck.

'Jesus Christ!' Andrewes swore – but it was more prayer than curse. Cautiously he took the man's place and peered out, keeping his head low. 'I canna see a damned thing.'

The open ground in front of him looked totally deserted, almost ghostly in the moonlight. Behind, Lt Smythe was quietly ordering the men to take up their positions, speaking as calmly as if on manoeuvres. The riflemen were stepping up to reinforce those on watch at the fence and the maxim gun, on a raised platform facing the forest, was already manned.

A movement . . .

Very slight, hardly more than a shadow changing shape on the edge of the scrubland a little to his left, but . . . And again. He waited, feeling the coolness of a slight breeze on his cheek, enough to cause the clouds to creep slowly across the sky; in another few minutes they would black out the moon and then the attack would come, no doubt about that. Then – a glint of something metallic, steady enough for him to draw a bead on it and fire. In spite of the cattle, the shot seemed sharp and intrusive against the quiet of night. The glint disappeared.

'If I were you, old man, I'd save your ammunition till you can see 'em,' Captain Burns commented in his ear. 'No point in shootin' at ghosts. You start, an' they'll all do it.'

'Someone's out there,' Andrewes grunted, 'An' not far away either, judgin' by that arrow.'

Before Captain Burns could reply they heard a shout from the far side of the *boma*. Leaving one of the railway *askaris* to take his place, Andrewes hurried across to see what was happening. As the major had pointed out several times already, he was a civilian and had no role to play in this strictly military affair; so be it, he thought, but there was no harm in keeping himself informed. He discovered that two arrows had been fired from the direction of the stream, both apparently aimed at the man on watch, though they missed, landing harmlessly at his feet. The Captain of the Maasai levy confirmed they were Gikuyu. But how many were there? It would need hundreds to surround this new *boma*.

The breeze was colder and the clouds now moved more swiftly over the sky. At the first hint of attack the fires had been doused, but the pungent smell of roast meat still lingered on the air, mingled with the stench of cattle. They dinna stand a chance against guns, Andrewes thought.

The clouds reached the moon, obscuring it. In that same second a swelling wave of yells came from every direction

197

and a shower of arrows descended on them from over the top of the high thorn fence. Andrewes ducked instinctively. Two or three men cried out as the arrows found their mark.

Between salvoes he mounted the parapet. The wispy cloud let some dim light through, sufficient for him to identify the gleam of a greased body. He put a bullet through it and dodged down again as the maxim gun opened up, firing a succession of short, harsh bursts. At its sound the cattle became momentarily quiet. The attack too died down, as though the enemy had given up and gone home, and the faint glimmer of the moonlight yielded to pitch blackness. Yet no one was in any doubt that they were still out there. Waiting.

'It's an attack! We're being attacked! Ali Wadi, get your men organized!' Tim Wilton's voice shrilled hysterically through the air, shouting a string of orders, at times rational at times wild, in a way that must have struck fear into every man who heard it on both sides of the thorn fence. 'Now save your ammunition, save your ammunition, don't shoot until you're absolutely sure . . .'

Andrewes picked his way through the darkness towards the tent, his heart heavy, stumbling over the body of a man lying across his path, passing Dr Hume, who was trying to help another who was not yet quite dead – though no one could survive the poison on those arrows. He found Tim Wilton sitting up on the camp bed, waving his revolver about as he chattered on in that terrible, mad voice, screaming out commands to men who knew they were not to be obeyed. To men who were dead, some of them.

'Mr Wilton,' he said firmly, asserting authority. 'Thank ye, Mr Wilton, but I'm in charge now, so ye can get some rest. D'ye hear me? I've taken over.'

For a short moment it seemed to work. He calmed down, muttering to himself. Then, outside the tent, the bright moon once more lit up the whole scene; there were shouts, scattered rifle fire, the *punch-punch-punch* of the maxim gun . . . Tim Wilton started wildly, and launched into a new series of orders, over and over again, shrieked out unbearably.

Andrewes tried coaxing him to be quiet, fearing the effect his screams would have on the men, on all of them. But with no success. That left him with no alternative. He bunched his fist, drove it hard into Tim Wilton's jaw, and knocked him out. The revolver slipped from his fingers.

'I'm sorry, lad,' Andrewes said, picking it up. He arranged him as best he could to lie comfortably. 'I only hope we can get ye out o' this alive.'

The shooting was now concentrated on the side of the *boma* facing the hill down which they had marched no less than twelve hours earlier. It seemed the main attack was broken. Some thirty or forty warriors could be seen retreating up the slopes and Andrewes counted seventeen lying slumped on the cleared ground, though not all were dead. One rolled about in agony, emitting a steady, horrifying shriek; another crawled a few feet then dropped down again, exhausted; one sat upright on the ground, gripping his shoulder, sobbing out his pain . . .

'Cease fire!' bawled the major. 'Sound the cease fire.'

The bugler tried his best to obey, ludicrously.

*Where does he think he is?* Andrewes brooded gloomily. *Bloody Culloden?*

But something else was happening. On the major's signal the Maasai spearmen slipped out of the *boma*. The larger group headed directly towards the hillside to pursue the retreating Gikuyus. The others inspected the casualties and methodically jabbed their spears into any who were still alive.

'Not a bad start, what?' the major said, reloading his revolver. 'Though I'm glad you did something about Wilton. He was getting on all our nerves. We lost three. The final count on their side'll have to wait till daylight – between twenty and thirty's my guess.'

Andrewes indicated the Maasai's slaughter of the wounded. 'D'ye really think that's necessary?'

'Bloods the young warriors – or *morani*, as I'm told they're called, what? – and that's good for their morale.

But look here, there's no way we could care for wounded prisoners even if we'd a mind to. What we've seen so far is only a skirmish. They'll be back for more, mark my words.'

'We could try to negotiate,' he objected, making no attempt to conceal his revulsion. 'They've seen our strength.'

'You volunteering, what?' the major snorted. 'They'd skin you alive.'

# FIVE

The following morning the clouds had gone and the sky was a clear blue. It had not rained but the grass and scrub on the hills glistened silver with dew and traces of mist lingered among the trees. Andrewes pulled on his boots and went to check up on Tim Wilton, only to find Dr Hume already in the tent.

'Sleepin' like a bairn, though how he can do so amidst all the clatter I dinna ken.'

They went outside in order not to disturb him. The whole camp was in a bustle with rifles being cleaned, a work party strengthening weak patches in the thorn fence, the Major and Captain Burns strutting about barking out orders, the Maasai tending the cattle in the inner *boma* . . .

'When can we move him?' Andrewes demanded.

'Gi' it a few days yet awhile, the longer the better. I imagine ye'll no be wantin' to risk those forest paths till ye can be sure ye'll no' be waylaid.'

'True enough.'

Though he had no wish either to stick around and witness a massacre. But he said nothing. He left Dr Hume to go about his business and decided to take a look at the lay of the ground outside the *boma*. He checked his Winchester just in case and selected two of the railway *askaris*, Shamte and Ali Wadi, to accompany him.

A work party was busy collecting up the dead, firing random shots to scare away the vultures, and carrying the mangled bodies on improvised litters to a spot near the trees where a pit had been dug as a mass grave. Ali Wadi – a Zanzibari who had been on many safaris even before the railway – was amused at this concern. He explained that the Gikuyu never buried their dead but left them out in the forest to be eaten, a story which Andrewes found difficult to accept.

But no one, he noticed, seemed to be going anywhere near the scrub where the previous night he had seen that glint of a spear. Out of curiosity he went over there himself to search among the stunted thorn trees and bushes, not really knowing what he hoped to find.

The two *askaris* spread out, reluctant to follow him into the thickest parts. Then one called a warning, pointing to something gleaming among the bushes – a spear, its blade highly polished and honed. He pushed through the undergrowth towards it, carefully parting the twining branches of shrub in case its owner might be concealed beneath, perhaps wounded. Somewhere to his right a twig snapped.

'Bwana!' Ali Wadi shouted, urgently.

The apparition leaped at him, human in shape but looking like one of the painted devils he had once seen in a cathedral. A mask, his mind told him, urging him to be rational. A short, bright blade flashed towards his neck. He parried with the barrel of his rifle and the creature swung around with a series of high-pitched squeals which turned the blood cold. Andrewes narrowly avoided the sword-point slashing at his belly, and he stumbled. With an unearthly shriek the creature sprang at him, but Ali Wadi brought him down with a blow from the butt of his Snider.

Before Andrewes could prevent it, the *askaris* had hit the man again, this time in the small of his back directly on the spine which cracked under the impact. Even then he did not die immediately; his almost naked body, painted white with weird patterns, writhed on the ground for several seconds before it finally went limp. They turned him over and Andrewes felt sick with shock at the sight of his face. A bullet – *his* bullet – had shattered the man's jaw, probably entering through the cheek and taking most of the teeth with it on the way through. This was what he had thought was a mask, this hideous wound which he had inflicted.

'We leave him here,' Ali Wadi stated, betraying no emotion.

Andrewes hesitated, feeling the warrior ought at least

be buried according to the rites of his own people – whatever they may be. He could not imagine that Ali Wadi was right. He turned to Shamte for his opinion.

'Bwana—,' Shamte began. Then he coughed, his face twisting in surprise, and fell forward with an arrow in his back.

Instantly, Andrewes dropped into cover and cocked his Winchester. Everything on the hillside was quiet. Cautiously he raised his head – no sign of any Gikuyu, but those trees and thickets could conceal an army and no one would be the wiser. On his hands and knees he eased his way towards the wounded Shamte who was lying face down, but still breathing. Ali Wadi joined him.

'We must get him back to the *boma*,' Andrewes decided, 'to let Dr Hume take a peek at him. It's a risk, but what choice do we have? Keep your eyes open, will ye? An' shoot if ye see anythin'.'

He managed to get Shamte on to his back and started to crawl through the thick undergrowth along one of the numerous animal tracks. It was a slow, uncomfortable business but at last he reached the edge of the scrub, with the *boma* only a few hundred yards away down the slope. Ali Wadi was immediately behind him.

'We'll have to make a dash for it, so if ye're ready . . .?'

'Ready, Bwana.'

As he got unsteadily to his feet he could feel the man on his back slipping as he slumped into unconsciousness – only the Almighty knew why he had to choose that moment. He hauled him up again, half-turning to see what Ali Wadi was doing.

The *askari* had raised his rifle and was taking careful aim. 'By that high tree,' he muttered.

High up the hillside a Gikuyu stood in full view, staring across at the thick tentacle of forest on their right. Until that moment he had not noticed them; then, a second before Ali Wadi fired, he glanced around and dodged back behind the tree.

'Run!' Andrewes yelled.

Hampered by the dead-weight of Shamte on his back,

he lumbered across the open ground towards the *boma*. He heard the click of the bolt as Ali Wadi, keeping pace behind him, reloaded. That shot must have missed – he *hoped* it had missed, as he was convinced it had been Kamau up there by the tree. A long way off, and dressed Gikuyu style rather than in his usual *kanzu*, but it could only have been Kamau – that sudden turn of the head, the way he moved when he dodged back . . .

Captain Burns and four men ran out towards them, probably alerted by the shot. 'Andrewes, this man's dead!' he exclaimed when they met. 'Two arrows in his back and look at his eyes.'

'Two?'

Shamte's body sagged heavily as he lowered it to the ground and saw that a second arrow had penetrated just below the left shoulder blade.

'Bwana, Shamte save your life,' Ali Wadi insisted.

It was almost a reproach and he was about to reply when they heard a low moaning noise from the hills, taken up right away in the scrubland behind them, and repeated once again in the forest to their right. It was an eerie, flesh-creeping sound like Scottish wind in broken chimneys, or the opening of old graves.

'War horns!' Captain Burns identified it briskly. 'Right, you first, Andrewes, with your askari – back to the boma. Smartly now! We'll follow behind, give you cover. Sooner we're all in there, the better. No sense meeting 'em outside while we've guns to do the job for us.'

As they started their dash for the *boma* the first line of warriors was already emerging from the scrubland, a frightening sight with their painted bodies and feathered head-gear, and more were coming out of the forest. The riflemen, well spaced out, went down on one knee to take aim. 'Fire!' came Captain Burns' voice, steady and businesslike. The volley was ragged but probably effective enough as a warning to the Gikuyus to keep their distance.

'Reload!' His orders seemed to float on the listless air, bodilessly. 'Take aim . . . steady now . . . *Fire!*'

Andrewes reached the thorn fence, with Ali Wadi close

behind him, as the second volley rang out. Glancing back, he saw the riflemen retreat a hundred yards or so, reloading as they ran, then turn to take aim for a third time. There was the sound of firing and yelling voices from elsewhere, too, perhaps on the far side of the *boma*. Captain Burns gesticulated to him to get a move on. Ay, this is no job for a railwayman, he thought as he ran around the outside of the *boma* towards the entrance, only to find it under direct attack.

Lt Smythe had been driven back towards the thorn fence by a sizeable party of Gikuyus. Three of his own men lay dead; the others were using their single-shot guns as clubs, having no time to reload. Hopelessly outnumbered, he was trying to hold the attackers off with revolver fire when a spear caught his right shoulder. The warrior who had thrown it immediately charged forward, a wide grin of triumph on his face, but a bullet from Andrewes' Winchester stopped him. Two more took his place, slashing at the young lieutenant with their short swords; he let out a long, agonizing scream as their blades twisted into his intestines.

Andrewes killed both of them, firing rapidly, but the enemy threw more and more men into the assault regardless of casualties. Then the magazine was empty; the gun clicked uselessly. He fumbled for more cartridges, but it was too late. Four Gikuyus surrounded him, taunting him with their shining blades, and he suddenly realized, bitterly, that he was not going to get out of this one. But he would make it quick . . . ay, they'd no' play wi' him . . .

Reversing the rifle, he gripped the hot barrel and charged into them, laying about him left and right like one of his Scottish ancestors – ay, an' yellin' murder at them . . . Two went down as the rifle butt smashed their skulls; a third attempted to fight back, a wee man an' no' up to it – the gun broke his arm, leaving him dazed but still on his feet. Andrewes grabbed the sword out of his hand, then shoved him forward on to the spear point of one of his comrades coming up behind.

He was fighting mad and never knew how many he

killed. The short sword in his right hand dripped with blood; so too did the spear in his left. And still they came on – until, quite unexpectedly, he stood alone. The sun dazzled his eyes but he was aware of several Gikuyu warriors lying dead around him, and of others moaning or screaming on the ground, blinded, or with gaping wounds in their bellies, their guts hanging out – had he done all that? He wanted to vomit, yet nothing came.

Then someone was at his shoulder. He swung around, his nerves taut, but it was Ali Wadi – also covered with blood – trying to tell him something.

Captain Burns was shouting too, though he could not see him. 'Get into the boma, man! King John, get back into the boma!'

Two other railway *askaris* came hurrying towards him, picking their way between the bodies, wanting to grasp his arms and lead him towards the entrance, which was now clear. Retrieving his Winchester from the ground he went with them. In the hills round about the war horns were sounding yet again and another wave of Gikuyus was charging down to attack – to die. The guns were firing steadily, one volley after another, with Major Arbuthnot yelling out his orders.

'Reload . . . take aim . . fire!'

And between each crash of the Martini-Henry rifles came the insistent reminder of the maxim gun.

'Well done, man!' Captain Burns greeted him. 'Now Dr Hume's taken over your tent as a casualty centre, so you'd best report to him right away. Two of you men, help King John over there.'

'I dinna need a doctor.'

'Suit yourself. I've better things to do than argue.'

The air was acrid with gunsmoke, stinging the lungs with every breath, while overhead the vultures circled. From outside came more of those blood-curdling war-screams as the Gikuyus attacked yet again, only to be repulsed by the riflemen remorselessly firing round after round. Andrewes reached for more cartridges but his pocket had been ripped away; for the first time he noticed his clothes were in tatters and sticky with blood. But the Winchester too was now useless, its lever bent and twisted. He threw it aside. Several of the cuts on his body were starting to throb; suddenly he felt very tired – and disgusted, too, at all the carnage. Each crash of gunfire murdered more men. It was a massacre, nothing less, even though the dead had attacked first.

At the fence a rifleman let out a surprised, frightened whimper and fell back with a spear through his neck.

'Ali Wadi – get him to the medical tent! Quick now!' He tugged the blade out. It had missed the artery and the bleeding was slow; there might be a chance of saving him. 'Carry him carefully now!'

Picking up the fallen rifle, he took the man's place on the parapet; in spite of his revulsion he knew they must not let the *boma* be overrun. That was the irony of it. The sight of the men lying dead or injured on the cleared ground beyond the fence was heart-rending. But by now the guns had done their work and the enemy – those who could still move – were in full retreat.

Behind him, the bugler sounded the cease fire. Then the gate was opened and a stream of Maasai warriors poured out, their faces and bodies stained with red ochre, their spears glistening in the sunlight, their long oval shields and feathered head-dresses giving the whole scene an air of pageant. The next stage of the slaughter was about to begin.

Andrewes rested his lacerated arms on the thorns, almost welcoming the pain as they pierced his skin, those long, thin needles. It was more than twenty four hours now since he had walked along that forest path and fired a random shot at a movement among the trees. That man had been the first he had ever killed and he had thought little of it at the time, perhaps shocked by the cruelty of those pit-traps, perhaps imagining himself to be tougher than he really was.

But since then, how many . . .?

Major Arbuthnot came up to congratulate him on his

fight outside the *boma*. Andrewes listened, nodded, and felt nothing but regret and nausea.

Kamau too was bitter. Many times during their long discussions he had warned the village elders, members of the *kiama*, against encouraging any attack on the red strangers until Muthoga had openly accused him of cowardice. But then Muthoga was safe in the privilege of old age.

In reply, Kamau had reminded them yet again of the prophecy, but they had scoffed at the advice; some even claimed it was not to be understood in that way. Patiently, he had then described the killing power of the rifle, and how a hundred Maasai had once died at the hands of a single red stranger between sunrise and midday. Muthoga countered this with the story of how he also had once seen a rifle in action. When he was a young man, he said, a red stranger had come to a village he was visiting and asked a warrior to set up his shield beneath a tree; then he had used his rifle to make fire and destroyed the shield completely. This he intended as a lesson to demonstrate how hopeless it would be to fight against him. But he reckoned without the medicine man of that place who had very special powers: first he caused the stranger to pack up and leave the ridge unexpectedly, in order that no blame should fall on them; then, within a week, to fall sick and die. Hearing this, the elders decided that provided the warriors were true to the traditions of the Gikuyu nation and did nothing to offend Ngai, victory must surely be theirs.

Even the doubters became convinced of the need for action when they heard about the latest red stranger to arrive in their land. This man had not come to trade for food or ivory. He had built his *boma* on Gikuyu land where cattle usually grazed. What was worse, he had been seen – a tall young man with hair the colour of the sun – supervising the cutting down of trees from the forest.

Word went out to even the most distant ridges of miles around that the time had come to expel the strangers. The warrior councils met and the *athigani* who had the duty of spying on the enemy came to report all they had observed. It was the general view that Kamau should teach the warriors about the sticks-that-make-fire. As Magana, the leader of the *athigani*, said, 'The warrior who knows the thoughts of his enemy has already won the battle.'

Kamau's young son, Ngengi – growing every day, taking after his grandfather, old Ngengi – was present when the message was brought. 'Baba, are you going to show—?'

Kamau had stopped him harshly. 'These are matters for men, not boys!'

Tears of frustration appeared in Ngengi's eyes but what else, thought Kamau, could he have done? His own gun must remain buried beneath the floor of his hut until the right time came; no-one else must know the secret of its existence.

'I shall tell them what I can,' he informed the messenger simply, 'and also how to fight men with these sticks-that-make-fire, perhaps even how to defeat them – but will they hear my words?'

All over the ridge the warriors were gathering together in groups, polishing their spears, sharpening their swords, making sure they had sufficient arrows for their bows. Using the bow as an example, Kamau tried to explain how a rifle worked, emphasizing how useless it was once all its cartridges had been fired. Therefore the best tactic was to lead the red strangers to believe they were being heavily attacked, while keeping the main force back until they were running short of ammunition. But this suggestion caused a great deal of argument.

'If our warriors are to skulk in the long grass until the red strangers are tired,' one man demanded, 'is this not the way of cowards?'

'A man can prove his courage a thousand ways,' Kamau said patiently. 'Faced with guns he can only die.'

Early the next day they heard that a party of warriors from the forest had attacked the *boma* – thirty men in all, of whom only ten returned. Moreover, the *boma* was still intact. He spoke to the council of warriors.

'Now the red strangers will send more men with guns. As a punishment, they will kill our warriors, steal our cattle and burn our homes. There are two courses open to us.' He paused, and they waited expectantly for him to continue. 'Either we go to them with gifts and ask for peace—'

'More cowardice!' One warrior declared, his eyes flashing angrily.

'—or we attack in the way I say,' he continued, ignoring the interruption, 'and when we have won our victory, we then invite the red strangers to talk peace, as one great nation to another.'

'How?' the same man demanded. 'They will all be dead.'

'More will come.'

After much discussion it was agreed to consult the medicine man and that Kamau was to accompany them. The medicine man specializing in military questions, heavy-faced and authoritative, gave the impression that he had been expecting them and knew what they were about to say. He accepted his fee of skins and a large portion of soda with scarcely a glance and listened as they stated their business, then he spread out his oxhide, took his divining gourd and cast the pebbles which were then counted into separate piles. Considering the piles carefully, and taking his time over it, he began to interpret their meaning. Some of the 'pebbles' were unblemished white stones of limpid purity, but with them were a lion's claw, beads, a spent cartridge case, arrow heads, cowrie shells, some human finger bones and pieces of metal. At first it seemed that the pebbles were against attacking the red strangers, but as he continued the message became clearer: there would be many difficulties but at last victory would be theirs. However, it was clearly indicated that Kamau must be appointed leader over all the warriors.

The members of the warrior council withdrew to cut twigs from various plants, each to represent its own special meaning relating to the coming battle. They took these now to the medicine man, spat on them, and asked him to choose which one represented an accurate forecast of what would happen. He listened to each in turn, holding it up to his ear, and in the end kept two which he handed back to them. The warriors nodded to each other, satisfied. The twigs foretold the same outcome as the pebbles. All was well.

Kamau met the councils of warriors from the other ridges, explaining his plan of attack, cajoling, training his troops as best he could. This was no sophisticated army of the type he had known on the coast during M'baruk bin Rashed's rebellion against the Sultan of Zanzibar, even taking on the British themselves. These warriors were accustomed only to small-scale cattle raiding, not set battles. But they were certainly brave enough, and he intended to reinforce their daring by having their shields annointed with *uumu* medicine made from a creeper bark known to be particularly effective.

Before he was ready, more red strangers arrived at the *boma*. He watched from a tree on the edge of the forest as the two columns marched down the hillside. The presence of Maasai among them was a sad sight. Was he not half-Maasai himself? Had he not taken refuge in a Maasai *manyatta* during his flight from Tsavo and remained there until his wounds had healed? He had warned then of how the red strangers would dominate the land unless all nations, clans and villages together rejected them with one voice, but they had listened without hearing.

The danger lay not only in the power of guns. He had seen how the strangers built their railway, bridged rivers, sent messages along metal wires, brought back the sick from the threshold of death, and even cut a man open to repair him inside, like a machine. They walked confidently across the country and claimed it as theirs; to expel them, such skills must first be mastered. On this matter he wished all Maasai, Gikuyu, Wakamba, and all nations could have heard the words of his father, old Ngengi, who knew the red strangers better than anyone.

'Never attack them, but always resist,' he once said. 'Learn everything, but reveal nothing. Know them better than they know you. Keep your mind open and your mouth closed.Co-operate whenever necessary – but for your own advantage, not theirs. While your strength is growing, allow them to think you a fool; the right day to show them otherwise will come in its own time.'

But the warriors had elected to fight, which left him no choice. His plans were carefully drawn up. They were to gather discreetly in the hilltops and forests surrounding the valley, taking care not to be seen. On his signal, the first group was to move forward and attack with poisoned arrows, while protected by warriors with specially-strengthened shields. Having drawn the enemy's fire, they would immediately fall back and the manoeuvre would be repeated by other groups approaching from different sides. The *boma* defenders would be constantly harried, never knowing where to expect the next onslaught, and forced to use up precious ammunition. When the time was ripe he would signal for the attack to be intensified from one direction, while simultaneously a reserve party of the toughest warriors would raid the *boma* entrance in an attempt to break through.

It went wrong from the very start. Perhaps he had expected too much from these fierce warriors.

The previous night, warriors from one of the other ridges had launched an independent raid. As the main party took up their positions in the cold light of dawn they could see the bodies scattered across the open ground. It was the worst possible omen. On his signal, the first group attacked as agreed, but instead of drawing the red strangers' fire from a safe distance, they charged into the hail of bullets, proving their manhood and dying in the same instant. The reserve party crept unnoticed towards the *boma* entrance, but had not waited. They had come up against King John and not one survived.

Bitterly he realized that had he merely selected men of his own and neighbouring ridges instead of attempting to co-ordinate this vast army, the death toll would never have been so great, nor the defeat so total. And if he had not broken cover to check whether the last group was already in position for the attack, he would never have been spotted by King John – the last man he had expected ever to see again. Well, King John owed him a life.

Sick at heart, Kamau observed most of the battle from his vantage point on the hillside until at last pride sent him too down into the valley, panga in hand, to seek death where the fighting was fiercest. He could never return to the ridge now. He cut his way into the middle of the advancing Maasai reinforcements, killing relentlessly, desperately yearning for the spear jab which would end it all. But these *morani* were too inexperienced to counter his onslaught; one after the next they went down before him.

At length he found himself isolated from the main fight – all that remained of it – in single combat against a tall young Maasai who was considerably more skilled than the others; every blow was met by that long Maasai shield; several times he was grazed by the blood-stained blade of that spear.

He tried to edge the young *moran* around to a position where the sun would be directly in his eyes, but he was ready for every trick and gradually Kamau felt himself being pushed nearer to the long narrow tongue of forest which reached down into the valley. His foot stumbled over some unevenness on the ground, a root perhaps, and in a flash that Maasai spear was thrust at his chest.

The point scratched against his ribs as he dropped down flat to avoid it, rolling over swiftly and slashing at the Maasai's legs with his short sword. The Maasai staggered back, blood streaming from him, then tried to recover by plunging the spear sharply down at Kamau, who again rolled over, escaping death by a miracle, and simultaneously jabbed upwards under the shield and into the young man's belly.

The blood spilled over him, blinding his eyes, choking his mouth and nostrils. Kamau spat it out and got to his feet. One glance showed him that the slaughter around the *boma* was practically over. Most of his own force lay dead on the ground with vultures settling hungrily on the bodies; a few remnants here and there could be seen fleeing into the hills.

And he was still alive, his whole world soured, arid, as if life itself was to be his punishment. He plucked some leaves from the nearest tree and tried to clean the blood from his face and arms, still in full view of the *boma*, not deigning to hide; then he wiped his panga and slipped it back into its sheath before retrieving the dead *moran*'s spear and taking refuge in the forest.

# SIX

Several days passed before it was judged safe for Andrewes to take Tim Wilton back to Nairobi. Before they left, a relief force of riflemen arrived with fresh ammunition and medical supplies. With them was a youngish civilian who introduced himself as Jeremy Smith, newly-appointed political officer for the district, a man of slight build, balding, and wearing spectacles which gave him a donnish appearance. His quiet but insistent manner of speaking reinforced this impression; within an hour of setting foot inside the *boma* he was expounding his view of how the situation ought to be resolved.

'Mr Smith, these people have just mounted a full-sacle attack on my camp, what?' the major barked at him, bristling. 'It's my duty to see that they're punished first, before we talk of political settlement.'

'Ye dinna reckon they've been through enough?' Andrewes protested. 'I'm no' squeamish but think how many died, man!'

The major dismissed the argument. 'With these fresh supplies we can now drive the lesson home on their own doorsteps – destroy their crops, burn their huts . . . Firmness, Mr Smith, what? Make the country safe for anyone to move about in.'

'That's something we'll only achieve with their agreement,' the new political officer argued.

'Exactly! And I intend to make sure they *do* agree.'

The first patrols were receiving their orders as Andrewes and his party left at dawn the following morning. He was glad he would not be around to see the result of the major's 'massive retaliation' policy. The killings – and the memory of his own part in them – disgusted him, although at least all that had been done in self-defence. They filed out of the *boma, askaris* first, followed by the porters carrying Tim

215

Wilton lying on the roughly-made litter they had knocked together. His face twisted with pain at each jolt.

'When ye feel ye need a rest, dinna hesitate to say,' Andrewes attempted to reassure him, though he knew full well they dare not risk stopping too often, not until they had reached a suitable spot where they could safely camp for the night.

Dr Hume had supplied a small stock of laudanum to help him on the journey if the pain became unbearable. 'I'd be happier if ye didna hae to move him at all, though ye're right he'll get better attention in Nairobi,' he had added. 'An' watch out that Swahili doesna pu' more o' his muck on the wounds.'

It was a slow tedious trek, though at least they managed to avoid the pit-traps in the forest, and there were no ambushes. Tim Wilton became weaker with each day's travel, hardly talking at all and at times not even conscious. At last, a week after leaving the *boma*, Andrewes saw the welcome sight of rusting rooftops on the horizon: Nairobi. Leaving Ali Wadi in charge, he pushed on ahead in order to warn Dr Carson to be ready for the patient, though he feared it might already be too late to save him.

Over the plain he saw many more tents than usual, but then new arrivals were always better advised to camp out in the open rather than risk the beds of Nairobi's one fly-ridden hotel. But as he approached, he spotted Gaby playing near one of them. Her long auburn hair was unmistakable. 'Gaby!' he waved. 'Hey, Gaby!'

Hearing his voice, she turned – unsure – but in the same instant Hester emerged from the tent and began to run eagerly towards him. He hurried on to meet her, clasping her at last in his arms, holding her tight, kissing her upturned face which was wet with tears.

'All right, lass, all right,' he conforted her, guessing she had probably heard news of the attack and been desperately worried. It can't have been easy for her. 'I'm back, as ye see. It's poor Mr Wilton we must take care of now. He's in a bad way.'

'But he's still alive?' she demanded anxiously.

'Ay.'

'Oh, thank God! Oh, John, I was so afraid!'

Her face was unnaturally pale and drawn, as though she had not been sleeping too well.

'Ye've no' been sick?' Those heavy shadows around her eyes made him feel uneasy. 'Why are ye all livin' in tents out here? What's gone wrong?'

'John . . . the tents . . . oh, they're . . . Dr Carson thought it was healthier . . . but John . . .' She looked at him pleadingly. 'I've had a letter from Liverpool. My father's died.'

'Och, my love!' He put his arms around her again, tenderly. 'My poor wee Hester – an' I had to be away when ye received that news! My love, I'm sorry.'

She clung to him, sobbing, her face against his chest, and he stood there solidly, the midday sun hot on his face, unable to find any words to help her.

'Nay, lass . . . Dinna weep so sore.'

'It was a heart attack. My sister wrote.' She broke away from him, trying to control herself. 'I'm sorry . . . I . . .'

Gaby had staggered after her mother with a baby gazelle in her arms, stopping every yard or two to talk to it. At last she reached them and held it up for him to see. 'Her name's Daisy and she's mine!' she announced importantly.

'Ay, she's a bonny wee thing,' he agreed gravely.

Hester wiped her eyes and blew her nose. 'Dr Carson gave it to her yesterday.'

'Mama's always crying,' Gaby observed critically. 'I'm not going to cry when I grow up. D'you like Daisy?'

'Ay.' He looked back, shading his eyes, to check how far the porters had got with the litter, but they were still some distance away. 'They canna move Mr Wilton too quickly for fear o' causin' him more pain. We'll need to prepare a tent an' . . .'

'It's prepared, John,' she stopped him gently, a hand on his arm. 'Oh, I'm sorry to receive you home like this, crying like a girl. The runner came two days ago with the news. We've put up a tent next to ours, and I've sent someone for Dr Carson.'

'Ye're no' countin' on nursin' him yesel', are ye?' Anxiously, fearing something he could not define.

'Who else? With the epidemic in Nairobi, Dr Carson hasn't enough staff as it is.'

'What epidemic?'

'You'd best speak to him yourself.' She glanced a warning in Gaby's direction. 'Almost everyone's moved out in the last few days.'

'Daisy's all right!' Gaby informed him importantly. The baby gazelle nuzzled up against her neck. 'She's my very own and I'm going to look after her.'

'Don't ye think ye should put her down awhile?'

'No.' The answer was blunt.

He turned back to Hester, troubled. 'I'm thinkin' o' the bairn – though I canna forbid ye.'

'That's right – *ye canna!*' She smiled at him fondly, half-mocking. Then her eyes clouded again. 'I'll be looking after him here, not in Nairobi, so there'll be no danger for the baby,' she tried to reassure him. 'John, if I'd been home in Liverpool to nurse my father, maybe he'd still be—' She broke down.

'Nay, lass, dinna take on now. These things happen.'

Hester watched apprehensively as Dr Carson cut through the bandages on Tim Wilton's injured leg and dropped them into the bucket. Beads of sweat gathered on his brow as he worked; she wiped them away with a handkerchief and cleaned his glasses, which had misted up. Then she took a damp towel and gently washed the patient's face and neck. He lay with his eyes open, staring up into the tent and sometimes chattering to himself, the same incomprehensible words over and over again, probably not realizing where he was, nor that she was there with him. She almost cried out when she saw the torn, jagged wounds.

'This gash here . . .' Dr Carson shook his head as he examined it. 'Lucky it didn't sever an artery. Very lucky. He's lost a lot o' blood as it is, and I don't want to remove the splints if the bone's—'

The splints – two spear-shafts held in place by twisted strips of blood-stained linen – allowed access for his chubby fingers to move over the bone, probing. Those cruel cuts, she thought, shivering with fear – as though they had been trying to hack his leg off!

'I might try to do something about that.' The doctor straightened up. 'But we'll have his clothes off first an' take a look at the rest o' the body. You're pale, Mrs Andrewes – are you all right?'

'Of course!' she lied. 'It was the thought of the . . . fighting . . . and how they . . .' She stopped.

'Looks like King John's picked up a few scratches too,' he grunted, opening the shirt and beginning to cut it away. 'Look, Mrs Andrewes, I'll call one o' the boys to help. You stay outside with young Michael an' Gaby.'

'A boy would be too rough.' Deliberately, she took the scissors out of his hand and set to work, changing the subject. 'What's happening in Nairobi? You're sure it's plague?'

'No doubt about it at all. Another death this morning, all the recognizable symptoms. And more have reported sick, but I'm certain there are others. Quite certain. They'll die off like flies, I'm afraid, till the epidemic reaches its peak, then eventually the numbers'll begin to fall, usual pattern. So you keep clear, Mrs Andrewes. You're better off out here.'

Tim Wilton's whole body was a mass of bruises and cuts, some frighteningly deep. Pressing her lips together, determined not to show her feelings, she cleaned the wounds as gently as she could; every moan from him went through her like a barbed knife. Across his right hip was one particularly long panga slash, and over his ribs . . . Yet in parts his skin seemed so white and pure. A light down of blond hair spread from his chest, thinning out over his abdomen.

He became delirious again. *Coming this way . . . must be twenty at least . . . how much ammunition . . . no, not enough . . . not enough to last . . .*

She took his head in her arms, pressing it soothingly

against her, whispering that the danger had past, it was all over, he was safe now, nothing more to worry about; and gradually he calmed down again, gripping her hand, until at last his eyes closed and he fell into an uneasy sleep.

Dr Carson had worked on stolidly, glancing at her curiously from time to time but saying nothing. He stitched up the worst of the cuts, having bathed them with iodoform, then applied the dressings. 'That mumbo-jumbo muck on his hands doesn't seem to have harmed him, which is something to be thankful for. All I can prescribe now is rest an' good nursing, though I'm sure he'll get plenty o' that.' He began to wash his surgical instruments before returning them to his bag. 'I'll drop by later to see how he's getting on.'

For the next two days there was no change. At times he lay quietly with his eyes wide open, yet unaware of anything going on around him; at others he talked to himself, confused, elided words. As she sat with him odd lines from a poem went through her mind, a Tennyson they had read together recently, 'Ring out the grief that saps the mind . . . Ring out the darkness of the land . . .' His gun-bearer, Sharma, shared the vigil with her, but she liked to stay with him herself when she could, holding Michael on her lap until he started to cry, when she had to take him out. Gaby often wandered in, usually with the gazelle in her arms. Once she startled Hester with, 'Is he dead?'

'No, of course not!' Hester reassured her, afraid.

'I'm glad,' she said, and marched out of the tent.

But he was so still, he might easily pass on without her noticing; to make quite certain she felt for his pulse, that throb beneath her fingertips. Was this how her father had gone? The letter had contained so few details, 'Collapsed in the pulpit . . . two deacons carried him into the vestry . . . a doctor called but Father was already with God.' Thinking about it, she bent over impulsively and kissed Tim on the forehead. For a moment his eyes flickered as though he understood – how could he understand? Or John who was so busy in Nairobi, taking the decisions while the Comptroller was away in Mombasa?

During her disturbed sleep one night she dreamed she was helping Dr Carson wash her father's body and was puzzled that he no longer had the dark hair and beard she remembered; instead, his hair was blond, his flesh strangely lacerated. As they uncovered him, the whiteness of his sex surprised her – yet this was her *father*, her conscience screamed, she should not be there with the doctor . . . The image had returned again and again until she woke up, confused, with so many feelings fighting to take her over.

Andrewes was only half-listening to Dr Carson's discourse on the plague as they stood in the emergency medical centre – one of the godowns which had been cleared of crates to make room. On the table before them lay the naked corpse of an Indian coolie, recently dead, and the doctor pointed to the swellings on his groin. *Buboes* he named them, puffing out clouds of smoke from his pipe to help disguise the smell of death.

'Bubonic plague, or the Black Death, as they used to call it,' he went on, leading the way to an adjoining trestle table where a female corpse was displayed, her thin legs apart, no doubt for the purpose of examination; her skinny breasts sagged against her furrowed rib-cage, motionless; her mouth open, blackening. 'This woman's from the same household – his wife, I imagine. The same symptoms: high fever, vomiting, giddiness, delirium, fur on the tongue, an' again these very painful swellings on the groin here.'

'Ay,' Andrewes nodded, nauseated.

'She was no beauty even while she was still alive,' Dr Carson observed.

'No more are ye.' He felt his stomach shift uneasily. 'But she's humankind when all's said an' done, so if ye canna bury her straight away, ye might at least cover her up.'

'I was about to start some work on her.' Huffily he indicated a bench on which he had set out a microscope and several glass slides. 'As yet, we've no satisfactory

221

method o' treatment. No vaccine, nothing, only the body's own resistance – where it exists, an' providing the disease hasn't reached the lungs.'

'Ay, very interestin' but dinna expect to impress me. One doctor against an epidemic – ye've no chance, man!'

The air was alive with insects attracted by the stench of decomposition. A fly explored the dead woman's blackening tongue; ants walked over her sunken eyes. Death had dogged him persistently, he realized gloomily. Those slaughtered warriors outside the *boma*, sacrificing themselves in a futile attempt to prove – what? That they knew how to die, but not to live? Then the news of Hester's father, and it was only a matter of time before Tim Wilton went. Now the coolies and their people . . .

'My research may be on a small scale, but that's no reason to scorn it, King John, none at all,' Dr Carson was saying as he refilled his pipe, his fat fingers stuffing the shredded tobacco into the bowl. 'Since Major Ross's success last year in identifying the mosquito as the carrier of malaria I think every doctor has been wondering if he does enough.'

'I've a wife an' bairns out there,' Andrewes reminded him impatiently, 'an' I say this epidemic must be stopped.'

'Tell me how.' He lit the pipe.

'Every bairn in school knows how!' Andrewes scoffed. 'Ye've ne'er heard o' the Great Fire o' London?'

'Burn Nairobi?'

'Ay. To the ground.'

'Railway property. And private. I'd not like to take that responsibility,' he said doubtfully.

'Then I shall.'

Once he had taken the decision Andrewes briskly set about arranging the details, issuing orders that everyone was to be out of Nairobi within six hours and riding over to discuss the operation with the commanding officer, King's African rifles, who agreed to reinforce the railway *askaris* in supervising the evacuation. Special squads of coolies removed the more valuable equipment from the workshops, though most crates of supplies were left behind to burn, including everything originating in Bombay. No-one could be certain how the disease spread – by insects, rats, or even in the air – but the evidence pointed to some connection with ports and ships. Drums of kerosene were placed in all major buildings and at strategic points throughout the bazaar. It was heart-rending clearing the Indians out, but no one doubted that the bazaar was the real seat of the epidemic. Finally, dynamite charges were laid to destroy the more solidly-built walls, which might act as fire breaks.

When all the preparations had been made and the soldiers were shepherding the few remaining people out of the township, Andrewes sat down to compose his lengthy message of explanation to Carpenter down in Mombasa. He worded it carefully, a formal request for permission to do what he intended to do anyway, and transmitted it himself. Carpenter would refuse, of course, he knew that even as he tapped the words out – but then he had not lived through that slaughter at the *boma*. If this prevented more deaths, Andrewes thought grimly, to hell with the cost.

While waiting for the reply he went over to the small, tin-roofed shack which Hester had made into their first real home. Their few bits of furniture had already gone, and her curtains, but the sight of her carefully-tended vegetable garden saddened him. She had the touch, no doubt about that, and things grew well in this climate; perhaps they could make a go of a farm, he could build her a proper house and . . . Ay, dreams . . . nothing more . . . And he was an engineer, not a farmer.

He gathered in the remaining sprouts, no point in wasting them, almost filling a whole box which he gave to one of the railway *askaris* to take out to her. Then he returned to the telegraph office where the bell was ringing persistently. He acknowledged, and immediately the message began to come through. Not the awaited answer, though.

'THE SAD NEWS HAS JUST BEEN RECEIVED FROM LONDON THAT HER MAJESTY QUEEN

VICTORIA PASSED AWAY YESTERDAY JANUARY TWENTY-SECOND AND . . .'

'Ay,' Andrewes muttered sarcastically, 'no doubt that's all very tragic, but meanwhile the lives o' some o' her subjects concern me more right now. Why's there no answer yet?'

He tapped out an impatient reminder, only to be informed that he was not to proceed until the full implications of his request had been studied. It reminded him only too well of the day Carpenter had refused to believe the true facts about the drought.

Outside, the men were opening the kerosene drums, drenching the woodwork and anything else that would burn. He ordered the first match to be struck.

The fire ran joyously along the walls of the two-storey shack known as Woods Hotel, then surged upwards to engulf the entire structure as if it had long been waiting for this day of release. He felt the heat wrapping itself around him as the flames spread to other buildings too, with separate blazes starting up in the bazaar quarter. Nairobi was purging itself – of the plague . . . of all slaughter . . .

He withdrew to the safety of the plain, where settlers and young officers were gathered, ready to shoot down any rats or other game which tried to escape the fire. Great dark clouds of smoke billowed over the burning township, while on the far side towards the swamp thousands of Indians had assembled with their belongings, dismayed at the loss of their homes, no doubt questioning if it was worth their while starting over again.

Andrewes became aware that Jimmy Hathaway had joined him, his lean face gleaming almost wickedly with enjoyment as the wind veered round and everyone fell back to avoid the fierce heat. 'Not every day we get to see a good fire!' he exclaimed, strutting about in his enthusiasm. 'Like November the fifth, or better! Back in Manchester, they'd steal your back door bonfire night if you didn't watch out. Know that?'

'Ay, ye told me before.'

'By gum, what's that?' He stopped and pointed. His

voice dropped in fear and awe. 'Oh, God! Oh, the poor thing!'

'Where, man?' Andrewes snapped impatiently. 'Is someone still—?'

'Between those building towards the station.'

Then he saw it. A rhino was charging about helplessly between the burning buildings, unable to find a way through. His first reaction was relief that it was not one of the men or a child, but as he watched the crazed animal crashing into a burning wall which collapsed under the impact, then retreating from it, he knew something had to be done. One of the officers had also spotted it, but Andrewes waved him back. It was his fire, his duty . . . His expiation.

As he ran back towards the township the heat became more intense. With the lack of rain everything was bone-dry and the fire had only to lick a wall for the flames to take hold. He reached the main road but now there was no trace of the rhino.

On both sides the buildings were burning fiercely. He took a few steps towards the station. A wall crashed down behind him, scattering flames where he had been standing only a second earlier.

'John Philip Andrewes, ye're an idiot!' he announced to the general inferno around him, though he felt oddly at peace in the midst of it, as if it no longer mattered whether he lived or died, not after what had happened at the *boma*. But then he knew it did matter. 'Now will ye get yeself out o' this before ye make Hester a widow!'

The rhino stood in front of him. Where it had come from he had no idea – from one of the burned out buildings perhaps, still as hot as furnaces – but it blocked his way, quivering, its skin singed, its jaws open, bellowing in distress.

Andrewes remained stock-still, fearing it would charge if he made any attempt to retreat. His new bolt-action Mannlicher, bought off Dr Carson only the day before, felt unfamiliar in his hands and he regretted not having the Winchester; though for rhino most hunting experts – the territory crawled with them – would have recommended something heavier. There was no way of escape either. The flames swirled around hungrily on every side, billowing out with each gust of the breeze; the smoke stung his eyes, stabbing into his chest each time he drew breath. One step nearer the buildings and his clothes, already unnaturally hot against his skin, would begin to char.

Slowly he raised the Mannlicher, praying it was as good a weapon as Carson had boasted. With that thick hide, a shot through the brain was his only chance.

'An' to think I came here to save *ye* pain an' sufferin',' he said to the rhino, taking careful aim at its right eye. 'Now it's touch an' go which of us gets out alive, so stand still a wee while, beastie.'

It came lumbering towards him as he squeezed the trigger. The shot stopped it for a moment and Andrewes backed away, cursing at his own clumsiness with the unfamiliar rifle as he fumbled at the bolt to get another round into the breech. He longed now to make a dash for safety but he found himself cornered with no room for manoeuvre among the fiercely-burning debris.

'Ay, lass!' he sighed regretfully by way of an apology to Hester as the rhino came straight at him. An apology she would never hear.

He fired, then immediately pulled back the bolt and slammed it home again with the next round.

The rhino was weaving about unsteadily, again checked by his shot, but not for long. Suddenly it charged, panic-stricken, forcing him to dive out of the way as it thundered blindly past him into the heart of the fire. Piteously it turned, roaring in agony, to make one last uncontrolled attempt to escape, but the flames had now taken over and the smell of its burning flesh reached Andrewes' nostrils as he raised the rifle for the last time, emptying the magazine at it. The rhino died hard, sinking down to the ground with a terrible slowness and finally rolling over. Whatever god had demanded that sacrifice must by now surely be satisfied, Andrewes thought desolately . . . drained out . . .

'Come on, lad, let's get moving! Quick!' Jimmy Hathaway, coughing from the thick smoke, was tugging at his sleeve. 'King John, we've got to get out o' here!'

Without Jimmy Hathaway's help he might never have made it. His lungs ached with every breath; the heat invited him to lie down to wait for the pain to end, curling up. But, spluttering, spitting, cursing, coughing, the little telegraphy wizard from Manchester bullied him back along that road between the savage flames ready to dart out at anything combustible, and refused to let him stop before they had put at least two hundred yards between themselves and the fire.

The smoke spread in a wide, mottled tail across the late afternoon sky, a fragrant smoke containing scatterings of grey ash from burning timber together with darker streaks from the mud, dung and wattle walls of African-built huts and greasy black patches from the heavy oil in the locomotive workshops.

Standing outside Tim Wilton's tent Hester gazed up at it, then over towards the fiery redness on the horizon. Everything in her life was changing again. For a time she had deceived herself into believing they might stay in Nairobi; now once more they lived in their shabby tent, their belongings folded and packed to make convenient head loads for the porters – a maximum of sixty pounds per man – even the tables and chairs. Nothing was ever permanent.

The pall of smoke hung in the air, catching at her throat. Inside the tent Tim was coughing. She hurried to his side, putting her arm about his shoulders to hold him up as, his face flushed, he struggled for breath, gulping it in, spluttering as the sharp smoke penetrated his lungs. Dampening her handkerchief, she placed it over his mouth and nostrils in an attempt to filter the air. Oh Tim, she thought; perhaps if he had come to Liverpool, met her first, and she had married him . . . But she loved John – no, she was over-tired, that was all, over-tired and confused.

His eyes stared at her, recognizing her at last. That boyish smile, the wisp of blond hair across his forehead, the exhaustion showing in the drawn lines of his face – was it possible, she wondered, to fall in love with two men at the same time?

Then, abruptly, his eyes closed and he lay back on the pillow so quietly, she was afraid it was all over. 'Another twenty four hours, I'd reckon,' Dr Carson had warned only that morning. 'Twenty four hours, no more.' But his pulse seemed steady and the flush drained from his face as, for the first time, he relaxed into real sleep.

Outside, the trail of smoke widened as it drifted across the borders of the plain. A lone Maasai herdsman looked up and wondered about it. In the *manyatta* his kinsmen speculated on what could produce so much smoke: was the whole forest burning?

In the forest itself and on the ridges they also saw it, though by now it had thinned until it was little more than a discolouring of the sky; but the Gikuyu people were still numb from the events of the past days. Many had lost their menfolk, their livestock, their crops, their homes; some felt, even, they had been robbed of their reason for living. And while they faced starvation, the red strangers pressed their demands for payment of the hut-tax. So what could it mean, this greying of the sky – an omen, perhaps, of worse to come?

But when, days later, they heard the true reason for the smoke, their joy was boundless. At last these red strangers had been punished for bringing their iron snake into the land, marching through like the black ants, devouring everything in their path. Ngai in his anger had visited their huts with fire, destroying all they had built by the side of the cold swamp. In spite of the people's own misfortunes, smiles now broke across their faces: their sacrifices had been great but Ngai had heard them. The red strangers could now only withdraw the way they had come, back towards the great water.

Though still only a child, Ngengi felt instinctively they must be wrong, though he said nothing: who would listen to a mere boy? His father Kamau would have spoken out in warning but he had not been seen since the great defeat, that day of shame, and many said he had died in the fighting. So Ngengi shared his thoughts with no one, not even his mother; she was so wrapped in her own sorrow, she hardly spoke a word.

Then, after three days, the sky unexpectedly darkened at noon, shaken by heavy thunder, jaggedly split by forked lightning, and the first isolated drops of rain fell. Even Ngengi began to accept that perhaps they were right as, within a few minutes, everything was drenched and the dry earth drank its fill for the first time in many seasons. Soon, water was gathering in wide, muddy pools; rushing streams were forming along the paths and, wherever Ngengi looked, he could see patches of soil breaking up, splitting, like a thousand mouths opening.

Yes, Ngai had spoken. It could only mean that the red strangers were leaving, and he wished his father were still there to witness it.

# SEVEN

With the few remaining buildings on both sides of Nairobi's main street charred and blackened, it was decided that the memorial parade for Queen Victoria should be held on the race course. Officials representing both the colonial administration and the railway assembled on the little knoll from which Andrewes and Hester had watched the races only a few weeks earlier and took the salute as the available platoons of King's – formerly Queen's – African Rifles marched slowly past. Near them stood the other European officials and settlers and the half dozen or so wives who had by now arrived in the Protectorate. Over to the right a large crowd of Indians – many of them dressed up for the occasion – looked on gravely, while a small number of Africans watched curiously from a distance.

The drums beat out the slow march until the whole parade had rounded the course and re-formed in the centre, facing the officials. Then a moment of silence before a voice rang out, Let us pray. Oh Lord God our Heavenly Father . . .

With Hester at his side, Andrewes contemplated the scene, hardly listening as the words flowed over him. It was the end of an era, the final passing of the greatest century yet known to mankind. Not that he had ever had much time for monarchy – or aristocracy of any variety – but that was all changing anyway; perhaps when another hundred years had passed, crowned heads would be as extinct as dinosaurs. That was the way it looked. With the advances in engineering, medicine and science, the old ideas of master and man were being blown away in the wind. Ay, an' a good fresh wind it was, too.

The prayers ended and the British sergeant yelled out his next commands. Six men stepped forward. There was a series of clicks as the bolts shot home, and then a ragged volley of shots into the air to salute the dead queen. From the direction of the swamp came the indignant squawking of the birds . . . raucously . . . to be answered by another volley.

Andrewes took Hester's hand, holding it gently. Hearing those shots he was once again in the *boma* . . . at the height of the battle . . . with the screams of men in agony . . . Then he pulled himself together; at least Tim Wilton was safe. He would live, though maybe he would never walk again. But it was something.

The sound of the shooting rolled away towards the hills and once again everything was quiet until another of the British sergeants raised a bugle to his lips to sound the Last Post. Andrewes felt strangely moved. The old queen had been on the throne all his life. He had never seen her, of course – other than her head on postage stamps and pennies – yet she symbolized something to him.

'God save the King!' Again that same voice rang out, and the response was even more ragged than the volley had been, as if the idea had taken everyone by surprise.

Hester murmured something and looked up at him, smiling.

'Ay, lass, I reckon they've just about finished.' The platoons of King's African Rifles were marching away. On the knoll, the higher-ranking officials – Carpenter among them – had started to chat among themselves now the formalities were over. 'It's time we took a look at the house. The place is no' so bad as I feared, as I was tellin' ye. It needs cleanin' up, but ye could move back in a few days if ye like.'

'When are you meeting Carpenter?'

'This evenin', mebbe. Or early tomorrow. He's no' too pleased now he's seen the damage. Carson's backin' me up, I'm glad to say. An' in writin', too.'

'But you'd no alternative, John – did you?'

'I doubt if that's the way he'll see it. Destruction o' property . . . But dinna fash yesel', lass. He'll come round.'

The fire had done its work thoroughly, destroying everything inflammable in the little township with the exception of the railway station, which was sited well away from the other buildings. Some of the European quarters had also been too far from the blaze to be seriously affected: among them, the row of bungalows for officers of King's African Rifles which had not long ago been constructed on a hillside two miles away. But the store, the hotel, some workshops and most of the shanties in the bazaar quarter lay in ruins; only those few with corrugated iron walls still stood, black and gaunt, completely burned out.

Their own house had been licked by the flames which had scorched the door and shutters facing the roadway, transforming them into slabs of deeply ribbed charcoal. But it stood slightly away from the main built-up area and the fire had been less intense at that point, or else the wind had veered around to save it from worse destruction, for the rear of the house was hardly damaged at all. The vegetable garden was much as he had left it, and the thorn tree still spread its shade as if nothing had ever happened.

'John, what a mess!' Hester exclaimed, brushing the back of her hand against her face where it left a grey smudge. 'Have you looked inside? It'll take weeks to put this right.'

'Och, it's no' so bad! Ye'll see – once I get the men workin' on it! What I've been wonderin', my love, is – what happens about Mr Wilton? He canna stay in that tent, no' wi' the rains comin'. An' there's scarcely room for him here.'

'He can't look after himself, he's not strong enough!' She was suddenly on the defensive. 'So he'll have to come here. There's no one else to take care of him.'

But he did not want to argue. 'Then I'd best build that extra room I was plannin' for the bairns, an' he can live there awhile,' he decided, placing an arm affectionately about her shoulders. 'It's no' a big job now the ground's levelled.'

She raised her face for a kiss, a contented smile hovering about her lips at having won her own way so easily. He knew well enough once Hester had made up her mind that someone was in need of nursing, not all the devils in hell could stop her. He had intended to put up that room sooner or later in any case: a couple of additional walls added to the side of the house, an extension to the corrugated iron roof which needed repairs after the fire . . . His main problem would be laying his hands on a gang of coolies not already ear-marked for the main reconstruction work.

'Ay, I'd best get on wi' organizin' that,' he said, kissing her again, then helping her back to the roadway over the charred fragments of what had once been the front fence. 'An' I'll be sendin' Patel down to Mombasa again to pick up a few items from Roshan, so if there's anythin' in the way o' new furnishin' ye want, my love, any odds an' ends, now's the best time to ask.'

Tim looked so different from the day John brought him in, Hester thought happily as Sharma and Abdul Hakim lifted him carefully on to the litter to be carried down to Nairobi. He was still unusually pale, of course, but he was smiling, joking even, and he had recovered that frank open look about the eyes which made him seem so . . . so boyish, in some ways.

As they set out, the thunder growled far away among the hills and the sky was a brilliant patchwork of dark moving clouds interspersed with pale, whispy gaps where the sun broke through. It was a short procession, their return to the township which was already taking shape again – growing, in fact. Ali led the way with half a dozen porters carrying what remained of their belongings, the greater part of which were already at the house. Then came Tim, with Gaby walking alongside, chattering away about her pet gazelle, which rode on the litter with him, snuggling up to him sensuously as he stroked its delicately-shaped head, running his hand over those dainty ears. Hester followed, holding her parasol over baby Michael to shade him from those occasional dramatic shafts of tropical sunlight.

John should have been with them – that was the way they had planned the move – but at the last minute he had been called in for another long session with Carpenter, who was gathering evidence for his report on the fire. John made light of it whenever she raised the subject, but she could sense he was worried. Or was *worried* the right word? At times he seemed more angry.

Unexpectedly, the next flash of lightning flickered dazzlingly across the plain, to be followed within a second by an explosion of thunder so violent, it seemed as though the ground behind them had been rent apart. She started, shocked, then hugged the baby protectively to her breast and called out to Gaby that it was all right, she should not be frightened . . .

But Gaby, wide-eyed, had already got over her initial spurt of fear, and actually seemed to enjoy the thunder as the next clap rumbled heavily over them. She held on to Tim's hand and jumped nervously at each heavy crash before laughing, apparently delighted, and shouting back, 'Mama, don't be 'fraid! Only thunder!'

They were a long way from shelter and had no choice but to walk on as the rain poured down on them. She struggled into her waterproof cape, anxious to ensure that at least baby Michael remained dry, and she had a smaller cape for Gaby, while Ali spread a ground sheet over the litter; but these precautions turned out to be completely ineffective. The wind lashed the rain against them; within seconds they were completely drenched. The groundsheet flapped about uselessly; the capes clung to them uncomfortably as the rain went through.

Tim called out something, laughing, and waving his hand in encouragement as she plodded on over the now-soggy ground. With each step her feet squelched the water her boots had let in. But at last she could now see the house. Another five minutes . . .

Once they arrived, she showed the porters where to take Tim and then left him to sort things out for himself; he could not stand up, but he had Sharma to help him get dry while she instructed Ali to get a fire going for hot water. Gaby was shivering and had to be stripped of her wet clothes and wrapped in a blanket; baby Michael too, until the water was hot enough to bath them both.

It was not until almost an hour later that she went along the veranda to Tim's room to see how he was managing. Sharma was with him and he looked worried. She hurried over to the bed, her heart sinking. Tim's eyes were bloodshot, his cheeks reddening; it was obvious at first glance that he had a fever.

During the next few weeks the fever recurred two or three times, but slowly he became stronger until the day came when Hester found him sitting on the edge of the bed trying to haul himself up with the help of a chair. One leg had healed completely, though it was badly scarred. The other – his right – was still in bandages; in Dr Carson's opinion, he would never be able to stand on it again.

It was understood he would be sent home to Britain as soon as Dr Carson judged him well enough to travel and a suitable companion could be found to accompany him, which meant someone already intending to make the journey and willing to take on this extra burden. Until then, the Railway Office was generously allowing him to remain on half-salary.

'Ye were no' coutin' on goin' yesel', lass?' John remarked one evening by way of a joke. He was just back after a week away at railhead and was in an expansive mood, sitting there with a good meal inside him and a glass of whisky in his hand. 'There are times I've been wonderin'.'

She felt herself flushing. 'Oh, John, you don't . . .?' She stopped abruptly, upset, not knowing how to put it. Not wanting to.

'Nay, I'm teasin' ye, lass!' His voice was warm and understanding – though understanding what? she thought guiltily. 'Ye're a born nurse, d'ye ken? Mebbe it's a pity ye didna study the subject properly in Liverpool. Dr Carson says so, at any rate. Young Tim would ne'er have pulled through wi'out ye.'

She snuggled up against him, watching the moths colliding with the lamp glass and throwing grotesque shadows against the wall as he talked. He was away so often these days now that construction work had started on the Mau escarpment on the far side of the Rift Valley, while Tim was there every day, always eager to talk to her, a real strength and comfort in spite of the fact he could not get around by himself. He hopped about the room now for twenty minutes a time, twice a day, leaning on her shoulder for support. It seemed so natural, his arm resting on her, like a second husband. She turned to him with all her problems too, relying on him when John was not there.

Yet with track-laying work going on through Nandi territory, where the coolies and engineers lived in constant danger of being attacked, John was never out of her mind. She knew that every work party now had a military escort but she still felt apprehensive whenever John visited that part of the line and ticked off the days until he got back. Too often news had come through of bad skirmishes, with casualties, and her heart missed a beat each time. She didn't want two patients on her hands, she told herself; then she woke up in the middle of the night wondering how it was possible this should be happening to her, this confused jumble of feelings about John and Tim. She loved them both deeply, each in his own way, yet . . . yet in the quiet of her own lonely bedroom she knew she loved John more. He was her husband, after all.

'. . . so then I thought, why not design some for him?' John was saying.

'Dearest?' She looked up at him enquiringly – his face set in its own strong lines, so individual, so firm and weather-beaten – and she felt she could not live without him. Not ever. 'I was day-dreaming, my dearest . . . not listening . . . sorry!'

'I've been designin' some crutches for Tim,' he repeated patiently, stroking her hair. 'They'll be knockin' 'em together at the workshops. Be ready tomorrow, mebbe.'

Not for the first time Andrewes was forced to cut short his stay in Nairobi. One of the new locomotives recently delivered from Britain was urgently needed up the line. It had come up from Mombasa under its own steam, but now they were faced with the tricky operation of lowering it down the funicular into the Rift Valley, and he had to be there to supervise it.

The main problem was the weight of the engine. He ordered it to be stripped down as far as they could outside a workshop and these lighter parts were sent down first. There was no possibility of carrying the main body of the engine on any of the specially-constructed wagons; it would have to run on its own wheels. The first section of the four-stage funicular would be tricky enough, with a one in six gradient, but the two middle sections with a gradiant of one in two would need very careful handling. The one and a quarter inch steel cable should be doubled, he decided, and additional wagons used to counter-weight the load.

'Right!' he called out briskly when everything was ready for the first stage. 'Now take it dead slow, d'ye hear? An' use the brake. Let her go, then!'

Gradually the drum of the steam winch began to turn. The engine tipped as it reached the start of the slope but its wheels kept to the rails and Andrewes breathed again. A de-railment had been his greatest fear; the thought of that weight plunging down into the valley out of control was a nightmare he did not wish to experience. The steel cables creaked, but held, as slowly they were paid out, lowering the locomotive to the first level staging point while the empty wagons on the parallel tracks balanced much of the weight.

A pity Tim Wilton canna see this, Andrewes mused as the men prepared for the next section. He had talked it over with him before leaving Nairobi; it was obvious what was going on in the lad's head – missing the challenge of the railway, feeling he'd lost his use in life. Ay, it was hard on him, lyin' in bed all day wi' nothin' to do but read books.

'Be careful there!' he yelled suddenly, spotting a man standing on the wrong side of the cable. 'Stand clear, unless ye want it to slice ye in half!'

The gradient on this next stretch was one in two; looking

down, it seemed the engine was almost end-on as it crept down the line. It was still one hell of a long drop to the bottom. Above, he heard the whistle of another train arriving with materials from Nairobi, but there would be a few hours' delay before the funicular was clear to take them.

'Take it easy now!' he bawled at the winch operator, sensing that the speed of descent was imperceptibly increasing.

But it arrived safely at the second staging point. There was a burst of chatter among the coolies as the tension eased. Andrewes went down to check everything was in order for the third section, also with a one in two gradient, but the *jemadar* clearly knew what he was about. It was all running smoothly.

Before they were ready to start lowering, there was a shout and the wagons immediately above them started moving again, contrary to Andrewes' orders that normal work was to be suspended until the engine had reached the bottom. He was not willing to risk anything going wrong, it was far too valuable.

'Who gave ye permission to—!' he bawled up the slope again against the clatter of the wheels over the rails.

Then he stopped. The descending wagon was empty; only the slim fastidious figure of a man neatly dressed in khaki came down, resting one hand casually on the safety rail. William Carpenter, Comptroller of Construction, Uganda Railway, thought Andrewes sourly, come to give me my marching orders, no doubt. It was nigh on three months now since his report on the fire had been sent to London; no doubt the decision had come through at last.

'I've arrived at an interesting moment, I see,' Carpenter greeted him, jumping down from the wagon. He looked carefully at the doubled cables, then nodded, apparently approving. 'No trouble so far?'

'As ye can see,' Andrewes replied shortly. He turned to the coolies. 'Stand clear now! Right, on the winch – dead slow! Lower away!'

He glanced at Carpenter, who had removed his wide-brimmed felt hat – a new one, too, and spotless! – to mop his brow. That part of the escarpment offered no shade at all from the sun. The Howard clip drum groaned and squealed alarmingly as the cables took the full weight of the locomotive; for a moment he considered stopping the operation to investigate the cause, but then the noise ceased and the locomotive rolled gently down to the next level. Beyond that point the gradient was less severe and within half an hour they had reached the bottom.

'This is no social visit, I'm afraid,' Carpenter apologized as they stood watching the men reassembling the engine. 'London's woken up again, agitating for answers.'

Andrewes tried to control his temper. 'I gave ye a full account o' how it was!' he exploded impatiently, then immediately checked himself. 'Do they no' think o' the lives we saved by burnin' the place down? There's been no case o' plague since.'

'My dear chap, it's not your fire they're pestering me about – they've had my report but it could be months before they deal with it! If I know Whitehall, it's probably sitting in someone's pending tray. No, it's the usual thing, I'm afraid. They're pressing to know how soon we expect to get through to the Lake. Seems there've been questions in the House of Commons again.' He rubbed his little blond moustache thoughtfully with a forefinger. 'So I've come on a tour of inspection, and I'd be grateful if you'd accompany me.'

Andrewes stared at him doubtfully, but there was no way he could refuse. 'Ay, well in that case we'd best spend today takin' a look at work on the permanent route down the escarpment here. In another two months' time I reckon it'll be complete an' we can start dismantling the funicular.'

'First-rate idea of yours. Earned its cost several times over.'

Andrewes nodded. 'Tomorrow we can take the first materials train to Nakuru, then on to the Mau range, where Jackson's in charge o' primary construction work. So if ye'll excuse me a wee moment, I'll be gettin' a message back to Mrs Andrewes to say I'll no' be home for a few days.'

'Of course . . . And I hope you'll convey my apologies. Nairobi is not the most salubrious town for a lady on her own.'

'Ay, true enough.'

Several times during the following days he caught himself thinking over that remark; he felt easier in his mind to know Tim Wilton was still with her. Not that he could get about too well even with the crutches, but at least his presence in the house would protect her from the unwelcome attentions of any lecherous roughneck tempted to imitate Muldoon one night and try his luck. Nairobi had plenty of them too, specially once they had liquor in their bellies.

The town was growing rapidly, as if the fire had released some secret spring of energy. New buildings were appearing almost overnight – a bank, two hotels, two or three other bars, and a couple of English-run general stores to compete with the Indian traders. The bazaar quarter itself was slowly being rebuilt along more spacious lines as an increasing number of the indented Indian coolies reached the end of their time and decided to settle there permanently. And Patel was soon to be one of them, Andrewes remembered contentedly: the idea that they might go into business, all three of them – though under the name of Patel & Roshan, with Andrewes himself staying very discreetly in the background – had been turning over in his mind for some time. As an insurance, in case that wee matter of the fire went wrong and he found himself without a job. He had not discussed it with Hester yet, it would not be right to worry her, but he had the title deed to a suitable plot of land already tucked away in the bank.

Carpenter's inspection was thorough, he'd say that much for the man. That languid air irritated him like a nagging tooth, and at times he could have wished to see him sprawling in the mud in those immaculate, well-pressed clothes, but he certainly knew his stuff when it came to railways. Work on the Mau escarpment was only slightly behind schedule, in spite of the heavy rains, and the line was already through, although there were numerous temporary diversions in use while the permanent viaducts were being built. Carpenter refused to pass one without stopping to examine it in detail, checking the give of the rails under the weight of the construction train as it was shunted backwards and forwards over some of the more troublesome sections, testing the ground beneath the sleepers, at times insisting on more ballast, or other changes.

At last they went on beyond the Mau range, and Jackson with them, boasting offhandedly of how many miles per day they could lay in the easier terrain and how he had his gangs working ceaselessly. Andrewes was surprised himself at the progress made during the six or seven weeks since his previous visit to railhead.

As the train moved slowly downhill over the newly-laid track he could feel the atmosphere gradually becoming hotter and muggy; but when it stopped, and they climbed down with the sweat gleaming on their faces, there in front of them – not two miles away – they saw a placid, white expanse of calm water, glistening in the sunlight.

'A sight you've waited for long enough, eh?' Jackson proclaimed with a sweeping gesture.

'Lake Victoria, by Jove!' Carpenter exclaimed, almost laughing in his delight. 'Then we've made it! Two more miles of track and we're there!'

Andrewes gazed at it, feeling unable to speak as an intense thrill of excitement pulsed through him. He had been with the railway since almost the very first days and now their goal – that impossible, lunatic goal for which men had sweated long hours, some had been maimed, some had even died – was only a step away. Already the ground had been cleared as far as the lakeside; already the coolies were laying out the sleepers for the next stretch of line.

'Don't know about you, Mr Andrewes,' Carpenter was saying, his face still animated, 'but I have it in mind to remain down here till the last rail's in place. What d'you think?'

'Ye're right, Mr Carpenter.' His voice sounded hoarse from the unexpected emotion. 'We couldna possibly leave till the job's done. An' I think, too, we should congratulate Mr Jackson for pushin' ahead so rapidly. It's no' been easy country.'

The final section of track reached the lakeside late the following morning. Andrewes, Carpenter and Jackson were watching in silence as the coolies worked on steadily. Then, out of the blue, they heard a lively discussion going on in Hindustani, and the *jemadar* offered Andrewes a sledgehammer.

'They're askin' me to strike the very last blows,' Andrewes explained, turning to Carpenter; he made no attempt to conceal how pleased he felt at the honour. 'But I've told 'em that privilege should be yours.'

Carpenter shook his head. 'You're the one they've chosen – King John! You mustn't disappoint them – must he, Mr Jackson?'

Jackson scowled. 'If that's what they want.'

'Ay,' Andrewes accepted, 'then on behalf o' every man who ever worked on the Uganda Railway . . .!'

He raised the sledgehammer to drive in the last bolts amidst shouts of approval from the crowd of coolies gathered around. It was a symbolic act only, as he realized only too well; another two or three months' work would be needed before the line could be opened for traffic. Even then trains would be running over temporary track in many places, all of which would have to be replaced by a more permanent alignment. But it gave him a warm, satisfied feeling just the same as he straightened up, glanced at the lake to one side of him, and then eastwards along those shining twin rails.

'Now, gentlemen, what about a little something to "wet the baby's head", as I think they say in Ireland? I've a bottle of champagne cooling in the lake which I'm sure you'll find acceptable.' Carpenter ushered them back to his tent and despatched his Goanese cook to retrieve the wine. 'We'll need to drink a special toast today. I don't know if you realize, but exactly forty three years ago to this very month the English explorer Speke first set eyes on this lake . . . looked out across this water . . . And now we've built a railway here. Incredible, don't you think?'

They sat for some time over the tepid champagne, listening to the crackling of the papyrus and the calls of the wildfowl, although Jackson left them after thirty minutes or so, muttering that he had work to do. Andrewes stared at his glass gloomily, wondering what people found to like in this insipid, aereated concoction; he'd have preferred an honest dram of whisky in which to toast the line. And his own dismissal, perhaps: there was no telling what Carpenter had recommended in his report.

'Hope you're not thinking of leaving us, Mr Andrewes,' Carpenter cut across his thoughts abruptly, almost as though seeing into his mind. 'Even when all the construction work is finished – and that's assuming we build no branch lines – there'll still be a need for first-rate engineers. The real difficulty, you know, has not been deserts or mountains at all, but the politicians back in London. They've been far the biggest obstacle. Let's kill the bottle, shall we?'

Andrewes contemplated him cynically as he emptied the last drops into their glasses. Ay . . . ay, an' ye're the most devious politician o' the lot!

If anything, Hester felt a sense of great relief at the news that a missionary returning home to Britain on furlough was prepared to accept the responsibility of looking after Tim as far as London. He would be spending no more than three days in Nairobi, and then they would be leaving on the Mombasa train. Tim might well be on his way even before John got back.

'Best thing for him!' Dr Carson declared, sucking at his pipe noisily. 'We've done all we can for that leg. The sooner a London specialist can take a look at it, the better. An' but for you, Mrs Andrewes, he wouldn't be alive at all.'

243

For Hester, it was an escape from an impossible situation. She tried – yet again – to think rationally about it as she prepared for bed that night, pulling the brush through her long hair in front of the rough, tarnished mirror. As long as he had been confined to his room, unable to get up, she had been able to convince herself she was firmly in control. Tim must have guessed how she felt about him – oh, she must have betrayed herself in a thousand ways – but she had always held back. It would not have been proper to do anything else. But now he moved about the house freely on his crutches, coming upon her unexpectedly . . . to chat as she sat sewing . . . to join in as she played with the children . . . and she was seized by a fear that he was supplanting John. A familiar glance . . . a shared laugh . . . and her guard was down, she knew it. Earlier that same day his hand had accidentally brushed against hers and something in that touch had surged through her like a charge of electricity. Her whole body had become receptive.

No, she thought, putting the brush down, she had been playing with fire and it would not do. She had deluded herself into imagining she could love him as a person – as *Tim* – without getting involved . . . *that* way . . . The way she had been brought up to believe belonged to a husband only.

It was right he should be going, she decided as she leaned over the children to check they were asleep and moved a wayward strand of auburn hair away from Gaby's face. She had been silly. Weak.

She got into bed, then turned down the lamp till it spluttered out. If only John were not away so much, she thought in the darkness as she tried to sleep. It would be so much easier to have him here all the time.

She must have slept, perhaps deeply, but then suddenly she was awake again and aware something was wrong. She half-sat up in bed, listening. All she could hear at first was the croaking of frogs from the swamp and the yelping of an animal in the distance. Yet her instinct insisted she had been woken by some other sound. An intruder perhaps?

And there it was again . . . A muffled clatter, a scraping, as though someone was trying to climb the wire fence near the house. A drunk? But whoever it was, he was moving cautiously. She heard a brief, creaking noise, and then once more silence.

Hester reached for the shotgun which she kept at nights by the side of her bed whenever John was away, but it was not there. She had been so pre-occupied with her own thoughts about Tim and her confused feelings and what she should do, she had forgotten to take it down from the wall pegs where it was kept out of Gaby's reach. And that meant it was not loaded, either.

But in her writing box she still had the little pearl-handled derringer. Fumbling in the darkness for the key, she at last managed to get the box open just as she heard the sound again – louder this time, and more determined. She took the gun and went out to the veranda, keeping her thumb on the hammer, ready to cock it instantly.

She stood, waiting. The air was chilly through her thin nightdress and she shivered. Then another sound – behind her! She swung around, simulataneously pressing back the hammer. Her finger curled around the tiny trigger as she pointed the gun squarely at the dark form standing only a yard away from her . . . coming towards her . . .

'Hester?'

He whispered the name. Her hand shook uncertainly, but still she held the pistol ready to fire.

'Hester, it's me – Tim!'

'Tim?' Everything inside her tightened with sudden fear. 'Oh, Tim, I almost shot you!'

'I heard a noise. Came out to see what it was.'

He moved to her side on his crutches. She touched his arm for reassurance as they both stared out into the darkness of her vegetable garden. The night was alive with noises. A hyena howled some way off; from the direction of the swamp came a throaty bird call repeated over and over again; and somewhere, perhaps over towards the bazaar quarter, an African girl was giggling and calling out as if trying to encourage the men she was with.

Then that nearer sound again, over by the fence.

'Wait here,' Tim said softly.

On his crutches he swung down from the veranda and began to move quietly over the soft ground towards the spot from which the noise must have come. He had his revolver with him, she had been able to see that much in the dim light of the stars, and for a few seconds she stayed where she was. But then, he was crippled, she told herself anxiously; without his crutches he could not even stand. If someone attacked him he'd be helpless. She went after him, keeping a good distance behind, but praying he would be safe.

Near the fence he stopped. To her surprise he began talking to the intruder. Laughing even. Then came – quite distinctly – the sound of a hard slap.

'Tim, what . . .?'

She hurried after him, her feet slipping in the loose soil

'A zebra!' he laughed, though for some reason still keeping his voice down.

He gave the zebra another hard slap across the rump. Indignantly, it retreated from the gap it had made in her wire fence and galloped off into the darkness.

'Found a weak spot, don't you know, and . . .' he started to say.

'Oh, Tim, I might have killed you!' She pressed herself to him, raising her face to his. They kissed at first hesitantly; then she felt a great sigh of contentment inside her as her inhibitions dissolved . . . might never have been . . . and she knew this was the man she wanted, at this moment. Gently she broke away from him to ease the derringer's hammer forward and make it safe. Then, as the kiss resumed . . . tender . . . exploring . . . discovering . . . inviting onwards . . . she said, 'Oh Tim, I didn't want to do this. Not ever. But—'

'But?' His voice seemed uncertain, yet at the same time he must have known by now.

'Oh yes – *But!*' It was like caressing the word, putting it all into that small syllable to make sure he understood.

Back in his room, she realized she was still wearing only her thin cotton nightdress; wherever he touched her she could feel the shape of his hands as on her naked skin. Every part of her responded and she felt no guilt, no more hesitation . . . This was right, what they were doing – her entire body was telling her it was right.

He lifted the nightdress and she helped him, slipping it off over her head, shaking her long hair about her shoulders. He sank back on to the narrow bed and they lay together, her skin alive with pleasure, as it glided against his, her shape made for him; and she took him to her, yearning for him, her mind empty of everything but Tim, his name, his person, his being.

Yes, they belonged together . . . She stretched, her body became taut, those feelings were more intense . . . fierce even . . . more . . .

Oh yes.

Yes.


Three days. She stood on the station platform to see him off, the arguments dancing through her mind as she tried to find some last words to say. She would not have yielded to him at all, she tried to convince herself, if she hadn't known for certain she would never see him again. He would go back to Britain and she would stay here with John, or find herself in some other distant country where there was a railway to build.

Three last days of pretending nothing had happened, that everything was normal. Three last nights when, once all was quiet, she had surrendered herself totally to this madness. This feverish dream.

No, they would never meet again, she thought as the train pulled out and she waved, briefly. Never – and from the bottom of her heart she thanked God for it. It was the only way. Now she had to face John and behave towards him as if nothing had taken place. He would ask about Tim, expect her usual answers, and . . . Would he know from her voice? An expression in her eyes, or in her manner?

For some time she remained standing on the platform, gazing at the tail of smoke spreading above the departing train as it took the long curve away from Nairobi. Then, numbed, she went through the station and signalled for a rickshaw to take her home.

*Book Three*

# ONE

As the train eased its way sedately across the Athi Plains, Nathaniel Catchpole perched on the cast-iron rail surrounding the narrow platform at the end of his compartment, notebook in hand, jotting down lists of the game they had passed: zebra, giraffe, oryx, impala, buffalo, gazelle – hundreds of gazelles – warthog, baboon, monkey . . . It was difficult to put a name to all of them; he had spent a year on his uncle's farm in South Africa, and later some months in Rhodesia, but nowhere had he seen anything to match this. No wonder the Protectorate was introducing Game Laws.

He was a quiet, shy young man, tall and thin, with outstanding ears and the habit of blushing whenever a stranger spoke to him. As the younger son of a Church of England bishop with a reputation for fox-hunting – though none for scholarship – he was in something of a quandary concerning his choice of career. He was rich in relations – one cousin was a belted Earl – but had very little money of his own. One evening over port his father had suggested the Law, with a seat in the House of Commons to follow, but there was the obstacle of his stammer. Animals had been his only boyhood friends and he had filled the Bishop's Palace with them – hedgehogs, rabbits, a blackbird with a broken wing, dormice, and a weasel which once escaped from its cage late at night and wrought havoc among the rest of the menagerie before escaping through the larder window. Then his brother suggested that farming in Africa might suit him – 'Plenty of wild animals there, old chap!' – and he had promptly agreed to spend a year travelling to different parts of the continent to test the water, so to speak. Already from the train the richness of British East astonished him, those thousands of square miles teeming with game. If anywhere, he thought, then here. 'Ee, they're funny, aren't they? Like striped horses – are they horses?' The woman who had just emerged from her compartment on to the adjoining platform was powerfully built, with a strikingly handsome face; wisps of hair stood out untidily around her head like a breeze-blown halo, darkened with red dust. 'I s'ppose they could be.'

'Th-the z-z-zebra?'

'Ay, I wasn't saying nowt about giraffes.' The North of England sarcasm was without malice.

'Z-zebra are th-the s-same f-f-family as h-horses,' he tried to explain, feeling the blood mounting to his face.

'Thought so.' She nodded, satisfied. After a while she added, 'Tha's no need to get hot an' bothered wi' me, young man. I'll not bite.'

'N-no . . .' He tried a laugh, unsuccessfully.

'Come to find me husband,' she confided, unperturbed. 'I ask at every station. He'll be somewhere along line.'

'Y-y-you've l-lost him?'

'Pining – could tell from his letters, he's pining for me.' She produced a crumpled scrap of paper from her skirt pocket, thrusting it into his hand. 'Judge if I'm not right.'

'I-I say!' he tried to object.

She would have none of it. 'Go on – read it!'

*My dear Ada*, he read, *I am penning these lines to convey to you and our dear children the compliments of the season and hope you can afford a goose this Christmas not like last year when money was scarce because of little Johnny being poorly. I am as well as can be expected here in Africa which is a miracle what with all the fevers about. Hoping this finds you as it leaves me I remain Your loving husband.*

'Canst see what I mean?' she demanded as he handed the letter back without comment. 'He's pining right enough, so I thought I'd let me sister look after children for a while an' I'd just run over to Africa to find how he is. Any wife'd do the same. Any proper wife.'

'H-how . . . how . . . how . . .' he tried to ask.

'Have a nut!' From another pocket in her skirt she fished out a handful of cashew nuts. 'Bought 'em down in Mombasa. Went into market an' they was all moidering me to buy something so I said I'll take some nuts, an' here they are. I know just what it's like – well, no harm in telling thee I've got a stall o' me own back home.' She popped a couple of nuts into her mouth and chewed vigorously as she talked. 'A'right, aren't they? Ay, not bad. Who'd've thought they had nuts in Africa?'

A piercing whistle from the engine prevented him from answering; the train jerked as the brakes were applied and it began to slow down. There, not a quarter of a mile away, they could already see the rooftops of the tiny settlement of Nairobi, silver in the brilliant sunlight. Catchpole looked down at his clothes and attempted to brush off some of the red dust.

'I h-hope . . . hope . . . hope . . .' he stammered politely, wanting to wish her luck in the search for her husband, but before he could get the words out she had seized his hand in an iron grip.

'I'll say goodbye,' she declared heartily, 'though this Nairobi doesn't look such a grand place that we won't be bumping into each other again. Tha's a nice lad, I can see that; well brought up. So tha' mustn't go an' do anything foolish now. I know what these places can be like.'

She nodded at him kindly, released his hand, then went back into her compartment to get her luggage together.

The little station was crowded with people meeting the train, but he made his way purposefully through them, ignoring all offers of help. Clusters of rickshaws stood beneath a great tree outside and were being allocated to customers by an imposing Indian in a turban; none of them risked contradicting him until Catchpole rejected the first of the selected African rickshaw pullers as too slight. The Indian's eyebrows shot up but he said nothing as Catchpole picked out the most muscular of all – who also looked less devious than the others – directing him to go with his companion to the train and fetch the bags.

It took five minutes or longer before everything was sorted out but eventually they were ready and the little procession of two rickshaws set off along the deeply-rutted track – road would have been too grand a name – towards the Norfolk Hotel. He insisted on the luggage going in the first where he could keep an eye on it. The rickshaw men raised clouds of fine dust as they ran, while the bells on their anklets warned other highway users of their approach.

The air was warm; the light, limpid and clear. It was hard to define his feelings, Catchpole decided as the rail in front of the hotel came into view with a couple of patient horses tied up at it, but some instinct told him he had come to stay.

'Mr Andwewth, do you not agwee,' one member of the Committee of Inquiry had drawled, a pink lisping inspector from London, sweating profusely in his dark, formal suit and stiff winged collar, 'that you tend to ovahweach yourthelf at timeth?'

The voice still echoed in Andrewes' mind as he strode furiously into the bar of the newly-constructed Norfolk Hotel and called for whisky. The boy was lighting one of the pressure lamps; before serving him, he pumped at it vigorously until the flaring white flame was bright enough to throw outsize shadows of his arm against the stone walls. Outside, the sky was reddening with the first flush of sunset.

'Whisky, bwana.'

The boy – Swahili, by the look of him, and old enough to be a young grandfather – placed the glass in front of him and waited. Andrewes let the sharp, clean spirit linger in his mouth before swallowing it.

'Another.'

'Yes, bwana.'

Not that he was normally a drinking man, but he had wasted yet another day giving evidence to the third Committee of Inquiry into the burning down of Nairobi – the Foreign Office in London having rejected the first two reports – and the outcome had left him in a sour mood which he felt he had no right to inflict on Hester and the children. Though sooner or later that evening he would have to tell her. *You ovahweach yourthelf*, he thought bitterly. He drained his glass again.

'Leave the bottle on the bar.'

'Yes, bwana.'

The air inside that Government office had been unbearably muggy. That grey corrugated iron used in the reconstruction of Nairobi's principal buildings offered no insulation against the warmth of the afternoon sun nor the coolness of the night, unlike the more sensible African huts of grass or mud.

'We ethtimate the damage at fifty thouthand poundth,' the inspector repeated, mopping the sweat from his face and neck. 'Almotht half the Pwotectowate's annual wevenue.'

'An' the disaster we averted – have ye tried quantifyin' *that*?' Andrewes had been seething with anger. 'That epidemic coulda decimated the population. Ye dinna think it money well spent to save 'em? Because I do.'

He had made no impression, though. The Committee did not even refer to his arguments in the summing up. The Foreign Office wanted a scapegoat, that much was obvious.

Across the bar near the window sat Hans de Jong's partner, Schwartz, an unusually small man for Cape Dutch, with dark weasel-like eyes, permanently scowling. He was deep in conversation with a young man Andrewes had never seen before. Fresh off the train, no doubt. With that wide-eyed expression, protruding ears, that air of puzzled innocence, it could only be a matter of time before he lost every penny to some rogue or other – if not to Schwartz himself, then to someone like him. A map was spread out on the table between them.

'Never vill you be short of vater on dis land,' Schwartz was explaining in loud guttural English, tapping the map for emphasis. 'Two rivers – you see? De railvay not far. I vish I could buy myself.'

Andrewes listened, refilling his glass. Tricksters and Government officials – that just about summed up the Protectorate these days. He remembered when Schwartz and Hans de Jong had first arrived at Voi. No one had expected them to make a go of it, but soon they had built up a flourishing business selling fresh vegetables to the railhead camps, and rumour had it that they lived riotously on the proceeds, with three concubines apiece supplied by the local chief, replacements when they felt like a change, everything they wanted; then, after some years, they had sold the estate at an outrageous profit to Italian missionaries – with the girls included, by all accounts. Now they were often seen around Nairobi sporting large bush hats, rifles slung from their shoulders, revolvers at their waists, proffering expensive advice to any newcomer fool enough to listen.

And every train brought more of them – younger sons of the well-to-do, cashiered army officers, men sent down from Oxford or Cambridge for gambling debts, escaping abroad to avoid some scandal, having perhaps made a housemaid pregnant or seduced a politician's wife . . . And Boers, now the South African War was over: the town's two sleazy hotels had no room for them all, so most pitched their tents on a stretch of land near Nairobi River which soon became known as Tentfontein, and where Afrikaans was heard more frequently than English.

Andrewes took more whisky. Time to move on, he was thinking, shaking his head at the bottle. No bloody choice now. But what the hell? The line has reached the lake, the bridges are built, the Rift Valley funicular dismantled . . . No more to do, anyway.

But where else could he build a railway? He had written to India – no vacancies. South America, perhaps – but what about Hester and the children?

'Y-y-yes, I c-can p-p-pay n-now!' the young man's voice floated eagerly across the room.

He opened his shirt at the waist, took a thick wad of banknotes from his money belt, and began counting them out on to the map. As a lamb to the slaughter, thought Andrewes in disgust; none of his business, though . . . but he picked up his glass all the same and lurched over to them. There was more than a year's salary on that table by the look of it. No wonder the young man seemed suddenly a little apprehensive.

'F-five p-p-pounds an a-acre – th-that's a g-good p-price, isn't-t-t-it?'

'Where lad? Near Nairobi?' Andrewes peered at the map but the banknotes covered most of it.

'A private transaction, Mr Andrewes,' Schwartz warned him unpleasantly. 'Between gentlemen. Not your bizzness.'

The anger which had been simmering inside him throughout that hot afternoon shot to the surface. 'Ye're no' implyin' now, Mr Schwartz, that ye're a genl'man? Lad, before ye hand over any money ye'd best let me take a peek at the map. My name'sh John Philip Andrewes, an' if I can help ye . . .'

'C-c-catchpole,' the young man stammered. 'N-nathaniel C-catchpole. I . . . I'm g-g-grateful for any ad-advice y-you . . .'

'Mr Andrewes, I tell you dis private transaction. Now please to go.' Schwartz, still sitting, drew his revolver.

'Ye're no' threatenin' me, Mr Schwartz?' Andrewes smiled down at the gun, almost inviting the man to try using it. 'D'ye no' think that'sh being' a wee bit foolish?'

He bent over the map, pushing the banknotes aside with a sweep of his hand. It seemed genuine enough, there was the Land Office stamp, but with all the whisky he had drunk in that short time he found it difficult to focus – ah, there it was! He grunted, satisfied, as he identified the line of the railway.

'Put your money away, lad,' he advised, straightening up. 'Mr Schwartz wouldna wish to cheat ye now.'

'Ch-cheat? I d-don't underst-stand.'

Schwartz cocked the revolver with a loud click, standing up and kicking his chair out of the way. Everyone else in the bar fell silent. Only the hiss of the pressure lamps could be heard, and the insistent croak of the swamp frogs outside.

'Gather your money up, lad,' Andrewes repeated, deliberately ignoring Schwartz. He was conscious that the whisky was slurring his speech and did his best to fight it. 'Three shillinsh an acre, that'sh the price for thish land.'

'Wit' de railvay only five miles?' Schwartz scoffed. 'Look at de map, man.'

'Believe me, Mr Catchpole, the railway ish fifty miles from thish place.' He emptied his glass and slammed it down on the table; Schwartz was about to use that gun, he could feel it in his bones. Recklessly, he went on, 'The map has been tampered with. Forged – understand?'

The bullet splintered the floor an inch from his toes and the sound of the shot, amplified by the iron roof, hurt his ears.

'Now you go,' said Schwartz, his face purple. 'De nex' bullet I shoot de leg.'

Man, thought Andrewes, stubbornly standing his ground, man, ye ovahweach yesel' again.

Then Catchpole intervened. 'Mr Schwartz,' he pleaded anxiously, 'th-there's no need to . . . I m-mean o-on m-m-my b-behalf . . . I . . . Oh!'

As he spoke, he stepped back from the table as if to go around to where Schwartz was standing, then stumbled against a chair. For a second Schwartz's eyes flickered in Catchpole's direction. Andrewes seized the chance, picked up the table in both hands and charged.

Taken by surprise, Schwartz's shot went wide, breaking a bottle behind the bar; then the flat of the table smashed into him, knocking the revolver out of his hand. Andrewes threw the table aside, hauled the man to his feet again, and sent him spinning across the room with a blow to his jaw. He fell against the opposite wall and stayed there. That's one crook fewer, he thought; but it gave him little enough satisfaction. What was worse, he was sober again.

'I thank ye, Mr Catchpole. If ye hadna helped. I mighta been killed by that madman.' He unloaded the gun, dropping the cartridges into his pocket. 'A .45. Could cause a lot o' damage.'

For a moment he considered leaving it on the table for Schwartz to find when he came around, but decided to pocket it instead. No point in tempting fate. Nay, this time ye didna *ovahweach* yesel' – but it was a near thing.

Catchpole was looking at the map again. 'Are y-y-you quite sure y-you're right?' he asked doubtfully.

'Ay, as sure as I'm standin' here still alive.' He regarded the young man thoughtfully. About twenty-five he would be. Tall. Ridiculously thin. And his manner was awkward too, as though he was not at ease with strangers. 'Stayin' here i' the hotel are ye?'

'Y-yes.' He blushed.

'I'll tell ye what, then – ye must come an' share a meal wi' my wife an' mesel'. I'm sure she'd like to thank ye in person.'

'W-w-what f-for?'

'For savin' my life, as I explained.' Seized by the idea, Andrewes pressed the invitation warmly. 'That's if ye can put up wi' three small bairns.'

'I-I-I l-like children.'

'That's settled then! I live jus' a wee step along the road, an' on the way ye can explain what made ye choose East Africa. It's a tough life, farmin', or so I'm told. D'ye have experience of it mebbe?'

Hester had known that John would be exhausted and irritable after meeting the Committee of Inquiry that day, whatever the outcome; for that reason she had taken special care over the cooking and tried to make everything nice for him. So she was not exactly pleased when he arrived home a good two hours later than expected, smelling of whisky, and bringing this awkward young man with him. She listened patiently to their account of what had happened at the Norfolk, then heard herself telling him sharply he was a fool to have interfered at all.

'You've made yourself one more enemy,' she added.

'Ye mean I *ovahweached* mesel'?' If it was an attempt at a joke she did not understand it. He bent down and kissed her. 'Ye look tired, my love. Ye've had a tryin' day?'

'Shou ... should I g-g-go?' The young man flushed scarlet.

'No, sit down, Mr Catchpole.' She was convinced John had deliberately invited him to put off having to face her alone. Something *had* gone wrong at the Inquiry, that was obvious. 'I'll see to the food. I expect you're both hungry.'

'As a h-h-horse!'

'An' the bairns?' John wanted to know.

'Asleep.'

It had been an unusually hot afternoon. Their iron bungalow had been like an oven and Robert, now almost eighteen months, had kept up a perpetual whimpering. She had picked him up, talked to him, tried to calm him down – and wondered once again, as she brushed that pale blond hair away from his brow and caught his attentive blue eyes following her every move, why John had never said anything. Surely he must have noticed? Though his own colouring was more fair than dark – 'That's the Viking in the Andrewes' blood,' he'd once remarked. 'An' I'd an uncle wi' the same eyes!' Of course she could not be certain; perhaps she was even deluding herself. There were times at night when she lay awake, thinking back on it all, blaming herself bitterly. And praying that Robert might be John's child, not Tim's – the dates tallied just as well – whatever she felt in her heart.

She had been so wrong, she now thought. So weak.

In the kitchen she was just in time to rescue the meat before it burned. Her new cook, now Ali had returned to India, was a young Gikuyu named Njoroge – Gaby had immediately called him Joe – who was quite bewildered by her array of pots, pans and cutlery. But he seemed willing enough to learn and the children liked him, specially Michael.

'Now carry this in,' she instructed, placing two dishes of hot vegetables on the tray. His command of Swahili was still weak and she knew no Gikuyu, but with the help of gestures she made herself understood. 'This. Carry – it – in!'

She followed with the meat.

'Simple homely fare!' John announced heartily as she set it down on the table, and the remark irritated her, considering the trouble she'd taken. 'We've none o' your

260

cathedral town sophistication here, Mr Catchpole. My
love, Mr Catchpole was tellin' me his father is in the
church, so ye've somethin' in common, the two o' ye.'

'A b-b-bishop,' Catchpole said, reddening again.

'Then I'm surprised at you keeping my husband out
drinking till all hours.'

She had meant the words to be lightly spoken, but as
soon as they were out of her mouth she realized her
tiredness and irritation had got the better of her.

'I . . . I . . .' Catchpole stammered in embarrassment.

'If you must know, my father was a Baptist preacher—'

'A very fine one!' John confirmed expansively.

'—who disapproved of the Church of England,' she went
on doggedly. 'And his views on strong drink were equally
uncompromising. Have some potatoes, Mr Catchpole. We
grow them ourselves.'

'Th-th-thank you.'

'My wife's no' that intolerant hersel', though.' John
rested his hand on hers for a moment, as though trying to
share some understanding with her. Or make it seem that
way. Oh, what *had* happened at the Inquiry, she wondered;
yet she couldn't ask him, not with Catchpole there.

'It has not been an easy day, Mr Catchpole, starting
with the zebra breaking through our fence again, trampling
the vegetables. And that's the way it went on.' It was only
a vague attempt at an apology, she knew, but her sharp
mood refused to soften any further. 'Oh, do eat your simple
homely fare.'

'My, love, I didna mean it like that, d'ye ken!'

'It's v-v-very g-g-g . . .'

She ignored both of them. 'I was about to tell you we've
a friend whose father is a Church of England vicar. In
some ways you're very alike.'

'Ay, Tim Wilton. Ye've come across a vicar o' the name
o' Wilton, mebbe? We'd a letter from him today, my love,
in the Office. Arrived on the same train as Mr Catchpole
here. Says he's walkin' again.'

'You mean without crutches?' She felt herself turning
hot and cold as she tried to control that tremble in her

voice. Deliberately she lowered her fork and looked directly across the table at him, speaking as coolly as she could manage. 'Then it was successful, the operation?'

'Ay, I thought that'd please ye. Still needs a stick, he says, but he can get about.' He spooned a generous quantity of mustard on to the side of his plate, much more than he usually took; she could have screamed at him. 'This roast's first-rate.'

'It's overdone.' She forced herself to eat again, then asked off-handedly, 'Is he coming back to the railway?'

'Nay, he canna expect that, he's disabled still. Seems he goes to see the specialist every month even now.' He turned to Catchpole. 'We're both very fond o' the lad, d'ye understand? Used to be my assistant up till a couple of years ago, an' then . . .'

She only half-listened as John began a lengthy account of how Gikuyu war parties had attacked the *boma*, playing down his own part in the story as usual. If it had not been for Major Arbuthnot letting slip one day that John might have been recommended for the Victoria Cross had he been a soldier, not a civilian, she would never have known herself what had really happened. Tim had told her nothing, having been only partly conscious during most of the fighting.

Since his return to England she had hardly had a word from him, not directly, other than a polite note at Christmas and for her birthday. Before he left they had agreed that was the way it had to be, although she guessed that these long, chatty letters he sent to his old colleagues in the Railway Office were really his discreet way of letting her know what he was doing. They would not correspond, not see each other again, try to forget everything they meant to each other – that had been the arrangement. Yet it was not possible, not that last part, however sorely she regretted it. She felt guilty towards John, and that made her often bad-tempered and irritable; above all, she felt she was marooned on some drifting raft on the ocean, not knowing where she was going.

You could leave John and come back to England with me, he had suggested before he went. But he was so wrong – that was something she could never do. Even the thought of it hurt her, in spite of all her feelings for Tim. At times, as she agonized over what had become of her life, she wondered if any of it would have happened if that animal Muldoon had not tried to rape her; before then, everything had seemed so innocent and straightforward. So uncomplicated. But then she always dismissed the thought, remembering one of her father's pet phrases when she was a child, 'None but yourself to blame, Hester!' And he was right.

A burst of loud, rough laughter broke across the silence outside the bungalow, receding slowly as a rowdy group of men made their way out of town in the directions of the canvas village they called Tentfontein. One was shouting something in Afrikaans, she did not understand what. These days Nairobi was so different. Since the fire it had developed into a wild frontier town with saloons, gambling dens, brothels, every kind of vice. The administration had already started work on a prison, choosing a site – oddly, it seemed to her – adjacent to the African hospital. There was no more nursing for her, either, now both hospitals employed professionally qualified sisters. She was not needed – and it had all happened so quickly!

With the completion of the railway, John's life too had changed. He was mostly confined to Nairobi these days, no longer meeting the challenge of deserts and dense forests, but planning maintenance schedules and mooching around the workshops, moody and unpredictable. She could understand that, too; it had all become so humdrum, and that old sense of excitement had gone.

She began to collect up the dishes and called Joe to take them into the kitchen. John was leaning back in his chair, quizzing Catchpole in that half-teasing, half-serious vein which she knew from experience meant that he was seething with anger, yet trying to hide it.

'Ye've seen somethin' o' farmin' in Africa, ye say?'

'W-with m-m-my uncle in S-south Africa.'

263

'My love, I was advisin' Mr Catchpole only an idiot would buy land to farm here in British East. D'ye no' agree?'

'I know one who has thought about it.'

'Och, the land's rich, the climate's right – but ye dinna think Mr Catchpole would be better off wi' a farm in England?'

'M-m-my f-father says i-it's our r-r-responsibility to extend the Empire,' Catchpole declared hotly, the blood flaring up in his face again. 'W-we Eng . . . English-speaking p-p-peoples must sh-share our . . . our advantages w-with the rr-rest of the w-world.'

'Ay, but let's stick to the facts, d'ye mind?' John seemed quite relentless, the way he was trying to pin the young man down. 'In the Foreign Office in London there are some fine, upright gentlemen who've ne'er set foot on African soil, yet they lay down the rules for those who have. Ye'd best pay attention. If ye buy land here, ye must fence it an' put at least a quarter o' the acreage under cultivation within an agreed period o' time, else ye forfeit the lot, wi' no compensation. But mark this – all standin' timber belongs to the Crown an' ye're forbidden to fell trees for your fence.'

'Th-there m-must be a r-r-reason.'

'Ay, no doubt – but listen. The Crown can build public roads an' waterways across your land, wi'out payment. An' ye're no' permitted to keep goats.'

'G-goats? B-b-but I've s-seen—'

'No *settler* may keep goats. What ye've seen belong to Africans.'

'D-d-don't the s-settlers ob-object?'

'Ay.'

'M-m-my f-father c-could ask a . . . ask a question in the Hou-House of Lords.'

'Ye're a man well worth knowin', Mr Catchpole! I'm glad I made your acquaintance.'

A moth fluttered around the oil lamp, knocking against the glass funnel. Hester scooped it up in her cupped hands and threw it out into the night. She had heard the arguments before when they had talked over the idea of taking up farming instead of the railway. She had wanted to pay for the land, too, once she had discovered how much her father had left – his printed sermons and devotional books had brought in far more than he had ever admitted – but John had refused to accept a penny of it, saying it was her security in case anything happened to him. Too proud, of course – that was the real reason. He wanted everything to be his own unaided achievement.

And his bitterness about officials from London, that was another thing. If only she knew what had happened at the Inquiry. They had not reached any conclusions, obviously: the first two Committees had taken months to finalize their reports. But something must have put him in this mood. She had passed one of the London inspectors on her way to shop at Patel's *duka* the other day – his *Emporium*, as he called it – and she was in no doubt who he was. A supercilious man in pince-nez glasses and a dark, thick suit, with stiff butterfly collar and starched cuffs to match, for all the world as though he were still in Whitehall.

No, whatever they did would not surprise her in the least. John was right.

'I'll walk ye back,' he said, standing up.

'Th-there's n-n-no n-need.'

'The fresh air'll be welcome.' Even now, she thought, he was putting off telling her about it. Then, to her surprise, he produced a revolver from his pocket and loaded it. 'I take it ye're no' armed? Ye'd best have charge o' Schwartz's gun.'

'John, what's going on?' she demanded anxiously. 'If there's going to be shooting . . .'

'Nay, lass, I'm jus' playin' it a wee bit cautious, that's all.'

'M-Mrs Andrewes, I t-trust I've n-not d-d-destroyed y-your evening . . .'

She cut short his thanks. 'I think I hear Robert crying, so I'll say goodnight. I hope no one bothers you, Mr Catchpole.'

As she went towards the bedroom she could hear John

saying, 'Ye've no' met our three bairns, but mebbe next time, eh? We'll be seein' somethin' of ye while ye're here.'

What was he up to, she wondered as she picked up the baby and began to walk up and down, patting his back and humming her little tune. His kingdom had gone, that was the main problem – the railhead camps, the coolies, his daily battle against the rough terrain, pushing the railway on. He missed it all. Perhaps that was why he spent so much time now down at Patel's *duka*. Perhaps they sat there talking over old days. He liked to speak the language, he said, and smell the spices in the cooking – well, she'd no objection to that. But Patel himself had changed now he had settled down. As a sepoy she had always thought him rather scruffy, disreputable-looking, but these days he wore new clothes and had put on weight, every inch a respectable businessman.

She shook her head at Robert whose face wrinkled into a big wide smile. 'What are we going to do about him, that father of yours?' she asked softly. His pure blue eyes gazed back at her.

Tim's eyes, she was sure.

Andrewes expected trouble. It was pitch dark, relieved only by a few faint smudges of light from occasional windows. Schwartz and his cronies could be waiting for them anywhere along the way. Keeping to the centre of the road, they made for the gleam of the safari lamps hanging outside the Norfolk Hotel and were about half-way there when he spotted a tell-tale move among the shadows.

'Ay, as I feared,' he muttered to Catchpole. 'A reception committee. Stick close to me, lad.'

'I . . . I . . . I . . . m-must ap-p-pologize I dr-dragged y-you . . .'

'Jus' keep your eyes skinned on your side o' the road.'

As he spoke, three men emerged ahead of them from hiding places between the buildings; simultaneously, he heard the crunching of footsteps on the murram behind.

'Take no notice,' he said, keeping his voice down.

But the men blocked the way. They were armed with heavy cudgels – pickaxe handles, by the look of them – which they held purposefully. And Andrewes could still hear the footsteps behind him, though not too close yet.

'In a hurry then?' Grinning, the man in the centre of the group of three stepped in front of him, raising the cudgel slightly to make sure he saw it. The other two moved in from the sides.

'If ye'll kindly allow us to pass . . .' Andrewes requested civilly.

'An' if we don't?'

'Ay, well in that case . . .' He tried an old trick, turning slightly as if about to retreat.

The thug on his left had started to guffaw when Andrewes' fist caught him unawares, knocking the laugh back into his throat. Any other man would have been flat on his back after that tap on the jaw, but he was thickset, solid as a rock, and merely staggered back momentarily before laying into Andrewes with his cudgel.

Andrewes tried to dodge away, but the other two came at him, aiming vicious blows at his shoulders and back; there was no way he could avoid them. Then, unexpectedly, a shot was fired.

'N-now st-stop this, or I'll sh-shoot!'

For a moment Andrewes' assailants were caught off guard; he turned on the nearest, wrenched the pickaxe handle out of his hand and sent him sprawling on the ground.

'I . . . I m-mean it!' Catchpole warned again. He had been pointing the revolver at the sky but now he levelled it at them.

The two remaining men glanced at each other uneasily but before they could react the tension was broken by a woman's voice booming out of the darkness.

'Ee, Jimmy, it's that young man I were telling 'ee about, an' he needs help.' Then she called out, 'Tha' be all right, duckie, we're here!'

She came striding towards them, a large buxom woman

in a big hat, with Jimmy Hathaway following anxiously behind.

'Giving 'ee some trouble, are they?' she demanded.

'It's all s-s-sorted out n-now, th-thank you,' Catchpole stuttered calmly. 'I th-think you s-surprised them.'

The burliest of the thugs shifted his gaze from the large woman to Catchpole, whose gun still pointed directly at his stomach. In disgust, he threw the pickaxe handle aside and started to walk away. 'Shit!' he swore. Andrewes persuaded him to stay with a well-placed punch; he felt the nose cartilege give way under his knuckles. His companion, too, tried to escape but Jimmy's woman friend stuck out a foot and tripped him up; then she retrieved one of the pickaxe handles and offered to brain him if he moved.

'My wife Ada,' Jimmy announced proudly. 'Just arrived from Manchester today.'

'Let's take a look at 'em.'

Advising Catchpole to shoot if they gave any trouble, he ordered the three men to move slowly towards the Norfolk Hotel where, under the light of the safari lamps, he inspected each one in turn. Two were Boers, hefty but overweight; the third, an Australian with a mass of tattoos over his arms and hands, looked more dangerous.

'I'll no' ask ye how much ye were paid, nor who set ye on to this,' he told them grimly, his fury still simmering, 'but I'll cripple any man who attempts t'interfere wi' me or my friends again – d'ye ken? I swear by God Almighty I will. An' I've a sharp memory for faces.'

Then he dismissed them. They made as if to go into the Norfolk but he barred their way; without arguing, they went off in the direction of Tentfontein. Somewhere in the darkness a fourth man still lurked – Schwartz, he guessed; or perhaps his partner, Hans de Jong. As Hester had so rightly observed, he had the knack of making enemies for himself.

'King John, I'd like 'ee to meet my wife Ada,' Jimmy Hathaway was saying, again attempting a formal introduction.

He grasped her hand; it was as strong as any man's. 'I'm pleased to make your acquaintance, Mrs Hathaway, an' grateful for your help. If ye'll excuse me for tonight, I've a few matters that need attendin' to.'

His shoulders ached and he could swear that his back was bleeding in several places. He was worried too in case they got to Hester. He cut through Catchpole's stuttered thanks, waving aside his insistence on buying drinks for everyone, and hurried back down the wide dark track towards the bungalow. No sign of Schwartz anywhere nearby but . . .

'Stop where you are! I've a shotgun aimed directly at you and I shall not hesitate to shoot.'

Andrewes chuckled, relaxing. 'It's me, Hester my love!' he called out of the darkness.

'Oh, John – thank God! I heard shots, but I couldn't leave the children and . . .'

'Nay, lass, ye did right.' He took the shotgun – his new Holland – from her and looked around carefully before going in. Ay, well maybe Schwartz had accepted defeat; revenge might be sweet but it put no money in the bank.

Her arms were around him the moment he had locked the door, hugging him as they kissed, deeply, longingly, the tension between them gone. Then he winced. He tried to laugh it off but she knew him too well for that.

'You're hurt!' she exclaimed, stepping back to examine his face in the light of the pressure lamp. 'Under your eye and . . . Take your jacket off.'

'A couple o' wee bruises.'

'And that shot?'

He explained what had happened, trying to imitate Catchpole's stutters and stammers as he challenged the three thugs, and telling her about Jimmy Hathaway's wife, who looked tough enough to take on any of them. 'I only wish ye'd been there to see it!'

She removed his shirt and flannel spine-pad as he talked, drawing a quick breath when she saw the great weals and bruises across his back and the ugly black and yellow patch spreading over his ribs. They tingled painfully as her fingertips touched them.

'I'll wake Njoroge, get him to boil some water . . .'

'Nay, lass.' He put a hand on her arm, stopping her. 'I'd like jus' us two, together – d'ye no' see what I mean?'

Gently he kissed her, exploring her upturned face with his lips, amazed at the smoothness of her skin, still as fresh and soft as when they first met in spite of seven years in Africa. He loosened her hair to let it tumble down richly over her shoulders, then kissed her lips again, probing gently with the tip of his tongue, inviting, confessing his love, until she broke away with a laugh to protest that his wounds had better be cleaned and dressed, else she would be failing in her duty.

'What duty?' he mocked her, teasing. 'My wife has no duties.'

'Repeat that tomorrow morning, I dare you!' She dodged away from his arms. 'If you still remember. No duties indeed!'

They fetched out the camp bath and she poured kettle after kettle of boiling water into it, while he watched her, remembering the eager expression on her face during their long talks in Liverpool, her excitement . . . Had he really lost touch with her, as he so often felt these days? Or was it all in his own imagination? Or a fault in himself, most likely.

When the bath was ready he stripped off the rest of his clothes and lowered himself into it, grimacing at the sting of the hot water on his wounds; she had added two handfuls of salt as a disinfectant. After a time she knelt down, took a soft flannel and began washing him gently, ignoring his half-hearted protests. He lay back contentedly as she went over his chest and stomach, moving down to the blue-black contusions on his thighs and hips. They had known what they were about, those ruffians with their pickaxe handles; it seemed all the dregs from the world's shipping lanes, all the outcasts from prospectors' townships and harbour brothels, were congregating in East Africa these days.

He gathered Hester's thick hair back from her face and she turned to look questioningly at him. Cupping his hand round the back of her neck, he drew her towards him to kiss her, savouringly; then, fumbling, he started opening the buttons of her bodice.

'Your hands are wet!' she laughed, her voice low.

But she helped him with the remaining buttons, slipping her clothes down over her shoulders to her waist until her breasts hung free. Spreading his hand with fingers apart he caressed her lightly, his palm brushing softly against her as again they kissed, and he felt her nipples hardening under his touch. Then he flinched as his ribs pressed against the wooden struts of the canvas camp bath.

'You need looking after,' she declared, breaking away from him to cover herself again. 'D'you always behave that way towards your nurses?'

'Stay like that!' He caught her hand to prevent her pulling the bodice straight. 'We've precious few times when we can be alone together, lass.'

'I reckon you should be ashamed of yourself, John Philip Andrewes.' She retrieved the flannel from the water, then looked mischievously at his erect manhood. 'Lying there like Adam without so much as a fig leaf to preserve the decencies. Though that's something we can soon put right.'

She draped the flannel over his sex, then sat back on her haunches to gaze at him. Drops of water trickled over her breasts, gleaming wet in the soft light.

He sat up in the bath, reaching out for her with both arms; but, mocking, she warned him off.

'You're badly hurt though you'll not admit it, so the best programme for tonight is liniment on those bruises, then sleep.' He stretched out for her again but she shook her head, teasing. 'No,' she said, 'the doctor would not approve. Besides, you're making a terrible mess of my skirt. It's soaking wet.'

'Take it off.'

'You forget yourself! I'm the minister's daughter!' As she spoke she was already loosening the waistband. 'It's a shame they don't make baths wide enough for two –

though maybe it's just as well! Is this what you wanted, m'sieur?

Her clothes dropped to her ankles as she stood up smiling wryly at him, but her eyes dancing. Stepping out of them, she stooped to pick them up item by item, draping them tidily over a chair. From her movements he could see she was very conscious of him looking at her.

'Now maybe you'd like me to put on some war paint and do a hornpipe?'

Before he could answer she was back at his side, kneeling again, her arms around him. His hands wandered over her body as they kissed. She murmured how much she loved him, how anxious she had sometimes been, not least when he had gone out with Catchpole and she had heard the shot; then she fell silent as he held her; her hands moved gently over the firm muscles of his belly, seeking him, throwing the flannel aside, closing around him.

He got out of the bath to gather her up and carry her to the bed, but he flinched again as the pain stabbed through his ribs. She shook her head and backed away.

'John, be sensible,' she said firmly. 'Until the doctor's seen that tomorrow.'

'A cracked rib, lass. Bind it up firmly, in time it'll heal itself.'

But she refused to take it so lightly. Bringing a towel from the chest, she dried him carefully before applying liniment to the worst of the bruises. As she bent over him, still naked, the lamp threw giant breast-shadows against the wall, firm and shapely.

'No one would think ye'd borne three bairns, my love,' he said, his hands straying over her as she worked.

'Behave yourself now, you'll make me spill the stuff!'

'Ye're the bonniest woman in Africa, d'ye ken? An' I love ye.'

'You'll wake Gaby if you're not quiet.'

For a moment she stood quite still as his hand lingered on her breast, then moved slowly down. 'Hester . . .'

'Raise your arms and I'll bind up those ribs.' She

unwound the bandage, passing it around him. 'Keep still now.'

The firmness of the bandaging already brought some relief from the nagging pain. He waited patiently until she had finished securing it with the safety pin before catching hold of her, sinking down with her on to the bed, kissing her lips, her eyes, the tip of her nose, his hands caressing her – until she protested once more, faintly, that with all those bruises, those cracked ribs, he would do better to sleep. And while she protested, and while he was agreeing with her, they made love – unhurried, sensuous, each totally aware of the other.

Much later, as they lay side by side, his leg across hers, he said, 'Hester, love, d'ye think if we applied for some land to farm we might make a go of it?'

A long silence. 'I don't know.'

'I checked again about India. Nothin' suitable, no' at the right sort o' level. But I told ye that.'

'Yes, you told me.'

'An' other places – well, it wouldna be right, no' wi' the bairns. But if we bought a farm here, mebbe wi' Catchpole as a neighbour, or even in together as a partnership . . . I havena thought it through yet, it's jus' a vague idea, but—'

She kissed him, running her hand slowly over his face. 'John, what went wrong at the Inquiry today?'

'I got the boot. Kicked me out. Termination o' contract.'

'But *why?*' She raised herself on her elbow, furious.

'There was this wee man from London,' he confessed, glad he could tell her at last; it was his own stupid fault, anyway.

'With glasses? I've seen him.'

'He was gettin' on my nerves all day. Kept sayin "Ye ovahweached yesel', Mr Andrewes!" till I couldna help tellin' him what I thought o' him an' his like. Och, nothin' clever – I said he was an idiot, an' that went for the rest o' the Committee too, an' they'd had two Inquiries already, so why did they want a third, except for a free trip out to Africa?'

'And that put their backs up?'

273

'Ordered me to wait outside like some wee schoolboy while they decided what to do. Och, they'd half made up their minds before today. When they summoned me in again, they said I'd a choice – either resign or be sacked. Summary dismissal. So that's what I chose to save mesel' the bother o' writin' out my resignation.'

For a time she was silent. 'Yes,' she said at last, thoughtfully. 'A farm would be something new, wouldn't it?'

'Ye dinna blame me, lass?'

A laugh bubbled up inside her, as if all her old sense of fun had suddenly flooded back. 'Oh, John, that was so like you!' Her voice danced. 'If only I could've seen that man's face!'

She snuggled up to him cosily and he felt reassured by her closeness. Ay, a partnership, that'd be the thing, he decided. Put it on a proper business footing. Cash crops – coffee, mebbe; or sisal. He'd have a word wi' Catchpole, sound him out; they'd need a man wi' farmin' experience. He'd write to Tim Wilton too, in case he'd like to come in on the deal once he'd finished wi' the doctors. They'd make a good team.

Ay, a first-rate team, he thought drowsily as he slipped away into a contented sleep.

# TWO

Hester anxiously supervised the loading of her precious household goods on to the long wagon which John had bought to transport them all to their new farm. Several months had passed already since his final quarrel with the Railway Office. During that time he had raised some capital of his own – she could not be sure how, he had spoken of it only airily, leaving all the details vague – and negotiated a large loan from the bank whose manager, he had explained approvingly, had shown sound business sense in his appreciation of the plans for the new estate. She did not mention that she had visited the bank herself several days earlier to offer her inheritance – he still refused to take any of it – as collateral for any sum he wished to borrow, on condition that they kept it secret. The bonds and share certificates had already been deposited at their head office in London.

'Careful with that box, Joe!' she cried out as Njoroge staggered under the weight of her carefully-packed crockery.

It was the set she had brought out from Liverpool, a wedding present; throughout those long years in railhead camps she had carried it with her, with only very few breakages – three cups, a couple of saucers, nothing more.

She felt disappointed that no one else seemed to share the excitement welling up inside her. At last they would have a place of their own; they would be answerable to no one but themselves! John was so calm, reminding everyone dourly that they would be travelling over rough country for at least three days and everything had to be securely lashed down. Gaby was looking after baby Robert, hugging her pet gazelle, and telling them both long, complicated stories which neither understood. On the veranda, Michael was still playing unconcernedly, ignoring the bustle going

275

on around him. Even the six humped oxen which were to pull the wagon stood docilely in the shade, uninterested.

They were already overloaded with pots and pans, oil lamps, a zinc hip bath, candles, camp furniture, an iron bedstead, some wooden chairs she'd had specially made, a sewing machine, a cradle on rockers – though Robert had already grown out of it – John's tool kit, spades, pangas, coils of wire, pickaxes, rope, a medical chest, a shining new plough recently acquired from P & R – why did he always have to buy everything through Patel? – buckets, laundry baskets, two framed pictures of Scottish glens, a carton of well-thumbed books – oh, a thousand things! Not forgetting the jars and tins of food, bags of *posho*, matches, seeds and other supplies to keep them going until the first crops could be harvested.

By contrast, Nathaniel Catchpole's wagon a few yards away seemed unnaturally tidy. He had packed everything into neat wooden crates, explaining, 'Cr-crates'll c-come in use-useful when w-wee g-get th-there, just s-see if they d-d-don't!'

She had been amused – and pleased – to see how he had dressed for the occasion too, in light trousers and a blazer, with a white pith helmet. Sarcastic remarks from John left him quite unmoved, and she was convinced he was just as intent on creating his own legend as any other man in British East. Why, she wondered, had the human male been born with such a high opinion of itself?

It was the most improbable partnership; no two men could be more dissimilar than Catchpole and John. As far as she could tell, the general opinion in Nairobi seemed to be that it could never work out, but she was not so sure. Once John's heart was set on something . . . And with an estate of six thousand acres of virgin country to bring under cultivation, there was plenty of space for each to get on with his own job without worrying the other. Six thousand acres . . . However hard she tried, it was impossible to visualize that amount of land. It was frightening even to think about it, but John had insisted. He always had such grandiose plans. Before they married it was

India; now it was the estate. 'Wi' young Catchpole, an' mebbe Tim Wilton, to help we can built it into a flourishin' business!' he had argued.

'Tim?' She had been startled. Shocked. 'You've asked Tim?'

'Ay – wrote to him. Letter went off yesterday.'

The thought of Tim and John working together again, living on the same farm, so close – no, that was something she could not take. She could feel them even now tearing her apart between the two of them; and not realizing it, that was the worst aspect. The moment she could, she slipped out to send off a secret telegram – breaking all her own rules – asking Tim not to decide until he had received a letter from her. It was a risk, but what alternative did she have? It was not until weeks later, when Tim's own wire arrived addressed to John to say he could not leave his London doctors for quite a while yet, that she began slowly to feel secure again. 'God bless you, Tim,' she had whispered gratefully.

At last the wagons were ready. John was about to inspan the oxen when a small zebra-drawn cart approached, weighted down with bundles and boxes, and driven by Ada Hathaway. 'Ee, I thought I'd never be ready an' tha'd leave without me!' she boomed, laughing. She surveyed the wagon. 'Tha's taking some bits an' pieces!'

She was a memorable sight, dressed in a man's suit but with a frilly blouse underneath, and a wide-brimmed felt hat. Hester had taken to her immediately – her loud, down-to-earth Northern manner, her no-nonsense way of cutting everybody down to size and that broad, earthy humour which Manchester shared with Liverpool. One night, reminiscing together, she had confided how much she missed the bustle of her own market stall; Jimmy was happy enough without her, she said, and she had considered catching the next boat home but somehow – well it didn't seem right, not after that long journey, so she'd rented a cart from Patel, spent her few remaining pounds on beads, blankets, mirrors, other trade goods, and intended to see what business she could pick up. Could she travel with them, she had asked, at least part of the way?

And John had laughed, as if he had known about it all along. Perhaps he'd even put her up to it.

'I'll no' be a couple o' minutes, Mrs Hathaway!' he called over his shoulder, red-faced. 'All I need's a wee sign o' co-operation from these beasties.'

'P-perhaps if I . . .?' Catchpole offered, hurrying across. Miraculously, his stammer disappeared as he coaxed the ox back towards the shaft.

'He's got the touch!' Ada Hathaway approved.

Around the corner came five rickshaws at high speed, each pulled by two Africans, their anklet bells jingling, raising clouds of dust. Their passengers, fresh-faced young bloods straight out from home, urged them on with promises of double money for the winners.

'Racing!' Ada Hathaway was disgusted. 'In middle o' town with kids about an' folk trying to earn an honest living! A few pounds they'll have bet, an' all! These young men, tha'll never guess what I've heard about them. They have black girls in them bachelor quarters, not a stitch on, not even when they're fetching food in. How they can eat it, beats me. As for what goes on afterwards, that's nobody's business.' Her voice dropped to a whisper. 'Two or three on bed at once, an' some no more'n eleven or twelve years old. Mere children. Should be stopped if you ask me.'

'I think John's more at home with steam engines,' Hester answered vaguely, watching him in difficulties with the oxen again.

There was a great shout from up the road as a rickshaw tipped over near the Norfolk Hotel; the others piled into it, unable to stop in time. Two rickshaw boys lay on the ground, obviously hurt; the young bloods, uninjured, were arguing and laughing as they tried to sort things out. 'I say! I say!' one shouted in a shrill, boyish voice. 'Send for fresh rickshaws, what? We must settle this now!'

'I'm glad we're leaving Nairobi,' Hester commented with a sudden intensity. 'I don't want my sons to grow up like that.'

With John driving, their own wagon took the lead; Hester sat with the children under the rounded canvas cover at the rear, feeling she could manage the oxen better herself, but not wishing to upset him by saying so. Next in line came Ada Hathaway on her zebra cart, every so often calling out some cheerful remark, or even bursting into song. She had a fine contralto voice and a vast repertory of music hall hits and drawing room ballads: *Come into the garden, Maud* and *Little Brown Jug* and *Our Lodger's Such a Nice Young Man* and – her favourite – *Ilkley Moor* rolled out across the plains, startling the gazelles.

Following her came Nathaniel Catchpole, controlling his own team of oxen with no more than a wink and a nod; sometimes walking alongside, sometimes riding on the wagon. His smart clothes – more suitable for Oxford picnics than for Africa – were soon covered with the same red dust which smothered everything.

It rose in great clouds wherever the wagons went, getting into their eyes, their ears, their nostrils, even causing Ada Hathaway to break off in mid-chorus – though she cleared her throat, spat, and sang on.

Gaby called out excitedly at the sight of giraffes feeding off the tops of the flat acacias; but after the first day she took no more notice, there were so many. Herds of gazelles and zebra grazing together raised their heads in curiosity as the wagon train passed. Only the nearest ran off to a safer distance. The buffaloes scorned them, as though knowing the plain was theirs.

If it weren't for the dust, Hester thought as they went on mile after mile. And how would they ever manage to tame this country? The very word *farm* brought a picture to her mind of gentle English meadows, haystacks, milking time – nothing like this! Should they even be trying? This land was – oh, in some ways so Biblical! As they travelled through it, she seemed to hear her father expounding Genesis: God created it in this manner and this was how He intended it to remain.

The few Africans they passed on the way stared at them neutrally. Who could tell what they thought about these heavily-laden long wagons rumbling over their country, bringing strangers to settle on the empty land? But at least there were no more armed attacks, not since that terrible battle at the *boma* when so many had been killed. John was always reluctant to talk about it; when he did, she was aware of the pain in his eyes.

'Mama!' Gaby burst impatiently across her thoughts on the third morning of their journey. 'What if a lion eats Mrs Hathaway's zebra?'

'Then she'll have to get another one, dear.' She held on to her double terai, while with her free hand she tried to steady Robert's sleeping basket as the wagon lurched over rills and pot-holes. He was sitting in it, good as gold, playing with some blocks of wood John had given him. 'And shoot the lion, I expect.'

'What if the lion eats Mrs Hathaway?' Gaby insisted.

'He'd need mighty sharp teeth!' Ada Hathaway shouted out cheerfully from behind them. 'I'm as tough as ol' boots, luv!'

Suddenly a strange chattering sound came from above them and Njoroge pointed up excitedly at a small grey bird. As they watched, it flew a little ahead of them, as if coaxing them to follow . . . follow . . . follow . . .

'That's good luck!' John exclaimed from the front of the wagon. 'That's a honey guide, Gaby, tryin' to lead us to where the bees are nestin'. It wants us to break open a hive, so it can feed off the honeycombs – an' takin' our road, it's a good omen!'

An hour later the track ended abruptly at the side of a sluggish brown stream. Its banks were one vast mud patch, pock-marked with scores of hoof-prints, large and small; across it were deep parallel runnels left by the wheels of wagon-trains which had been there before them.

'It's where the animals come to drink,' Hester explained to Gaby and Michael as she watched John jump down to lead the oxen across.

He went forward to the leading pair and grasped the harness. 'Off we go, then!' he called out to them, but they remained stubbornly rooted to the spot, refusing to move.

Hester pressed her lips together to suppress a laugh. She could not get down to help him, not with Robert crawling over her, and she could see from his face it had become a battle of wills between him and oxen.

'What's ailin' ye, ye daft beasts?' he demanded, exasperated. 'If ye two in front make a start, the others'll follow . . .'

A giggle escaped, and although she stopped it immediately, she was too late: Gaby took the cue and her hearty laugh rang out across the quiet African landscape.

'Ay, ye can laugh!' John exploded at them darkly, as Ada Hathaway joined in.

The sudden noise goaded the two leading oxen into moving and the others followed suit, twisting almost at right-angles to the direction he wanted them to take. The wagon lurched frighteningly.

'John, stop them!' Hester clutched Robert tightly while holding on desperately to the side as the loads shifted on the tilting wagon. 'Do something!'

Michael lost his balance; he might have been hurt if Gaby hadn't caught him. They both staggered back against Hester's legs and sat down heavily on her feet. Meanwhile Catchpole had seen what was happening and he ran towards them, plunging up to his knees in mud.

'St-stand cl-clear!' he stuttered, taking charge. 'I'll . . . I'll . . .'

He gave up attempting to explain and began talking instead to the oxen who were now motionless again – in fact, looking rather smug, Hester thought, as one turned its head and seemed to stare at her. Gradually he coaxed them to reverse slowly, step by step, the whole team of six, until the wagon had gently righted itself and stood on solid ground once more.

'We're getting down!' Hester declared firmly, now convinced that crossing the mud on foot was the lesser evil. She called Njoroge to her. 'Joe, you can take Michael, and Gaby can climb down by herself.'

'I've ne'er felt such a fool,' John confessed ruefully as he watched Catchpole still talking quietly to the oxen. 'They'd no' go the way I wanted.

'Not everyone does, John,' she commented tartly, thinking, what if one of the children had fallen off – been killed even?

A bellow of laughter came from Ada Hathaway behind them, easing the tension. 'Ee, lad, tha looked a right Charlie! An' I could do nowt to help, I'd only've made matters worse! Now, how are we going to get across this mud, then?'

Catchpole took charge of fording the stream while John and Ada Hathaway lent a couple of broad shoulders to heave from behind and wind on the brake whenever they felt it was about to slip back. Hester left them to it and wandered upstream to search for a less muddy place to cross, finding a spot where the water parted gently around a cluster of flat, protruding rocks. She sent Njoroge over first, then carried the children to him one by one.

Sitting down afterwards to wring the water out of her soaking wet skirt, she longed to strip everything off and plunge into that cool water to wash away all the dust and mud and sweat. She could imagine their faces, though, if she did anything of the kind! And her father would look down from Heaven – oh, she'd no doubt he was up there! – to voice his disapproval at her even thinking such thoughts.

Though – did people wear clothes in Heaven, she wondered irreverently, or did they walk about dressed only in Innocence, as in the Garden of Eden before the Fall?

John was studying the survey map with Ada Hathaway, pointing out several settler farms not far away. He had already been out on safari in this direction a few weeks earlier to verify the land he was buying – 'To check it's good farmin' country, lass,' he had explained, 'an' make some arrangements regardin' accommodation.' Though goodness knows what that meant: she had expected to be living in a tent again for the first few months.

'This is where Mrs Hathaway parts company wi' us, my love,' he said as she approached, her wet skirt clinging to her ankles. 'She goes on northwards for a mile or two, while we've another ten to cover.'

'Today?'

'Ay, it's early still. A half-hour break here, a bite to eat, an' then let's see how far we can get. Any snags, we can always camp one more night.'

It was late afternoon when they arrived; by then, the children were tired and squabbling, though fortunately Robert had fallen asleep at last. The country had become hilly and the wagons moved forward with difficulty through grass and low scrub, following the contours of the land. Then, dramatically, she saw a wide valley spread out in front of her. Its beauty was breathtaking, with the hills on one side bathed in golden sunlight, while on the other the slopes were dappled with soft-edged shadows. There were occasional trees standing in majestic isolation, as well as stretches of forest and – high up – bald patches of moss and smooth rock. And a stream, its water pure silver, with a little group of three African huts nearby.

'Whoa!' John cried loudly, reining in. He turned towards her with a great smile of contentment on his face. 'How d'ye like it, lass?'

'This is it?' All sorts of contradictory thoughts crowded into her head. It was beautiful beyond all description, but how would they ever manage to clear enough land to grow anything?

'Ay, this is it.' He waved his arm to embrace the whole valley – oh, it seemed like a wilderness now . . . 'This is the farm. An' there ye see three wee houses where we can live. For the time bein', that is. 'D'ye remember, lass – Buckingham Palace?' He laughed happily. 'Ay, it'll be all right here, d'ye ken – once we get organized!'

Hester looked around and slowly her apprehension subsided again. She scrambled down from the wagon, catching her skirt on the corner of one of the boxes and giving it a tug which ripped it, but that didn't seem to matter now! She ran around to where John was winding on the brake. 'Oh, John, it's lovely!' she exclaimed, suddenly overwhelmed. 'Like a dream! I just can't believe we're going to be living in a place like this. After that terrible iron house in Nairobi – or, come to that, those dismal streets in Liverpool. Oh, this is a fairy tale!'

'It'll be a lot o' work, my love.' He was unexpectedly serious again, and so abruptly! Oh, why could his mood never match hers? Why must he always pull back? 'It doesna do to be too romantic about it.'

'Och, dearest John, are ye no' yesel' the most romantic soul I ever met?' she mocked him in lighthearted desperation. She kissed him, a whole series of kisses that set Gaby giggling. 'Is that no' the reason we're both here, plannin' to bring up a family on a grand scale – in a couple o' wee grass huts?'

He laughed, cupping her face in his hands. 'That accent's terrible. Ye'd ne'er pass for a genuine Scot, d'ye ken? As for the huts, they were built specially for us by folk from the village up yonder.' He pointed vaguely towards the hills. 'An' I've arranged wi' the chief – if that's what he is, though it seems there's some doubt – to hire gangs o' young men to come an' help on the land. We'll hang out a safari lamp tonight as a signal we're here. Now I reckon there's jus' two hours o' daylight left, so we'll see to the beddin' first for the bairns if ye're agreeable.'

'I c-c-can g-give you a h-hand,' Cathpole called back from where he was outspanning the oxen. 'M-my th-things c-c-can w-wait till m-morning.'

Michael and Gaby were already busy exploring the huts, shrieking with laughter as they ran from one to the next. While they were unloading the wagon, Robert woke up and wanted to join them. 'Keep away from the stream!' she warned as she gave Njoroge a large bedding roll to carry, taking the next one herself. Yes, whatever happened with the farm, she thought practically, they should at least be able to grow enough food to live on. It was good for John, too, she decided; she had already sensed a change in him as he pointed out where he thought the first vegetable fields should be, where they might try coffee, and where eventually – down at the far end of the valley – Catchpole could have his dairy herd. He was his old self again.

# THREE

Watching from a hill-top, Ngengi had observed the two ox-drawn wagons making their slow progress towards the valley and he had scrambled down, keeping to the cover of the shrubs, to take a closer look. He recognized King John the moment he set eyes on him. He had not seen him again since that terrible day when his father had been manacled to a tree and whipped, a day he would never forget as long as he lived, but there was no mistaking King John. It could not possibly be anyone else.

So he was to be one of the settlers in the next valley. Well, his father had forecast that changes would come to the ridges, brought by such men as King John. They were *siafu*, he had once said, using the Swahili word for those vicious safari ants which marched like soldiers over the country, devouring whatever was in their path. Ngengi knew what he must do. One day, he swore, he would search for that red stranger who had used the whip on his father almost to death; he would complete that punishment which King John had left unfinished.

In the meantime, he must prepare himself for the new ways which the red strangers were already beginning to impose upon the people.

All along the ridge where Ngengi lived with his mother Njeri and his uncle Wanjui, her older brother, people had talked of nothing but settlers for months past – ever since, in fact, the red strangers' medicine men had come to examine the land through their iron tubes. In this way, it was rumoured, they could foretell the best crops for future years; yet, oddly, they ignored the crops of the past – the snatches of millet and sorghum now growing wild where once there had been well-tended farms, abandoned during those bad years of drought and disease when thousands had died. Before they left, the medicine men hammered pieces of angle iron into the soil over a wide area to ensure that only red strangers' crops could be successful there.

Then a few days later a caravan of some fifty porters and *askaris* arrived on the ridge, led by a young red stranger dressed in light brown clothes decorated with shining beads. On his head he wore a pointed pith helmet to make him look taller.

'My name is Jeremy Smith!' he introduced himself through an interpreter. 'I am your District Commissioner. I have come to hear your complaints and problems. And also to collect the hut tax.'

Old Chege answered him. 'First you will wish to rest after your journey.' he said peaceably. 'Tomorrow we can discuss these matters.'

This 'hut tax', they discovered, was no simple matter. He demanded a gift of two rupees for every hut on the ridge and, as everyone could see, his *askaris* were armed with rifles, which made it unwise to refuse. They led their visitor by such winding paths, he could no longer be certain which huts had been counted and which not, while the young men ran ahead to strip the thatch off a few of them to show they were no longer in use. But at last they handed over the payment. To everyone's surprise, Mukiro produced two rupees tied in the corner of his cloth, but most paid in kind and offered the District Commissioner any hens, goats or sheep which looked as though they would not do well.

It was the District Commissioner himself who raised the topic of the settlers. 'They will need plenty of men to help clear the land. Then there will be planting, weeding, harvesting . . .'

'Weeding is women's work,' old Chege explained carefully, as though speaking to a child. 'Some work is for men, some for women. That is the Gikuyu way.'

'Men or women, they will all be paid wages!' The District Commissioner declared enthusiastically. 'Rupees for the hut tax! And something left over for yourselves! Of course, I must tell you, your own land will not be touched.

This is yours for ever. The Great King in London has made that promise. It will be a reserve for the Gikuyu alone.'

While his words were being translated, he looked at them benignly, as if waiting for their gratitude.

'Haiya, the land was given to the Gikuyu by Ngai,' Muthoga broke the silence at last. 'When he showed our father Gikuyu the woods, the streams, the valleys and ridges, did he say, "This is a reserve for you and your children, but over there, that side may be taken by red strangers"?'

A buzz of approval greeted these words. Ngengi, with the others who were present, waited for him to reply to this infallible argument, but he had no ears. He merely said that pieces of angle-iron had been placed in the land – he called them *beacons* – to define the boundaries of the settlers' farms.

Before he departed from the ridge with his *askaris* and porters, he gave old Chege a fine wooden staff which he said was a sign that the Great King recognized him as the 'chief' of this village. Old Chege now carried it wherever he went. It helped steady him on the uneven paths, as his legs were no longer as strong as in his youth.

For a long time no more was heard of settlers until a rumour was carried on the wind that two red strangers had arrived in the district, the people of the next ridge had built huts for them, and then they had left again as suddenly as they came, no one knew why. Now Ngengi had discovered the reason with his own eyes: they had returned with women and children.

The elders summoned him, wanting to know everything in detail. He felt very young and vulnerable as he faced their cross-examination; after all, he was still a boy and his voice was not yet a man's. He tried to recount everything accurately, concealing only the fact that he had recognized King John. It was better not to mention the time before they came to live on the ridge.

'My grandfather's wives cultivated land in that valley,'

old Chege remembered. 'It belongs to the clan. Yet if we attack . . .'

Muthoga shook his head. Everyone knew what he was thinking. So many young men had been killed in the great battle; so many had died later of their wounds; so many still hobbled with the aid of sticks. True, a man's duty was to risk death in war, just as a woman's was to plant seed and transmit life. But . . .

'Our day will come,' he said at last. He was known as the greatest warrior of his time and the others heard him with respect. 'So let us wait with patience.'

'The man who waits never arrives,' old Chege retorted.

'But the hunter who looses his arrow while the lion is too far off, ends his life in the lion's stomach.'

It seemed they had forgotten Ngengi was still there. Listening to them, he remembered those long evenings in his father's *thingira* when these same men went over the self-same arguments. Now, if they spoke of Kamau at all, it was disparagingly. They no longer used his name even, but called him *Mwebongia* – the one who walks alone. They had been wrong, they all now agreed, to accept him on the ridge in the first place.

Such talk always hurt Ngengi. Since the day of the great battle his father had not been seen again. It was assumed at first he had been killed, but then came reports that he was living with another Gikuyu clan at the very foot of Kere-Nyaga. Later still came other stories, claiming he was working for red strangers in Nairobi, or that he had returned to Mombasa and the great water.

Yet how he would have spoken in this debate! Ngengi could almost hear his voice. *First learn the red strangers' knowledge* . . .

'Wherever the rhinoceros wishes to go, man cannot prevent it!' cried Muthoga heatedly, his voice rising above the others.

'Who invites the rhinoceros to walk where millet is planted?' old Chege countered triumphantly.

The following day a great meeting of all the people took place. Ngengi was there with his two friends Gatheru and

Mwando. Among the girls he recognized Nyambura, whom he particularly liked. But he would tell no one of his secret plan, he decided; not even his mother, to whom he owed a duty.

Old Chege addressed the meeting, leaning on the staff which – Ngengi recalled ironically – he had accepted so eagerly from the red strangers. Now he spoke out against them, reminding his audience of all the misfortunes suffered by the clan since they had first been seen in the land – drought, disease, defeat in war, death. Then he came to the settlers in the next valley, warning that these were the first of many: if their farms were fruitful, more would come, and more again, until all was lost to the Gikuyu.

'Therefore,' he cried, 'our young men must not work on their farms, nor go to their mission school, nor—'

'Nor accept their chief's staff as a gift!' someone called.

'The purity of the Gikuyu must be kept unsullied!' he concluded with a flourish, and Ngengi sensed that most of the crowd was on his side.

Ngengi's heart sank, for he knew that after this speech it would now be unwise even to say goodbye to anyone.

He looked across the crowd towards Nyambura, but she was talking to his sister and two other girls. Only twice or three times had he ever succeeded in speaking to her alone, but on this day he would have liked to do so; he did not feel at ease at the idea of leaving the ridge like a thief stealing away.

'Ngengi, what are you dreaming about?' Mwando cut through his thoughts, mocking. 'Not planning to work on a red stranger's farm, are you?'

'If he does, he will answer to all of us!' Gatheru was known for his hot temper; unfortunately he was also the strongest of his age group and the best wrestler. 'You heard Chege!'

'You have seen them – what are they like, the red women?' Mwando demanded eagerly. 'Do they have red buttocks and red boobs and red – you know! Do they?'

Gatheru's anger subsided into laughter. 'Next time,

bring one back here, why keep them to yourself? Anyway, I heard the men have red cocks and if our women go with them they become ill with the itch.'

Ngengi laughed too. An indistinct picture of King John bathing in the river came into his mind, though his memories of the railhead camp were now very distant. 'I think their cocks are white,' he said.

'White?' Mwando snorted, amused. 'I don't believe it.'

'You are inventing that!' Gatheru asserted. 'Red men with white cocks – that's impossible!'

'Their bodies are really whi—' he started to say.

Mwando interrupted him again. 'The itch! It must be the itch makes them white!' He stared down at his own black penis. 'It is hard to imagine,' he added.

Long before dawn the following morning Ngengi got up and crept outside, pulling his short skin cloak closer around him. The air was cold and not a sound could be heard from the other huts, nor from anywhere on the ridge. Stepping cautiously through the darkness he made his way to the edge of the village. The trees ahead stood dark and quiet, as if disapproving; behind, over the sleeping rooftops, he could see the faintest shimmer of light already spreading thinly across the sky. Soon, he knew, the sun would be rising.

Quietly he moved away among the trees, skirting the maize and bean patches to take a path which led directly down into the valley. After a time it branched off towards the stream where he had sometimes waited to see Nyambura, but on this occasion he chose the other route, which eventually led to the places where they grazed the cattle. He needed to cross that open country before the sun was too high.

Then a twig cracked and Gatheru stood blocking his way. 'So – you go to the red strangers after all?'

'I must look for Wanjui's cows,' Ngengi lied.

'Have they strayed? I shall come with you.'

'No, that is not . . .'

'Hyena!' Gatheru hissed at him between his teeth. 'You're going to the red strangers.'

He tried to throw Ngengi to the ground and they wrestled fiercely till they both fell down, rolling over and over; but there was no doubt he was stronger and knew more tricks too. At one moment, with Gatheru on top of him, pinning him down, Ngengi thought he would never escape. Lying there breathing with difficulty, he was ready to give up, he *did* give up but then changed his mind, seizing the opportunity of Gatheru relaxing his grip, and managed to tip him over.

They both got to their feet again and Ngengi began to realize there could be no easy outcome to this fight; he might even have to kill Gatheru – yet that would bring so many problems, he would never get away. Gatheru now had his arms so tightly around him, he thought his ribs would crumble. But then Ngengi managed to bring up the palm of his hand under Gatheru's chin, pressing it back with all the strength remaining to him.

Gatheru still held on and they swayed, backwards and forwards, as he tried to force Ngengi sideways to the ground. Then his foot slipped, his grip shifted, loosening slightly, giving Ngengi a chance to bring up his knee sharply into his opponent's groin. Losing balance, they tumbled into the undergrowth, Gatheru's face twisting with pain. But he was not finished yet; his fingers found Ngengi's throat and squeezed hard.

Ngengi thrashed about on the ground trying to break out of that killer hold, but the fingers merely tightened and he felt himself choking, unable to breathe, struggling for air; his eyes lost focus and once more he seemed to be back at that scene of his father's humiliation when King John had arrived and knocked down the torturer, The-Man-of-Thirst. Reliving that moment, Ngengi bunched his fist and drove it hard into his own torturer's face, as King John had done.

The fingers loosened at last.

He hit him again, and Gatheru rolled away, unconscious.

Ngengi got unsteadily to his feet. Leaning against a tree

he coughed and puked until slowly – it seemed to take for ever – the air entered his lungs again and, painfully, he began to breathe. Gatheru was sitting up too, shaking his head from side to side as if trying to clear it, muttering that others would hunt Ngengi down and bring him back.

Ignoring him, Ngengi stooped to pick up his skin cloak and it was then he noticed the long, slim, dark root on the ground near Gatheru's thigh. It was a snake and it was moving closer, lazily, the ripples seeming to run down the whole length of its body. If it killed Gatheru – the ideas tumbled through his mind – then no one would know about the fight, nor his own escape . . .

But, even as the thought came to him, he instinctively grabbed a stick lying on the ground near his cloak and brought it down heavily on the snake's head . . . once . . . twice . . . three times . . . Even then he was not too certain it was dead; he found a heavy stone and crushed its head to a pulp.

Gatheru, standing, had backed away, horror-stricken, as he stared at the snake's mutilated body, as long as a man's arm. They both knew this was a particularly venomous kind, whose bite could kill within seconds.

'Go,' he said to Ngengi, his voice shaking. 'I shall tell no one. Ngengi – go!'

It was already evening when Ngengi arrived at his destination. The sun had sunk behind the trees; the sky was pale yet smeared with red, like patches of blood dissolving over limpid water, and these colours were reflected on the gleaming metal roof of the mission station. A welcome, perhaps? Or a warning? But he did not slacken his pace. He went steadily towards the house, then up the steps to the door where he stood waiting for someone to notice him.

'Gracious, you gave me a turn!' a woman's voice exclaimed at last. 'What are you doing here?'

She wore a long skirt down to her ankles and a long-sleeved blouse which fastened at the neck; her pale face was set in a frame of flat, fawn hair covering her ears and drawn into a thick, round clump at the back of her head.

Ngengi looked at her gravely, saying nothing, not wishing to betray the fact that he had already learned a few words of English from his father.

'Henry!' she called. 'We've a visitor – a boy!'

She sent for one of the boys already living at the mission and through him she asked her questions. Where did he come from? Why had he come? And he answered that he intended to stay at the school until he had learned what they could teach him, and then he would go.

'Well, I suppose we could take him . . .' the woman said doubtfully, pursing her lips. She looked him up and down; he wore only that short skin cloak draped over one shoulder and hardly reaching his waist, nothing else apart from some bangles on his legs; her eyes lingered briefly on his genitals. 'We shall have to put some clothes on him first. Henry, d'you agree we take him?'

# FOUR

For two years they did not hear from Tim Wilton, two years during which the face of their valley changed as it slowly became a farm.

At dawn each day Hester stood outside her hut to look with amazement at how much progress had been made since the previous morning. This was the best time, she found, to take account of it all; by evening she was so tired, she had no desire to do anything more than sit watching the stars with John, talking it all over, planning the next day's work.

Some patches of scrub they had burned where it stood and the smoke had drifted across the valley, a pungent witness to their attack on the land. But John had also devised a modified harrow of iron claws and chains which could scratch the low vegetation out of the soil as it was dragged slowly forward by a team of oxen – with Catchpole in charge, naturally. John had an uncanny genius for persuading people to work for him – at any one time he had at least thirty Gikuyu youths employed, and willing, as well as some twenty girls who came down into the valley from time to time for weeding and transplanting. Njoroge explained one day that the older men on some of the ridges were opposed to their people taking work with white settlers, but John experienced none of these difficulties. Yet when it came to handling oxen, he was lost. Whenever he approached them, they turned to stare at him so malevolently, it was plain to everyone that they disliked him as much as he loathed them.

And the farm grew. Each morning, looking out as the first rays of the sun glistened on the dew, she could see how much more scrub had been cleared, how many more rows of maize and vegetables had been planted. It was a miracle, their farm. When she thought about it, everything else which had happened in her life receded like a faraway tide. That time with Tim – oh yes, a very *live* memory, what with Robert growing to look more like him every day – but that sharp regret had softened and with it her intense longing for him, which she had once felt might destroy her whole world if she ever gave rein to it.

Then, when John was in Nairobi for supplies and also to buy a Somali pony for Gaby's birthday, he found a letter from Tim waiting for him. He had been discharged by his doctors, he wrote, and decided to try his hand at farming after all. Not in partnership, though, but if John could manage to buy some land for him in the same neighbourhood, five or six hundred acres maybe . . .? John had acted immediately, taking up an option on land in a subsidiary valley bordering their own, and wired Tim to confirm the purchase.

Hester knew nothing about any of this until he got back, by which time it was too late. When he told her, every thought in her head stopped dead, leaving her mind completely numb. She stared at him, not able to find words.

'Ay, I said i' the cable ye'd be pleased,' John blundered on, mistaking her reaction. Why could he not *see*? Yet even as the thought came to her she knew he must never know, not if she was to keep him. 'We could do wi' some fresh faces round here,' he was saying. 'There's little enough company, jus' the missionaries, who are too far off . . . Och, an' Jackson has taken a farm, I hear, farther up i' the highlands – ye remember Jackson o' the Railway, my love? But I dinna think we'll be seein' much o' him.'

She took a deep breath which felt like a sigh at the inevitable. 'When do we expect Tim?'

'Jus' as soon as he can get himsel' organized an' book a passage out. Meanwhile we must see about recruitin' some labour to build a hut for him. There's a good place I have in mind – high ground, an' wi' fresh water nearby. No' too far from here.'

'Will the Gikuyus there work for a settler?' She recalled what Njoroge had told her. 'Joe says some are refusing.'

'I dinna think they've yet been asked, no' the right way.'

They rode over a week later to inspect the site for Tim's hut. It took them about an hour to get there and the moment she arrived she pronounced it unsuitable, using whatever excuses came into her head. She could not prevent Tim coming out, it was too late for that now, but at least she could make sure he did not live too close. John was puzzled, but he gave in to her as he so often did, and they eventually agreed on another spot a full half-hour's ride farther on. In fact it was ideal, with fresh water, good views, and a big old fig tree which stood proudly dominating everything around it.

But when it came to contacting the Gikuyu villagers on the ridge he was oddly reluctant. 'In roughly two weeks time from now, I reckon – that'll be about the right time for it.'

'Why?' she demanded suspiciously.

'Ye'll see. It's a wee surprise I'm plannin' for ye.' He smiled at her, his eyes tender, full of affection, as if trying to penetrate this strange mood she had been in ever since his return from Nairobi. 'I wouldna wish to spoil it.'

She rode on in silence, wondering if he had guessed the truth. But that was impossible – not the *real* truth! As if he had not surprised her enough already with his news about Tim – she wanted no more surprises from him, not like that. All the joy in her had died; in its place she experienced only fear. At nights she lay awake listening to the insects busy in the thatch above her head, knowing that the very roots of her new life here in the valley were menaced. If John found out . . . noticed at last how Robert had Tim's eyes, his way of inclining his head . . . Or, worst of all, if she discovered she could not hold back, that she still loved him . . . was unable to stop herself . . . loved both men . . .

She reined in and dismounted, stretching out her hand to John, longing to be kissed, enclosed in his arms, shutting out everything else and made to feel secure again. As they stood there amidst the scrub, their horses grazing nearby, she reconized again it was not security which John offered her, but a quickening of the blood, a challenge, stimulating

296

her own inner strength. Was not this the reason why she had wanted him from the start? And why she could never leave him, whatever happened?

During the days that followed they were all kept busy transplanting some three thousand coffee seedlings into the newly-ploughed fields. It was the biggest risk Andrewes had yet taken. They might easily die before reaching maturity; or some untreatable blight might render them useless as a cash crop. Either way, his investment could turn out to be money squandered on little more than a dream. Only the fact of Hester's presence gave him any real confidence in the venture; of the two of them, she was the one with green fingers. Since coming to the valley he had witnessed many times how she could coax life out of the soil where he would have given up in despair.

Catchpole too had that special gift, but then he had farming in his blood, his father the Lord Bishop being himself the son of a landowner, while Hester had natural genius. If young Tim Wilton had half the talent of either of them he'd not starve when he came out to try his hand.

He straightened up to watch her as she inspected the rows of young plants, pausing to demonstrate to one of the Gikuyu workers just how firmly the soil was to be packed about the roots. She was wearing her usual mud-bespattered skirt, kicking it out of the way as she stepped over the furrows, though there had been occasions recently when she had preferred breeches as being more practical. Ay, he thought contentedly, they made a good pair, he an' Hester; between 'em they'd do somethin' wi' this valley, no doubt about that. Though it was strange, the way she'd reacted on hearin' Tim Wilton was to be one of their neighbours, as though she didna welcome the idea.

He called his headman over – a tough-looking Gikuyu named Mwangi, who could scare the daylights out of the work force when he was angry, yet could also coax them to put in an extra hour's effort even when they were on the point of dropping from exhaustion.

'Mwangi, when this job's finished, mebbe Memsabu an'

I go on safari two, three days, d'ye ken?' Andrewes spoke his usual mixture of Swahili and English, with a scattering of Gikuyu words and gestures to help out. 'Ye make a start next on that hillside over there – clear the scrub, everythin', ready for ploughin'. Bwana Catchpole will show ye.'

'Yes, Bwana.'

If Tim Wilton could not get his labour from that village he would stand no chance, Andrewes reckoned, as there was no other within miles. According to the District Commissioner, they were likely to prove more than difficult; Njoroge's stories, too, were not encouraging, and many a man would call him a fool for what he was about to do. That night he spent a couple of hours cleaning his guns in readiness, though he did not expect he would have to use them, save to hunt for meat.

Ada Hathaway arrived the following morning, a full day earlier than they had arranged, but that was all to the good. Her voice rang out across the valley singing – inevitably – the chorus of *Ilkley Moor* while she and her zebra-drawn cart were still little more than a misshapen dot in the distance. The children were delighted and Gaby rode out to meet her on the Somali pony, carrying Michael with her.

'Ee, tha's made a difference to this place!' she exclaimed in admiration as she pulled up before their huts, where Andrewes and Hester were waiting to greet her. She stood on the cart, a magnificent figure clad as usual in the man's suit she always favoured when travelling, and surveyed the fields around her. 'I envy thee, Mrs Andrewes – know that? Whatever King John touches always turns out right, no matter what it is. Wish my Jimmy had that gift.'

'Ye musna under-estimate Jimmy, now!' Andrewes protested, and he meant it, too. 'As for what ye see here, Hester's done more'n her fair share o' the work. An' Catchpole. Now, have ye brought the things I asked ye for?'

'Tha's loyal, I'll say that much for thee!' Ada Hathaway roared with laughter, and Andrewes knew he must have been flushing red in his indignation. 'Everything's here, an' more! I've brought mail, mostly for Mrs Andrewes an' Mr Catchpole, though there's a big envelope for thee from Patel & Roshan's Emporium. An' a wire for thee as well, King John, before I forget.' She fished it out of her jacket pocket.

Andrewes tore it open. 'From Tim Wilton,' he told them. 'He's managed to get a passage sooner than expected. Landin' in Mombasa six weeks from now. The timin' couldna be better, to my way o' thinkin'. Mrs Hathaway, I hope ye feel up to carryin' straight on tomorrow mornin'?'

'John . . .' Hester intervened, hesitating. She looked worried about something, he thought; or maybe just tired. 'You don't think Mrs Hathaway might like to rest for a day or two first?'

'Sooner we move, sooner we'll know result!' Ada Hathaway said briskly. 'Now, King John, if tha'll lend a hand wi' these boxes . . .' She noticed Gaby hovering about. 'What is it, luv?'

'Michael wants to know why you wear men's clothes.' Giggling – and Michael, in the background, put his hand over his mouth.

'That's when I'm travelling on cart, luv, to help men forget it's a woman they're dealing with.' She chuckled. 'Unless I feel inclined to remind 'em. Ee, what a question! Here, take hold of this basket . . . careful, now!'

When they left the valley next morning, the sun had not yet risen above the hill-tops; the air was misty and cold. Robert, as the baby of the family, rode with Ada Hathaway and her Swahili factotum on the cart, while Michael went with Njoroge on one of the mules. Gaby, still excited that she now had a pony of her own, constantly cantered off to put it through its paces, until Hester had to warn her not to tire it out. This was a family outing, Andrewes proclaimed once they were clear of the farm. A holiday from all the hard work. No need to force the pace either – it was high time they took things easy for a day or two.

On the far edge of Tim Wilton's land, where the grass was thick and clusters of giant trees threw plenty of shadow, they found a place to camp. A few yards away was a clear, swiftly-flowing stream, gurgling and bubbling as it came down the wooded hillside. Up there, Andrewes knew, was the Gikuyu village; a few round, thatched rooftops were just about visible.

'I reckon this'll do fine for today!' he announced, dismounting. He turned towards Hester as she leaned forward, laughing; grasping her slim waist, he lifted her down from her horse. 'Lass, I'm thinkin' we made a wee mistake bringin' company wi' us! If we were on our own now . . .!'

'Ay, but we're no'!' she teased him, dodging away.

He pretended to lumber after her while Gaby and the two boys squealed with laughter, joining in the chase, until the entire family tumbled into a heap on the ground, happy and breathless.

'Bwana, we stay in this place?' Njoroge's expression betrayed not a flicker of amusement.

'Ay, ye can get a fire started for the meal, an' tell the others to pitch the tents.'

Through his field glasses he searched the hillside but saw no sign of movement. Yet their arrival must have been noticed.

'When do we pay our first call?' Hester asked, straightening her clothes.

'First thing in the mornin'. An' tonight we'll hang out the safari lamp in case they've no' spotted us already.'

'An' the kids?' Ada Hathaway demanded, looking up from her inspection of the damage the cart had suffered over the rough ground. 'Somebody's got to look after 'em.'

'They come wi' us,' he explained patiently. 'As I said last night it's a family visit – that's the idea.'

'I hope you know what you're doing, that's all,' she commented darkly, going round to check the other side of the cart. 'If something went wrong . . .'

But there was no more argument about it. They spent the rest of the day in the camp, with the children playing among themselves and Hester using the field glasses to try and identify some of the dozens of brightly-coloured birds darting about among the nearby trees. Andrewes attempted some rough and ready repairs on the cart while Ada Hathaway transferred a good selection of her trade goods into saddle bags, ready to be carried up the hillside.

'I'm very grateful, d'ye ken?' he said as he worked.

On his last trip to Nairobi he had found her kicking her heels with nothing to do, having given up her petty trading safaris after the first two. Almost everywhere she visited, Indian traders had been before her, setting up their *dukas* in the most out-of-the-way places. At first, she had not been too keen to undertake another one.

'It's a great help havin' ye out here,' he added.

'I've been thinking over that daft idea we were talking about. It was serious, wasn't it? I never know wi' thee, King John.'

'Ay, 'twas serious enough. An' it's no' so daft. That land where our old bungalow stands is a prime site, there in the heart o' Nairobi. I could sell it as one lot – I need more capital for the estate – but I thought to mesel' that's no' the way.' He did not mention that, having bought his title to the land right at the very beginning while the railway line was still being laid, he had paid no more than a few pence per acre; now Nairobi was a flourishing boom town, it might bring in as much as twenty thousand pounds in an auction. 'Nay, if I sell half that'll be sufficient, an' build a hotel on the other half to provide an income for Hester an' the bairns in case – ay, well ye understand me – in case the farmin' goes wrong.'

'Even saying I could raise enough to put down my share, what makes thee think I can run a hotel?'

'Lass, ye could run a railway, if I'm any judge. A business head, that's what ye've got – an' attractive enough to pull in the customers too.' He hammered in the last couple of nails and stood up. 'Ada Hathaway, ye're a handsome woman an' ye're tough enough to make a success. Do I need to tell ye more? Now about tomorrow – ye keep the blankets till the end, d'ye ken? I dinna want 'em seen till I give the word.'

They set out early the following day, slowly climbing the

winding paths up the hillside, their horses' hooves dislodging the loose stones, sending them sliding and bouncing down behind them. Among the trees they came to the first of the *shambas* where the Gikuyu women looked up in astonishment from their weeding, calling out to each other as they saw the children. Robert rode this time with Hester, while Gaby and Michael were together on the pony. Ada Hathaway and Njoroge were on mules, but the other African boys had stayed behind to guard the camp.

After a while, as they approached the homesteads, which were well concealed behind the trees, Ada Hathaway began a hearty rendering of *Ilkley Moor*, with Gaby and Michael – laughing – joining in the chorus.

'Let's 'em know I'm here, like,' she excused herself, one verse completed. 'It'll bring 'em running, just see if it don't.'

Ay, no doubt she's right, thought Andrewes, aware of movement among the trees on both sides of their path.

By the time they reached the wide clearing a considerable number of people had gathered to receive them. The young men took the centre ground, their serious faces framed by well-greased locks of hair twisted as into little tails, their spears held ready. Behind them stood the women, most of them dressed only in a short leather apron, and some with babies on their hips. Stopping at the edge of the clearing, Andrewes dismounted and stepped forward a couple of paces ahead of the others.

The young men stared at him suspiciously. In addition to their spears, they all wore short swords in red leather sheaths at their waists, and some had bows. Andrewes waited patiently until eventually they parted to allow four or five older men to come forward through their ranks. One carried a long staff: obviously this must be the chief of whom the District Commissioner had spoken. He greeted Andrewes solemnly.

'He asks why you have come here,' Njoroge interpreted, standing at his shoulder.

'Tell him we have come in peace to pay our respects,'

302

Andrewes instructed, without taking his eyes off the old man.

Njoroge did so, and waited for him to answer. 'He says you are welcome. He invites you to drink beer with him. It is freshly brewed.'

Andrewes was about to accept the invitation when his son Robert came trotting forward, stared up at the old man with a friendly, curious look in his eyes, and trustingly held out his hand to him. The old man's face wrinkled into a great smile of delight. He leaned forward on his staff, gently touching the boy's light blond hair and exclaiming – as Njoroge translated again – that it had the same colour as the sun at midday.

Then Hester and Michael joined them. And – more shyly – Gaby too with her long auburn hair spread about her shoulders, much to the astonishment of the young women who now jostled around them. They reached out to finger it until the old chief admonished them and led his visitors to the shade of a large old fig tree where they sat down. He offered Andrewes a drinking gourd of sugar-cane beer, eying him slily as he sipped it. Its taste was sweet-sour, with a tang like rotting apples.

His name was Chege, he explained with Njoroge's help, ignoring the other elders gathered around. Andrewes introduced himself, Hester, the bairns and Ada Hathaway, and presented him with an enamel plate and a mug, both decorated with painted flowers, saying he was honoured to meet him. The elders passed the gifts from hand to hand, discussing them, as Chege encouraged Andrewes with signs to try the beer again.

He had to be patient. No point in trying to rush things. They discussed the crops, the weather, the uncertain rains, and after a while Hester got up to admire the babies of three of the more persistent young women, hardly more than girls themselves. His granddaughters, Chege said.

He had already described his own farm, how it took up the whole length and breadth of one valley and how he was helped in the work by young men, Gikuyus, from another ridge who earned many rupees in this way. 'There could be a chance for young men here,' he suggested tentatively. Briefly, he told the elders about the new white settler who was coming to farm in the valley below their ridge, adding, 'You will know him when he gets here. He also has hair the colour of the midday sun.'

'This man is your friend?' A cackle of laughter spread among the elders and to the women beyond.

Andrewes looked around the group, bewildered; then, suddenly understanding, he felt the blood rising to his face and tried to disguise it by gulping more of that foul beer. 'Many people from my country have that colour hair,' he said calmly, master of himself again.

It was the oldest joke in the history of mankind, but it never failed to hurt, however fantastical. Men had killed for it. But they intended no malice, he could see that; if anything, they now looked less on their guard than before.

'You have your customs, we have ours,' Chege put to him, his eyes gleaming. 'If our young men work for you, they neglect the customs of the ridge. They learn new ways which are not always good. For this reason they do not wish to work.'

'Ay,' Andrewes nodded almost placidly. 'If a man doesna wish to sell his labour to another – that I can understand. Now our friend Mrs Hathaway here, she has no *shamba*, she plants no crops, but she travels through the land buyin' an' sellin'.' He turned to her. 'Will ye no' show 'em what ye've brought? I'm sure Chief Chege will no' object if ye sell a few wee items to his people now.'

Ada Hathaway had sat quietly until this moment, waiting for his cue, but now she stirred herself and came to life. He watched contentedly as she opened her saddle-bags and began spreading out her beads, mirrors, bangles, tin plates, bottle tops, and other knick-knacks, holding forth about each item in her flat Manchester accent, giving her sales pitch without bothering about translations, holding things up for them to see better, describing them, laughing, coaxing, cajoling, until the crowd around her had tripled in size with people pushing and elbowing through to see what she had to offer.

'Nay, lass, I can't take that!' he heard her refusing good-humouredly. 'Rupees! Only rupees! No bartering!'

There was a murmuring among the crowd, a buzz of explanations and disappointment as she made it plain she would take cash only; she would not exchange her wares for *posho*, fruit, vegetables or anything else. One or two people managed to find some coins and went off clutching a mirror or a coveted knife; the rest merely retreated a yard or two and looked on sullenly as – apparently as disappointed as they were themselves – she packed up her goods again and loaded the saddle bags on to the mule.

Andrewes stayed with Chege and the other elders, smiling benignly despite the headache which that terrible beer was giving him. In the background he could see a heated discussion going on between Njoroge and some of the young men from the ridge, and he could guess what it might be about. Then Hester came over to him carrying Robert whose face was hot and tearful.

'What's the matter, Robbie lad?'

'Getting tired,' she said, smiling. 'Don't you think . . .?'

'Ay, we must be on our way!' He stood up and, tipping his head back, drained the gourd empty. The elders clearly approved of this gesture. Then, summoning Njoroge to interpret for him, he remarked, tongue-in-cheek, 'It's a pity your people couldna buy more. O' course, on the other ridges the young men are no' so short o' cash as here.'

As a final gesture he opened the remaining saddlebags, realizing as he fumbled with the buckles that he had drunk too much of that excruciating beer. No matter – he took out the red blankets, five in all, and distributed them among the elders.

'A farewell gift,' he declared expansively, 'to thank ye for a most enjoyable mornin'.'

As they rode down those twisting paths again, he could feel that beer slurping around inside him with every jolt. The women should be grateful they were not offered any, he thought hazily; saved, they'd been, by the Gikuyus' sense of propriety. Behind him, Gaby and Michael were chattering away, giggling about something, and he heard

Hester warning them not to bother him just now. From her voice he guessed she was probably laughing at him, but he did not risk looking back.

That afternoon Andrewes retired to his tent to sleep it off, although when he eventually emerged, bleary-eyed, the headache was still with him. He took his rifle and set out along a path through the trees, leaving the women and children to their own devices. About half an hour later he came to a wild hill-slope covered with thick scrub where, some yards ahead, he spotted a small buck grazing beneath a stunted acacia.

He was still too far off, but he crept carefully forward, making a wide detour to keep downwind of it, and then crouched behind a bush well within range. He took his time about the shot, holding the buck in his sights until it turned slightly towards him. Then he squeezed the trigger and the sound bounced off the hillside, echoing across the valley.

The buck lay twitching pathetically on the ground. He broke its neck and slung it over his shoulder with a sense of deep satisfaction. He was no lover of slaughter for its own sake, but when it came to obtaining food, it always seemed to him that stalking and killing his prey was a considerably more rewarding occupation than sticking seeds in the ground and then waiting weeks for some result to show itself.

On getting back to the camp he found three Gikuyus from the ridge had arrived to return that morning's visit. Two were young warriors, still dressed in their warlike finery and fully armed; the third was an elder whose name, according to Njoroge, was Muthoga, seemingly a man of some influence. After some polite exchanges, they came fairly rapidly to the purpose of their call. Not all men on the ridge, Muthoga explained, were opposed to helping the new settler; in fact, it might be possible in time to supply him with whatever labour he needed.

They discussed the matter at length and, by the time they left, Andrewes had made arrangements for the building of two huts as a first step. He watched them go back towards the path up the hillside. Muthoga's red blanket, draped over his shoulder, stood out brightly against the duller green of the scrub.

'Ay well,' he said at last, knowing he had won, 'I reckon Tim Wilton will be well pleased. What d'ye say, my love?'

She looked up at him, putting her arm through his. 'I feel,' she began; and then she paused. 'I feel in some obscure way that we've corrupted them.'

'Is that no' your Baptist upbringin' showin' itsel'?' he commented with a laugh. The sun was dipping behind the hills, his headache had gone, the buck was roasting over the fire and he felt very much at peace with the whole universe. 'I wouldna worry about other folk desirin' to share a few of our worldly goods, d'ye ken? Is it no' born in us all?'

Hester was supervising the girls weeding between the rows of coffee plants on the far slopes when Tim arrived. From where she stood near the candelabra tree she could see the ox-cart approaching from the far end of the valley and someone – Catchpole, she assumed – riding out to meet it. This first meeting was the moment she had been dreading most. As she watched the cart nearing the huts she rehearsed once again in her mind what she intended to say, how she would conduct herself – as if nothing had ever happened between them, that was the way it had to be, at the same time making quite certain he understood nothing would ever happen again.

Although – what if he brought a wife with him? He had said nothing about a wife, not in the letters John had shown her, but what if...? She shaded her eyes in an attempt to see the cart more clearly but it was piled up so high with his belongings, she could not tell whether he was alone or not. There was an African driving the oxen and ... yes, that must be Tim beside him ... yet ...

She turned away and walked along the rows of girls who were chopping away at the weeds with their pangas, every movement of their wrists so economical, and singing while they worked. They seemed so carefree, she thought enviously. Their naked breasts quivered and danced, gleaming black in the brilliant sunlight; their flashing teeth made every smile seem warmer.

No, she would not go down to say hello just yet. That could wait an hour or so; the coffee was more important.

But half an hour later she changed her mind and rode down towards the huts, telling herself she had to face this reunion sooner or later, so it might as well be sooner. She found the whole family gathered there – the children playing, John pointing out to Tim which parts of the valley were already under cultivation and where he hoped to build their house, while Catchpole was showing the driver where to take his four oxen to graze. Tim broke away and hurried forward the moment he saw her.

'Hester!'

She slipped down from her horse, her heart beating wildly, and handed the reins to Mwangi's *toto* before turning to face him. Still that same boyish grin, still those searching blue eyes seeking hers.

'Well, Tim!' she said. Everything she had rehearsed deserted her. 'We . . . didn't know quite when to expect you. I was up with the coffee.' She waved vaguely in the direction of the hillside.

They shook hands formally — what else could she do? — and his grasp was unusually firm, as if trying to communicate something; but she dropped her eyes from his.

'It's been a long time, Hester,' he started to say, but she cut across him.

'John, you should have sent someone to tell me Tim was here!' she cried, breaking away from him a pace or two. 'Doesn't he look pale when you think of that deep tan he used to have? Oh, but Tim, it's so good to see you without crutches! Does the leg bother you at all now?'

'There's no pain any longer, if that's what you mean,' he answered, smiling at her, his eyes wandering over her face, *understanding*, damn him! He was not making it any easier for her.

She linked her arm through John's — very deliberately — and suggested they show him the hut where he was to spend the night. His limp was very noticeable, particularly where the ground was uneven, and she was conscious of how heavily he sometimes had to lean on his stick. She could not help wondering how he would ever manage the farm, even with the help of Gikuyu labour, but then she remembered how determined he could be beneath that pleasant, nonchalant manner of his. It must have taken plenty of that same determination for him to learn how to walk again after his injuries. Glancing at him — it was odd how young his face still seemed, with no sign of those years of pain! – his expression was so relaxed and confident, she knew he was bound to succeed.

'Here we are!' she announced as they reached the end hut, which they used sometimes for guests, sometimes as an extra store-room. 'It's not quite Claridge's, but it's the best you'll find in these parts.'

The mud floor was damp and the thatch was becoming wispy.

'I should warn you,' she went on – and there was a little laugh in her voice as she began to feel more confident, 'you may have to move your bed around a bit if it rains, because it comes in through the thatch. In fact, all our huts let the rain in when there's a real downpour. The children have the driest.'

'A little rain does no harm!' Tim said cheerfully. 'Know what I missed most? The flavours.'

'Ay, the smells,' John nodded.

'No, England has smells – the coal fires in people's houses, the smoke from the railway heavy with sulphur, the factory chimneys . . . But Africa is quite different. Africa has flavours – to my way of thinking, don't you know?'

'Still writin' your poetry then?' John commented drily. 'Ye'll be pleased wi' the land ye've got in that case, wi' Mount Kenya visible most clear days.'

During their meal that evening the two men sat talking over their time on the railway, reliving all those fascinating engineering problems which she did not even wish to understand. But – to her own surprise – she felt very much at peace. The fire flared up, crackling noisily as the flames wrapped themselves around a fresh log; above, an almost full moon flooded the valley with cold light.

Catchpole had come over to join them and was showing the children some of his magic tricks with a piece of string, patiently teaching Gaby how to do them herself, when Robert took it into his head to go and sit between John and Tim. Looking across at them in the firelight, she began to wonder if he was really like Tim after all. Perhaps she'd been wrong, she thought, seeing them side by side. They had the same colour hair, a similar look about the eyes – but no more. The ears could easily be John's; perhaps the mouth, too.

It would be so much easier if only she felt guilty, but she couldn't. And now they were sitting together, both her men, with herself and children – well, what could be more natural?

'Tim, I'd have expected by now you'd have found a wife,' she said casually, stopping John in mid-flow as he was describing how they had dismantled the funicular in the Rift Valley.

'No.' He looked at her steadily through the dancing flames, almost mocking her.

'But you must have met some girls in England.' Illogically, she felt a rush of relief when he laughed – what could it possibly matter to her now? 'A farmer's daughter would have been useful.'

'A p-p-practical s-suggestion!' Catchpole spluttered, his high-pitched laugh exploding out of him. 'P-please f-f-f-find w-w-one f-for m-me t-t-too. V-v-very useful!'

'My love, an' I thought ye were a feminist!'

'A pragmatic feminist,' she confirmed, unruffled. 'And I stick by the word *useful*. There's no point in bringing a wife out here who isn't.'

Tim had intended to stay for one night only before going on to his own farm. In the event he extended his visit by an extra day in order – so he said – to take a closer look at how they managed things on the estate. But the real reason, Hester was convinced, was that he wanted a private word with her – he made that plain enough – and she did her best to avoid him. Instead, Catchpole accompanied him around the fields to discuss the crops and give him a few tips from their own experience, even offering to ride over to lend a hand when he was ready to start ploughing. Catchpole was a blessing, she thought – not for the first time.

Towards late afternoon, when the thunder was growling gently in the distance and the lightning flashes were just visible above the hill-tops, she was crouching down beside her precious potato crop, examining the spots which had appeared on some of the leaves, when she heard the sound of a horse behind her and looked up to see Tim.

'I was beginning to think we'd never get a chance to be alone together,' he said with a disarming grin. He slipped his feet out of the stirrups to dismount and she noticed how he had to hold on to the saddle until he had retrieved his walking stick. 'Hester, it means so much to me, seeing you ag—'

'I think we have blight,' she interrupted him. She had not moved and still held the leaf between her fingers and thumb. 'It looks like the whole field's affected.'

'Hester, I came back for you. No other reason.' He spoke quietly, as if pleading with her.

'Then you made a mistake, didn't you?' That sounded harsh, much harsher than she had really wanted, but there was no other way. She had to do it.

He stood there leaning on his stick and holding the horse's head with his free hand, confessing his unhappiness. 'I tried to forget you in England – oh, because of King John and your children and because people don't do the sort of thing that . . . that we've done. But oh, my darling, it was just not possible! I had the feeling that at any moment, all I had to do was turn round and you'd be there – and of course all that was just self-deception. D'you remember when you sent me that telegram saying I should turn down King John's offer to come and join you all out here? Well, I did what you said, and I've spent every day since then regretting it. I love you, Hester – so deeply that I—'

She got up angrily and faced him. 'Tim, if you go on like this,' she said in a cold fury, 'I shall make sure we never meet, even though your farm *is* next to ours. I didn't want you here. I don't want you here now, but you've arrived – against my wishes – so you'll just have to accept that it's all over.'

Her anger was genuine, it coursed through her like a fever, but it was not Tim she was angry with. It was herself and her own stupidity. It was all her own fault, she knew, for having given in to her feelings instead of resisting them as she should. She kept her voice hard, as sharp as a whiplash, afraid that if she softened she would give way completely.

'It's over,' she repeated. 'Now we're just neighbours. Friends if you like. That's all that's left.'

She untied her horse and pulled herself up into the saddle. 'No, don't follow me – I don't want you!' she told him scathingly as he made a move to remount.

She slammed her heels into the horse's flanks, heading farther up the hill along the muddy paths skirting the fields. At that moment she felt she could take no more. She just had to be alone for a while, away from everybody. Beyond the fields the ground was treacherous and steep but she urged the horse on relentlessly.

At last she reached a place where the hillside levelled out slightly and she could see across the entire valley which now lay, gloomy and menacing, under dark, heavy clouds. A sudden cold breeze had sprung up too, and the thunder sounded much closer. Her horse shifted uneasily at each flicker of lightning. The first fat drops of rain were cool against her skin. Then the downpour came, soaking instantly through her thin blouse, and with it her tears flowed freely, uncontrollably, her shoulders heaving. There she sat, keeping her restless horse on a tight rein, her back straight, while her own private storm ran its full course.

It solved nothing, she knew that.

Nothing.

And as the sobbing eased, she felt if only she could stay up there, away from them all, at least for a while longer . . . But then John would come in search of her and questions would be asked – those inevitable questions. She leaned forward to pat her horse encouragingly as an apology for keeping it out in that storm so long, and then turned back down the hillside to face them again.

## SIX

Time on a Kenyan farm – the name Kenya was now increasingly being used – could be wily and deceptive, Andrewes often thought. There were days when it seemed not to exist at all. You could stop what you were doing, wait, listen, and everything was unhurried . . . unchangeable . . . endless . . . Then, unexpectedly, came the realization that more seasons had passed, more harvests been gathered in, more years gone, and still no work had been started on the stone house he had been promising for so long.

But now he had made up his mind the right moment had come. The estate was producing sufficient vegetables, apart from potatoes, both to meet their own needs and supply Patel's Nairobi outlets. Coffee, too, their main cash crop, was at last beginning to show a return. He picked out half a dozen of the stronger men and took them over to the quarry he had started some years earlier when he needed stone to build the stables and to give their road a firmer surface for the rains.

The men stood around watching him as he carefully packed his sticks of dynamite into the cleft between two major seams of rock. He tried explaining to them why he'd chosen to start at that particular point, but then gave up. It was ninety per cent instinct, and only experience could give them that.

Of course, the family had stopped believing in the house and an incredulous little smile always appeared around the corners of Hester's mouth whenever he mentioned it, however clearly he described what he had in mind, even making rough sketches for her. On the other hand, she never grumbled that they were still living in those small thatched huts as on their very first day here, with reed mats on the walls and animal skins spread over the hard mud floors. Cool when the sun was hot; cosy when the weather turned chilly.

'We should do something about the thatch, though,' she would comment from time to time. 'It lets in a lot more rain than it used to.'

Ay, well now he was doing something – he began playing out ten feet of fuse – something constructive.

Altogether, The Kingdom – as they now called the estate locally – was turning out well. He had been going over the figures on the previous evening. There was a steady improvement on the income side; in fact, more than he had expected. It was largely Catchpole's and Hester's doing too, he felt. Hester was in her element; she could even – he often thought – bring life to the Sahara if she turned her mind to it. And now Catchpole was experimenting with a dairy herd, cross-breeds with local cattle. When, once in a while, the two of them got together with Tim Wilton – another born farmer – and they all sat discussing potato blight, or the plague of beatles, or whether or not to plant more maize, or why the coffee on the lower slopes was not doing too well – ay, on those occasions he felt completely out of it.

Not that it worried him. He had too much to do clearing land, road-building, fencing, digging irrigation canals, with pipes and a steam pump to raise water during the dry season – all good engineering work which he understood to the tips of his fingers.

And now the house. A kingdom needed a palace, he'd told Hester.

He straightened up. 'Right, ye can blow your whistle! Everyone out o' the quarry! Quick! Upesi! We're about to start blastin' – *boom!*'

The headman, proud of the whistle which Andrewes had recently brought back from Nairobi, blew a long blast with the full force of his lungs.

'That'll do! Ye've no need to ruin our eardrums, man!'

With the quarry cleared, Andrewes squatted down to light the fuse. As the intense little flame began to burn steadily along the wire towards the detonator, he took cover behind the broad trunk of a cedar and waited.

'Michael! Mi-i-chael!' Unaware of the danger, Gaby cantered up on her Somali pony. 'Michael! Where are you?'

'Gaby, get down!' Andrewes roared, dashing forward to hold the pony's head. 'We're blastin' - *get down!*'

In that second the flame reached the detonator. The pony reared up at the explosion, uttering a series of short, frightened screams. Andrewes hung on to it, fighting to prevent it bolting. Any other rider might have been thrown but Gaby kept her seat, seeming to communicate her calmness to the bucking pony until it gradually quietened down again.

'Are ye crazy?' The fear that she might have been killed by some flying fragment of stone twisted in him like a hot knife. 'I warned ye all I'd be blastin' today, an' to stay clear. Ye canna say ye didna hear me?'

She flushed with annoyance, her eyes blazing at the injustice. 'Njombo said Michael had come this way. I wasn't being stupid, Papa, but somebody's got to look out for him and Njombo doesn't seem able to manage.'

'Then I'll gi' him a talkin' to!' Andrewes declared grimly.

His mouth was dry as he surveyed the scene. The cloud of dust still hung in the air; the birds still circled, screeching indignantly. Surely there was no chance Michael might have been hiding in the quarry, no chance at all, or . . . Even as the thought came he realized it was just what Michael might do. Out of curiosity as much as mischief. Once while he was still only a toddler they had found him stretched out on the ground watching a puff adder only a couple of feet from his face.

'No, he'd have more sense!' Andrewes tried to convince himself. They went in among the broken stones. 'Michael, are ye hidin' somewhere? Come out at once, d'ye hear?'

'M-i-chael!' Gaby called again.

No answer.

'He talked about nothing else when you explained about the blasting,' she said. 'Mama told him to stay away.'

Treading carefully over the rubble, Andrewes went farther into the quarry. The charge had done its work well and he should be setting the men to cutting and trimming the larger blocks for use as foundations for the house, while he needed all the small debris for strengthening the road over towards the stream. Yet if Michael *was* there . . .

'Nay, he'd have more sense, lass,' he repeated, cupping his rough hand under her chin and turning her face gently towards him.

'He's only ten!' Her eyes flashed. 'If he's lying hurt?'

The expression on her face was a mixture of anxiety and stubbornness, her lips pouting slightly. Just like her mother, he thought; she was already as tall as Hester and her figure had rounded out too in the past year. Though in other ways perhaps she took after him. For her fourteenth birthday he had bought her a .22 rifle and given her some shooting lessons. She had a good eye.

'Njombo was holding Michael's pony when he jumped on and rode off before anyone could stop him,' she was explaining. 'You can't blame Njombo. He's always a bit slow.'

'We pay Njombo to stay wi' him an' if he canna do so—'

'You can't sack him!' She was indignant again. 'Papa!'

He smiled, liking the way she always jumped to the defence of their staff. It was a feudal trait in her, quite unsuited to industrial society. If part of an engine ceased to function properly it had to be scrapped, no two ways about it – though maybe her instincts were right for Africa in a way that his were not. He was about to reply when they heard a scrambling noise up the hillside beyond the quarry.

'Michael!' she yelled furiously.

A pony appeared through the trees ridden by his ten year old son who obviously had no intention of stopping. Gaby swung herself into the saddle and charged off to meet him. Michael spotted the danger, changed direction and headed for the flatter ground some distance away, but she pulled her pony around and broke into a gallop to cut him off.

His children rode like Cossacks, fearlessly, as though born in the saddle, and their ponies needed no spurring on but seemed able to read their riders' thoughts. Gaby gained ground until eventually she drew level, caught hold of his rein and took control. It was magnificent riding, he thought as they slowed down to a trot and came back towards him.

Ay, but it was time he made plans for their schooling. Gaby had probably read more books than most girls of fourteen; she had a fine hand and a fair knowledge of reckoning through helping him with the calculations for the estate and the new stone house, but she needed the company of other girls and now this new Young Ladies' Academy had been opened in Nairobi maybe they had better enrol her. He knew Hester thought so, and she also talked of sending the boys to stay with her sister who had moved to London and married a solicitor. Yet for a man to be parted from his own children for so long, it didna seem right.

They dropped down from their ponies and Gaby pushed Michael forward to face his father.

'I told ye to stay clear o' the quarry,' Andrewes began.

'I did!' Michael defended himself vigorously. 'I was up there at the top, miles away from your dynamite.'

He pointed to the clump of trees above the quarry where the ground began to rise steeply towards the summit of the hill, explaining how he had crawled there on his hands and knees, leaving his pony tied to a bush some distance away.

'I wanted to hear the bang in the earth,' he said.

Andrewes was foxed. 'To hear what?'

'Your dynamite shaking the earth inside,' he repeated. 'I pressed one ear to the ground and put my finger in the other . . .'

'That's silly!' said Gaby scornfully.

'*It isn't!*' he shouted back at her. 'It does shake the earth. It sounded like . . . like thunder far away.'

318

'Ay, ye'd good reasons I've no doubt, but next time I tell ye to stay clear – do it! Now run an' see if ye can help Mama.'

'Oh!' Gaby turned slightly red. 'Mama's talking to Uncle Tim, I forgot to tell you. He rode over just after you'd left and says he's heard rumours Mr Jackson's planning to divert the stream. Our *stream!*'

'Ay, an' plannin's as far as he'll get.' Andrewes sent Michael off. 'That stream touches three different estates an' he'll need agreement before he can do anythin'. Now, Gaby, I've been wonderin', lass, if ye'd no' like to help wi' the house? D'ye see, these stones have to be trimmed to the right size an' shape. Once the men've got the hang o' how to do it, they'll still need someone to keep an eye on 'em.'

Get her involved, he thought; get her interested. That's the way. He had noticed how the colour mounted in her cheeks when she mentioned Tim Wilton's name. On the odd occasion when Hester had cause to ride over to see him she invariably took Gaby with her, but maybe more had been going on than she realized. The man was attractive to women, no doubt about that, with his blond hair and pale blue eyes. And that limp seemed to make him irresistible, hard to understand why. It must be something of a nuisance needing a walking stick wherever he went.

Yet Andrewes remembered Ada Hathaway's reaction when she first set eyes on him. 'Who's that? Ee, I could eat 'im!' she had exclaimed, sitting stock-still on her zebra-cart – and for all to hear. Time he found himself a wife, and that was the truth of it.

No' Gaby, though. Nay, certainly no' Gaby.

'Ye see,' he demonstrated, 'ye take one o' these measurin' sticks I've made an' ye place it against the edge o' the stone to make sure it's quite straight. If ye find it's jus' a wee bit . . .'

To his relief it worked. She joined him every day to help at the quarry while he laid a length of track as far as the building site. It was old railway stock which he had picked up cheap, together with a small wagon which could be loaded with stone and pushed by hand.

She became genuinely enthusiastic about the work too and at times he felt he had never been so content as when she was helping him peg out the ground, checking everything meticulously against the plans he had drawn up, taking all the measurements afresh – as he insisted – and doing her own calculations. 'In case I made a wee mistake, d'ye ken?' he explained, though she probably saw through the ruse.

Then the first stones were laid and they finished work that day feeling it would not be long before they saw the walls rising, the roof on, the house complete, even. But the next morning they got up to find most of the pegs pulled out and the string between them chewed away. He stood there and surveyed the scene in dismay, wanting to swear with frustration – only his daughter was with him, so he refrained.

'A bush pig – must've been!' she declared with evident disgust, but not at all downcast. 'Africa strikes again! We'll just have to start at the beginning once more, won't we? But watch out, bush-piggie! If I catch you, we'll be having you roasted for supper!'

He was proud of her, this daughter of his. As they worked side by side he felt he was getting to know her as a different person – not as a child any longer, either.

This would be the only stone house for hundreds of miles around, she commented one day as they began on the walls of the large, rectangular living room which he planned to complete first, before adding the smaller rooms at either end. And what she said was true enough. Most settlers lived in simple thatched huts, though they had stone-built stables to protect the horses, and a few – very few – luxuriated in pre-fabricated, metal-framed bungalows with corrugated iron roofs, courtesy of Patel & Roshan.

They joked about it, made derogatory remarks about such short-cuts to comfort, confident that their stone house would be a real palace in comparison with anything other settlers might build. But for once his heart was not in the banter. A reply had come from Nairobi at last to the effect that there would be a place for Gaby at the Young Ladies' Academy, and when might they expect her? So far she knew nothing of it, but later that afternoon he and Hester would have to tell her.

As time went on that day he became increasingly depressed, knowing in his bones how she was bound to react. He was right, too. At first she listened in silence, her lips tightening, her eyes becoming dark and hostile with shock. Then the hurt protests burst from her.

'And what about the house? Aren't we building the house? You said last week you could never manage it without me, but that was all lies, wasn't it? Just lies!'

'Nay, lass – I meant all I said . . .'

'You're living lies, both of you, and now you want to get rid of me!' her anger whipped them, and her face became a flaming red. 'At least I thought we were working together, I was really helping, but all the time you were plotting to send me away. I despise you, both of you! I really despise you!'

'Now, Gaby, that's enough!' Hester tried to assert her authority. 'We'll have no more nonsense—'

Beside herself with fury and what she saw – Andrewes understood only too well – as her parents' betrayal, Gaby pushed past them and marched towards her pony.

'You'll never see me again!' she yelled. 'Never!'

She vaulted into the saddle, scowled at them, quivering with bitter resentment, and then galloped off across the valley.

'John . . .' Hester looked up at him, troubled, but also clearly annoyed. 'What got into her? I thought it'd be a nice surprise, she's always reading those school stories in her magazines. And I don't know what she meant by "living a lie" – don't we try our best for her?'

'Let her get it out o' her system, love,' he tried to calm her, as gently as he could. He had always been convinced there was a special bond between him and Gaby, and now he felt it had been ripped apart; as though his skin had

321

been flayed off, leaving him raw. 'Mebbe we should've discussed it wi' her sooner.'

'She gets too much of her own way, that's what's wrong.' Hester's soreness was getting the upper hand. 'And you spoil her, John. You always did. I'll be giving her a real talking to when she comes back.'

But a couple of hours passed and Andrewes began to get worried. He rode up to a point on the hillside where he could overlook the valley, yet saw no trace of her in any direction. Fear writhed through him at the thought of what might happen to her if she left the estate and went off into the wilds somewhere. A rhino in an ugly mood . . . a lion . . .

Grimly, he set off down the hillside again to organize the search. He'd ask Hester to ride over to Tim Wilton's place in case she had gone over there; Mwangi could try up in the direction of his own village; and Catchpole towards the north perhaps . . .

Hester felt sick with anxiety and remorse as her horse picked its way through the scrub, taking the short-cut to Tim's farm. It was just possible John was right and Gaby had gone over there to cool off her temper, though in her heart she did not believe it. Recently Gaby had been distant towards Tim, as though she had noticed something. Yet what had there been to notice, Hester thought desperately. She and Tim had been so careful of each other, frightened even to stand too close together.

At the top of the incline she stopped to scan the landscape through her binoculars – every direction – but there was no sign of her. There was no alternative but to go on.

Eventually she passed the coffee fields. He was going to have a good crop, too. The white flowers looked so pure in the sunlight, the rows of bushes so straight, following the contours of the land. Oh, if only she could arrive at his hut to find the Somali pony tied up outside and Gaby . . . But no, when she got there he was alone. He looked up from his writing, surprised to see her.

'Just doing another article for *The Field*, don't you know!'
He stood up and pulled a canvas chair over for her,
perhaps wondering – it flashed through her mind – why
she had for once ridden over alone.

Ignoring the chair, she blurted out that Gaby was
missing, everyone was out searching for her, and had she
been seen over in this direction? 'She's never run away like
this before.'

'I'll ask my people,' he said immediately. 'Oh, do sit
down. You poor thing, you look worried to death. I shan't
be a sec.'

She heard his voice out in the back as he questioned his
headman and his Swahili *fundi*. Even before he came back
she knew what the answer was going to be. If Gaby had by
any chance been over in this direction, no one had noticed
her.

'Well, she's not here, as you probably heard,' he
announced as he returned to the shade of the fig tree in
front of his hut where he had his table set out for his
writing. He gathered up his papers into their folder and
yelled for the syce to saddle his horse. 'So we'll have to go
out and look for her. She's impulsive, don't you know –
but she can't have gone far. What caused all this? Was she
in a paddy about something?'

His tone was so practical and reassuring, as though he
could take the whole problem out of her hands – which, of
course, he couldn't. But she explained about the Young
Ladies' Academy, following him as he limped into the
enlarged thatched hut which served as his living room.
Why, she wondered, wiping her eyes while his back was
turned, why did she find it so easy to cry when she was
with him? With John, she was always dry-eyed whatever
happened.

He put the folder into his sea-trunk, still one of his main
pieces of furniture, then loaded his rifle and took a pocketful
of cartridges.

'It must be that auburn hair of hers!' he remarked
lightly, trying to cheer her up. 'Often goes with a quick

temper, don't you know? But it burns out just as quickly. I think she's going to be quite a handful.'

Anxiously, Hester began listing the places which were already being covered by the search. 'And then I think I should perhaps go back to The Kingdom in case she turns up there . . . Oh Tim, if that pony's thrown her and she's lying injured somewhere and . . . supposing the hyenas scent her . . . you can hear them at night sometimes . . .'

He stopped her. 'Hester, oh my sweet Hester, don't make it worse for yourself than need be. Things never turn out the way we imagine them. We just don't know.'

'But . . . oh, I can't stop thinking of it!'

Unconsciously she had moved closer to him and then his arms were around her, so comforting, so understanding, as though he instinctively knew all she was going through. She turned up her face, her lips parting, meeting his in a kiss which was gentle at first but becoming more urgent . . . seeking him . . . filled with an insatiable longing for him . . . wanting far more than was possible, then or ever, she felt.

Tim broke away from her first, but lovingly, considerately, holding her for a second by both shoulders, at arms length, his eyes on her. Then he turned, supporting himself against the table until he had recovered his stick.

'I'll search lower down beyond where the two valleys merge,' he said crisply, as though nothing had happened. Then, with his rifle slung from his shoulder, he limped over towards his horse.

But it *had* happened. She stood there confused, bewildered, as she watched him ride away. She was despicable, one part of her mind insisted. When it came to the test, every one of her good intentions had dissipated like smoke in the wind. Yet she now felt a sudden warmth flowing through her, a tenderness, a kind of blossoming out; her nerve ends had become alive with her need for him. Oh God, this was not what she had wanted.

And yet it was. Every time she had seen him she had known the feeling was there, and suppressed it. And now . . .

She became aware that the African syce was staring at her curiously. Remounting, she made her way back to the incline where she had stopped on the way over, forcing her horse not to slacken its pace even as it climbed the steep slopes. She needed to be alone, right there on the top where she could feel the cool of the breeze around her and allow her thoughts to wander freely. About Tim . . .

About John . . .

Again she searched the rolling countryside through her field glasses, looking for Gaby and not finding her, then lingering on the figure of Tim as he rode off towards the south, well beyond the area so far under cultivation. From time to time she heard his voice calling.

'Ga-a-aby! Ga-ab-eee!'

And she prayed desperately that he would find her and bring her back to them. In person.

Darkness fell, a pitch blackness with no moon or stars, and still Gaby had not returned, nor had there been any word from Tim. Hester made sure Michael and Robert got to bed, and then sat outside with John and Catchpole, keeping their voices low. They had been forced to abandon their search at nightfall, but were now planning a much more systematic combing of the whole area for the following morning using all the field labour, every single man of them. In the distance an animal howled, and she shuddered as she heard it.

John picked up the sound of the hooves first. 'My love, listen!' he interrupted something she was saying. 'Is that no' . . .?'

Two horses, she could swear. 'It's them!' she exclaimed delighted, her tensions dropping away from here. 'Oh, John, it's them! Tim's found her!'

'I c-can s-see them c-c-coming!' Catchpole stuttered, his face beaming with relief. 'Oh, th-thank G-god!'

The light bobbed and waved as it approached. John ran down to meet them, with Hester close behind. But the man on the horse, carrying a safari lamp attached to a bamboo pole, was broader than Tim and more thickset; as he came closer she recognized him – Jackson. Gaby rode demurely beside him on her Somali pony as if nothing in the world could possibly be wrong.

'Found this lass o' yours wanderin' o'er my farmland,' he announced as though he thought the whole idea entertaining. 'I imagined at first she'd come to honour me wi' a social visit, but it seems she was lost. So I'm sorry to say I've brought her back. How are you, Mrs Andrewes? Still as pretty as ever, I see – though you've a rival here in Gabriella. Gabriella o' the Gabriella Cup – them was the days, eh? An' you, King John – I'm told you're buildin' some kind o' baronial hall. I'd like to see that, if you've no objection.'

Gaby had slipped off her pony and run to Hester, hugging her close, but not in the least upset. She tossed back her long hair and ran her hand over it with all the confidence of a young woman who knew exactly what she wanted.

'Ay, ye can see the house, an' welcome!' John was saying to Jackson. 'I dinna ken how we can thank ye for bringin' her back this late, but I've a bottle o' fine malt whisky jus' waitin' to be opened, an' this seems the right kind o' night to demolish it, if ye'd care to join me? An' a bite to eat, mebbe? It's no' all that often we get company oursel's.'

## SEVEN

For the first time in his life, Andrewes had the feeling that everything was falling into place. From the building site he could gaze out across the estate, field after field already neatly under cultivation, and now the house itself was becoming a focal point in the valley. The walls of the large living room – Gaby dubbed it the 'baronial hall' – had reached their full height and the men were already raising the joists which were to carry the roof, chanting as they worked, or breaking out into sudden bursts of Gikuyu chatter. To one side were the first of the bedrooms he also aimed to complete in this stage of construction; later, he intended to add a bathroom, kitchen, storeroom, perhaps another bedroom or two, while Hester had already started to lay out the extensive garden which the rear veranda would overlook.

It all gave him a strange, unfamiliar sense of permanence. After years of working on the railway, first in India, then here in British East, conditioned to think of his life as one continuous process of change, moving on from one camp to the next, he realized – with surprise – that he had at last arrived at a destination. In this stone house, this mansion, he would spend the rest of his days, he felt. Die there too, probably.

'Ay, an' that's no' too bad, John Philip Andrewes,' he said to himself, more than once. 'Grandson o' a poor Scottish crofter driven off his land by the enclosures – an' ye end up a laird yesel'!'

Gaby was still helping him supervise the work and he was glad about that. She always got on well with the young Gikuyus and she'd a sharp eye when it came to checking that the carefully drawn plans were being followed exactly. After that childish business of running off and being brought back by Jackson she had stayed away for a few days, but she turned up at the site again eagerly enough once they had agreed she need not go to the young Ladies' Academy until this stage of the building was finished, and then they would talk it over, perhaps even take her there to have a look at the place before any decision was reached. Besides, building a house – Andrewes had argued, shifting his ground – was an education in itself which could never be matched by any school, however good.

But for his two sons there was no alternative. They had to be sent to Britain, whatever his feelings on the subject. Even Catchpole had insisted on the importance of putting them through good schools – quiet, unassuming, stammering Catchpole who had acted as the sympathetic mediator in the Gaby business! Uncle Nat, as the bairns called him. He had written off to his father the Lord Bishop, requesting he use his influence to get them places.

Of course, Hester was behind it too, stressing that her sister would care for them in the holidays – had already offered to do so, in fact – and in the end Andrewes had reluctantly agreed.

'Th-think, K-king John – they're g-g-going to inherit all this one day! W-what s-sort of m-men are they g-g-going t-to be w-with n-n-no f-formal education?'

'Ay, very well, I'll leave the choosin' o' schools to ye an' Hester. But wi' a good reputation for learnin', mind! I dinna want any sons o' mine to come back wi' little more than fancy accents an' empty heads!'

There were times when Catchpole amazed him. He lived down at the far end of the valley in his own hut, struggling to make a success of that pathetic collection of half-breed cattle he grandly called his 'dairy herd', and for days he might not be seen at all – save by Hester, perhaps, when he came up to the fields. It was easy enough on occasions to forget he even existed: yet, without him, the Kingdom would never have flourished the way it had, Andrewes was in no doubt about that. Ay, Catchpole was worth a mint more than his one third share, there was no denyin' it.

He walked round to the side of the house to shout up his instructions to the Gikuyus, who were attempting to slot

328

the last of the joists into position, but it was not necessary. There was a great shout of triumph as it suddenly slipped into the gap in the top layer of stones, and the men straightened up to admire their own handiwork. Andrewes offered them a few words of praise, and then Gaby came across to him with a scrap of paper in her hand.

'I've been looking at the magazine pictures for an idea for the fireplace, Papa. All the really grand houses have carvings cut in the stone, so I thought why can't we? Like this.' She thrust the paper at him, then laughed, embarrassed. 'I mean, it's not perfect, but it's a Grant's gazelle. Meant to be. For the big stone in the middle.'

'The keystone. Ay.' He glanced at the sketch. 'Who can carve it, d'ye think?'

'Can I try, Papa?' Her voice was intense; her face serious. The idea obviously meant a deal to her. 'If I make it simple – you know, not too *real* – it might turn out all right. I've worked out how to get the rough shape already.'

He laughed indulgently. He was astounded himself at the mellow mood he was in. Was it the sight of the house, perhaps? Or maybe he was getting old. Settling down at last.

'Ay, lass, we've no shortage o' stone. But ye've two weeks, no more, mind, as I'll want to be finishin' off that fireplace. I reckon on us movin' in before the rains.'

During the next six weeks, progress on the house was rapid. It took less time than he had estimated to finish the carpentry for the roof and apply several generous coats of creosote before laying the sheets of corrugated iron. Once the place was rainproof, he set the men to fitting a ceiling. Window frames were already in position, using heavy wire mesh in place of glass and shutters which could be closed when the weather was chilly. To Gaby's obvious delight he approved her rough carving showing the animal's head with vague indications of ears, horns, and two scooped-out eyes. She helped him complete the wide baronial fireplace, which had been her idea too.

In the meantime, Catchpole had been to Nairobi to buy seed and brought new furniture with him on his return, including a secondhand sofa acquired by Patel from some over-ambitious settler forced to flee the colony to avoid bankruptcy. Hester gave it pride of place in the centre of the room facing the fireplace. She hung a lion skin, with crossed spears and a shield next to it, on one of the bare stone walls, and spread new mats on the floor. On the adjacent wall, between two windows, she put the framed photograph of her father she had kept constantly by her all those years, ever since they left Liverpool. There was a new double bed too, with an iron bedstead.

Yet she delayed moving into the house until the very last minute, wanting to make sure everything was absolutely right. Wanting too – Andrewes gathered – to spend one last night in their hut and hear that familiar whispering in the thatch before they fell asleep. Naturally he humoured her, though he did not see the point of it himself; she had complained about that same noise often enough over the years.

But it also gave the move the feeling of being a very special occasion in their lives. He would have set up his camp bed there the moment the roof was on, but he was forced to acknowledge – she insisted, laughing at him affectionately, leaning up to kiss him on the cheek – that this way was better. They loaded their remaining belongings on to their old covered wagon and Hester drove the oxen with Andrewes beside her while Gaby and the two boys rode excitedly on the back.

When they arrived, they found Catchpole and Tim Wilton there before them with a couple of bottles of champagne waiting to be opened.

'A libation to the new house, don't you know!' Tim Wilton declared amid the general clamour. He untwisted the wires on the neck and the cork shot out, startling the life out of Njoroge who almost dropped the box he was carrying. 'And God bless all who live here!'

'Is it c-c-cold enough?' Catchpole stuttered anxiously, flushing. 'I d-don't kn-know m-m-much about ch-champagne, but I k-k-kept th-the b-bottles in the s-stream overnight.'

'It's lovely, Nat!' Hester said, her face radiant with happiness.

Andrewes observed her contentedly. If only he had been able to offer her a place like this right at the very start, he thought, instead of the railhead camps, the mud huts, the tin shack in Nairobi . . . But now at last she had a place of which she could be proud; or it would be, once he had added the kitchen and bathroom, though for that he needed pipes from Nairobi. But he had reason to be satisfied, he felt as he looked around that spacious living room. Ay. He sipped his champagne and tried not to grimace at the taste of the stuff; he'd have preferred whisky, but Catchpole was already offering him more, which he had to accept out of politeness.

'Ye're next on the list, d'ye ken? Soon as I've finished here. So ye'd best start thinkin' o'er the kind o' house ye'd like, an' pickin' a site.'

'B-but th-there's n-no need—' Catchpole started to protest when Hester's voice was heard from the far end of the room.

'Everybody! Everybody, listen! Tim wants to propose another toast! Go on, Tim!'

Gaby and the two boys fell quiet. Catchpole and Andrewes turned and waited.

'This is a personal toast, but I hope you'll all join me, don't you know. Gaby, Michael and Robert as well.' He held up his glass. 'I've known and respected and *liked* King John since our very first meeting years ago, when I was quite new in British East and we worked together on the railway. He has that special quality of inspiring people to work with him and to share his vision. So I'd like us all to drink – To King John and The Kingdom!'

'K-k-king John!' stuttered Catchpole as they all drank. 'I . . . I dinna quite know what to say.'

'Then say nothing, John.' Hester slipped across the room and kissed him. 'It wasn't meant for you to make a speech. We did it because we all love you very much.'

'Ay . . . well . . . I must say somethin', my love, if it's only that *ye've* made The Kingdom, an' Catchpole, an'

Gaby . . . ay, an' Mwangi an' all the Gikuyus who knew this land long before we set foot on it . . .'

'But you're King,' Hester said firmly, putting her finger across his lips, and she added lightly, with a laugh, 'Why d'ye think they call ye King John?'

'Well, there'll be no speeches,' he conceded. 'But I'll tell ye one thin', my love. Your Scottish accent's no' improvin'!'

The only incident to sour the day occurred after Catchpole and Tim Wilton had left and the empty champagne bottles had been cleared away. Perhaps without the champagne it would never have happened. They were none of them accustomed to it. Robert, his cheeks unusually flushed, had declared he was going off to arrange his things in the bedroom. Michael lay stretched out full length on the sofa, chattering about all he intended to do when he got to school in England, while Andrewes himself only half-listened. Out on the veranda, Hester and Gaby appeared to be arguing.

'I don't see why Uncle Tim doesn't get married.' Gaby's voice was loud and challenging, as if she was intent on annoying her mother. 'Or if he doesn't want the bother, he could have an African mistress. Mr Jackson's got three, I've seen them! So why doesn't Uncle . . .'

Hester slapped her face. The sound was sharp and uncompromising.

Andrewes got to his feet and strode to the veranda. He found the two facing each other hostilely, standing about a yard or so apart. All the colour had drained out of Hester's cheeks.

'You'd better go to your room,' she said coldly, trying to control herself. 'I never hit you before – *ever* – but then I never expected to hear that sort of filthy talk. Go on. Go to your room.'

Gaby turned dramatically and went into the house, glowering at John as she brushed past. A moment or two later they heard her bedroom door slam.

'I don't know what's come over her these days,' Hester muttered, almost to herself. She sat on the veranda rail and stared out at her raw new garden. 'She never used to be like that.'

'She's growin' up, lass,' Andrewes attempted to comfort her, though sensing that he was not succeeding. 'She's growin' up, that's all.'

They had seemed like two grown women confronting one another rather than mother and daughter, he thought as he went over it all in his mind later on. A difficult age, people had warned him, though he had scarce believed them. The trouble was, Gaby had never experienced the rough and tumble of mixing with other children of her own age, and maybe they were about to pay the price for that. If she still refused the Young Ladies' Academy he'd no idea what to do.

But the next morning she took matters firmly into her own hands. She rode out to the quarry to speak to him, fanning herself with her soft felt hat and shaking out her long auburn hair about her shoulders. She was a beauty right enough, and very well aware of it. Before long she'd be turning many a young man's head. Older men too, if they didna watch out.

'I've apologized to Mama,' she stated in her most matter-of-fact manner. 'Before she'd a chance to ask me to. I told her I'm ready to go to the Young Ladies' Academy now. I *think* she was pleased.'

'Ay, she would be.' Andrewes eyed his daughter suspiciously, wondering what she was up to this time.

Suddenly she relaxed into a laugh, though behind it she remained deadly serious. 'Oh Papa, I've just got to get away – you see that, don't you?'

It was however a few months before the Young Ladies' Academy in Nairobi got in touch to say they once more had a vacancy and could at last take Gaby. By then it was time for Michael and Robert to leave for Britain and, as a special treat, Andrewes suggested they should all go down to Mombasa for a week to see them off.

'No.' Hester was emphatic and her eyes were troubled. 'No, John. It may be cowardly of me, but the thought of watching their ship going off into the distance and knowing they were on board – that's more than I could stand.'

'But you insisted they should go, my love,' he objected, puzzled, wondering if she were about to change her mind.

'We've no choice, they have to go to school,' she said, sadly. 'I want to say goodbye to them here. Oh, I know it's silly, John, but that way I'll feel more certain they'll be coming back. Besides,' she dodged any further argument, 'Mombasa will be hot and sticky, and I've far too much to do on the farm just now.'

So they left for Mombasa without her: first, a day's journey by ox-cart; then by rail to Nairobi on the new Thika 'tramway' – built, much to Andrewes' disgust, and that of all other railwaymen, by the Public Works Department, though he had to admit they had not made too bad a job of it; and, finally, from Nairobi to the coast by the familiar old Uganda Railway. The boys soon got over their initial, uneasy sadness at leaving their mother behind, when they had not been too certain whether to fight back their tears or not, and were full of questions every mile of the way. As Andrewes tried to explain some of the technical problems they had faced when building the railway, vividly reliving those old days, Gaby pretended to be superior to it all and withdrew into her own thoughts. Yet he noticed from an occasional flicker of her eyes that she was listening all the same.

'Why did they start calling you King John?' Robert asked, once they had settled down again after the excitement of seeing the man walking along the carriage-tops of the moving train to light the lamps as dusk approached.

'Och, it's a silly nickname,' he answered easily. 'I dinna ken why.'

Did Hester, he sometimes wondered, still remember it had been Ed Muldoon who had first used that name? It was years now since she had even mentioned the man, though he knew for a fact she kept the derringer well-cleaned and with ammunition to hand. Maybe he should buy her something more up to date if it helped her feel safer. One of the new pocket model Colt automatics he'd

334

seen in the catalogues. Though there was little enough risk these days.

'It's Tsavo!' Michael announced importantly when the train at last slowed down to a stop, reaching its destination for the night. 'Where Papa shot the lion! Will you tell us about the lion, Papa?'

'Ay, after we've had a wash an' a bite to eat, mebbe.'

Altogether, it was a nostalgic journey and he indulged the boys' curiosity as much for his own pleasure as theirs. Gaby too, he suspected, had half-forgotten memories she was trying to piece together again, though she had only been a wee bairn at the time. Looking back, it seemed like a different world. They had something solid behind them now. The Kingdom – ay, it was a good name. The estate . . . the house . . . Ay, mebbe that was the reason he felt so . . . och, so contented in spite o' the boys goin' away.

In Mombasa, he handed them over to their companion for the voyage, a settler's wife whose fare home Andrewes had agreed to pay in return for her looking after them. Then he spent some time showing Gaby the sights – the old Portuguese castle, the lagoon, Freretown – and several long hours in business discussions with Roshan about the possibility of opening further branches of Patel & Roshan's Emporium in other parts of the Protectorate, while Gaby picked over the latest consignment of silks and cottons, selecting some for herself and Hester.

Back in the train as they travelled up to Nairobi he began telling her more about the business and was pleased at the interest she showed. One day, he thought, he would have to set about drawing up a new will. Maybe this side of his affairs would be something for her, leaving The Kingdom to go to the two boys; though he had made the estate into a limited company right from the start, with Hester, Catchpole and himself having equal shares, and they would need to be consulted.

But och, who was thinkin' o' dyin' anyway? They'd all have farms an' business o' their own long before he reached his deathbed. An' Gaby'd marry a lord, mebbe. Or one o' those American millionaries who turned up regularly in British East on extravagant hunting safaris.

He ran into one within two hours of arriving in Nairobi. He had taken Gaby and her luggage to be received into the bosom of the Young Ladies' Academy – she said goodbye light-heartedly enough, just a moist kiss on his cheek and she was gone – and come out on to the pit-holed murram road where his rickshaw was waiting, when he saw the caravan approach from the direction of the Ngong hills.

There were three white men whose safari suits and pith helmets looked brand-new in spite of the red dust which covered them from head to foot. Following them were more than a hundred porters carrying tents, boxes, cooking utensils, ivory tusks, rolled-up skins and animal heads that attracted swarms of flies which crawled over the canvas wrappings and exposed horns. Their guns – the very best from Holland & Holland, Andrewes estimated – were borne by gun-bearers, but with them also were some fifty or sixty armed *askaris* dressed in dark blue jumpers embroidered with the initials of the safari firm employing them.

The headman – a tall, commanding African with slight traces of grey in his hair, his arm in bandages, and carrying his rifle with the casual ease of an experienced hunter – walked alongside the main column and slightly apart from them. But there was no mistaking him. Andrewes would have recognized Kamau even in the midst of a crowd.

Kamau passed with hardly a glance towards the rick-shaw, yet Andrewes felt convinced the *askari* had seen him. The caravan was probably returning after several weeks on safari; no doubt later that day the men would be paid off. There was time.

'Ada's!' he yelled to the rickshaw boys, settling back on the narrow, uncomfortable seat. 'Upesi! Quick!'

The rickshaw tipped forward, rocked, jolted, skidded, swayed alarmingly from side to side and almost collided with three others before finally depositing him in front of Ada's; by that time he was wishing he had walked instead. He paid the boys off and strode up the steps.

336

The official name was Hathaway's Hotel, painted in large letters across the front, but everyone called it simply Ada's. She had made a big success of the place – and on her own, too, as Jimmy was still with the railway. Andrewes' share in the business was kept very quiet; only the bank manager was in on the secret, as well as Roshan, who had put up part of the money. Newcomers to British East might still patronize the Norfolk, but it was to Ada's many of the settlers flocked when they were in town. They liked the elegance of the bar with its dark wood panelling, its engraved glass shades over electric light bulbs and its gilt mirrors. They liked the spreading thorn tree outside – still that same thorn tree near which he had once camped with Tim Wilton. Above all, they liked Ada.

He pushed his way between the men crowding the bar and went straight through to the back to find her.

'Heard tha wast in town!' she greeted him, interrupting her haranguing of one of the room boys and sending him about his business. 'Tha usual room's ready, an' water's hot for a bath. Ee, it's good to see thee, King John!'

'Good to see ye an' all, Ada!' he responded warmly. 'Ye've made a few more changes, I've noticed. Place is lookin' grand. An' Jimmy – is he in town?'

'Gone off to Nakuru,' she said placidly. 'Always off somewhere, is Jimmy, ever since I first met him.'

She asked if the children had got away without any bother, and for the next half hour or so they exchanged their news. Then he went up to his room for a bath and a change of clothes before going out to find the manager of the safari firm.

The *askaris* were to be paid off the following morning, he discovered, although some could expect to be re-engaged almost immediately for the next client, due to arrive in Nairobi within the week. Not Kamau, though: there would be no more safaris for him until the gash on his arm had healed up. The manager could promise nothing, but if Andrewes wished to speak with him, his best course would be to turn up the next day when the pay was doled out.

Andrewes thanked him briefly, and made his way to the

337

Patel & Roshan Emporium, where he spent some time selecting the pipes and other items he needed for the W.C. he planned to instal at the house; they still used the old, outdoor pit latrine, and he had repeatedly assured Hester that the W.C. would be the next job he would tackle. Afterwards he sat drinking tea with Patel who was full of his latest idea – to invest in a workshop where they could manufacture agricultural tools themselves cheaper than any imports. He was looking very sleek and prosperous, Andrewes reflected as he enlarged on the details; it was hard to recognize in him the thin, sad sepoy with betel-stained teeth that he had once been.

Andrewes' thoughts wandered, going back yet again over those early days. They had all changed over the years. Matured – was that the word? And could that be the reason for the mood which had gripped him now for so many months, since building the house, in fact?

*I reckon I've reached the stage when a man has to sum up what he's been doin' an' where he's been. Like strikin' a trial balance, mebbe.*

Saying he would be back again the following morning, he left Patel to return to Ada's. As he rounded the corner, he spotted Kamau – now dressed in his familiar white *kanzu* – staring up at the front of the hotel, as though reading the name painted over the ground floor windows. At that same moment, two young bucks in spotless safari clothes and new bush hats came blundering across the road and collided with him.

'I say, watch out, you!' one of them protested loudly. 'What are you doing here anyhow? You can't go in there! Round the back if you're looking for a job.'

'Practisin' his alphabet, what?' his companion joined in, a sallow-faced youngster with a drooping moustache. 'It's my opinion he deserves a whippin' for bumpin' into his betters like that. Teach him to look where he's goin'.'

Andrewes joined them in a few strides, twisted the still-coiled raw-hide whip out of the young man's hand and tossed it away. 'Ye'll no' be needin' that in Nairobi,' he said, reproving them. 'The man's done ye no harm.'

'I say, you saw him push us!' the first one protested vehemently. 'We could have him run in for assaulting a white man. A whipping's letting off lightly.'

'If you were a gentleman – though from your foul Scottish accent I judge you're not – you'd pick that whip up now an' return it to me with some suitable apology,' the sallow-faced young man drawled, slapping his clenched right fist against the open palm of his other hand. 'Because if you don't, I'll be forced to teach you a lesson.'

During this exchange, Kamau remained absolutely still, neither intervening to help Andrewes, nor making any attempt to withdraw. One or two other men, attracted by the prospect of a fight, came out on to the hotel veranda to watch. Andrewes ignored them.

'Ye can pick up the whip yesel', but dinna let me see ye usin' it,' he said contemptuously, about to turn away.

'Then you've asked for this, old man!'

His right fist shot out, but Andrewes blocked it, knocking it aside. But the lad was serious, boxing according to the book, dancing around him lightly, and Andrewes began to realize he was no longer so agile as he used to be. His friend too looked as though he was ready to join in at any moment, given half the chance. He had to finish it off, and quickly. Feinting with his right towards the lad's chin, which brought his guard up, he lashed out hard with his left below the navel, following it up with a punishing blow on the neck behind the ear which laid him out.

'I say!' the other one was loud in his condemnation, paling as Andrewes turned towards him. 'I say, that's not cricket!'

'Ay, ye're right!' Andrewes grinned suddenly, relaxing. 'Kamau, I'm delighted to see ye again!' he added in Swahili, grasping the *askari*'s hand and shaking it warmly. 'I'm hopin' we may have a wee talk. Old times, d'ye ken?'

'You still fight like an angry rhino, Andrewes,' Kamau said gravely. 'But that is not always good.'

'Ay, ye're right.' He could already feel the bruises spreading on his fist and forearm.

'Ee, what's been going on?' Ada exclaimed anxiously as

she came bustling out of the hotel. She took it all in with one quick glance at Andrewes and another at the sallow young man sitting doubled up on the deeply-rutted roadway while his friend bent over him. 'Tha's not been tangling with King John surely? Ee, tha daft buggers! Did nobody warn thee?'

'I say, Gerry's Oxford University boxing champion, you know!'

'An' much good it's done him!' she declared cheerfully. 'Come on, I'll help thee up. A free drink on house'll put thee right.'

Andrewes turned away and led Kamau into the hotel, ignoring the muttering and hostile looks as they went through the main bar. For a second he was tempted to sit at one of the empty tables and have their chat there, just to see what they would do about it; but he desisted and chose the private room at the back instead.

# EIGHT

Hester stumbled as she stepped over the newly-ploughed furrows and caught hold of Tim's arm to steady herself. 'Sorry!' she laughed, her eyes darting to his face.

He was gazing at her seriously, without moving. In that moment they seemed to be completely alone, shielded by the trees from the eternal curiosity of the Gikuyus working among the maize only yards away. Her sense of freedom made her almost light-headed. Michael and Robert would be on the boat by now, Gaby was at the Young Ladies' Academy at last, John was still in Nairobi – and now she had time to be herself again after all those years! With neither children nor husband to make demands on her, however much she loved them! Even Catchpole was away for a few days to buy cattle.

'Hester?'

Her hand still rested on his arm; embarrassed, she drew back a little. 'You should go for potatoes again,' she said, trying to pick up the threads. 'It's newly-cleared ground. You might be lucky, and they always fetch a good price.'

'Hester, listen to me!' Tim hobbled after her.

'Sisal takes years before it shows any return,' she went on stubbornly.

He gave up. 'All right, we'll talk about potatoes if that's what you really want. But I don't think it is.'

His face was sad, she noticed; it made him look very young and vulnerable. Yet he had been so considerate since that time when Gaby ran away, helping her to keep a proper distance however much it hurt. True, he had asked her once more to leave John and go away with him. He'd sell the farm, he said, and they could live in England, Australia, Canada, anywhere she liked . . . But that was impossible and she had spelled it out so clearly to him, he had never dared bring it up again.

Oh, at times she had dreamed she might explain everything to John and he would understand and they would settle down happily together, all three of them . . . Well, it was only a dream. She knew she would never succeed in making John see that Tim could take nothing away from him. Nor he from Tim, for that matter.

Tim limped back to the horses with her and held the stirrup as she mounted. 'Will you come over to supper this evening?'

She shook her head. 'I'm sorry, Tim. No.'

'Hester . . .'

'Not behind his back. I couldn't stand that again.'

It was a strange day: cold, with banks of grey and purple cloud creeping across the sky. Then towards late afternoon a drizzle started, more mist than rain really, and the Gikuyus huddled in their warmest clothing.

Hester asked Joe to light a log fire in the living room and she sat there alone after her meal that evening, staring into the constantly-changing colours of the dancing flames. Remembering. This was the time she had looked forward to every day since they left, when she could be on her own with no one to disturb her. She thought about the boys, probably tucked up in bed on board ship, and Gaby, and how proud John was of this big stone house, as though it compensated in some way for that bitterness he still felt at how shabbily the Railway Office had treated him. It had worried her ever since they came out to start farming here. It had never been enough for him to see a whole field of green shoots where before there had only been seed. He had seemed fanatically driven on to prove he was bigger and tougher than anyone else. Oh yes, The Kingdom was aptly named. Other settlers scratched a living from the soil, and were content to do so; but he had to dominate it.

He still loved her, she was quite sure of that. Perhaps even more now than in the early years. She often caught the expression in his eyes . . . something in his voice . . . and then . . . *With my body I thee worship.* He really savoured those moments, carrying her along with him, exploring her skin with his strong hands, which were hardened and calloused through work . . . till she arched her back, hungry for him, opening to him sensuously, longingly . . . but not too quickly . . . wanting him to go on for ever and never stop.

No, she could never face the thought of losing him.

And Tim?

Tim, who could relax her tensions with one glance from his sympathetic eyes, who could share her thoughts so intimately, they often found themselves saying the same words . . .

'*Memsabu! Memsabu! Tembo!*'

The urgency of Joe's voice shocked her out of her reverie. She could hardly believe her eyes when she got to the window and looked out. Looming through the misty darkness came the largest elephant she had ever seen, with at least two more behind it. They moved silently, placing one massive foot in front of the other with slow deliberation, their trunks swaying gently and their giant ears occasionally flapping.

In a panic, she dashed to the bedroom for a rifle, fumbling desperately to load it; cartridges scattered across the floor. Shoot through an elephant's left eye, John had once told her – or was it the right? She could remember him explaining how a shot through the wrong side would merely hit solid bone without penetrating the brain – but which?

Back at the door, trembling, she watched as the biggest elephant investigated the edge of her veranda while still more came unhurriedly out of the darkness, knowing no one could stop them. A fence was carried away; her young, scarlet erithrina trees snapped in half as one brushed against them; the others trod the branches underfoot. She counted at least six of them . . . no, seven . . . and one only a baby.

And yet more came.

But what could she do? Her hands shook as she held the gun and she prayed she would not have to use it. They were all waiting to see how *Memsabu* would deal with the situation, relying on her – Joe, Mwangi, Njombo, Gatema, their wives, their *totos*, behind her in the room, crowding at the

343

window . . . It was a nightmare. That big bull elephant stood blocking the veranda front, sideways on with two others, and she felt completely dwarfed by them. And beyond – she could only just see them through the gaps – the rest of the herd quietly trampled her garden to mud.

That terrible silence, too, was so hard to bear, punctuated only by an occasional grunting rumble, as though nothing in the world existed but them. If she ever found herself in their path she knew they would walk over her without even noticing. She held her breath as the great bull turned, almost as if checking that his whole herd had arrived, almost counting them . . . Then, unbelievably, it let go a string of steaming wet droppings on to the veranda itself.

When it had finished it moved away and, behind her, everyone sighed with relief, a sigh which changed to a sudden clamour of dismay as they realized the elephants were heading around the side of the house towards their own huts.

Undecided, Hester went to the end of the veranda, fidgeting with the rifle. Then she remembered that Wanjiku and her new baby would still be in her hut.

'Oh, no!' she cried, hurrying back through the house, pushing her way between the fearful Gikuyus, calling out to Joe and Mwangi to come and help her.

Emerging through the door at the rear of the house she ran over towards the huts, hoping frenziedly to head the elephants off, but there were so many of them – at least ten now – their great ears waving like sails in a breeze, their tusks gleaming. If she fired they might stampede and then . . . yet if somehow she could change their direction . . .

Within a few yards of the bull elephant she stopped, perplexed. It seemed even more enormous from ground level, and with the others approaching gravely out of the darkness, unperturbed, the whole scene carried an air of eerie majesty. Oh, it was out of the question to shoot them, even if it were practical, yet she had to find some way to divert them away from the huts.

'Shout!' she called out. 'Anything – as loud as you can!'

Setting an example, she started yelling at the top of her

voice, but it had no effect. Instead of veering away, they continued stolidly in the same direction; she could have reached out and touched the leader, he was so close. She would have to use the rifle after all: perhaps if she pressed the muzzle against him, pulled the trigger . . . But no, she'd heard enough hunting stories to know that even a shot directly through the heart might leave him with enough impetus to charge forward that fateful few yards towards the huts.

She fired into the air, taking the risk.

The elephant gave a lumbering start of surprise, its pace quickening for a couple of steps, then it stopped completely. The Gikuyus too ceased their shouting; the silence was unnerving. Again she fired, and was then forced to jump back, retreating several yards to avoid being trodden to death as the herd surged forward. But they *were* changing direction! She fired a third time to make sure, then – catching her foot in a tangle of something on the ground – she fell, rolled over and scrambled out of the way on hands and knees until she felt her arms seized and someone helped her to her feet.

'Is Wanjiku safe?' she panted, seeing nothing in the darkness. 'And her toto?'

'Safe, memsabu!' Njombo grinned.

With her day-old baby in her arms, Wanjiku was sitting on one of the large stones John had placed to demarcate the Gikuyu living area. She seemed hardly more than a child herself.

'Shouldn't she be lying down?' Hester objected.

But no one answered.

The elephants were still moving among the wattle-and-daub huts, demolishing each one as they brushed against it. Yet not deliberately; this was no orgy of destruction. They pushed through these simple homes with no more thought than she would have given to walking through grass, and then disappeared into the darkness and mist, making for the coffee fields. In a few minutes – her despair returned, she was almost in tears – they would destroy the work of years.

345

Then, from among the ruined huts, she heard someone groaning in pain. 'I thought everyone was out?' she snapped, turning to Joe and Njombo. 'You two come with me. Gatema, light a safari lamp and bring it – quick! Upesi!'

She picked her way in the darkness through the tangle of crumbled walls and thatch towards the sound which came from the rear of the little settlement. More than one person must be buried there, she realized; as well as the man's groans, a girl was sobbing. Mwangi went berserk as they reached the spot, urgently pulling the debris aside and muttering to himself hysterically. From somewhere in the distance she heard several shots . . . reverberating . . . rolling like faraway thunder through the black mist. Then Tim's voice, calling out of the darkness as he got closer – oh, thank God!

'Hester, are you all right? What's been going on?' At that moment Gatema hurried out of the house with the safari lamp; its light played over the remains of the wrecked huts. 'God Almighty . . .! It looks like you've had an earthquake!'

'Someone's hurt.'

'But you're all right?' He got down from his horse, unfastened his walking stick from the saddle and limped towards her. His tone was anxious, 'Are you?'

'How could I not be?' she challenged him, brushing the hair from her face with the back of her hand. 'You didn't see the elephants? That wasn't you shooting?'

'To let you know I was on my way. Heard your shots.'

Instead of answering, she set to work again, trying to clear away the broken thatch and ravel of interwoven sticks from which the hut walls were made. Clumps of hardened mud and dung came away in their fingers, disintegrating into fine dust in spite of the dampness of the night. Underneath, the girl was still sobbing. As they removed the last of the wreckage they found the girl and the young man, both naked, clinging together; it was obvious they had been making love when the hut fell on them.

Mwangi's concern changed to anger. He stood abusing them both furiously, refusing any more help, while Tim

346

improvised stretchers from sections of the broken walls and had them conveyed to the house.

'Girl Mwangi daughter,' Joe explained cheerfully, with a good-humoured flash of white teeth. 'Kabogo come from far, far 'way. Always night. Very quiet.'

Hester cut him short. 'I need plenty hot water,' she told him briskly. 'You take plenty debe and make hot – understand?'

'*You* look like you could do with a bath,' Tim commented.

'Later,' she said briefly.

She examined the girl first, questioning her, for there was no blood visible as far as she could see under all that dirt, so perhaps she was merely bruised. Then Tim pointed to the dark mess caking her ankle. The girl whimpered as she carefully lifted it away. The skin had been torn off, exposing the bone.

'Oh God, what can we do?' She felt helpless. 'We need a doctor.'

Tim had stripped off his jacket. 'It'd take three days to get a doctor, that's if he'd come at all. You'd best have a look at the man while I hurry that hot water along.'

'Tim, I'm glad you're here.'

Her voice must have betrayed all her self-doubt. He said encouragingly, 'Heard shots, don't you know? Couldn't be sure where they came from. But *you* know what to do, my darling. You helped doctor Carson often enough.'

The man's foot had been crushed when one of the elephants had walked over the collapsed wall of the hut; there were several open gashes on his legs, too. The first task, she knew, was to wash both patients, who were covered in mud and filth; then she cleaned the wounds, splashing them liberally with permanganate while Tim tore up a sheet for dressings. She had taken a flat piece of timber from John's workbench and was holding it against the young man's foot as a splint, considering how best to bind it in position, when she became conscious of Mwangi standing in the doorway, observing her.

'Elephants caused much damage,' he said awkwardly. Then he stepped forward to examine his daughter's

wounds; and the young man's. He shook his head gravely.
'Bad. And Kabogo's leg . . .! I have sent Njombo for
Gikuyu doctor.'

For a moment Hester did not fully grasp what he was
saying. 'You mean there's a doctor nearby?'

'Please wait. He will come. Such wounds are well
understood by Gikuyu people.'

'Oh, a witch-doctor!' She felt defeated again. 'Tim, we
can't allow that, surely? Just think if there's gangrene . . .'

'If they trust him, what else can we do? Tim sounded
just as doubtful. 'I imagine King John would agree with
them.'

'Yes . . .'

She was still hesitant.

When the Gikuyu doctor arrived she was even more reluctant to let him touch the wounds, although Mwangi and the
others seemed so relieved to see him there, she could do
nothing to stop him. He was a wrinkled, older man whose
skin hung loosely from him, and he smelled strongly of
rancid oil. As he laid aside his red blanket and approached
the patients, she began to explain that they both needed
stitches and Kabogo should have a splint for his foot.

He took no notice of her. Instead, he issued his own
rapid instructions to the Gikuyus crowding around, and
they ran off to obey them. Then he investigated the solution
of permanganate she had been using as a disinfectant and
seemed to approve of it. To her amazement, when Mwangi,
Njombo, Gatema and the others returned they bore
branches sharp with long, needle-like thorns. He looked at
them with approval, and then set to work.

Hester's mind was in a turmoil as she watched, wondering if she was right not to intervene. She would never
forgive herself if anything went wrong and they died. Tim
touched her arm but she moved away from him, intent on
checking everything the old man did.

He dealt with the girl first, drawing the edges of the skin
together and pricking a series of tiny parallel holes in it
through which he then threaded the long thorns. To hold
them in place he wound banana fibre around the protruding

348

ends. Mwangi looked on intently and nodded, satisfied, as he finished. Perhaps noticing the doubt on Hester's face, he showed her a neat scar running up the inside of his arm, with rows of prick-marks on each side.

'I also was once healed in this manner,' he explained to her reassuringly. 'He asks you to wash the wound again with the brown water.'

She picked up the bowl of permanganate to swab the girl's ankle once more and the old man grinned at her; he was practically toothless.

He turned next to the young man, Kabogo, and stitched up the gashes on his leg in the same way, using the long thorns. Then he took the crushed foot between his hands, said something in Gikuyu, and began to stretch it until Kabogo – for all his braveness – screamed out fearfully, and fainted.

Hester felt sick at the sight of it. She glanced away and saw how Tim was biting his lip as he watched. Yet he had always sworn he would have died of his wounds at the *boma* had his Swahili *askari* not treated them in his own traditional way. And perhaps, she thought, some of the Gikuyus standing around at that moment – people she now knew well – had also fought at the *boma*; had been the enemy, in fact. It was so strange.

Under instructions from the old man she held the splints in place – a flat piece beneath the foot, and bamboo at either side – while he tied them in position, then covered them with a length of hide which he laced up tightly like a boot.

And when he had finished, he turned and pulled his blanket about his shoulders again, then left the house without ceremony.

At last, exhausted, half the night gone already, Hester went into her bedroom and closed the door. She was grateful to be alone once again. Grateful, too, that Tim had volunteered to stay until morning and sleep on the lumpy sofa in the living room. The two patients had been put into Gaby's room for the time being; her belongings had been moved into the boys' bedroom which was already in use as additional dry storage space since they left.

Getting into bed, she turned down the oil lamp until just the tiniest of blue flames danced on the blackened wick. Even as a child she had always enjoyed watching the light burning this way for those last few seconds before she blew it out. Then she lay listening to the quiet sounds from outside and heard the rasping protest of the springs in that secondhand sofa as Tim tried to find a more comfortable position. Her bedroom opened directly into the living room; every little noise was sharp and clear.

Those elephants, she thought.

As she had stood helplessly watching them trample over her garden, that sense of security she had gradually acquired over all her years in this wild country – John's achievement, really, with his intense passion for building and order – had dissipated and she was more frightened than she had ever been. In a few seconds they could have demolished her 'safe' stone walls without even bruising themselves. Even in her worst moments she had known nothing like that fear before; except perhaps when Muldoon attacked her; that, too, had stripped away all the certainty in her life.

The sofa springs creaked again. Thank God Tim had been not too far away. It was ridiculous, she thought, both lying awake. Then she turned over, determined to get to sleep and pulling the bedclothes more comfortably around her. What a shock it must have been for those two when the hut suddenly collapsed on top of them – and at a moment like that! Would they ever feel safe again?

Any of them?

She made no conscious decision. One minute she was cosily in her bed; the next, she was getting up and feeling for her slippers. Then she crossed to the door and opened it, looking into the dark living room, saying nothing. A creak from the sofa told her Tim knew she was there.

His outline was faintly visible as he sat up. Then he waited, uncertain. Silence. Long, long silence. Hesitantly, groping first for his walking stick, he limped over to her . . .

stretching out to touch her arms . . . her shoulders . . . her neck and throat . . . His hand was rough on her skin as it moved gently up to her face.

So often she had refused him, held back from him, pretended at times to scorn him – anything to keep him away from her, however much she had longed for him. Now, in the darkness of the new stone house of which John was so proud, she took Tim's arm and guided him to her bedroom, shutting out everything else.

Inside, they stood for long seconds close together, neither moving nor speaking, conscious only of each other's presence. Still without a word they found the bed. His arms were around her as he caressed her; he kissed the tears away from her cheeks, tears of happiness as she took him to herself, surrendering all that reserve which she had tried to build up as a protection from him. *If Love be Love, if Love be ours* . . . The words went through her head wildly as they once again realized the love that *was* theirs, and had been, and would be . . . and she recognized things, little things her body had half-forgotten yet now were there again, and it was like returning home after a long voyage.

As they lay quietly afterwards, their arms about each other, knowing they could never part again, whatever happened, Tim murmured, 'I've been sleeping at Catchpole's hut while he's been away, to be closer to you.'

'Tim . . .' She snuggled up to him, her head against his shoulder. 'Oh Tim, how could I ever have turned you away? How could I have done it to you?'

He kissed her again tenderly; and the kiss lingered, grew, became a whole world of new sensations as his body hardened against her until all other thoughts fled before that one yearning, glorious and timeless moment of their love.

## NINE

*Praise the Lord, the King of Heaven . . .*

It was Ngengi's favourite hymn. Normally he would have joined in the singing wholeheartedly at the daily service in the big mission hut they called 'the church', but that morning other thoughts were buzzing around like angry bees inside his head. Since Mungai had arrived with the news that his father Kamau was back on the ridge, all his old doubts had returned.

Until that moment his mind had been made up. Soon he was to be baptised as a Christian, with five fellow pupils at the school, and he had been concentrating all his thoughts on the full meaning of that great event. He would be an outcast, he knew. It was a momentous step to turn his back on all the traditions and beliefs of his own people and embrace the faith of the red strangers. Yet if he was to learn their knowledge . . .

Then Mungai had come – Mwando's younger brother – and waited outside the perimeter fence, nervous in case one of the missionaries spotted him.

'Kamau has returned,' he announced simply through the wire. 'He sent me to tell you. Did the missionaries give you that?' Enviously he fingered the sleeve of Ngengi's white shirt.

Ngengi felt a quick thrill of joy at the news, but it was followed – inexplicably – by an uncomfortable sense of dismay and uncertainty. 'Does he know I am here?'

'They have told him. Will the missionaries give me a white shirt?'

'Perhaps. Tell me about my father. What did he say when he heard? Was he angry?'

Instead of answering the question, Mungai began describing all the unimportant details – who first spotted Kamau when he reappeared on the ridge, what they had done, how they had reacted – and as he spoke, his eyes darted this way and that, taking in the mission buildings, the pupils, the vegetable gardens they tended ... His body, naked but for the usual few bangles and his short cloak, was dusty from the journey. This is how I looked the day I came here, Ngengi remembered, seeing himself unexpectedly through others' eyes.

'And soon the irua is to be held,' Mungai was going on. 'Mwando and Gatheru will be circumcised and people on the ridge are asking, where is Ngengi? Though some say you are Kamau's son, so not truly one of us.'

Before Ngengi could reply, *Bwana* Taylor approached. Mungai gaped at him, uncertain whether to turn and run, or stand his ground. Thin and scrawny, the missionary walked with hurried steps and stooped shoulders, as if convinced that the world moved too slowly for all he had to achieve.

'A friend of yours, Peter?' he called out in English, upon which Mungai dashed off to take refuge among the nearest trees. 'You must persuade him to join us. We're not so frightening he has to run away, are we?'

'No, bwana,' Ngengi answered dutifully.

'Remember you are Peter – *Upon this rock will I build my church*. We rely on you, you know!'

'Yes, bwana.'

The missionary had given every pupil a new name. 'New names for a new life,' he had said, though perhaps remembering their scornful laughter at his attempts to pronounce Gikuyu names.

Now, a few days later, he stood in front of them as usual at the morning service, his little black moustache wriggling up and down as he sang. *Praise Him Praise Him* ... Since his last illness his clothes sat loosely on him; his pale, unyielding face was more haggard than ever as though he – not Lord Jesus – bore the sins of the world on his shoulders. No use asking him for permission to visit his father, Ngengi decided. Nor Mrs Taylor – straight-backed, her expression serene as she accompanied the singing on

353

the harmonium, especially if she heard about the circumcision ceremony.

Her face would redden with anger as it had done on that famous occasion two years earlier; her eyes would widen, glaring as she spoke out against it – though every Gikuyu knew *irua* was the initiation into full adulthood, the most important day of their lives. According to her, all Gikuyu customs were wrong. The pupils had listened in silence as she told them this; only Ngengi had dared to speak up, with the result that he was caned before the whole school. That same night he had left the mission compound, vowing never to return.

In his rage he had stumbled through the forest, not caring where he was going, until at last, worn out, he climbed a tree and slept for long hours. The sun was directly overhead when he awoke. He went on aimlessly, uncertain what he should do, and eventually came to the clear pool fed by a waterfall not far from the ridge. Stripping off those hated clothes, intent on cleansing himself of the mission and all its works, he was about to plunge into the cold water when he saw a girl bathing there.

So white – whiteness beyond anything he had ever imagined; and her skin so smooth, her lithe figure, her firm yet delicate breasts, her gently swelling hips, and that tumble of russet hair spreading about her on the water as she crouched down. She must be King John's daughter, he guessed. The mission boys knew all the settlers' names, all the details of their families. Besides, he remembered that rich hair.

She was like a dream in the night . . . like a song on the air . . . a wisp of white cloud . . .

Bitterly he realized such girls would be well beyond his reach if he abandoned the mission school. Learn from them, his father Kamau had said, but expect nothing. He had dressed once again in those clothes he despised and retraced his steps.

*Praise Him, Praise Him . . .*

Guiltily, he started singing again as the missionary

354

caught his eye. On the front row he could see Mungai, coaxed into the mission by the promise of a new white shirt, his lips moving hesitantly as he tried to pick up the words of the strange hymn. Had he perhaps intended to come to school all along and merely used the news of Kamau as an excuse to get away from the ridge?

But none of that mattered. Ngengi's mind was made up.

It was still dark the following morning and long before anyone else was awake when he slipped out, moving like a ghost across the compound, parting the wire strands of the fence to make his escape. As he reached the trees his heart felt about to burst with joy. He was free of the mission – maybe for ever! He had become a star pupil in their eyes – they had said so themselves – and was being prepared for baptism, the final step. But now he was turning his back on it all. The dense forest opened to receive him and the birds welcomed him with their dawn chorus.

Throughout the long day he travelled, hardly once pausing to rest, and the sun had already set by the time he neared the ridge. Then he was struck by fresh doubts. How would he be received after all this time? He stopped, identifying the familiar shapes of the rocks and trees by the thin light of the quarter moon lying on her back low in the sky. Near the place where he had once fought his friend Gatheru he took off his mission clothes and hid them in the undergrowth before continuing along the dark paths to his mother's hut.

Njeri stood outside talking to another woman as he approached. 'Ngengi!' she cried out in surprise and delight, her dark eyes lively. 'Everybody, come quickly! Ngengi is here! My son has come back!'

A burst of excited chatter and laughter surrounded him. His hands were seized, his arms touched, as though they could not believe their eyes – after all this time! Then they took him towards the cooking fire where his sisters and his uncle stared at him from every side to discover if the mission school had changed him in any way, and expressing their satisfaction when they found he was still the same Ngengi after all, only a little older.

His mother brought him food and withdrew a little with his sisters while he ate it. The firelight flickered across their faces. He listened to the night sounds among the trees, the distant murmur of voices, the sudden laughs. The scent of the burning wood caressed his nostrils. He was home at last. Home!

'You have come for irua,' his uncle – his mother's brother – stated.

Ngengi did not contradict him. Only a few days ago his thoughts had been on baptism, but now he had left the mission and come here, where he belonged. All his age group would be preparing themselves for initiation.

'Where is my father?' he asked, thinking it strange no one had mentioned him yet.

'He has built his thingira on land farmed by the red stranger,' his uncle Wanjui explained, shaking his head in disapproval. 'But his ways were never ours. Truly they call him Mwebongia, for he has always been one to walk alone.'

Njeri sighed, busying herself with the fire. 'It is the man they call King John. Kamau works for him again. This man – while you were away, he came once to the ridge with his wife and his children. Do you remember his wife? You were very small, but I knew her. She knew *me* in those days. Now everything is changed. As I was working, she stopped and looked, but without seeing me. I might have been the wind, she was so blind.'

'And King John?'

'He drank beer with Chege, I am told.'

'Will you not join my father?'

Njeri laughed comfortably. 'Join that man again? Why – I am happy here, this is my home, I have my children. Do I lack for anything?'

'A wife's duty is to her husband,' Wanjui remarked.

'Did I not follow him to Mombasa? Besides,' she added, quite without resentment, 'I hear he has other wives now to bring pleasure to his bed.'

Most people on the ridge, Ngengi noticed during the days that followed, seemed to regard his return with indifference. They greeted him whenever they met, but had little to say. At first he imagined they had not forgiven him for having run away to the red strangers' school; at that time they had all agreed that no one should ever work for the settlers, yet he soon spotted signs that their resolution had weakened. Every elder now wore a new blanket, while old Chege had become fatter and drank from an enamel cup in place of a gourd.

'Chege and the elders decide who will work,' Gatheru explained to him enviously – even their fight, it seemed, was now forgotten. 'But they send only age-groups who are already circumcised, and the rupees they earn must be handed over to the kiama.'

'Soon it will be our turn!' Mwando grinned happily. 'I shall keep some to spend with She-Who-Sings. She is a red stranger woman who travels in a cart drawn by a zebra. Twice she came here and brought many things to sell in exchange for rupees.'

'You mean Memsabu Hathaway. I saw her at the mission.'

Gatheru regarded him slily. 'Will you be circumcised?' he asked. 'They say the missionaries are enemies of irua.'

'Who asks their permission?' Ngengi retorted. Then to cover his embarrassment, he said, 'If the missionary woman had been circumcised herself, perhaps she would be happier.'

Gatheru was curious. 'Her man does not satisfy her?'

'How could anyone satisfy her?' Ngengi joked, and the other two laughed.

Once, he remembered, a boy had peeped into the mission bungalow at night and seen Mrs Taylor in bed – fully dressed, as far as he could judge – while Mr Taylor was on his knees praying aloud. But he kept it to himself. It would all be so meaningless to them – the sheets on the bed, the iron bedstead with its chamber pot beneath, Mrs Taylor's white cap to keep her hair in place. And in that

357

moment, Ngengi felt the gulf between him and the others on the ridge.

'Will you go back there?' Mwando demanded.

'I don't know.'

'If you need help with this woman, you can send for us.'

He laughed, but his heart was not in it. He would leave the ridge, he decided, and go in search of his father, who would understand all these things. With him, surely, he would be able to talk. *Mwebongia,* they called him: the One-Who-Walks-Alone. But was not he also walking alone?

Was not this the only way?

Kamau noticed the young man approaching while he was still some distance away but did not give him a second thought. He sat outside his hut, cleaning the Winchester rifle which Andrewes had given him – that same old Winchester he remembered so well from those early days on the railway. It had been damaged in the great battle, Andrewes had explained; then it had been completely stripped down and rebuilt. Now it was as good as new again.

He had hesitated for some time before accepting Andrewes' offer to let him have land for a *shamba* on the edge of his own estate. He was an *askari* and hunter, not a farmer. But then, there would be no more work for him until his arm healed and his wife Muthoni was dissatisfied with the life he led, always away on safari somewhere while she was left behind in Nairobi, so he had come out here after all. She was content, particularly when he agreed to take her friend as second wife to live with them.

As for Andrewes, the moment he had heard about the damage wrought by the elephants he had declared it was high time they employed a hunter on the estate, and he had presented Kamau with the Winchester.

It was still an excellent gun, he thought, giving it one last rub with the oily rag; if only he had been equipped with a few of these at the great battle! But that battle had been wrong from the start – the wrong time, the wrong place, wrong in every way.

He looked up suddenly, aware that the young man was standing now only a few yards from him, his eyes fixed on him. A tall, well-built young man with a fine, sensitive face and intelligent eyes. A Gikuyu from one of the ridges, to judge from his dress.

'If you have something to say, then speak,' he broke the silence, puzzled. 'Were you sent to find me?'

Still no reaction. Then a memory stirred deep inside him. Something familiar about the young man's face . . . the shape of the lips . . . of the head . . .

'You are Ngengi!'

'Yes, Baba, I have come to find you.'

Kamau started up, his heart about to burst as he greeted the son he had not seen since he was a small boy, so bitter had been the price which fate had exacted from him after his defeat. In those first months, unable to return to the ridge himself, he had three times sent messages to Njeri, asking her to rejoin him with their children, but no word ever came back. Now his son stood in front of him, old enough already for the initiation ceremony – yet a stranger.

He called Muthoni to prepare food for Ngengi who must be tired and hungry after his journey, he said.

'We have many things to talk over, my son and I. To recall the years that were lost, and learn to know each other anew.'

During the days that Ngengi stayed with him, they spoke together for many long hours; yet at times they were silent, as if they had no more need of words. Kamau heard all that he said about the mission school and questioned him closely on some points concerning the missionaries' belief that their own ways were superior, that their God was white and that all should serve Him. Of Ngai they had never heard; about the followers of the Prophet Muhammed they were scathing. Only they were right, they taught – and to that extent, Kamau reflected, they were no different from any other people.

He showed Ngengi the whole of the estate known as The Kingdom – the big stone house, the pipes conveying water to the fields, the steam pump, and the long, straight rows of vegetables, coffee plants and sisal covering the whole valley. As they stood watching the Gikuyu girls weeding and hoeing, Catchpole rode past – tall, very thin, and wearing a wide-brimmed hat to shade his face which was the colour of a promising sunset.

'G-good morning, K-kamau!' He did not stop.

Kamau raised his hand gravely in reply, than hitched his rifle more comfortably on to his shoulder. 'They call him C-catchpole. He helps Mrs Andrewes with the farming.'

'A man?' queried Ngengi, but he showed no surprise.

They climbed the hill, skirting the great wound in its side which was caused – Kamau explained, anxious that Ngengi should understand everything – when Andrewes dug out rock for his house. The whole land was scarred, he pointed out when they reached the summit: those straight fields with their fences and their rows of coffee like railway lines; the long drying trays like passenger platforms; the stone house; the wide roadway cutting across the entire estate . . .

'They call this The Kingdom!' He indicated the entire landscape with a sweep of his arm. 'As far as you can see in every direction. They subdue the land as they subdue everything else.'

'Like a vast spider's web!' Ngengi seemed over-awed by the sight. 'And they're all caught in it – Gikuyu warriors bending their backs to dig the land, Gikuyu girls over there, singing as if they don't realize how those long, straight threads are holding them prisoner. And now you, Baba?'

'That could be true,' Kamau agreed. The image appealed to him; but it was not only the Gikuyus who were entangled in that web. Andrewes himself was gripped fast by it, too. He understood now why the man had altered so much. The Andrewes he had seen so often standing on some rock promontory, his Winchester ready, or carrying that wounded *askari* back through the scrub to the *boma* – such was the man he remembered, not this hero of the coffee fields.

But he said nothing to Ngengi about this. Instead, he pointed across to a distant line of hills. 'Over there Wilton has his farm. Do you remember him? He worked on the railway.'

'They speak about him on the ridge. They say he shares Mrs Andrewes' hut when Andrewes is away in Nairobi.'

'That I have heard too.' Kamau adjusted the strap of his rifle again. 'Come, I shall take you to the stone house. Think over these things when you return to the ridge. The elders see nothing. They send their young men and women to work for rupees while the strangers destroy their land and grow more powerful.'

'But you work for them!' Ngengi protested.

'For that reason, I know their hearts better than any man.'

As they approached the house he noticed how impressed Ngengi seemed by its thick, solid walls. Through the windows they could see rooms as large as forest clearings, with high ceilings and stone floors. At one end, work was still going on, supervised by Mrs Andrewes, whose thick brown hair tumbled untidily over the shoulders of her white, long-sleeved blouse.

'Good morning, Kamau! My kitchen will soon be finished, you see?' Her eyes rested on Ngengi questioningly – brown, smiling eyes. 'I'm afraid you've caught me at a busy moment.'

Kamau explained that she had known Ngengi as a *toto* at the railhead camp. She remembered instantly, but her face clouded.

'He doesn't live with you then?' She nodded abstractedly as he answered and then said, still in Swahili, 'Well, Ngengi, we must find you a job when you've finished at the mission school, mustn't we?'

Dismissed.

On their way back, Kamau sensed that Ngengi too had recognized that tone of voice. Yet Mrs Andrewes was not so unlike a Gikuyu woman. She cultivated her *shamba*. She bore children. And her arrangement with Wilton – the talk of every ridge for miles around – did not a Gikuyu woman also have the right to invite any man of her husband's initiation group to spend the night in her hut?

'Baba,' Ngengi said on his last day, shortly before he left. 'You buried a gun on the ridge. Shall I bring it to you?'

That gun with no cartridges, he remembered; useless when he most needed it. Yet perhaps it might still serve a purpose.

'No, let it remain there,' he decided. 'The time is not yet.'

Nyambura was unusually silent amidst the excited chatter of the other girls as they approached the sacred fig tree with their escort of chanting warriors. She had been looking forward to the initiation ceremonies and her heart had quickened with joy when Ngengi reappeared on the ridge, for she naturally assumed he too was preparing himself for *irua*. Then a rumour spread that he intended to obey the missionaries and refuse circumcision after all. Everyone said it was the greatest scandal ever known on the ridge, and an ill omen for all others in the age group. She just could not believe it; it seemed so terrible.

But the rumour persisted until – only two or three days ago when all initiates were called together – Ngengi joined them, proving them all wrong! In the dancing she chose him as her partner, and they gazed delightedly into each other's eyes as they abandoned themselves to its urgent rhythms and freely joined in those wild songs with their open, shameless references to the secret parts of men and women, and their detailed descriptions of all they might do together.

Strangely, Nyambura felt no embarrassment at singing such words. On the contrary, her pulse beat quickly, her whole body opened as if to receive him; though, naturally, they did not cease dancing, for such contact was strictly forbidden.

Now the girls were nearing the fig tree, each with her head newly-shaved and her body naked save for the beads supplied by the older women of the family. The warriors' chanting reached a high pitch of excitement, the ceremonial horn sounded to start the race – oh, let Ngengi be first to reach that tree!

The boy-initiates charged forward with fierce cries as if going into battle, at first closely bunched together, but later straggling out with two or three ahead of the others and – yes! – Ngengi was in front! His arm rose as he threw the wooden spear over the tree and Nyambura – surging in front of the girls – knew her heart was singing. Ngengi was the one chosen by Ngai to speak for his age-group; not Gatheru, whom she disliked.

Climbing to the highest branches, the boys began to break off the twigs and leaves, which they threw down for the girls to collect while their families and friends sang yet again of the intimacies between man and woman. But Nyambura hardly listened to the words. She stared up eagerly into the tree, then darted to catch the twigs Ngengi dropped specially for her. Even later, during that solemn moment when they took the oath and swore always to behave in a manner befitting a full member of the tribe, she never ceased to be aware of Ngengi's presence.

The next morning before it was light they went to the stream – the girls in one place and all the boys together in another. A white mist hovered over the banks and the water was painfully cold. As she bathed, Nyambura gritted her teeth to stop them chattering, which the observers might have interpreted as a sign of fear. By the time she left the water her limbs felt completely numb.

Holding her fists clenched with her thumbs protruding between her first and second fingers in the prescribed manner, her hands level with her shoulders, her elbows pressed into her sides, she walked in the slow procession towards the homestead where the circumcision was to take place. A fleeting shiver of apprehension crossed her mind but she controlled herself immediately, banishing all thoughts. When she got there she sat down on the cow-skin which had been laid out on the ground, and spread her legs wide apart. Directly behind her, with her own legs wrapped over Nyambura's, sat Wanyaga, her sponsor. Nyambura leaned back against her, comforted by her warmth, waiting . . .

An old woman came forward out of the crowd; she bore

363

a gourd of bitingly cold water which she splashed against Nyambura's sex to numb it still further. Then more waiting, and she stared up at the sky, emptying her mind.

Out of the corner of her eye she just saw the weirdly decorated face of the operator as she approached, and she heard her leg rattles clacking out her rhythmic dance, coming closer. Then those hard fingers touched her vulva, parting the lips, wider, and suddenly Nyambura felt a quick, burning pain as the sharp knife removed the end of her clitoris. It was done. The old woman returned, clucking away unintelligibly as she washed the wound with water and herbs, then Wanyaga covered her up while the watching crowd of women burst out singing about how brave she was.

Nyambura allowed herself to be helped to her feet. She walked in a daze to the hut where she was to stay until the wound head healed; in spite of her numbness from the cold water she felt sore at every step. But she gave it no thought, relieved that she had shown no fear and also intensely proud that now she was a full initiate, able to take her place in the tribe as an adult woman.

Ngengi lay on his bed of banana leaves in the hut set aside for male initiates. His agony grew as the night wore on, yet it was nothing compared with his feeling of deep satisfaction that he had taken the right course. He had not flinched when the circumciser took hold of his penis, shrivelled to a mere stump after immersion in the cold water, bunched up the skin and then cut – once . . . twice . . . From the joyful sound of the crowd of women and men looking on it was clear that not so much as a flicker of fear had crossed his face: it had been his one anxiety. Now he was a full member of the tribe, a junior warrior, shorn of his foreskin, but with the small skin still hanging beneath the penis in traditional Gikuyu fashion. And with the privileges it brought, there were also duties and responsibilities; Mikiro, his sponsor, never tired of going over the details of all he had to learn.

Kamau had given him no advice on the subject of *irua*,

saying it was a matter he must decide for himself. But he added, 'It is good, if you can, to know where you belong. I have come to realize that my roots are among those who have no roots; I am at home in many places, though none would wish to claim me as theirs. My father tried to tell me this, but it was many years before I understood him. In some ways, Ngengi, you are different, and you must learn how to use this difference.'

And Ngengi had been glad that his father no longer dressed in Gikuyu fashion, but again wore the long white *kanzu* and small skull-cap he still vaguely remembered from the railhead camp. In these clothes Kamau had the appearance of a lord, beside whom *Bwana* Taylor was a mere worm. A worm with a moustache.

They had discussed again the straight lines across the estate – row upon row of coffee, maize, beans, pineapples, sisal, and fruit trees such as pawpaw, mango, oranges . . . 'Don't you know how to draw a straight line?' the missionaries had often cried out in exasperation; now he could guess what must have been in their minds.

That great spider's web!

He dozed off fitfully and found himself dreaming about it, seeing Gikuyu girls and warriors helplessly enmeshed in its threads, and there – almost in the centre – was Kamau, his back bared to receive the lash, each blow cutting more straight lines into his skin until at last Ngengi could stand it no longer. He rushed forward to try and stop it. Then a spasm of pain snaked through his penis and he woke up again.

He shifted to find a more comfortable position, but whichever way he lay that open wound stuck to his skin – against his leg . . . against his belly . . . against whatever it came into contact with, other than the banana leaves themselves.

But at least he had been initiated, he thought, in spite of all the scepticism of Gatheru and the rest. In fact, only Nyambura had truly welcomed him. Only Nyambura . . .

# TEN

For those who have ears to hear, there are no secrets in Africa; news spreads quickly in its own mysterious way, no one knows how. So the rumour soon reached The Kingdom that Jackson was once again talking of diverting the stream, regardless of the effect on anyone else. Mwangi reported the story to Andrewes, who decided he had no alternative but to go and confront the man right away.

He rode up there early in the morning, taking Kamau and Ngengi with him for company. Jackson's farm was difficult to find as he had not bothered to build a good road, only a rough track which was already partly overgrown again. The fields, too, had been unevenly hacked out of the bush and his ploughing was obviously erratic, the furrows curving and buckling, though the crops looked healthy enough.

Jackson himself he found drinking whisky – although it was not yet midday – lying in a hammock slung between two posts on the veranda of his prefabricated frame-house; his rifle was near to hand and from time to time he raised himself to stare across at the Africans working in the nearby field.

'Come an' sit down! You'll take a drop o' whisky?' he called out as Andrewes dismounted. He turned towards the house and bawled orders for another glass and a fresh bottle to be brought. 'An' to what do I owe this honour, *Mr* Andrewes? You don't bloody like bein' called King John, do you?'

The man's speech was slurred and Andrewes ignored the question. He found a chair, brushed the debris off it and sat down, glancing around the veranda with distaste; it must have been several weeks since it was last cleaned. Jackson shouted again, impatiently, for more whisky and an African girl came out to hand him the bottle and a smudged glass. She was very young, Andrewes noted, and wore just a strip of leather over her sex, nothing else. A second girl lounged at one of the windows, giggling.

'You'll drink wi' me?' Jackson rubbed the glass on his shirt before sloshing a generous measure of whisky into it. His words sounded more like a challenge than an invitation. 'I imagine it's the stream you've come about.'

Andrewes raised his glass briefly, then took a mouthful. At least the man bought decent whisky, he thought. 'Ay, it's the stream. I reckon, d'ye ken, we can work somethin' out. Irrigation is an engineerin' problem, when all's said an' done.'

'An' you've got all the answers, I s'ppose?'

'Some.'

Andrewes began by setting out plainly the reasons why the stream should not be diverted. Jackson listened suspiciously, pursing his thick lips and shaking his head each time he disagreed. Then he interrupted.

'There's nowt you can do to stop me, King John, an' you know it!' he retorted cheerfully, taking another drink. 'Not that I've no sympathy, but you're not the man to make me change me mind. Now if you'd sent that girl o' yours – different matter, eh? She's in Nairobi now, they tell me.'

'She's at school,' Andrewes said shortly.

'I don't know, King John – you an' your women, eh!' Jackson laughed, as though sharing some sort of understanding. 'Tell you one thing, though. I'd not let any wife o' mine behave like that.'

Andrewes put his glass down. His voice was ice. 'Behave like what?'

The man grinned, his heavy-jowled face creasing with pure enjoyment as he realized he had Andrewes where he wanted him. 'Why, you're never tellin' me you don't know?' he mocked, settling down comfortably in the hammock. The girl who had brought the whisky stood next to him and his free hand wondered over her hips. 'You must be the only man who doesn't. Her an' young

367

Wilton – the moment your back's turned, hoppin' into bed together?'

Andrewes was on his feet. 'Get out o' that hammock!'

'Must'be been goin' on for years, an' you didn't know!' Jackson said lazily, staying where he was. 'How old is that young boy o' yours – the one wi' hair like Wilton's? Robert, isn't that him? General opinion, *King* John, was you jus' closed your eyes to it – but fancy not knowin'!'

'Either ye get out o' that hammock an' stand up, or I'll tip ye out,' Andrewes threatened him, his voice deadly quiet. Drunk or not, the man had to be taught a lesson, he told himself grimly; yet he felt a sudden fear, too, that it might be the truth he was telling. Hester was fond of Wilton, always had been, that was no secret, but surely she would never . . . 'I'll give ye one more second!'

'An' then what?' The rifle was in Jackson's hand and he swung his legs out of the hammock, one either side, sitting up. 'If you'd like a bullet through your shoulder, jus' step one pace near, your *fuckin'* Majesty. I'm not surprised your wife gets more out o' young Wilton than you can give her. Maybe I should shoot your balls off instead, they're fuck all use to you.'

Maddened, tortured by doubts, Andrewes left the veranda and came towards Jackson from the other side, halting a short distance away. The rifle was still trained on him and Jackson was a good enough shot to be dangerous, however much he had been drinking. Kamau, who had probably heard their raised voices, approached from the side of the house, his Winchester already in his hands. Andrewes stopped him.

'Bring the horses,' he ordered. 'We're leavin'.'

'Quite right – you are!' Jackson jeered at him. The rifle did not waver. 'I never liked you Andrewes, not since that first day when I was lyin' on me bed wi' a cracked skull. Always too big for your boots, to my way o' thinkin'. An' that name – *King* John! Christ, whoever thought that one up? Well, now you're bein' cut down to size for a change.'

Andrewes held the reins, ready to mount, and his hand

368

brushed against his own rifle in its saddle holster. Jackson noticed it.

'Leave that where it is, an' keep those mitts o' yours where I can see 'em!' he said sharply, standing up. Then he grinned, relaxing slightly, and placed his left hand beneath the African girl's bare breast, displaying it. 'See that? Finest pair o' tits south o' the Sahara – an' two more pair to match 'em in the house there! You're a fool, King John. Why marry, if you can get 'em without?'

Andrewes looked at him with contempt. 'Ye'll hear from me again, Jackson, when ye're sober. On both counts.'

He swung up into the saddle. With a nod to Kamau and Ngengi, he rode off without looking back. At any minute, he felt, he might get a bullet in his back, but that was a risk he preferred to ignore. Any other time he would have torn the rifle out of Jackson's hands and beaten the hell out of him with it – so what was so different now? That rubbish about Hester and Wilton, made up on the spur of the moment to goad him into losing his temper? No sense in it, none whatever. Hester an' Wilton – why, they hardly ever saw each other these days in spite o' the closeness o' the two farms.

Yet Wilton had been there the night the elephants created all that havoc amongst the crops, he remembered. He had helped her with the two injured Gikuyus. Andrewes recalled no despair on her face when he got back a few days later and saw the damage; on the contrary, she had glowed with a sort of inner happiness, as if having to meet this challenge had stimulated her in some way – that's how he had interpreted it, anyhow. But had he been wrong? Had there been some other reason?

But no, it was impossible.

Yet . . .

Jackson's accusations had been like a vicious blow with a long, barbed spear, deeply penetrating his guts, the poison on the tip sending its numbness to creep through him.

He glanced at Kamau's face as they rode on, but he could read nothing there. If such rumours had been flying about among the Gikuyus he was bound to have heard. And how long had they been talking like this? When the Gikuyu girls had tittered among themselves in the fields, was this what they had been gossiping about?

He tried to dismiss the thought, to force himself to think about the problems of the estate, clear, logical problems with straightforward answers which could be worked out, but each time the fear came back to nag him . . . scratching away at his peace of mind . . . What if it was true?

What then?

He found Hester at the drying trays, examining the pale coffee beans. She looked up with a quick smile as he approached commenting that this year's crop was the best yet.

'Ay,' he responded brusquely, his nervousness clawing at him. She looked so confident as she stood there, so much in her own element. She'd put up her thick brown hair again, so most of it was concealed under her terai, but a few unruly wisps escaped. He wanted to reach out and touch it, frame her face in his roughened hand as he had done so often. 'Ay, my love – but can ye come up to the house for a wee moment? We've somethin' that needs discussin'.'

'The stream?' she guessed. 'Jackson refused?'

'He was drunk.'

But he said nothing else until they were back in the living room. On one of the stone walls Hester had recently hung the skin of a leopard which Catchpole had shot when he discovered it ravaging his cattle. Its eyes seemed to stare at him, sullenly.

'What is it, dearest?' she asked anxiously. 'It's not the stream, but something else worrying you? John . . .?'

'Jackson was makin' remarks about ye an' Wilton . . . I thought it best ye should know.'

'What about me and Tim?' she challenged him hotly. But then she stopped and looked at him, troubled, as if trying to come to a decision. The colour left her face; her eyes were tender, almost pleading. 'I love you, John.'

'Ay.' Then it's true, he thought desperately; it must be true. The numbness from that poison penetrated deeper; he stared at her, not knowing what to say or do.

'I want you to . . . to understand,' she went on, her voice betraying her own uncertainty. 'It *is* possible to love two people. But then of course it must be, mustn't it? I love you . . . I love the children . . . and . . .' She paused; then said firmly, her chin set determinedly. 'And I love Tim.'

Hester stood there before him, *his* Hester, every line of her face so familiar, so much part of his life – and now suddenly he no longer recognized her. She was telling him something, that she was in love with Wilton, young Wilton, and had been for many years, but the words blurred into each other, making no sense. It could not be Hester talking, but a stranger, someone he had never known in all that time of living together. *I love you, John,* she repeated – but how could that be true? *I don't want to lose either of you.* And those many times they had declared their love for each other – with their words? With their bodies? Each knowing that only one other person in the world existed for them?

Or that's what he'd thought: now he knew it all to be a lie.

He sat down, his mind dead, his whole world gone, understanding nothing any more. The poison had done its work thoroughly; the numbness was in his brain, his thoughts blank. Before him he saw nothing, only Gaby's rough carving on the fireplace arch. That animal head, its scooped-out eyes mocking him pitilessly.

After a while he became aware that she had stopped talking. He stirred himself. 'Robbie?' he asked dully. 'Jackson implied he was Wilton's child.'

'Oh John, can't you call him Tim?' she pleaded, her face animated. 'We all belong together.'

'Is he Wilton's child?' he yelled at her, losing his temper.

'He has the same hair,' she admitted, almost complacently. 'But he has your mouth – have you noticed?'

'Ye mean ye canna bloody tell?' Her answer shook him. All those years she'd been making a fool of him. 'An' ye

371

stand there like ye're proud o' what ye've been doin'. Ye're a whore.'

'I'm not a whore, John.' She spoke calmly, without raising her voice. Her tone was quite firm. 'I love two men, that's all. Each of you differently. All I've done wrong is to keep you in ignorance all these years, because I was afraid of how you would react. Not to avoid a scandal, John – don't think that! – but because I truly and honestly love both of you, and above everything' – she dropped to her knees by his side, leaning her head against him – 'I don't want to lose *you*.'

Defeated, empty, bewildered, he stroked her hair as he had so often done in the past, until the hairpins loosened and it all spread itself out beneath his fingers like a thick mane. Years ago they had once sat like this together – Gaby's gargoyle leered at him as he remembered it – in front of the smoky fire in her father's study in Liverpool. What had happened to them, he wondered, as the pain within him took over, sharpening; what had made it all go so wrong?

Even then he knew what he had to do, though he said nothing. He spoke very little that evening, yet he was constantly aware that her eyes were on him, worried. She went to bed early and he waited patiently until he judged she was asleep.

Then, in the night, he collected his guns, a good supply of ammunition, his usual safari gear, and left The Kingdom for good.

*Book Four*

# ONE

They headed north.

With him were Kamau and Ngengi, together with four other Gikuyus whom they recommended as good hunters. It was a hunting safari, he told them; they could all expect to be away for many months. No further explanation was necessary. They probably all knew the full story already, he thought; there were no secrets in Africa, and only fools believed otherwise.

Under his orders, they pushed on relentlessly through the night, with scarcely a pause for rest, intent on getting as far away from The Kingdom as possible. It was hard going in the darkness, but by daylight he reckoned they had put ten miles or more behind them. Even this did not satisfy him. They had to go on despite the heat, which became more intense as the sun climbed in the sky.

Then the forest thickened and some relief came from the close, roof-like foliage above them; but there were no paths, only animal tracks which frequently petered out in impenetrable bush and they had to hack their way through inch by inch. Andrewes wielded a panga with the rest of them, refusing to admit they should turn back to seek a better route. That was one thing he would never do – turn back. He slashed at the tangle of twisting fern, grass and tendrons in blind anger, never letting up, always first in to attack the densest bush.

The Gikuyus followed him without daring to grumble, as if they could sense that darkness in his soul, that desperate force which drove him on without mercy. Between themselves they arranged a relay system, taking turns at working beside him to clear the undergrowth ahead, while others looked after the horses and mules strung together in a line behind them.

The sweat poured off him, drenching his clothes and

attracting thousands of tiny insects which fed on him, sucking his blood, crawling over his neck, into his ears, up his nostrils, even into his mouth and over his tongue as he gasped for breath, gulping in the hot air.

'The men need rest, Andrewes,' Kamau informed him, stating a fact.

Andrewes glanced at him, and tried to wipe the sweat from his brow with the back of his hand, ineffectively. Over all the years Kamau had not changed. He never called any man *Bwana*, nor did he usually challenge an order. He was as solid and reliable as Mount Kenya itself. If only he had not gone his own way after Muldoon's whipping. If only Hester had not been left alone that day. If . . .

None of it might have happened.

If.

'Let 'em rest,' he said roughly. 'Ten minutes. No more.'

He continued hacking at the undergrowth, with every stroke trying to kill that relentless pain . . . the memories . . . the realization. But wherever he looked he seemed to see them watching him, Tim and Hester, Hester and Tim, their faces appearing in the dappled patterns of the sunlight filtering through the leaves . . . laughing . . . enticing . . . inviting him to join a disgusting threesome . . .

'Och, madness,' he muttered, attempting to concentrate his thoughts on the job in hand. 'Ye always were an idiot, John Philip Andrewes, an' she saw through ye a'right.'

He told the Gikuyus their ten minutes were up and the sooner they got back to work, the sooner they'd be through this jungle. Reluctantly, they picked up their pangas and once more attacked the twining undergrowth, which seemed to get thicker with every step. It was another three hours before they heard the sound of running water ahead of them and eventually burst through a dense wall of leaves and twiners to find themselves on the bank of a stream.

They threw themselves down flat, hanging their heads in it to gulp in the cool water and let it wash over them, laughing and spluttering as they came up for air. Andrewes stripped off his shirt and splashed handfuls of the water against his burning skin.

376

It looked an idyllic spot, with every shade of green among the high, lush vegetation on either bank, the tall creeper-covered trees and thick lianas; even the rounded rocks scattered here and there like little islands in the stream were green with tiny plants growing all over them. But the air swarmed with insects and he decided they should move on to find a more suitable place to camp.

They followed the stream down, at times scrambling over the bank, at times plunging into the water itself despite protests from the animals. One mule slipped on the uneven rocks, or caught its hoof maybe in a root, and broke its leg, whinnying pathetically as its blood stained the water. Andrewes had to shoot it and distribute its load among the others.

At last they reached a glade where the trees gave way to bare rock and patches of low scrub. They would camp for the night here, he decided, giving the order for a fire to be lit. The men's sullen mood changed miraculously; the air was suddenly alive with their chatter as they set about preparing to stay there. A fire was soon blazing; the animals were freed from their loads and left, hobbled, where each could take advantage of the limited grazing; water was fetched from the stream; a meal cooked.

Andrewes had expected they would eat the usual *posho* porridge, but then he smelled meat roasting over the fire. He went across to investigate.

'The mule was still young.' Kamau's face was serious, betraying no trace of humour. 'And you shot nothing else today.'

He repeated his words in Gikuyu for the sake of those who could not yet follow his Swahili, and they grinned broadly.

'Ay, well I hope it's tender,' Andrewes commented tartly, looking around the circle of faces. 'That's all I can say.'

The meat turned out better than he had feared, though strongly flavoured, and there was plenty of hot tea to help wash it down. As he sat afterwards picking the shreds from between his teeth, he felt a nudge at his elbow and saw

377

that Kamau had unpacked a bottle of whisky for him. He uncorked it and poured a generous amount into the tin mug. The burning in his throat was soothing as he drank it, and so too was that quickening in his veins as it began to take effect; if only, he brooded, he could drink something to dissolve that whole aching cancer inside him, to make him forget Hester and the marriage which had been the very breath of his life; and that desolation which was now all he had left.

Before trying to sleep he emptied the bottle, but it was no help. He lay awake most of the night while the forest breathed around him, alive with the sounds of millions of insects, shrill cicadas, rubbing, scraping, whispering, humming, with quick, harsh calls, suddenly urgent then not heard again; and the noises became louder, more menacing, a murmuring that approached and receded like waves of people crowding through Indian streets – yes, it *was* India! He could smell the spices from their cooking, hear the familiar shouts . . .

Gita was there too, smiling at him as she adjusted the sari on her shoulder. 'I must at least try to help them,' she was arguing . . . pleading with him . . . 'You do understand, John?'

She floated away, carried by the crowd, only her face still visible, her eyes dark and worried. But then the crowd disappeared and her face lay drawn, exhausted, against a pillow and he knew she was dying. Fighting for life, yes – fighting to stay with him, yet all the while going from him. Wasting away.

'Trying our best, ol' man! Don't hold out much hope, though!' That voice he had hated, unreasonably; and hating himself too. 'Trying our best!'

He woke up. How long he had slept he had no means of telling. Not long, probably; it was still dark. He lay there, his confused thoughts darting about in uneasy patterns, wondering why he should have dreamed of Gita again for the first time in so many years, not since the railhead camps, the Taru Desert, Tsavo, and seeing her face . . .

378

No, *that* was Hester . . . and Tim Wilton . . . 'Trying our best, don't you know? Trying our best . . .'

A change in the rhythms of the forest announced the approach of dawn long before it was light. He got up, thankful it was time to be on the move again. His mouth was dry. He went down to the stream to plunge into the stinging cold water. He had become soft, he thought; had to harden himself again.

The men were packing up ready to leave when there was a shout of laughter from Ngengi and one of the others, followed by a cry of dismay. Andrewes swung around in time to see half a dozen baboons loping off towards the trees, having snatched some of the things Ngengi was about to pack. His Mannlicher was already in his hand and he brought down the first two before the rest disappeared, chattering, into the forest.

'At least we've saved the cooking pot,' he commented wryly as Ngengi picked it up, and also the drinking mug the second dead baboon had been clutching. 'What did they get away wi'?'

'A knife.'

'Ay, ye've got to watch out for baboons. Steal the false teeth out o' your grannie's mouth if ye let 'em.'

Ngengi looked at him, uncomprehendingly, but Andrewes did not bother to explain. He was the only one of the Gikuyus who spoke any English, though in a limited way, and Andrewes liked to encourage him. Not at that moment, though, when they had to finish packing and make a start.

By midday they were clear of the forest altogether and in more open country. He scanned the landscape through his field glasses, then almost at random chose the direction they should take. He had no fixed plan in his mind. What did it matter where he went? He pushed on, keeping up a hard pace, until towards late afternoon he spotted a movement among the distant bushes.

Through his glasses it looked like no more than a couple of twigs shifting in the breeze, but the space between them remained constant. Ordering the Gikuyus to remain where they were, he dismounted and ran forward, half-crouching, to get closer. Then, unexpectedly, he caught a clear glimpse of the curved horns; he ducked down as the animal's head turned in his direction.

Where it stood it could not scent him, he knew; but if its hearing was sharp he might still not be able to get close enough for a kill. The bushes seemed unusually brittle, making it impossible to move quietly. Slowly he crept forward, following the scattering of hardened animal droppings, freezing every yard or so before raising his head to take another look.

He was almost within range when the beast took it into its head to wander off – not quickly, and no more than a couple of dozen yards, but in the wrong direction. Andrewes cursed it under his breath as he watched.

It stopped again.

He had no alternative now but to make a wide detour in order to approach from its flank. He set off cautiously, keeping his head well down and pausing every yard or two to make sure his quarry had not moved. It was not even feeding where it stood, merely standing motionless as if contemplating the landscape.

It was a greater kudu, he could see that now – the first he had ever come across, though he had examined the head of one displayed on the wall of the Norfolk Hotel. Hunting for its own sake had never appealed to him before, but now he could feel that excitement thrilling through him, that hard determination to win.

Ay, an' to kill.

He went on, moving even more stealthily now he was so close. Even from where he stood he could have risked a shot, but this one had to be dead certain; another three or four yards, maybe . . . Then some instinct made him glance over to his right, only to discover he was not the only hunter marking that kudu. He had a rival – a lioness, crouching tensely between the bushes, observing its every move.

The kudu seemed quite oblivious of the double danger threatening its life. It stood, completely visible, on a patch of higher ground. Every movement sensitive and superbly controlled. Noble. Aristocratic, even. A real monarch o' the glen!

Ay, thought Andrewes, satisfied that he had only to squeeze the trigger to bring the beast down if he so wished, I'll let ye go now, but dinna think ye've seen the last o' me!

Instead, he took careful aim and put a bullet through the base of the lioness's skull. With a slight jerk she slumped forward, still in that crouching position, lying so naturally anyone might think she was only sleeping.

As for the kudu, it was half a mile away already.

During the days and weeks that followed Andrewes lost count of the number of animals he slaughtered as they moved on through that wild, untamed country. It was not that the killing in itself gave him pleasure. Squeezing that trigger was no more than the logical conclusion of the whole operation, the last piece slotted into place, the final nut tightened. What mattered – what blotted out everything else in his mind, giving him relief from those torturing thoughts – was the intense concentration of stalking his prey, pitting his wits against it, until at last he was within range; or following fresh spoor, the droppings which were still warm, the hoof-print which had not yet lost its crispness, until the beast was in his sights. And then the conclusion: its head and skin carefully prepared – one of Kamau's special skills – to join the collection.

But he never saw the greater kudu again. Twice, maybe three times, he spotted its imprint in the dust, the shape of a punctured heart, but it was too cunning to show itself. As if it realized there were no second chances.

Then – they were nearing the Rift Valley, but far to the north of the railway – a group of Laikipiak told them of a large herd of elephants they had met heading south. Andrewes cajoled his men with promises of extra pay to endure yet another forced march to catch up with them. They grumbled but in the end agreed, no doubt recognizing there was no way they could thwart that demonic fury which was driving him blindly on.

After the first day they came across a trail of broken

bushes and trampled scrub, with a string of droppings showing the direction the elephants had taken. But the droppings, each the size of a blackened haggis, had already baked hard under the hot sun. They must still be some distance ahead, Andrewes judged and he urged the Gikuyus on.

Progress became slower. The men were exhausted. The horses and mules were also tiring under their additional loads of animal skins. Impatiently, he decided to push on alone, leaving Kamau in charge; but when he announced his intention, Ngengi volunteered to accompany him as gun-bearer.

'Ay, ye take after your father well enough,' Andrewes said by way of acknowledgement. 'Now see ye stay wi' me, where I need ye.'

He gave him the Mannlicher to carry, with two bandoliers of ammunition, while taking the large-bore double-barrelled Frazer himself. It was an old gun he had picked up in Nairobi for next to nothing, but still serviceable.

Take after your father . . . His own words twisted in his mind like a red-hot knife as they tramped along that wide, debris-strewn path left by the herd. Ay, if any man could be certain a child was his own.

He could forgive her least for that. For not even knowing herself. For not even caring, it seemed to him.

*I love you both, John!*

And she expected him to believe it. To . . . to do what? Congratulate her? Call in the local missionary for a triple wedding? Champagne?

He stopped dead in his tracks, unslinging the Frazer and indicating to Ngengi not to move. Directly in front of them, just beyond a bare thorn tree whose branches were decorated with bulbous weaver nests, was a large cow elephant snuffling at the earth. As they watched, it lifted its trunk high and emitted a thick shower of dust over itself, spreading its ears as it did so. Even from several yards away its size was overwhelming.

Andrewes pulled back the hammers for both barrels and walked slowly forward. The elephant was facing half-away from him and he estimated he should be able to get a shot directly into its heart from this angle, but he had to be sure. If it turned on him, he would not stand a chance. He went closer still, and a spasm of fear suddenly churned in his guts as he realized he was facing a creature more than twice his own height and with enough strength to nudge even the heaviest locomotive over on to its side.

He raised the rifle, half-deciding to let it have both barrels in the same spot, when a second, much smaller elephant, hardly more than a calf, appeared out of nowhere. The large one began to turn towards it. He fired and felt certain the shot had gone home, seeing the dull mark on its flank.

But it did not fall. Instead, it lumbered forward, then checked itself, turning, as if trying to protect the younger one. Andrewes ran around in a half-circle to finish it off, but this move upset both of them. There was a great yammering and trumpeting, then the giant elephant charged directly at him. There was no way he could escape. Those tusks gleamed dully in the afternoon light; that powerful trunk was ready to seize him; those massive feet could crush him to death in seconds.

He went down on one knee to take a quick aim. The spittle was acid in his mouth, yet his mind gained a frightening clarity. This was how it was to be; this was the end. Even if he killed the elephant with his one remaining shot, the impetus of that charge would bring it down on top of him. His hands shook; his eyes refused to focus.

With an unformulated, desperate prayer to whatever deity existed – *anywhere* – he discharged the remaining barrel as the enraged animal bore down on him. He felt the recoil jarring through him; then he dropped the rifle and attempted to roll clear.

The ground shook under him as the elephant fell. He heard the great crash and knew something was on top of him, entangling him, tearing into him, lacerating his flesh. What it was, he could not see at first; his eyes were blinded with dust. But he was not dead, his mind told him persistently. He was not dead!

'Andrewes?' Ngengi's voice, some way off.

'Ay.' The sound rasped in his throat. Everything pained him, every little move. 'Where are ye?'

'The big elephant is dead.'

'Ay, an' the wee one? Watch the wee one.'

The impact of that elephant hurling itself at him must have uprooted the thorn tree, he reckoned; ay, that's what had happened – it collided wi' the tree, bringin' it down on top of him. Its branches were spread out over him, pressing him to the ground like a shroud of thorns; they cut into him like needles. He could feel the blood running down his face and taste it as it reached his lips.

Then he heard more voices as Kamau and the Gikuyus arrived. How they got him free he never discovered – Kamau's doing, for he heard him constantly giving instructions – but some branches were lopped off and eventually he felt the tree being lifted slowly away from him. He sat up, cautiously testing both arms and legs before attempting to stand. His clothes were in tatters, caked with blood and dust; every muscle ached and there were pains in his chest and back. He looked around for the rifle and found the tip of the barrel protruding from beneath the bulk of the dead elephant.

The calf stood nearby, quivering and pathetic. He should put it out of its misery, he thought; yet he was reluctant to do it. Overhead the vultures were already circling. They should take the tusks and go. Let nature get on with its own work.

'We kill the calf?' Ngengi asked.

Kamau waited expectantly, fingering his gun.

Before Andrewes could make up his mind, one of the other Gikuyus grabbed his arm and pointed. Not far away, a second large elephant was approaching, its ears fanning lazily. The calf let out a whinnying call for help, or sympathy, no telling what, and the big one replied.

Andrewes took his Mannlicher from Ngengi – the Frazer was still on the ground – and he pushed the bolt in, cocking it. He indicated to the others to fall back as far away as possible without drawing attention to themselves.

At that stage he was still undecided, though he was in no mood to risk another fall. From the sharp pains in his chest he guessed he must have cracked some ribs. His whole body ached and smarted; his mouth was dry, his eyes hot. The elephant came nearer, not quite as large as the first, but with magnificent tusks. Its leathery breasts swung between its forelegs as if full of milk.

A shot through the eye, he estimated – straight into the brain. But he hesitated. The large cow elephant went directly to the calf which nuzzled against her. Then, though the calf was uncertain at first, she coaxed it gently away from that massive carcase, encouraging it with her trunk until it followed her back the way she had come. The whole episode took ten, maybe fifteen minutes, and Andrewes looked on quietly, his rifle lowered.

They waited until the elephants were well out of sight before returning to the spot to cut out the tusks and recover the .405 Frazer leaving the rest for the vultures and jackals. Before camping for the night he insisted they should go on for another three or four miles to get as far away from that place as possible. For the last mile he was barely able to walk, but staggered alongside his heavily-laden horse, holding on to the harness.

The only water they found was a muddy stream. They strained it through one of his old shirts before drinking it, but it tasted foul. But he still had half a bottle of whisky left – after that first night he had drunk very little – and he got out of his rags and called Kamau to clean up his wounds with it. The raw spirit stung like hell, burning into him, but it was better than risking gangrene. As for tetanus, the best he could do was pray.

It was impossible to go on, he realized. Supplies were getting low, particularly ammunition, the men were worn out and he needed to lie up for a few days. Before setting off the next morning, he took some readings and then headed for Nakuru. He could just about totter along, his legs and feet were so swollen. The loads were redistributed to free his horse and Kamau helped him up into the saddle.

As they walked, the men began to sing, chanting some

Gikuyu song he had never heard before. Then an argument broke out between them and Kamau, which Kamau clearly lost, for they started singing again. When Andrewes asked him about it during one of the rest breaks, he replied shortly that it was not important: simply a foolish song about a woman who invited a different man to her hut every night.

'They walk better when they sing,' he excused them.

For the next three days he lived with that song, yet made no move to forbid it. It kept the men cheerful, and why should they not enjoy themselves at his expense after all? Was it not true enough? Riding through that shadowless country, his thoughts were as bitter as the strained mud they were forced to drink from the water holes. His cuts bled again, his bruises deepened, stiffening the muscles, and every jolt in the saddle seemed like a concentrate of all the torments of hell together.

But at last they arrived at Nakuru. The town consisted of a mere handful of buildings clustered near the railway. One, claiming to be a hotel, looked as though it had recently been laid waste by rioters; it had a view across the wide, flat soda lake where thousands of pink flamingoes congregated, preening themselves or skimming gracefully over the soda-encrusted mud flats along the shore.

Andrewes rented a room behind one of the *dukas*, instructing the owner – a short, dapper Indian with features as delicate as a girl's – to make sure his Gikuyus were well cared for. He had some sort of a bath, the best he could manage with those bruises almost paralysing him, and sank back gratefully on to the lumpy bed. It was not much of a room – just four rough walls and a roof made of old kerosene cans opened out and hammered flat – but it was all he needed. He refused the Indian's offer to fetch a European doctor and closed his eyes, letting his mind slip mistily into oblivion.

He was out for twenty four hours, though at times ghosts fleeted through the darkness – Gita walking through the stone house, but when he called her, reaching out, her face merged with Hester's; her voice too was Hester's, he could

386

not understand why she was speaking that way; then there was no more doubt – she *was* Hester, her eyes full of laughter, her shoulders white, her breasts quivering as she held out her arms to him – and they were together in their room, her breath quickening, her nails digging into his back as she murmured his name . . . urgently . . . Tim . . . Tim . . . The darkness must have returned, blotting it all out for a while, but again the ghosts came to haunt him. And again. When he regained consciousness, blinking uncertainly at the unfamiliar room, those hauntings were as vivid as opium visions.

The dapper Indian looked after him discreetly, offering some concoction of his own for the bruises, then serving him tea with chapattis and fragrantly-spiced vegetables, and leaving a dish of mangoes and paw-paw sections in the room. The fruit tasted fresh, and the Indian explained proudly that it had been brought up by train from Mombasa earlier that same week.

And he nodded at Andrewes, smiling knowingly, as if they shared some secret, the two of them.

For the next three or four days Andrewes did not set foot outside that room. Each morning he attempted to bully some life back into his muscles with a series of slow, painful exercises; for the rest of the day, he lounged partly-dressed on the bed while Kamau carefully unrolled the animal skins for his inspection. There was a good market for skins and visiting hunters often paid high prices for the heads of any species they had not managed to slaughter for themselves – just to complete their collections. In his notebook he wrote down brief factual descriptions, dimensions and grading according to quality. Then, too, he had the ivory tusks which he was keeping by his bed for safety. Altogether, he should earn a fair amount from that safari. A parting shot perhaps, before he left British East for good.

Not that he had yet come to a firm decision. Maybe he would go directly to Nairobi when he felt inclined to move on; maybe continue the safari southwards to the soda lakes of Natron and Magadi. He had often wondered about setting up a company to exploit the soda deposits. There was money enough to be made by anyone with the drive to do it. He let the ideas play idly through his mind as he worked on, but said very little.

One thing was certain, though – Hester would never defeat *him*, however hard she tried.

Unusually for him, Kamau took Andrewes' silence as an encouragement to talk. Andrewes only half-listened to his comments on the hunting of the past weeks and his anecdotes about previous safaris. Yet he felt that in some ways they had grown closer during that time. Kamau must be much the same age as himself and seemed able to read his moods instinctively. Then – Andrewes' thoughts were elsewhere, again working out where he would go if he left British East – Kamau said something which jolted him back to paying attention.

'Ye were in Dar es Salaam? Because o' Muldoon?'

'I have spoken to no man on this subject, but now is the time to say certain things.' He had been rolling up one of the skins, but he left it where it lay and took a seat on a tin trunk against the wall. His face bore the first lines of approaching old age, and it made him look very dignified, like a highly respected elder. 'After Muldoon used his whip on me, I knew I had to kill him. But he was a white man, so I chose the other course. I went to live among my own people, to help them steel themselves to meet this new danger.'

'Ye were no' too successful.'

'I was not the right one for this work, as the great battle made plain to me. And in my heart I still wished to see Muldoon die. In order to look for him, I went to German East, as you say, as askari for a white hunter.'

'Ye didna find him, though.'

'He was there. I heard his name, but I never saw him.' Kamau paused for a moment, remembering. 'I witnessed the hanging of two men who had killed a trader. I thought, Muldoon injured more than my body with his whipping, but should I also hang for him? We each have our own lives to lead, regardless of what others do to us.'

'Ay,' Andrewes sighed. 'Ay, that mebbe so. The Gikuyu call ye by a special name, they tell me.'

'Mwebongia – One-Who-Walks-Alone.'

'Ay, dinna we all?' Andrewes agreed thoughtfully. 'Though mebbe we two more than most. If ye've finished that skin, Kamau, d'ye think ye could ask our Indian friend if I could have some whisky?'

# TWO

Patel arrived in Nakuru by the next train, his face full of concern as he bustled into the *duka* to find Andrewes, exclaiming how everybody had been exceedingly worried at reports of his long absence without one word, but now there was much relief following receipt of telegram from his good friend here.

'Of course, you are now returning to Nairobi, I am sure,' he added, eyeing the tusks of ivory near the bed. 'There are many matters needing your urgent attention. Some papers I am bringing with me for your perusal. Your safari met with much success, I am thinking. They are very fine tusks.'

'Ay, I reckon we'll show a profit. Though as for goin' to Nairobi, I canna say.'

But Patel was persuasive and he had plenty of time. Passenger trains ran only twice a week, the next one down not being for another two days. His face glowed from the heat as they sat going through the details of an agreement for P & R to become the exclusive suppliers of milk and fresh vegetables to the Nairobi Hospital. Then they went over the accounts of the shipping and forwarding branch of the business – one of Patel's pet schemes – which had hit unexpected costs and might have to be abandoned.

'There is much talk, too, of the danger of war in the eastern Mediterranean.' His now almost portly figure shifted uncomfortably on the narrow wooden stool provided by the dapper *duka*-owner. 'Mobilization has been ordered by the Czar. And the German Empire also, the reason being that one Archduke Ferdinand is dead, having been murdered. Are you knowing about these matters?'

'I canna say I've heard. It's serious, d'ye think?'

'Indian sources are telling me it could result in closure of Suez Canal – exceedingly disastrous for our business.

But no certainty is possible. We are having so little news in Nairobi.'

'Ay, I think mebbe ye're right,' Andrewes agreed reluctantly after mulling it over for a while. I'd best go back wi' ye to Nairobi. Jus' in case.'

Nairobi was crowded. Settlers from all over the Protectorate were streaming in for the races and bringing bulging wallets. They found no shortage of things to buy either, including the very latest in ploughs, water pumps, electricity generators, bicycles and the first motor cars to reach East Africa – though, in spite of an aggressive trading policy, P & R were content to allow their more reckless competitors to burn their fingers on these latter items.

After dark, the attractions of the newly-installed electric street lighting made Government Road seem like Piccadilly Circus on a Saturday night, though its surface was still a porridge of red mud and horse dung. According to Ada Hathaway, the bars, billiard rooms and brothels were raking in the rupees faster than they could count them, and there was not a hotel room to be had.

She welcomed Andrewes in her usual matter-of-fact manner, though he could see from the expression in her eyes that she knew all about it – and what she didn't know, she could probably guess.

'Been expecting thee, King John!' Her smile was genuine – a big warm smile that said everything. 'Weeks ago, but tha never showed up. Tha'll need a drink – whisky?'

'Ay, but no' here in the bar. Upstairs where we can talk. An' I could do wi' a bath too. The room's available?'

'I let no one else use it, tha knows. Always there for 'ee.' She led the way through the back and – in the doorway – the light caught her wispy fair hair which, as always, defied her well-meant attempts to confine it. 'People have been here looking for thee. Hester come first – in a real state, too. Couldn't understand why tha'd gone. Had to stay up all night trying to calm her down.'

'She spun ye some yarn?'

'Things she told me, King John, I never expected to

hear from anybody,' she declared, unlocking the door to his room. 'Where I come from in Manchester, I didn't exactly lead what tha'd call a sheltered life, but – nay! Nay!' She shook her head. 'I'd never have believed it possible from a minister's daughter.'

On her way up she had brought an unopened bottle of whisky from the bar which she now set down on the table. She turned to go.

'Ye'll no' take a dram?' He fetched two glasses from the chest of drawers.

'Later on, not now. I'll see about bath first.' But she paused with her hand on the doorknob. 'I was shocked, I don't mind admitting it. I mean – leaving one man an' taking up with another, that sort o' thing happens. But wanting to have both at once!'

'She told ye that?'

'What didn't she tell me? Things I never knew about. But I'll see to bath.'

'Who else came here?'

'Catchpole for one, wanting to speak to thee. Straight after Hester he come. Then he was back again some weeks later an' I'm told he's in Nairobi now, though I've not seen him.'

'An' Wilton?' His tone was acrid.

'Nay, he'd not dare come here. I'd have a thing or two to say if he did. But tha daughter was one who turned up, making me promise I'd let her know when I'd news o' thee. An' from railway – Lord-God-Almighty Carpenter – though what he wanted he didn't say. Anyhow, I'd best do summat about that bath, or tha'll not get it.'

She closed the door, leaving him alone.

He poured out a whisky and went across to the window which looked out towards the spreading thorn tree, its umbrella shape never changing over all the years. A couple of white birds perched on it briefly, but then flew off: egrets, perhaps. They had watched that tree through all the seasons, he and Hester, during the time they lived here in their tin shack. The land beyond had been her first vegetable patch.

Ay, in those years already she an' Tim Wilton were . . .
An' he'd known nothin' about it.

Abruptly, he drained his glass and returned to the table
to pour out another. The practicalities, that's all that
mattered now. The choice was his alone: either stay on,
give more time to building up the business, maybe start
that soda company, or else quit British East, put the whole
lot behind him, and begin again in . . . China, maybe . . .
Australia . . . South America . . . Either way, his share in
The Kingdom should be held in trust for the children, and
that was something he intended to fix up with the lawyer
that same week.

A knock on the door. The room boys came in carrying
the big enamel bath between them. They positioned it near
the foot of the bed and then returned with tall jugs of
steaming hot water to fill it, mixing in the cold until he
was satisfied the temperature was right.

Then he dismissed them, tugged off his clothes and
lowered himself with relief into the soothing water, soaking
those aching bruises which still bothered him when he was
tired. With the whisky bottle to hand, his glass topped up,
he lay back to work it all out. His rage was still with him,
simmering beneath the surface − rage with himself more
than anyone else − but he kept it forcibly under control.

*Ay − so the next move?* He reached for the bottle to refill his
glass. A generous slug.

Maybe he dozed off, or slipped unawares into a stupor,
but the next knock on the door startled him. 'Ay, come in!'
he called impatiently when the knock was repeated. The
bath water was lukewarm, almost cold.

Ada came in, her big frame filling the doorway. 'Ee, I'm
sorry, King John! I didn't think tha'd still be in bath. 'Ere,
tha's not been down in dumps, now? That whisky bottle's
looking worse for wear.'

It was three quarters empty. 'Nay, Ada, I was jus'
thinkin' things over, that's all. An' ye always did keep the
best malt in British East.'

'Meal's laid for 'ee an' ready in my sitting room. An'

393

Catchpole's here. Would 'ee like me to send him up? He won't go till tha's seen him.'

'In the bar.' This was something he could have done without on his first night back in Nairobi. Ca-ca-catchpole, come to plead with him, no doubt. 'I'll meet him in the bar in thirty minutes, tell him. If I must.'

'We'll be right busy tonight, there's a crowd in already,' she said doubtfully. 'Still, tha knows tha own business best, I dare say. But not a drop more whisky till tha's eaten, mind, or I shall begin to worry about 'ee.'

She nodded at him with an amused grin as he sat in the low bath, trying to conceal his nakedness for decency's sake.

Once she had gone, he pulled himself to his feet and stepped out to the rug to dry himself on one of the giant-sized towels she provided – the biggest in Nairobi, any-where. A magnificent women, he mused; perfectly propor-tioned, as perfect as Hester in that respect, only a lot bigger. The Almighty alone knew how she ever came to marry Jimmy, who was shorter than most. One o' the oddities o' Manchester life.

The sound of a piano floated through the hotel as he went along the short corridor to her sitting room and sat down to the meal of cold roast meat and hot vegetables. One of her music hall songs, he recognized, and he started to hum the tune as he spooned mustard on to the side of his plate. The whisky had put him in a mellow mood.

But he still had to meet Catchpole. Ca-ca-catchpole the peacemaker. He was not looking forward to it.

*Just a little bit! Not too much of it!*

The roar of men's voices, topped by Ada's throaty contralto, drowned the tinkling of the piano and was loud enough to have been heard down in Mombasa. It was their favourite Marie Lloyd music hall song, and they made sure everyone knew it. Andrewes joined in lustily, though out of tune.

'Nat, ye're no' singin'!' he complained after the final emphatic chord. He slopped more whisky into Catchpole's glass, then into his own. 'An' ye're no' drinkin'! Will ye no' drink to – ay, to Gaby! No harm in that now, is there? Come on, man – to Gaby!'

In one gulp he drained his glass, then slammed it down again on the table. Catchpole sipped his.

'I n-n-need t-to t-t-talk t-to you.' His face was set, his eyes dark with determination.

'Ay, we've no' had a good talk in many a long month. Ye were explainin' now about this Archduke assassinated in Sarajevo – is that the place? – while I was away on safari. D'ye really think it'll come to fightin'?'

'K-k-king J-john – about H-hester . . .'

'Nat, I've been away, d'ye ken. I've no' heard any news. I'm serious now. Your father's in the House o' Lords, what does he say?'

'L-letters t-t-take t-two m-m-months. In G-government H-house they th-think it's s-s-sabre-rattling.' Catchpole refused to give up. 'C-c-can't we g-g-go s-somewhere else t-to . . . quieter?'

'I've told ye a'ready, no' tonight. We can talk business in the mornin'. Tonight ye drink up an' enjoy yesel'.'

'B-but H-hester is d-d-desperately un-unhappy. Y-you c-can't refuse to s-see her. Sh-she's your wife.'

'Ay, she was.'

'She still is,' Catchpole insisted, flushing.

'Till she chose otherwise.' He stared at the whisky in his glass, wishing it were anyone but Catchpole who had come as Hester's emissary. He liked the lad too much. 'Nat, ye grew up in the church – now I ask ye, is it right what she's wantin'?'

'I'm n-n-not d-defending her. B-but she d-d-does n-need you.'

'Ay, an' I need to get away from her, as far away as possible. D'ye no' understand that?' He emptied the glass, then pushed it away from him to the centre of the table. 'As for the estate now – The Kingdom – that's a business enterprise we three undertook an' ye've a right to know where I stand. So first thing tomorrow mornin' we'll call on the lawyer an' get it sorted out.'

From the men at the far end of the bar a great shout went up, drowning his words. '*I'm shy!*' someone shouted. '*I'm shy!*' Ada played the first notes and then seemed to explode into the new song, sweeping her audience up with her until everyone was singing. Everyone, that is, except Catchpole, who was regarding Andrewes across the table, misery written on his face as he realized that this time his diplomacy would come to nothing.

As the song ended, with a final flourish on the piano from Ada, a massive cheer of approval shook the windows in their frames, followed by laughter and calls to the bar boys to fill up the empty glasses.

'I say, Ada! Let's have another song, what?"

Andrewes recognized the young boxing champion from Oxford standing at the bar, waving a half-empty beer glass and looking very red in the face.

'Ee, there's no rest!' she declared good-humouredly. 'Give us a chance to get me breath back. Mind them corns, now!'

She pushed through the crowd, a laugh and a joke for everybody, heading in the direction of Andrewes' table. Reaching it, she sank on to the chair with a big sigh. One of the bar boys had followed her across with a glass and a bottle of cool beer. She watched him pouring it, keeping her eye on the froth, then drank a long mouthful before she spoke.

'Ee, I said we'd be busy tonight, remember? I haven't had a minute to call me own, not all evening.'

'Ada, ye're a genius!' Andrewes started to compliment her, when he caught sight of Carpenter coming in through the swing doors and hesitating, his eyes scanning the bar-room. 'Ye'd ne'er guess who's jus' arrived.'

'We get all sorts!' said Ada.

Carpenter had already spotted Andrewes and was making his way between the tables towards him. He had put on no weight over the years, but was as thin as ever, meticulously dressed, holding himself very tall and straight, his hair – now snow-white – immaculately groomed.

'Good evening, Mrs Hathaway. Good evening, Andrewes. I was told I might find you here. D'you mind if I sit down?'

'Ee, come an' join the party!' Ada winked at Andrewes, but made room for him. 'What'll tha drink – whisky?'

'This is not a social visit I'm afraid, Mrs Hathaway.' He sat uncomfortably, obviously ill at ease in the rowdy bar. 'I'm sounding out as many people as I can, but I'm hoping you'll volunteer, Andrewes.'

'Ay, an' for what?'

'For the railway, don't you see? According to our information, the Germans intend to disrupt traffic between here and Mombasa. Sabotage the line. As you know, the track runs within striking distance of the German East border for some considerable way and—' He stopped, noticing the blank amazement on their faces. 'I beg your pardon, you've obviously not yet heard. I'm afraid we're at war.'

'W-war?' Catchpole blurted out. 'B-but I understood th-that . . .'

'A signal came through to Government House three hours ago. Not much in the way of detail yet, but France is involved and it seems the Kaiser has sent his troops into Belgium.'

It was even worse than Patel had feared. With the major European powers at each other's throats, trade would come to a complete standstill. And if the fighting spread to East Africa they could lose everything.

'Is there no' an agreement,' he asked slowly, trying to piece together something he remembered from years ago, 'that in the event o' any European conflict, the colonial territories in Africa should be regarded as neutral.'

'Gone by the board, I'm afraid.' It was almost a personal apology from Carpenter. 'We're in this game up to the hilt.'

The men over by the piano were beginning to get restless. 'Ada! Come on, luv, let's have another song! One o' your Marie Lloyds!' One man tried to pick out a tune on the keys, clumsily.

'We'll have to tell 'em,' she said to Carpenter. 'Tha'll have to make an announcement. They've every right to know.'

'Andrewes . . . I mean, King John . . .?'

'She's right, Carpenter, so up on the bar wi' ye!'

He tried to refuse, nervously. 'It's hardly my place . . .'

Ada grasped his arm and propelled him forward through the press of drinkers. 'Here, mind out! Gangway! Make room, will 'ee, lads! Will tha shift out o' bloody road?' Then she helped him climb on to the bar. He stood there clearing his throat and making several attempts to speak above the row, a lonely elegant figure as out of place as a saint at a Roman orgy. His voice was lost under a deluge of catcalls and whistles.

'Now shut up, the lot o' thee!' Ada boomed above all the din. 'He's summat to say as affects us all. Right, Mr Carpenter – there's nowt stopping 'ee now.'

'His Majesty's Government has informed us,' he started hesitantly, clearing his throat again, 'that as from midnight last, the British Empire is at war with Germany following the violation of—'

The spontaneous cheer that went up from every man present – with the sole exception of Andrewes – made it impossible for him to continue. He stayed on the bar, half-smiling, half-bewildered, while they got to their feet, shouting, waving their glasses, declaring their intention to cut the upstart Kaiser down to size.

Gradually, the sound of Ada's hefty strumming on the piano, which was the nearest approximation to a drum-roll she could manage, penetrated the clamour and they quietened down expectantly, straightening up to attention, to join in singing *God Save the King!*

'Ay, they dinna understand,' Andrewes thought gloomily as he reluctantly mouthed the words. 'It could mean the ruin o' everythin'.'

# THREE

With the news of war, all British East was in a turmoil. Every able-bodied man, it seemed, had enrolled in one or other of the private volunteer forces, armed with their own rifles and dressed in whatever crazy costume took their fancy. Arnoldi's Scouts, Monica's Own, Wessel's Scouts, Bowker's Horse, Plateau South Africans – there were a dozen of them, for the most part encamped on the race course, harrassing Colonel Arbuthnot of King's African Rifles with demands to be sent into action immediately, though no one knew where any Germans were to be found.

Intelligence reports – which, in Andrewes' estimation just meant *rumour* – had it that an attack on the railway was definitely planned, with the bridge at Tsavo named as the probable target. For many long hours he pondered Carpenter's invitation to rejoin the staff – on a temporary basis, to be sure – in order to take charge of repairing any damage caused by enemy sabotage; in the end, having weighed it all up and decided against, he went over to the station to see Carpenter, changed his mind on the spot, and accepted. It was the sound of the shunting perhaps, the smell of the locomotives' acrid smoke, or merely the sight of the rails themselves – but he felt he had not sweated out years of his life on that railway to have it blown up by anybody.

A couple of days later he was ready to leave. For his commando he had selected eight men, all Indian, from the regular maintenance gangs, together with two Swahili *askaris* from the Railway Police. Kamau and Ngengi were also with him, though – at their own request – he let the remaining Gikuyus return home to the ridge.

Gaby came down to see him off, and he reflected how beautiful she looked in her modest white blouse and full-length linen skirt, her double terai neatly held in place over her sophisticated hair-do by a light scarf tied in a flowing knot beneath her chin. The Young Ladies' Academy had already done her some good, controlling some of that wildness, though her lively brown eyes still promised mischief.

She had said very little about the business with Hester up until that moment; then, abruptly, she brought the subject up shortly before the train was due to leave.

'I'm sure you'd rather not talk about it, Papa. Of course, I knew all the time something was going on.' She was all poise and brittle woman-of-the-world, but that was no more than a fragile outer shell. He began to realize what she must have gone through from the other young 'ladies' at the Academy once they got their innocently malicious tongues around the scandal. 'I could see it in Mama's eyes when he was around.'

'I thought once ye were interested in him yesel'?' he confessed awkwardly.

'Urgh, spare me!' She pulled a face, protruding the tip of her tongue between her lips. 'He gives me goose flesh! The living dead – like some vampire had sucked all the blood out of him. I don't know what she sees in him. There – I've got it off my mind!'

'Ay, ye can often be mistaken about a person,' Andrewes said, out of his depth.

'Oh Papa, you're too good-hearted, that's your problem!' Impulsively, she hugged him, kissing his cheek. 'Now don't go being kind to those Germans, d'you promise?'

'If I see any,' he laughed.

'You're dressed like you're going to fight the war single-handed!' She eyed the Webley service revolver – official issue – at his belt and the Mannlicher rifle slung from his shoulder. 'At the Academy, we're talking about enrolling as auxiliary nurses – three of us.'

'Ye dinna think ye'd best have a word wi' Mama first,' he began to say, but an impatient, throaty whistle from the engine blotted out part of it.

He kissed her, then climbed up on to the step to his compartment, turning to add something else. But it was already too late. The train was pulling out. Ay, she left it till the last minute before mentioning it, he thought, amused. Still the same Gaby – she's no' changed.

Tsavo was alive with rumours of German patrols lurking just over the horizon, awaiting the signal to attack, but no one could be found who had actually seen them with his own eyes. Detachments of King's African Rifles scoured the country on both sides of the river, finding nothing. In the meantime, Andrewes kicked his heels in idleness, inspected the stores for the twentieth unnecessary time and sat of an evening drinking too much whisky while Jimmy Hathaway brought him up to date on railway gossip.

But it was good to get the feel of the railway again, to hear the clacking of wheels over rails, to have the whiff of the smoke in his nostrils, and know he was back in charge. Carpenter had done a good job, too, in organizing the Railway Volunteers. They were mostly clerks, accountants, other administrative staff; he pushed rifles into their hands, gave them some minimum training and set them to guard every bridge and station along the two hundred miles of track which ran parallel to the border with German East. Yet how effective could they be, Andrewes brooded, against a really determined, professional enemy?

He had been at Tsavo for about four weeks when a report came through that a small party consisting of two white men and three or four Africans had been sighted lurking among the hills near a bridge some forty miles away. It had a ring of truth about it, Andrews decided. Two white men – not the whole German Imperial army. It might be worth getting up there, just in case. He sent a runner to contact the nearest unit of King's African Rifles, and ordered the special Inspection & Repair train to be got ready.

He found the bridge intact and the guards, alerted by telegraph, nervously awaiting his arrival. It had not been a difficult bridge to build, he recalled when he saw it; certainly not one he would choose to sabotage if he wanted to bring the railway to a halt for long. It crossed a sluggish river which at this point was little more than a narrow stream between two muddy banks; through his glasses he could identify several lazy, log-like crocodiles sunning themselves.

Nearby was a small, sleepy station – just the usual single building, a water tower, fuel for the engines, and a dak bungalow. Andrewes strode into the office. The sun on the corrugated iron made it as hot as an overn. He threw his hat on the table and stripped off his jacket while the Gujerati clerk – a slim, nervous man – called up Jimmy at Tsavo.

The signal came back in Jimmy's rapid morse. All quiet, everywhere along the line.

Outside, nothing moved. The air was so still, there was not so much as a whisper through the high grass. The hills were some five miles away, their jagged outline timelessly silhouetted against the sky; but there were other, nearer hills too, rocky outcrops on the other bank of the river, and the railway line swept around them in a long curve like a giant scimitar.

He felt proud at the sight, reliving those weary weeks of track-laying; here it all was, looking so permanent. Hester had never appreciated the problems, he mused, though she'd had faith enough it would all happen. But maybe he had expected too much.

'We'll stay here the night,' he announced briefly. 'We'll double the guards on the bridge an' see if we canna catch the Germans at it.'

He assigned the two railway *askaris*, Hamisi and Amami, to the bridge itself, while keeping Kamau and Ngengi with him on a flat section of the station roof which offered an extensive view over the plain. During the hours until midnight, the moon was so bright, it might have been daylight; towards the river he could make out the dark shapes of buffalo, waterbuck . . . possibly even rhino. He did not envy the German patrol attempting to cross that plain through the high grass after dark.

Who were they, after all, these Germans? Probably settlers like himself, or engineers from their own railway in

German East, men with whom he'd be glad enough to share a drink under different circumstances. If they were wise, they would not stick around for long, either. A quick strike and then away, that would be their best tactic.

He trained his glasses on the bridge, then on the ground leading towards it on both banks of the river, but saw nothing.

It was well after midnight and the moon had already set when he heard the explosion – a dull thud far away in the distance. Kamau touched his arm and pointed away from the bridge.

'Many miles,' he judged.

Andrewes climbed stiffly down and went over to the bridge to check with the guards. They too had heard the explosion and seemed uneasy. Was it a diversion to lull them into a sense of false security? Were there two parties of Germans? With the two *askaris*, Andrewes inspected the bridge thoroughly but found nothing.

Then he ordered total silence and returned to his eyrie on the telegraph office roof, straining his ears for any hint of movement in the darkness.

Dawn came at last and the bridge was still standing. Its steel girders looked solid enough to last for ever, yet he knew better than anyone how a couple of correctly-positioned charges could bring the whole structure crashing down into the mud within seconds.

'Ye heard nothing at all?' he questioned the *askaris* as they ambled towards the station.

'Nothing, Bwana.' Hamisi yawned. 'We waste the night.'

'Ay, an' ye're about to waste the day too!' Andrewes responded sharply. 'We leave in five minutes.'

There was no doubt in his mind that the explosion must have been on the line. The Gujerati clerk tried calling up the next station, but the telegraph was dead. Andrewes bawled at the men to get a move on. He checked his rifle as they scrambled on board. Maybe the Germans were still up there among the hills, he thought, keeping watch from hiding places among the rocks.

403

He rode on the footplate, peering ahead at the track and instructing the driver to hold the speed steady. For the first two or three miles the grass was high on either side; if the enemy chose to ambush the train, this would be the place to do it.

Then it climbed slightly and the grass gave way to stretches of exposed rock and reddish soil. Immediately ahead he saw a rail bent upright like a slim column, glittering brightly as the sun's rays caught it. The driver spotted it in the same second and applied the brakes hard.

The enemy had chosen the spot well, where the track crossed a narrow gully. It was less than the span of a single girder, not a big job to repair, but it still meant no traffic over that section of the line for three days at least.

'He was no engineer, though, we can be sure o' that.' Andrewes pushed back his slouch hat and rubbed his fingers over his tired scalp. 'He used enough dynamite to bring down Fort Jesus.'

'Horses, Bwana!' Hamisi called out excitedly, examining the ground a few yards away. 'Three horses!'

Andrewes went over to look for himself. No one could have guessed the *askaris* had been on watch all night. Their dark blue jumpers were immaculate, their belts polished, the khaki shorts pressed, their pill-box hats at the correct angle. Beside them, he felt grubby and in need of a bath. One of Ada's generous baths, with a bottle of malt whisky for the inner man.

'They went back to the hills, d'ye reckon?'

'To the hills, Bwana.'

They looked bare and sun-baked, those hills. He stared at them through his field glasses. No sign of any movement. They could be miles away by now.

There were several attacks of the same kind. Pin-pricks he called them in his written reports, yet they were enough to disrupt traffic for days at a time. He found himself forced to go back to some of the short-cut techniques they had used in the early stages of construction – makeshift repairs just to get the line open again, with more permanent work to follow weeks later.

Whoever chose where to attack next, it must be someone who knew the line well, he was convinced. He talked it over with Jimmy, outlining his ideas as they sat one night outside the dak bungalow at Tsavo.

'A German?' Jimmy shook his head in disbelief. 'Ee, I don't remember no German working on railway. Dutch – or a couple o' Boers, rather, from South Africa. An' that Greek contractor, but he's dead.'

'It's no' someone who's been o'er the line as a passenger, Jimmy – they'd ne'er notice half the places. It's a man who's had to tramp every inch o' that route, I could swear.'

'I think they're just bloody daft,' Jimmy declared flatly. 'They've only to destroy one major bridge an' they could close railway for rest o' war.'

'The bridges are guarded.'

'By pen-pushers wi' popguns.' He sighed and sipped his drink, then leaned back on his canvas camp chair and stretched out his legs. 'P'rhaps tha's right – how'd I know?'

He seemed tired these days, all trace of the old spirit gone. Andrewes said nothing, but topped up his glass.

'At times,' Jimmy went on after a while, 'I feel like chucking all this in an' going back to Manchester. An' I would an' all, only Ada's settled with 'er pub an' that. Not that she sees much of me. Never has done. But we've been happier this way – an' she's always glad to see me, I'll say that much for 'er. Now she's talking about bringing kids out after war's ended – did she tell thee? – setting 'em up out here.'

'Ay, she mentioned it.'

'She's got the money. Always did have a head for money, our Ada. Could be she's right, specially now. It's no life for 'em – lads in army, lasses in factory.'

'When did ye last see 'em?'

'Our kids? Ee, they were nowt but babies. I sent money regular, like. But they never knew a father, not really. Upsets me when I think about it.'

'Ay, it must do.'

405

'I like Ada, that's a fact. No nonsense about her. But I weren't cut out for married life somehow. Never settled to it.'

Jimmy talked on, but Andrewes' thoughts wandered away to India, his first years there, and Gita. If she had not died, if he had married her – how would that have turned out? Would they too have gone sour . . . taken someone else . . . separated . . .?' Or if he had returned from leave bringing Hester with him? Maybe Jimmy was the wise one after all.

And he had never once mentioned Hester – not even to ask after her, so he must have known about the situation. Everyone throughout the whole of Africa probably knew by now, from Cairo to the Cape. Since he came to Tsavo she had written to him – three letters with envelopes addressed in her handwriting – but he had pushed them to the bottom of his box without opening them. What was the point?

'Ay, I'll be turnin' in, Jimmy,' he said, emptying his glass and standing up. 'An' mebbe if ye do decide to leave this God-forsaken country, mebbe I'll come wi' ye. What d'ye say to layin' track across the Gobi desert, eh? Better than patchin' an' darnin', which is all we're doin' now.'

Early next morning a mounted platoon of King's African Rifles under the command of a pimply young second lieutenant passed through Tsavo, pausing only long enough to requisition new supplies of *posho* and telegraph a long message to Mombasa. In spite of the sabotage, they had come across nothing suspicious on their patrols, the officer told Andrewes.

'Met up with one of you railway wallahs two or three days back – man called Lynch.'

'Lynch?'

'Track inspectorate, so he said. I imagined he might be based here. No? Anyway, he was clearly no German. A small party on horseback – Lynch himself and three Swahilis.' The lieutenant hoisted himself back into the saddle. 'Sorry I can't hang around but I've a rendezvous to make and still quite a bit of ground to cover. You'll let HQ know if you need assistance?'

He saluted smartly and the patrol rode out, heading east.

Andrewes went in search of the Indian station master to enquire if he had ever heard of 'one Lynch Sahib, of the Permanent Way Inspectorate'. He had not. The regular inspector, he pointed out, was one Hargreaves Sahib who was expected at Tsavo the following day.

'Hargreaves? Ay, I've met Hargreaves. As for Lynch – well, I canna say I've come across him, though I've no' been back wi' the railway all that long mesel'.'

The question nagged at him. This was where he needed Jimmy – Jimmy knew everybody – but he was a couple of miles away up the line and not expected back for an hour or two. He'd ask Nairobi, he decided and went to the telegraph office, only to find the line was dead. No doubt Jimmy was still working on it. He tried raising Mombasa.

No trouble getting through, though they made him wait half an hour before requesting him to confirm the name 'Lynch'. Then another half hour passed before they replied that Lynch was not known in Mombasa, but he was to expect Hargreaves to arrive as notified.

For the rest of the morning Andrewes busied himself with sending out messages to Mombasa, the army, the police, anyone he could think of, warning them of the bogus Lynch. It was possible there might be nothing in it, that Lynch might be smuggling ivory, prospecting without a licence, or merely on the run from his wife. Or the pimply lieutenant might have made a mistake. No harm in finding out, though.

'Lynch?' said Jimmy when he got back. 'Can't say I've ever heard of Lynch. There was a Finch years ago – accountant, he were – but he went home. We'll ask Hargreaves tomorrow, he's bound to know.'

Hargreaves did not arrive. Feeling uneasy, that question still nagging at him, Andrewes tried telegraphing the next station down the line, but without success. No chatter of morse; no reply to the call signal: only silence. While Jimmy took over, Andrewes ordered Kamau to get the horses on the train. This time he was determined not to be left immobile at the track-side.

Within twenty minutes the commando train was ready to leave. As usual, Andrewes rode on the footplate where he had a good view of the track ahead, but he placed his two railway *askaris* – armed with rifles – on the cow-catcher in front. Kamau and Ngengi, also armed, were in the brake van; Jimmy and the maintenance men travelled in a passenger coach, watching the sides of the track.

Almost an hour passed, with the train moving cautiously ahead, and no sign of anything unusual. Then suddenly there was a great clamour from the *askaris* on the cow-catcher.

'Inspection train, Bwana!' they yelled excitedly. 'Inspection train!'

It was only the coach and it stood in one of the old construction sidings which had been kept in service as a reversing station. The locomotive was about a quarter of a mile ahead, lying on its side across the points.

Andrewes instructed Jimmy and the maintenance men to remain where they were, while he took a look around with the *askaris*. He approached the coach carefully, his revolver cocked in his hand, but there was no sign of anyone about and the land around offered very little cover. Before deciding to go aboard he checked the exterior carefully for wires, but found nothing.

Signalling to Kamau to take the far end, he climbed up to the platform and kicked the door open, flattening himself immediately against the side. But the coach seemed deserted.

Cautiously he went inside. That living compartment so shocked him, he almost retched. It looked like a slaughter house, with smears of blood over the walls and bunks, and deep panga cuts scarring the timber fittings. The report pads and inspection log were torn up, the medicine box overturned, its contents strewn across the floor . . . among them a man's broken spectacles, part of a leather belt,

408

fragments of ripped clothing, and black ink splashed over everything.

Kamau came through from the kitchen end of the coach and stood, motionless, taking it all in. It was a few seconds before he spoke. Then he said 'No one here many hours.'

Andrewes retrieved the log-book cover from the debris on the floor. It bore the name Arthur Hargreaves inscribed in fine copperplate handwriting. He threw it down again, sickened. Outside, he found Jimmy examining the telegraph wire which lay, cut, curling on the ground like a long thin snake. He told him what had happened. Against his advice, Jimmy climbed up to take a look for himself and returned within a few seconds, his face pale.

'We're dealing wi' a madman,' he said. 'That's not war, not what he done in there.'

An urgent shout from Ngengi cut him short. Vultures were swooping and circling over a spot about four hundred yards from the track and he had gone over to investigate. He waved his arm and called again.

Andrewes ran across the dusty red ground, with Jimmy and Kamau close behind. On an area of parched grass lay four dismembered human bodies, practically eaten away already, their exposed bones bleaching in the hot sunlight. They all stood stock-still, unable to believe what they saw. Jimmy turned aside and vomited, while Ngengi began to attack the vultures, clubbing them with his reversed rifle.

'Hyena,' Kamau judged, his voice sombre. 'First hyena, then vultures.'

The arms and legs of two of them had been tied together with lengths of telegraph wire; from the few shreds of skin and clothing left on the bones they must have been Indian railway staff – trussed up alive by the look of it, then left out there to feed the hyenas. The other two had clearly resisted. One – Indian, to judge from his hair – had a bullet-hole through his skull and a broken arm; the second was Hargreaves, mangled and unrecognizable. Only a pocket diary in the rags still clinging to his bones gave a clue to his identity; it had been written up in that same copperplate handwriting.

Andrewes contemplated the scene, his mind paralysed, his eyes seeing yet not seeing, as the terrible anger simmered within him.

'What are ye bloody waitin' for?' he roared furiously at the maintenance gang, who were standing there stupified. 'Fetch tarpaulins! Upesi! Get these bodies to the train, an' handle 'em decently now! They were men like yesel's!'

As they scampered back to the commando train, Jimmy came over to apologize.

'Ee, King John, I'm no hero, tha knows that. It just turned ma stomach, the sight o' them.'

'I'm goin' after 'em, Jimmy.' There could be no argument about it; it was the only thing he could possibly do. 'I'm leavin' ye in charge wi' the two askaris. Ye ken well what has to be done. Whoever was responsible, they've made for those hills. I canna let 'em get away wi' this.'

Kamau had already found their tracks – not fresh, but not all that old either – clear hoof-prints in the dry red soil. Four, he estimated, though they crossed and re-crossed each other confusingly. Ngengi brought their horses down from the train, fresh and eager to go. Andrewes swung himself into the saddle, his face set and grim.

'Jimmy, ye'd best inform the military as soon as ye can get a signal on that telegraph,' he shouted across. Then, to Kamau and Ngengi, 'Let's go.'

The farther they left the railway behind them, the clearer the trail became, and leading directly towards the hills. It was flat, barren country, and the horses needed no encouragement to cover those first few miles at a gallop. As they got closer, Andrewes noticed a scattering of brown spots among the southern-most hills – thatched rooftops, no doubt – but the trail was already edging northwards towards the bleaker, greyer end of the range.

The ground became hard and stony until the hoof-prints disappeared completely. Only the discovery of horse-droppings reassured them that they were still on the right track. Their pace slowed down to a stumbling walk as they climbed and the landscape seemed to close in on them.

They were entering a steep, curving valley, with high inhospitable slopes on either side.

Eventually, when they looked back, they found the plain was no longer visible. They were hemmed in on all sides, while the way ahead narrowed to only a few feet, yet continuing to lead upwards. Kamau grunted, pointing. In the shadow of a boulder just above their heads, a wild cat watched them intently, crouched, ready to spring.

Two shots rang out, echoing among the rocks.

Instinctively, Andrewes dropped down from his horse and made for cover. Ngengi was slower, but reached the boulders just behind him. He looked around for Kamau and saw he had not been so lucky. One of those shots had hit the mare he had been riding and she now lay thrashing about in her death throes, with Kamau's leg trapped beneath her.

More shots threw up fragments of stone around him. Andrewes fired back blindly, unable to mark where the shots were coming from, though at least he forced the enemy to keep their heads down long enough for Kamau to free himself. He limped towards the safety of the rocks, leaning heavily on his rifle.

Two snipers, Andrewes estimated. His eyes searched the hillside; it offered ideal cover. Then he noticed a gun-shot flash seeming to come from the heart of a stunted bush about half-way up. He drew a bead on it, taking his time before gently tightening his trigger finger. The Mannlicher did its work: the body rolled and bounced downwards over the rocky slope like a dislodged stone.

Before it hit the bottom Kamau had also fired. The sound reverberated through the valley. Then silence. Overhead a lone bird circled. The wild cat had disappeared.

'It could be ye hit him,' Andrewes said softly. 'Or why are they no' firin', since they ken well we're here.'

They waited. Still silence.

'Give me some cover, will ye?'

He risked a scramble from one boulder to the next over the loose rocks as Ngengi and Kamau fired three or four rounds. Each shot echoed through the valley with a sharp *crack-Crack-crack* . . . From the other side came no response.

'Is the foot badly hurt?' Andrewes asked, reaching the boulder behind which Kamau was crouched.

'I can walk.'

'Ay, but no' too well.'

He stared up the hillside, seeing nothing. The man lying dead was African; a Swahili maybe, from farther up the coast. But it was not Swahilis he was hunting, he was sure of that. It was . . . who? This man Lynch, maybe? Some renegade Englishman – or a German with a good command of the language? Andrewes thought of those whitening bones, the last shreds of meat being torn off them by the vultures . . . His anger flared up, like an intense white flame.

'I reckon there's another wee valley beyond that big crag over to the right there. That's where the others'll be holed up, an' those two shootin' at us would be look-outs.'

Kamau said nothing. He had finished reloading his Winchester and was gingerly massaging his ankle.

'I'll try a wee recce. Ngengi. ye'd better stay here wi' Kamau. I'll jus' take a wee look, then come back.'

He moved cautiously from one boulder to the next, pausing for a few seconds behind each one to survey the hillside opposite. It was uncannily dead. Maybe Kamau had killed that second man; maybe not. Glancing back he could see the two of them, father and son, ready to open fire at the first sign of trouble.

The last few yards to the foot of the crag were the tricky ones, offering no cover whatsoever. Taking a deep breath, he loped across the bare rock, half-doubled, and reached it without a shot being fired.

Again he stopped, waiting. Nothing. Even their two remaining horses looked peaceful. During the shooting they had run off, but now they stood patiently at the far end of the valley.

He examined the crag and found a deep fissure running through it, leading upwards like a chimney. And wide enough, too. Slinging his Mannlicher, he began the careful climb upwards, using footholds on either side of the gap. After a few minutes he had to stop for breath; his heart thumped out its protest against his ribs.

Ye're no longer so young as ye were, John Philip Andrewes, he thought to himself, glancing up to see how much farther he had to go.

A giant lizard snoozing on a ledge level with his face darted back, startled, then disappeared into another crack. He almost lost his grip as the tail swished past his nose; desperately he hung on.

He started climbing again, hauling himself upwards with fierce determination to reach the top. Then at last the chimney widened, opening on to a rock plateau. Loose stones spun away beneath his feet as he scrambled clear. He was right about that other valley. The moment he stood up he could see it – narrow, even steeper than the first, and in it were four horses, closely huddled together.

'Sure, an' didn't I say King John would come snoopin' round by the back door?' a soft Irish voice greeted him.

A voice Andrewes recognized. He swung around. In front of him stood Ed Muldoon – that same Muldoon from years back, with those same small mocking eyes, that leering mouth. This was the man responsible for the slaughter; ay, an' for much else besides. He lashed out in blind fury, but the Irishman ducked, backed away – grinning – and coolly fired a shot from the business-like Luger he held in his fist. The bullet passed close to Andrewes' ear, grazing it.

'A warnin', King John!' he gloated. 'Don't think I won't be puttin' the next one somewhere nice an' tender. I promise you'll die slowly whichever way.'

'Like Hargreaves?' Andrewes watched him like a lynx, just waiting to smash his fist into that mouth. If there were any justice he should leave Muldoon spread-eagled over those rocks, alive, for the vultures to tear out his guts. 'An' the rest o' the crew on that train?'

'Sure, an' wouldn't they still be in the land o' the livin' if they'd not tried to put up a fight? All I was after was the train itself.'

Muldoon's gaze seemed to wander and Andrewes grabbed the chance, closing in on him recklessly, lunging for the hand holding the gun. It was a stupid move, as he realized even as he was making it. Muldoon could have put a bullet through him without so much as blinking – so why didn't he? The answer came a split second later when a violent blow against the back of Andrewes' knees sent him sprawling.

'I could kill you before you could say Holy Mary,' Muldoon informed him reasonably. 'Added to which, Juma is right behind you wi' a very itchy finger. You've shot two o' his friends, d'you realize, so he's not by way o' bein' in the best o' moods.'

Andrewes felt the Mannlicher being wrenched from his shoulder. It was tossed aside. Then, with the muzzle of Juma's rifle ticking his neck, he was made to remove his gun-belt.

'Mother o' God, will you never learn sense? You're no fighter, King John – sure, you're as strong as an ox an' you've lived on your strength all these years, but you've no finesse. That one fight we had, you an' me, if I'd not been as drunk as a lord I'd've murdered you, now.' He kept the Luger aimed steadily at Andrewes' solar plexus as he reminisced. 'Sure, that was the fault all along. If I'd been sober, that sweet wife o' yours would've lain down on the bed, quiet as a lamb, jus' askin' for it.'

Andrewes reacted – just the slightest of moves, but enough to offer Juma an excuse to slap him across the back of the neck with his rifle muzzle. The blow dazed him. Muldoon had him just where he wanted him, and there was nothing he could do about it. No chance of help either, with Kamau injured, Ngengi inexperienced . . . He lay back on the rocks, not daring even to raise his hand to massage his bruised neck.

'Ye realize ye'll no' get away from here?' he tried to bluff, but not even believing it himself. The odds were all on Muldoon's side. 'They'll be takin' ye to Mombasa to hang as a traitor – an' quite right too.'

'Holy Mary, a traitor to what?' Muldoon's face turned

puce with rage. He had coarsened with age and put on weight. 'Not to Ireland, I tell you! As for the bloody British Empire on which the sun never fuckin' sets – isn't it my patriotic duty now to stuff my boot up its fat arse whatever chance I get? A traitor, is it? Try sayin' that in Dublin an' see how long you live. Even the priests'd have the balls off you.'

Andrewes watched him narrowly as he went on, raving about his father being hanged as a Fenian, his great-grandmother raped by British soldiery and God knows what other indignities he claimed his family had suffered, but the Luger never once shifted away from him. Most of the sabotage along the line had been his work, he boasted; an', sure, at times he'd gone under the name o' Lynch – was it not his own sweet mother's name before she married his father? An' as he'd been sayin', that fool Hargreaves would still be alive if he'd not resisted: such a brilliant plan it was an' all – to ride into Tsavo as a newly-appointed Inspector o' the Permanent Way an' blow up the bridge under their very noses.

'A traitor, is it?' he repeated vehemently, his eyes sharp with hate. 'Right, King John – on your feet!'

'Ye're an idiot, Muldoon,' Andrewes scoffed, not moving.

'You always thought that, didn't you? Right from the very first day in Mombasa, wi' you fresh off the boat, knowin' nothin'. Treatin' me like I was dirt.' The deeply-felt rancour must have been rusting into him all those years; he'd best take his chance now, Andrewes decided uneasily. *'Get up, I told you!'*

To encourage him, Juma slammed the rifle barrel sharply across his ribs. Andrewes began to struggle to his feet, stalling for time. Juma had not stepped clear and if he could get his hands on that barrel . . .

He grabbed it, tugging it forward with the muzzle pointing away from him, though the recoil jarred through his wrist as the gun went off. Using both hands, he swung the rifle around. Juma still held on, yelling in agony as his finger – looped through the trigger guard – snapped and was practically torn off. He crashed against Muldoon.

Muldoon staggered back, knocking the Swahili out of his way with a sweep of his left arm. But Andrewes now had the rifle. He brought the butt crashing down against the Luger before Muldoon had a chance to use it. It went over the edge, an almost sheer drop. Somewhere far below a spur of rock probably caught the trigger, for it fired – just once – and the sound continued to reverberate through that narrow valley until slowly it faded to nothing.

'As ye were sayin', Muldoon?'

He tossed the rifle over the cliffside and faced the man with his bare fists. The pain in his ribs was persistent, jabbing him with every breath, but he ignored it. He ignored everything except Muldoon in front of him, his face sullen with hatred. Again and again he dodged that fist, taking it easy until he saw the right opening; then he went in hard with his left . . . felt it crunch home . . . followed it with a right to the jaw . . .

It purified him. It sweetened the air he breathed. That white-hot anger burning within him now took him over completely, its fierce flames licking those old scars, cauterizing, cleansing, bringing back life.

Muldoon lumbered forward – they were neither of them quick, neither of them young any longer – and closed with him, his left working like a steam hammer into Andrewes' already-damaged ribs. Andrewes was forced back until he felt the edge of the rock with his foot, only just managing to keep his balance. But he led him round, feinting, manoeuvring, until again he was ready to take the offensive . . . and again it was sweet . . .

Not for Hargreaves any longer . . . not for Hester . . . Andrewes' mind was empty of all thoughts, all memories; it was taken up solely with this fight, heightened, ecstatic in its total awareness of this one outlet for his triumphant anger. His tension went, a sudden moment of release, but then again an uplifting, a winding up to heights he had never known before.

Muldoon used his left again, aiming low. Andrewes'

eyes misted over, he was swaying, giving way. But his fingers groped for the Irishman's throat, squeezing the cartilege tighter . . . tighter . . .

When he heard the first shot, Ngengi glanced at his father uneasily. 'Do you think Andrewes needs help?' he whispered, his nerves taut. It was like encountering ghosts in the forest, this fighting with an unseen enemy. He wanted to get up and dash over to the big crag where Andrewes had disappeared, but Kamau restrained him.

'Listen!'

Faintly he could hear men's voices arguing; one might be Andrewes. There was nothing he could do but settle down behind his boulder to wait. Those had been the orders.

Kamau was bending down to examine his injured ankle again, seeming to stroke it with his fingertips. 'The bone is broken,' he pronounced after a time. He shifted on the rocks until he could lie more comfortably, though still able to survey the valley from the cover of the boulder.

The second shot sounded farther away, but amplified like a charge of dynamite detonated in the distance. The effect of the rocks, Kamau commented; he pointed to the top of the crag where two eagles were circling indignantly.

'Go to him,' Kamau decided, though his eyes expressed doubt. 'Give me your rifle, and take my Winchester. Remember, first you must see and not be seen. Then you will know what you have to do.'

Ngengi ran from one boulder to the next, using what cover he could, until he reached the foot of the crag. He stopped, uncertain which way to go until he spotted how – in that wide crack in the face of the rock – some of the moss had been scraped away in places, and the stone scraped by someone's boots. He began to climb.

The scene at the top was something he would never forget for the rest of his life. Andrewes and another man – both heavily-built, ponderous, with greying hair – were pounding each other mercilessly. It was like a death fight between two ageing bull elephants. To one side, watching

417

them, sat a Swahili *askari* nursing an injured right hand from which the blood was dripping.

The moment he spotted Ngengi the Swahili tried to grab Andrewes' Mannlicher which lay near him on the rocks. Ngengi was there before his fingers even touched it; he saw a shadow of fear in the other man's eyes as he knocked him unconscious with the butt of the Winchester.

He turned, and it was only in that moment that he recognized the other red stranger as Muldoon – The-Man-of-Thirst. He had only been a young child at the time, but the memory was branded on his mind. He could still see every lash of the whip, his father manacled to the tree, Muldoon's face ugly and brutal. He checked the Winchester, and waited.

Andrewes had dug his fingers into Muldoon's throat until he had recoiled, choking, his face purple; then he released him and smashed his fist into that gasping mouth. Oddly, the blow helped him recover his breath. Shaking his head, blinking, he charged back at Andrewes, his eyes vicious.

Both men were exhausted; neither would give up. They battered away at each other, one punch after another, never stopping.

'Ay, one more wee tap,' Andrewes muttered, tasting blood in his mouth, his whole body screaming out its rawness. There was no elevated feeling now, just a hard stubbornness.

Again he lurched forward; his fist met bone.

Then he stumbled.

Too close to the edge, his mind told him – but by then it was too late. His foot trod on air. His arms flailed about as he tried to keep his balance, throw himself forward to safety, and perhaps . . . Disbelieving, he felt the rush of cooling air around him as he fell, a sheer drop down; then a sharp blow across his shoulders, another cutting into his hips. Rocks, his mind told him, racing. Bouncing against the rocks. Like that body – he saw it again, the man he shot.

Falling . . . unable to stop himself . . . nothing to catch on to . . . just falling . . .

A cascade of small stones came down with him as he landed against a slope – still conscious – still aware of every little detail of what was happening – slithering, rolling over, his legs snapping, somersaulting, his skin tearing away, blood, his back . . .

Oh, that pain in his back as the hard ground hit him.

Hit him.


Muldoon stood on the edge of the cliff, stupefied, staring down as Andrewes tumbled like a rag doll over the rocks until he finally came to a stop, his body distorted. Slowly he turned, grinning to himself, to find Ngengi watching him.

'If you're one o' Andrewes' *askaris*, he's dead. I s'ppose you'll be wantin' a job wi' me.'

'Your name is Muldoon.' Ngengi spoke in English.

'Mother o' God, it's a mission boy we have here!'

Ngengi raised the rifle. 'Stay where you are. I have something to say to you.'

'You'll put that gun down first.' Muldoon went straight towards him, slow but without any hesitation. 'None o' your kind ever threatens me wi' a gun, I'll have you know. Jus' down out o' the bloody trees, an' you think you can bloody do what you like!'

'Stop where you are!' Ngengi ordered, but his voice trembled.

'Sure, now jus' hand over that rifle, nice an' easy . . .' He kept on, looking directly into Ngengi's eyes.

'I—' He squeezed the trigger. 'I told you, stop.'

Muldoon crumpled to the ground, still breathing, his eyes bulging, but unable to move or speak. Ngengi stood paralysed, his heart thumping. Then, dimly realizing he might still be in danger, he used the lever to pump another round into the breech. Shooting a man . . . it felt quite different from killing an animal.

'I want to explain why I have to kill you,' he began,

keeping a wary eye on Muldoon. 'You have to understand, or there is no point. I want you to listen.'

But the eyes were staring at nothing; the breathing had stopped. Ngengi looked down at him, uncertain if he were truly dead, remembering how it was when hunting, how a badly-wounded animal could sometimes recover its strength unexpectedly, and then it was at its most dangerous. Biting his lip with fear, he took aim and, with a deep shudder of horror at what he was doing, he put a bullet through Muldoon's brain.

# FOUR

John still lay in the freight wagon in which they had brought him back to Tsavo. The sliding doors were wide open for coolness, with dusty mosquito netting draped over the openings. Inside, they had made some attempt to clean up in addition to providing a folding camp table and a couple of canvas chairs as furniture. A strong smell of antiseptic lingered on the air.

Hester stood by the bedside, the tears starting into her eyes at the sight of that poor battered face grizzled with two days' growth, swollen so badly she hardly recognized him, and scored with cuts and scratches. His legs and arms were held stiffly in splints; his back and chest encased in dressings also soiled by the inevitable red dust.

She turned on Dr Carson, her voice choking. 'But you told me he was still . . . still . . .'

'He *is*,' he reassured her gruffly. 'It's a miracle, but your husband's still breathing. Here, sit down, Mrs Andrewes.'

'You're sure?'

'Sure as I'm standing here.' As if to calm her, he felt for John's pulse on his neck, then guided her fingers towards it. 'We've known each other a long time, you an' me, else I wouldn't risk telling you what I'm about to say. But you've helped me on enough cases to understand – you get my meaning?'

'You're saying there's no hope?' She heard herself speaking the words, but her mind was numbed. Looking at him lying there so still, so lifeless, she felt only a long cry of anguish inside her. She pulled over a canvas chair and sat down to watch for the slightest sign on his face that he might know her; but it was motionless, as though his soul had already escaped. 'Oh John . . .' she whispered.

'While he breathes, there's always hope,' Dr Carson said, but only to comfort her, she knew. He was not telling

421

the truth; she could hear it in his tone of voice. 'But I'll leave you alone with him for a while. I'll not be far, mind, if you need me.'

By sheer chance Hester had been in Nairobi when the news came through that John was seriously injured, maybe dead, after a fight with an Irish republican saboteur caught laying explosives to blow up Tsavo bridge. He had killed the Irishman, it was said, but the story was vague in its details. She had run to the Railway Office immediately, ignoring the jibes from the men crowding the streets, and insisted on seeing Carpenter. Fear for John gripped her like a gauntlet of ice. Nothing else mattered – her business in Nairobi, Tim, the coffee crop, Gaby, it was all forgotten. She *had* to get to Tsavo, and oh please God John would still be alive.

She boarded the next freight train, riding in the brake van, her thoughts confused. The van swayed and jolted; the dust covered her as she sat on the hard floor boards; the wheels clackety-clacked over the rails in a nightmarish rhythm until she almost screamed at the way they scraped against her nerves. *Is-he-alive-Is-he-alive-Is-he-alive . . . ?*

Then at Tsavo Dr Carson had met her, puffing his pipe as usual, trying to give the impression that everything was under control, no need for panic – though he of all people knew nothing was ever under control. Ever.

But he persuaded her at least to wash and tidy up before going in to see John. Even eat something. 'In a coma,' he explained. 'Ten minutes'll not make that much difference.'

John stirred.

She leaned forward, looking at him intently: had she been mistaken? His eyes were still closed – almost closed – his face set as if frozen in that terrible, neutral expression. Afraid, she sought the pulse in his neck . . . and . . . and . . . yes, she found it – a steady beat sending its message through her fingertips. Not strong, though.

She sat with her man, thinking of no other, resentful even when Dr Carson looked in – showing it, so that he withdrew after only a brief check on John. Her tears had dried on her face. The salt tasted on her lips.

422

A deep sigh, almost as if he were trying to say something; his eyes opened, puzzled. Another heavy breath, struggling.

'John?' She hardly dared hope.

'Hester . . .' He attempted to move, but then sank back. 'Where are ye?'

'I'm here, my dearest.'

'Och, Hester lass . . . I canna see too well.'

'It doesn't matter. Just lie still awhile.' She wanted to shout out her joy! To sing, dance, anything! Again her cheeks were wet with tears, but of pure happiness. 'You're going to need looking after.'

His head was not to be raised, the doctor had said; not until they knew more about his injuries. She dunked a clean cloth in the drinking water and held it to his lips to suck. He blinked his eyes as she bent over him, complaining he could see naught but mist.

'Hester, love . . .' At times he seemed to breathe with difficulty. 'Will ye tell me the truth now?'

'Oh, of course, John,' she assured him, praying he was not going to ask about Tim, because he would never believe the truth, however often she repeated it.

'Have they amputated both my legs?'

'They've amputated nothing,' she said firmly, her heart going out to him, longing to take him in her arms, and to have his strong arms around her again. 'They don't know yet what's wrong.'

He smiled, the edges of his face puckering up with sudden amusement. 'I can see ye're in charge!' he teased, the way he had always done.

But as he tried to move his head, she saw his lips suddenly twist at another spasm of pain. The breath rasped in his throat. His eyes closed. She should fetch Dr Carson, she thought; but she could not bring herself to leave him like this. She might only be out for a second or two, and then come back to find him dead. Oh no, she could not face that.

He calmed down. His breathing became quieter. More regular. She stayed with him, resting the back of her fingers against his cheek, just to let him know she was still there. It was all she could do. She had no doubt now what was going to happen; in a way, the very certainty of it strengthened her, dulling the raw pain at least for a time. If only he had been able to understand . . . or if it had never happened . . .

His eyes opened again, and she knew immediately he could see her. He even smiled. 'Hester lass, I . . .' he gasped for air. 'I ne'er did . . . take ye . . . to India, did I?'

'You loved India. Your eyes used to light up when you talked about it.'

'Ay . . . Now I'll ne'er go back there.' He was breathing in great gulps of air, as if unable to get enough of it. 'Och, I meant to tell ye so much more.'

'But you never did,' she said gently. His breathing worried her – at times quiet, at times a fight to draw the breath inside him. She stood up, undecided whether to call the doctor or not. But what could he do? A morphine injection, to take him away from her again? She sat by the bed: just a last few seconds and then she'd go. He could still see her.

'I . . .' Another breath. 'I want to tell ye about it.'

'All I know is, you must have loved her very deeply.'

His eyes widened; then again looked amused, almost proud of her. 'Did ye ken all along? I mighta guessed.'

'Oh, John, I've been so much in love with you all the years we've known each other, I could sense every mood.' She leaned down to kiss him; as their lips met, she knew he had not long to go. To master her feelings, she tried to laugh. 'Besides, you used to talk to her in your sleep.'

'Ay . . . those dreams . . . many a long year . . .' He sucked in the air through his open mouth, long and steady. 'Gita. She died, d'ye ken. An epidemic. Always practical, goin' out to help folk – ye're alike in that. Then she went down sick hersel' – same as those she'd been nursin' – poor souls – an' she died like 'em too. I wanted to tell ye . . . och, many a time . . . I couldna talk about it.'

'And me?' As soon as she asked the question, she regretted it. She had no right.

424

'Hester lass, from the moment I met ye... I thought...' His breathing was difficult again. 'I thought... I... we were made... made... for each other... other... I... I... dinna... ken... if I was... right... Och... nay, lass... I ken only too well... I was right...'

Hester dashed to the door, pushing aside the mosquito netting so violently, it came loose in her hand. 'Dr Carson!' she called almost hysterically. 'Bring Dr Carson! Quick! Oh God, bring him quickly!'

She stood by watching, biting her lip until the blood came, as the doctor examined John as best he could. His presence seemed to have a calming effect on him and the breathing gradually became quieter again, though he remained conscious. He complained of the bandages, saying he was sweating inside them, and again asked if his legs had been amputated, as he had no feeling in them.

'I'll give you an injection,' Dr Carson told him briskly, 'to take away some o' the discomfort. Best I can manage. An' no, your legs are still there, though I'm makin' no promises.'

'Ye... always... were... a bastard,' John said, and he sounded so normal, she looked at him in surprise. But then he spoke with a sudden urgency. 'Hester, love...?'

'John?' The doctor was still preparing the syringe. She pushed past him. 'What is it, dearest?'

'I want ye to... promise me...' His eyes had become grave and his voice considerably weaker. 'Hester... ye'll be marryin'... Tim Wilton... will ye no'? Promise me... ye'll marry him... an' be happy? D'ye ken?'

'We'll talk about it again, John.'

'Nay, lass.' He seemed to realize he had only a few moments left. His eyes flickered over her face the way they had always done... in Liverpool... on the boat coming here... 'I reckon... I ovahweached mesel'... d'ye remember? I'm sorry... Gaby's... no here... wi' us.'

His gaze went blank; the breathing stopped.

Dr Carson felt for the pulse, then straightened up, shaking his head. 'I'm sorry, Mrs Andrewes,' he said very

425

gently. He took her arm, suggesting she should go to the dak bungalow to lie down; he'd give her a sedative.

'No.' She felt so desolate, so desperately lonely, she did not want to leave him just yet. 'No – you're right, of course, but . . . just two or three minutes. Alone with him.'

The telegraph clerk, an Indian, appeared in the doorway with a scrap of paper in his hand. He looked at them both, puzzled, not knowing what had happened.

'Sahib?'

'What d'you want, man?' Dr Carson barked at him impatiently.

He handed the paper over – a message addressed to King John to say Gaby had been contacted at the hospital. She would arrive in Tsavo on the next train, though that would not be until the following day.

Hester stared at the paper dully. 'It's too late,' she said at last. The words sounded as though they no longer belonged to her. 'King John is dead. He's *dead* – d'you understand?'

The Indian backed away.

It was too late for everything, she thought as Dr Carson, too, left her and she sat by the bed again in a daze. No tears now – only that terrifying sense of emptiness, which she would have to live with for the rest of her life.

They laid him in a rough coffin which they sealed and made watertight with pitch before placing it in a strong, outer case for the journey.

In Nairobi, it was draped with a Union Jack and borne through the town by six stalwart Indians resplendent in turbans and long robes. Kamau walked alongside on crutches. He wore a fresh white *kanzu* and carried the Winchester slung from his shoulder; his son Ngengi was with him, also in a white *kanzu*.

Hester and Gaby, both in black, followed immediately behind the coffin. Gaby had hardly addressed a word to her, still blaming her for the unhappiness of those last months. Yet when Hester stumbled over a deep rut in the road, Gaby's hand went out instinctively to help her; and

426

they walked like this, with Gaby holding her arm, until they reached the church.

After them came Jimmy Hathaway and Ada, weeping uninhibitedly until Carpenter – tall, distinguished Carpenter – offered her the spotless white handkerchief from his breast pocket. Then more railway people, officials, settlers, the solicitor, the bank manager, a detachment of King's African Rifles under the command of Colonel Arbuthnot, Patel and other leaders of the Indian community, African *askaris*, workers from the hotel . . . the procession seemed endless, the longest Nairobi had ever witnessed.

The church service was brief. As John would have wished it, Hester felt as she stood for the last hymn – *Lead, Kindly Light* – determined not to break down in front of all these people. Carpenter had been appreciative about his work building the railway – John would have liked to hear that – while the missionary spoke of this 'vale of tears' and the need for forgiveness. Hester glanced at her daughter, still stern and unyielding – but at her age how could she possibly understand? If only life were that simple . . .

She had refused burial in the Nairobi cemetery, insisting that John would have wanted to be taken home to The Kingdom. So the cortege went from the church to the Thika Tramway for one last journey to railhead, where Catchpole met them with the ox-drawn wagon.

The route no longer took them over untouched countryside; there was now a road of sorts, roughly hacked out and always in need of repair after each heavy rainfall. As the wagon jolted along it, Hester sat upright by the side of the coffin, refusing to move into the shade offered by the rounded canvas cover at the rear. Her place was with him, nowhere else.

For the first night after their arrival at The Kingdom she had the coffin carried into the living room of the stone house – the 'baronial hall', as they had once proudly called it. Tim was there, anxious about her, concerned, but she sent him away, wanting to be alone. She had no thought of sleeping, but stayed up with the coffin throughout all the hours of darkness. Njoroge and the other Gikuyus crept

427

about uneasily, discomforted by the presence of a dead man in the house.

Catchpole and Tim came over early in the morning to supervise the final ceremony. The coffin was conveyed up the steep hillside to that narrow plateau from which the entire valley was visible. There they buried him.

Each in turn said a few words – Catchpole . . . Tim . . . Kamau . . . Mwangi . . . Then each fell silent, lost in his own memories. And at last Hester spoke – for Gaby, who had returned to the hospital where she was helping out, just as Hester had done before her; for Michael and Robert far away in London, who did not yet know their father was dead. Then—

'We'll build a cairn,' she announced, taking a deep breath and forcing herself back to practicalities. It was over now – she seemed to hear John's voice instructing her gently – and she had to take control once more. Oh, she'd learned so much from John! Why did it have to turn out like this? 'Yes – we'll build a cairn over the grave, but cement the rocks in place to make it permanent. And his name on the centre rock – John Philip Andrewes. Nothing else. The dates perhaps, but nothing else. And Tim—'

She turned to him and was touched by that intense sadness in his eyes.

'Tim, when it's my turn,' she went on, her voice as brisk and businesslike as she could make it, 'I want you to bury me just here. With John.'

She strode off down the hillside to hide her grief among the coffee bushes where they could not see her tears. The delicate white flowers were now full in bloom – in his honour, she thought. Poor Tim! He obviously longed to comfort her, but he knew these few days belonged only to John. When they had passed she would need him all the more.

Had she wanted too much – just to live with both her men, happily, and together? Yet on the ridge were Gikuyu men with several wives – Kamau, even – and no one thought it odd in the least. Was that really so different?